Tartufo

Also by Kira Jane Buxton

Hollow Kingdom

Feral Creatures

Tartufo

Kira Jane Buxton

GRAND
CENTRAL

New York Boston

Copyright © 2025 by Kira Jane Buxton

Jacket design and illustration by Jarrod Taylor. Jacket images by Getty Images and Alamy.
Jacket copyright © 2025 by Hachette Book Group, Inc.

Grand Central Publishing
Hachette Book Group
1290 Avenue of the Americas, New York, NY 10104
grandcentralpublishing.com
@grandcentralpub

First Edition: January 2025

Grand Central Publishing is a division of Hachette Book Group, Inc. The Grand Central Publishing name and logo is a registered trademark of Hachette Book Group, Inc.

The publisher is not responsible for websites (or their content) that are not owned by the publisher.

The Hachette Speakers Bureau provides a wide range of authors for speaking events. To find out more, go to hachettespeakersbureau.com or email HachetteSpeakers@hbgusa.com.

Grand Central Publishing books may be purchased in bulk for business, educational, or promotional use. For information, please contact your local bookseller or the Hachette Book Group Special Markets Department at special.markets@hbgusa.com.

Print book interior design by Marie Mundaca

Library of Congress Cataloging-in-Publication Data

Names: Buxton, Kira Jane, author.
Title: Tartufo / Kira Jane Buxton.
Description: First edition. | New York : Grand Central Publishing, 2025.
Identifiers: LCCN 2024025659 | ISBN 9781538770818 (hardcover) | ISBN 9781538770832 (ebook)
Subjects: LCGFT: Humorous fiction. | Novels.
Classification: LCC PS3602.U9825 T37 2025 | DDC 813/.6—dc23
    /eng/20240614
LC record available at https://lccn.loc.gov/2024025659

ISBNs: 9781538770818 (hardcover), 9781538770832 (ebook)

Printed in Canada

MRQ-T

1   2024

Per la mia famiglia—Em, Pops, and Rinny

And to the treasure of a Tuscan village
where we planted seeds and grew roots

A ogni uccello il suo nido e bello.
To every bird, his nest is beautiful.

—Italian proverb

The Visitor

The wisest souls say that pure mountain air makes us all go a little mad. A wind—lawless and long tailed—slices through the snow-stippled Apuan Alps and the Apennines with all the wantonness of La Befana, the winter witch. Swifts catch this wind on their wings, carving up the crisp blue morning. Dipping down into the valley, the wind now worries over the murmuring blue tongue of the Serchio river on its journey to the Tyrrhenian Sea. It slips—an unseen spirit—under the Devil's Bridge. Shivers along the great gray hunch of the Devil's back. Hissing over every ancient stone. Rising from the river, the wind picks up speed, hastening toward the woods. Hurtling toward chestnut trees spaced like the pews of a great duomo. The wind now weaves between golden leaves. Whispering quick consonants between the branches, borrowing an autumnal aura. Sweet sighs of ripe chestnuts and shed leaves. And here—where the wind steals woodland scents—hides a curiosity. Cloistered by soil, moss, stone, and leaf litter, a thing unseen—a thing quite mysterious—lies in waiting.

A thing that sits buried, like old bones.

What lies under the soil has stayed secret. It is an underground barterer. A schemer who has set a trap in the soil. A sylvan swindler. A tormentor.

A tiny god.

Swelling to irresistible bulk, it has ripened into a knobbled fruit of corruption. And now the time has come. The tiny god releases a lusty sigh, soundlessly unfurling a phantom into the wind.

No more visible than the notes of nightingale song.

No more audible than a wordless wish.

The tiny god has released a cipher.

The breath of the tiny god is whisked away by the breeze, slipping through the damp woodland of chestnut worship. Deeper into the woods, the breath in the breeze paints the pupils of a fallow deer into great glistening lakes. Fur stiffens along a back freckled with the white of first snow. The doe salivates in answer to the call of the stranger she can smell but cannot see. Her nostrils flutter, messages flood her bloodstream. But the breath blows on.

Now a wild sow lifts her moist snout from the leaf litter and inhales a slip of the wind. Instantly intoxicated, her muddy snout snuffing. The grunting sow is aroused into a frenzy. Bristled legs stab at the soil as she arranges them to assume her stance, ready to receive the boar she smells. Turning her head toward her tail, she hunts for him, but—and here is the trick, here is the olfactory deception—there is no boar, and the breeze blows on through the woods, fanning the sensual scent along with it.

See-through scarves of scent curl from the forest and swirl toward a beautiful medieval village, perched upon a peak. Its tallest point an eleventh-century bell tower with memories of steel swords and shields. The wind, pickled with flavors of the forest, ridden by the breath of the tiny god, tickles trees of olive and cypress. Until it dangles its string of little calamities above cobblestone streets and terra-cotta roof tiles.

And it settles upon the medieval village like a spell.

Down in the village, past the sleepy post office, past the boarded-up *ristorante* and the sixteenth-century church and the water fountain. Past the teeny-tiny grocers and a ginger tomcat slinking under an archway to go make mayhem, Nonna Amara shuffles slippers over cobblestone on her morning walk. The breeze and the mysterious thing it carries slip under her shawl, bright and invigorating, a sonnet read to her skin. Nonna Amara tightens her floral shawl, the silver cirrus of her hair aflutter. She lifts the lovely lines of her face to the sky. Squeezes her eyes shut. As she inhales, a memory whirls her off her feet, whisking her all the way back to her childhood.

She is sitting at the table in the *cucina rustica* of her beloved home. Blue snakes of smoke coil around young Amara, up toward the wooden ceiling beams. Some hang themselves in her hair. Her papa, Babbo, leans in, his spice of sweet smoke, the powdered sugar lingering like a second skin, his hands thick from pummeling pastry. Babbo with his feral hair and his hands and his hairy chest and his heart, oh, his heart...

"Close your eyes, sweetheart." That voice. The rumble, the rasp.

Amara closes her eyes, makes a wish for a thing with wheels. Her papa leans close, smelling of a glossy white soap cake, sweet tobacco from his pipe. Babbo's pipe. Babbo's hands wrap around the waist of her summer dress and she lifts into the air with a shriek. Babbo and Amara are a two-headed creature that blunders blindly out of the *cucina*, through the arched doorway.

"Open!" bellows Babbo. And Amara opens her eyes to a courtyard stippled with sun. The planters popping with red geraniums. Babbo's potted herbs and their aromatic whispers of lavender and rosemary. The old black-and-white cat staring at them from a stone wall with blatant disgust in its green-eyed glare. And a bicycle, glossy and red, with a wished-for basket in the front and a seat on the back. Amara kicks her legs and screams in delight, slipping from Babbo's shoulders, held by those hands, held by that big, rumbling laugh, until she is running toward the bike, the sun, toward Babbo running beside her yelling, "That's it, pedal! Keep going, *piccolina*, keep going!" toward Babbo holding Amara's delicate hand so she does not fall, toward scraped knees, toward firsts and falls, heartbreaks and hurdles, all the way through time toward Amara holding Babbo's delicate hand so he does not fall.

The breeze blows on and Nonna Amara opens her eyes. She smiles, lifting the lines she has earned with years of laughter.

"Babbo."

She rubs her hands together and shuffles ahead, averting her eyes from the crudely nailed planks of wood boarding up the *pasticceria*. From cobwebs on windows. She smiles, lets in birdsong instead of sorrow.

The breeze and the breath of the tiny god, ahead of Nonna Amara now, make a mad dash down a winding cobblestone street, across a sleepy piazza, and finally—with a devious bluster—slip under the door of Bar Celebrità.

The breath of the tiny god is now, to many a nose, undetectable. Indeed, all the current inhabitants of Bar Celebrità have missed the secret cipher slithering into their midst.

All but one.

At a table by the window, nestled up to the muddied boot of her person, sits Aria, a dog-shaped burst of brown and white corkscrew curls, woolen and wiry to the touch. She peers up at Giovanni's flatcap and thick white mustache with alert, almost-human hazel eyes. Giovanni Scarpazza gives his dog a reassuring nod—*Not long now*, it says—inducing a doggy yawn of excitement. Quick pink flash of a tongue.

Aria lifts her nose to the height of the table. She reads the room in sentences of scent. First, she takes in Giovanni's breakfast *bombolone*, fried dough bulging with Nutella. The pastry sits on a napkin next to a cup of strong coffee. She sniffs the spiced soil of those coffee grounds—bitter beans with a roasted raisin lilt that lifts the spirits of the humans in here. Aria smells a mist of milk as Giuseppina—*carnevale* incarnate and incidental human—manhandles the steam wand, yelling loud enough that all the hunting dogs of the village can hear. Aria leaves Giovanni's side briefly to visit the neighboring table and sniff the pant leg of Leon Rosetti. A musky reek from billy goats clings to Leon's jacket and jeans. A small map made by the urine of a young female goat dried to his boots. The farmer's skin smells of beetles and unearthed roots. He is in good health, though filled with a sadness that smells like the resin of a sick tree. Sadness the color of crushed irises. Aria reads that Leon did not sleep well last night, smells the story of his tending to an old donkey, feeding the dogs and geese breakfast after splashing his face with freezing spring water. She reads that farmer Leon woke up alone, since Aria can no longer smell the creamy vanilla flowers of fragrance that bloom in the wake of the farmer's wife.

"Good morning, Aria. Beautiful dog," says the farmer. His breath glitters with sweet stars of grappa. Thick farmer fingers tousle Aria's head curls. Fingers stained purple from harvesting grapes, a metallic tang of goat bells trailing from them. Aria pushes her head into Leon's hand to comfort him. She knows she is very good at comforting those who need her. And she always knows who needs comforting.

Curls bouncing, Aria pads back to the table by the window, where Giovanni is biting into the *bombolone*. Nutella oozes out, plopping onto the napkin. Aria licks her lips, then sweeps her snout under the table and across the terra-cotta tile. She sniffs a crumpled napkin with an angry smear of *arrabbiata* sauce. The spot where some tangy salt-and-vinegar crisp crumbs were swept up. Peach juice poured by a colicky child. Her nose hovers just above a dried patch of cleaning agent, chemical and sharp. And a tidy trail of dried blood droplets—human in origin, spilled by a male filled with pungent rage. Things the cleaning agent did not catch. Out of sight, in the *cucina* behind Giuseppina and the bar, Aria smells bones bubbling in a pot to make a rich broth. Stale bread tensing on a counter. Mold violating a hunk of mozzarella. The ghost of roasted garlic. The last tomatoes of summer simmer in an earthenware pot with a green potpourri of freshly chopped herbs. On the *cucina* tiles, scents tracked in on the soles of shoes—cigarette butt with a sweet stamp of lipstick, gum spat hastily onto the marble church floor, a squashed scorpion. Aria smells the stacked crates of belching onions. The metallic menace of the shotgun hidden in a cupboard under the antique stone sink. A bowl of jellied cat food, partially licked by the mischievous ginger tom who was already full from hunting mice all night but just didn't want any other cat to enjoy it.

When Aria fixes her muzzle on the table in front of her once more, just as Giovanni is swallowing the last lump of *bombolone*, a strange summoning from the forest holds her nose hostage. Aria's eyes light up with longing. She gives a gummy, open-mouthed grin, her curls quaking. Her tail takes on a life of its own, thumping terra-cotta.

The breath of the tiny god is here.

An earthy burp, a miasma of cheese and funky sweat. A sweet fizz of fermented fruit. A message. This breath of new life sets her heart racing. A rush of passion strong as gunpowder. She whines, panting, placing her front paws onto Giovanni's leg. She lifts to her hind legs to stare into gentle gray eyes.

"Calm, Aria. Wait." Giovanni winces at the acerbity of his coffee. He pats Aria, feeling waves of vim floating from his canine companion.

Aria cocks her head at the window. She stares beyond the piazza at the arched outline of the Apennines. She will be very good and she will wait, as Giovanni has asked. Though they cannot and must not wait too long. Soon, she will follow her nose to show Giovanni what is out there. The cipher that is summoning her. Calling for her in chemicals. A tease. A treasure.

A story sent to her on the wings of the wind.

Struggling to keep her wiggly bottom on the ground, she stares out the window, pining. Possessed.

She will find the tiny god. She will do it before anyone else has a chance.

And it will change everything.

Chapter 1

Since the *ristorante*, the best café, and the *pasticceria* shuttered their doors, Bar Celebrità has become the heart of Lazzarini Boscarino. A heart whose pulse could perhaps use one of the potent espressos made by its bartender, Giuseppina. *Bar Celebrità*—a bold name for a place that has never actually hosted a celebrity. It sits tucked behind a lonely piazza where umbrellas sing longingly of gelato in loud colors. Daffodil-yellow chairs ring rickety tables. The bar itself is nestled inside a rustic limestone building. Emerald-green shutters and potted planters. Charming vintage doors. Plaster flaking like good pastry. A bar whose stone walls glitter under the sun. Whose quaint lanterns cast it in a golden glow under the stars.

On this autumn morning, the piazza is empty but for one being. A cat—best described as a cross between a crumpled tuxedo and a well-used toilet wand—sits vigilant. Seven unplanned litters of kittens have tested her patience and her personality, so that she has matured into the kind of cat that will take a crap on the carpet before she takes crap from anyone else. The kind of cat who knows where the sensitive skin of an ankle is and how it can fell a full-grown man. The kind of cat who instills bewilderment into the heart of a mastiff. The kind of cat who is sitting next to a wine barrel holding a WELCOME! sign outside the last bar of a doomed medieval village. Ready to unleash hell upon any tourist who dares to smuggle an exposed ankle in through its door. For what is a tourist, truly, but an invader with blinding white crew socks and a selfie stick?

The cat chooses to sit out on the piazza alone to steal a moment of morning peace. And to avoid an aroma that is dogging Bar Celebrità. The smell of longing is sharper than the long-gone lemons of summer. A horrible yearning hangs in this bar. That and Giuseppina's perfume, which could deflea even the most verminous of felines. So the cat sits outside and sniffs at maddeningly fresh mountain air.

And she realizes something is coming.

Something snarky. Sensual. A gambit.

A quiet riot.

The cat purrs in anticipation of anarchy.

It is well on its way.

Inside, Bar Celebrità is filled with the music of chiming cups and the beautiful burble of *la bella lingua*. On one side of the bar sit colorful shelves of Nutella, Baci chocolate, gum and Mentos, brightly colored jelly candies flavored limoncello, fruits of the forest, and CBD. On the other is a fridge filled with juices and soda. A freezer filled with long-forgotten gelato.

Giuseppina leans on the bar itself, her bosom spilling over its surface like two jellyfish in a battle for hegemony. She idly molests the bar's wooden surface with a rag, sighing loud enough to suggest some sort of respiratory distress. Dusty bottles line shelves against the stone wall behind her, as well as a large mirror and framed photographs of various celebrities.

Postcards from Milan, Florence, Rome. Big cities, where big things are happening. And, most prominently, a tacked-on flyer inviting one and all to join in the twenty-second birthday party and celebrations for Maurizio, who happens to be a donkey.

At the end of the bar, scowling over a cup of rocket fuel, is Duccio Berardinelli, somber and sporting a thin silver ponytail. He is a wet weekend of a man and the village's disgraced postman. Some say Duccio has not smiled in seventy years, but most certainly not after his scandal.

"Giuseppina, where is my coffee?" pleads Padre Francesco, who has been languishing on a barstool in front of Giuseppina, watching her not make the coffee he ordered twenty minutes ago.

"I'll get to it; I am very busy."

Padre Francesco is a plump man of God, blessed with biblical black eyebrows like two Pekingese guarding the temples of his bald head. He looks around the bar in bafflement. The current patrons of Bar Celebrità—hunter Giovanni with his dog at the table by the window; Duccio, the ex-postman, brooding at the end of the bar; Leon, the forlorn farmer— are all grimacing as they sip potent coffee. Giuseppina flaps dismissively at Padre with arms so tanned she could camouflage against the coffee grounds with which she has carpeted Bar Celebrità. This particular tan was born at the Versilia seaside at the end of summer, where she faced the ocean eating a bowl of *cacciucco*—tangy tomato-and-white-wine stew with mussels, cuttlefish, squid, and prawns the size of puppies. Seafood as sweet as the sea. Between sips of a velvet Chianti, she savored the salt breeze stinging her lips, a kiss of coconut from someone's sunbaked skin. She abandoned her clothes, running toward waves. A skinny dip in a cerulean sea. After bobbing in Tyrrhenian salt water, she took a lengthy nap on the sand, breasts sunny-side up, thighs and buttocks achieving the reddish searing every chef worth his salt wants for a *bistecca alla Fiorentina.*

Giuseppina turns to the mirror, jostling the warring jellyfish in her beige bra. She is wearing a floral singlet and a plethora of emotions where a sleeve would be if she was not wearing a singlet.

"I could be famous, Padre," she states. Sure, Giuseppina has had a healthy serving of hardships, but she is not one to wallow in the wet sands of nostalgia. As a young woman, she was self-conscious of her curves, of every eye tracing her silhouette. At fifty-three, she couldn't give a flying fig about what any eye is up to. She has honed her keen nose for nonsense. Let them feast upon every fabulous feature.

She manages Bar Celebrità. Took over for owner Lorenzo as he and his beloved wife traveled all over Italy for her career in veterinary medicine. And now he has returned under the saddest of circumstances. Giuseppina stepped in because she loves this village. She grew up here. Met a Boscarini man and married him at the little church. Had her daughter, Elisabetta, and raised her in this beautiful medieval village where a sunset turns the stone walls pink. Where a labyrinth of lovely cobblestone streets are patrolled by old-age pensioners and an inordinate number of cats.

Giuseppina inhales the ambrosia of life, sweet as all the seafood in a perfect bowl of *cacciucco.* Her passion for the making of merriment and love, for the smell of a storm and the shimmer of summer heat, for everything, cannot be contained. She wants to share all of it, just not with Padre right now.

In the mirror she is met with a goddess. Giuseppina admires her adventurous eye makeup. She does not hold back with a brush, not with her tongue, not with living her life out loud.

Still, she is tortured.

She wants to see her village thrive. In her younger years,

she was entangled in the thrill of ambition, forever running a rat race. But the demanding days of accomplishment and accumulation are gone. As the years go by, she wants to take less and appreciate more—all the tiny miracles she missed in her youth. Slow down and savor the fragrance of every flower. Giuseppina just wants everyone to fall for the charm of Lazzarini Boscarino. For the magic and beauty in the simplicity of small village life.

But everyone leaves. All the children. Giuseppina's own daughter, Elisabetta. Grown and gone. Mayor Benigno—gone to heaven. Farmer Leon's wife, Sofia, who has, she suspects, run away with a lover. Her husband—*no grazie*, she won't think about him.

If only everyone could see what she sees in Lazzarini Boscarino.

If only everyone would stop leaving her.

She piles her supernova of hair—bottle blonde in a fight with five inches of black root—on her head. Padre Francesco waits, quite saintlike, for her to be less busy. He clears his throat, swipes a hand over those consecrated eyebrows. He will not complain. He has no intention of angering Giuseppina after the incident in church all those Sundays ago, so he stands by the bar and sweats as silently as possible.

From the mirror, Giuseppina's eyes float to the postcards she'd tacked to the wall. She snorts. Why do all the tourists flock to these overpopulated places like foolish flamingos? Elisabetta told her that hotels in Venice are issuing tourists tiny orange water pistols to spritz seagulls who keep swooping down to steal their sandwiches. Orange is apparently a very offensive color to the gull *comune*.

"Here in our little medieval village, we have staggering mountains," she thinks out loud. "In Rome, what they have is staggering mountains of trash. *Che schifo!*"

And as well as sinking, Venice is also suffering a plague of ghosts, including the late painter Lorenzo Luzzo, who committed suicide over a doomed love affair and now wafts about the palace Casino degli Spiriti on the Canale Grande, quite unalive. Not to mention the dead of the mental asylum who wander about Poveglia Island in the Venetian Lagoon and are said to have thrown the doctor who tortured them plunging from a tower to his death. There is even a house on the canal—Palazzo Dario—that murders people! A homicidal house! And Milan, well, her Elisabetta is in Milan, so it had better behave itself or it will have Giuseppina to contend with. Giuseppina makes the sign of the cross. Padre Francesco instinctively copies her and crosses himself without knowing why; he needs very little provocation.

Giuseppina ignores Padre's woeful sigh of a man who is being deprived of coffee. She stares at the celebrity photographs; Virna Lisi sandwiched between Sophia Loren, Monica Bellucci, and her favorite—the late Raffaella Carrà. She swims into a daydream—silken and warm as the Tyrrhenian Sea. It is summer. She envisions Bar Celebrità teeming with tourists all the way out to the piazza. All in beautiful beach ball colors and straw hats stippled with sun. Aperol spritzes flank bright yellow bowls of crisps and salted peanuts. Sophia Loren walks into Bar Celebrità, smelling of sunflowers and giant sacks of money. Giuseppina regales *i turisti* with a tale of the time an eight-year-old Elisabetta stole cash from her father, smuggling it in a Christmas panettone. How she was only discovered because Dante—hunter Ugo's dog and agent of chaos—stole the panettone sitting on this very table here at Bar Celebrità and tore around the village with it, lira notes fluttering behind him. Nonna Amara has made *pasta fritta* with *stracchino* cheese, the salted dough glistening with hot oil. Now Giuseppina is serving glasses of L'Orso, the village of Lazzarini Boscarino's very own liquor. Farmer Leon gets out his guitar and sings and Lorenzo is fatter and Duccio is nowhere to be seen and we dance and dance. Beyond the beautiful village, cypress trees are propped against the horizon, golden hills of smiling sunflowers rolling into an ocean of olive groves. It is a Tuscan summer of wine and sun and sex, lungs breathless with laughter, sweat beading between breasts, everyone warmed by sunshine that sweetens the tomatoes and many a soul.

Giuseppina's daydream dissolves and she is back to the present, Padre staring at her like one of Leon's goats. She is struck by the painful pang of desire, of longing for the fortunes of the village to be different.

The terrible loneliness of being left behind.

Thoughts of Nonna Amara's *pasta fritta* and creamy smears of *stracchino* cheese have made her hungry. She plucks a Kinder Bueno from the sweet shelf next to the bar, tucking the chocolate into her cheek.

"Giuseppina!" Lorenzo Micucci has emerged from the *cucina* of Bar Celebrità, standing with both hands thrust into the air.

"What! I'm wasting away!" She slaps both thighs eight times for emphasis.

Lorenzo Micucci rubs his forehead in exasperation. Sleepless nights have left him feeling hollow. Lately, when he glimpses his reflection in the bar windows, he thinks of carrion. Of a carcass picked over by vultures. He will tell no one, but there is a tightness in his fifty-year-old heart. His very veins feel like sucked straws. Funny to think about his body. He has given all of it to this bar since he moved back here, has he not? Certainly his blood, sweat, and tears. But he is the owner of Bar Celebrità, the last bar of the village. The survival of this bar, and therefore the village, falls on his shoulders.

Everyone is alerted to commotion outside Bar Celebrità. On the road across from the piazza, a blue bus coughs up the hill with a belly full of tourists. Everyone in Bar Celebrità— with the exclusion of a fly who has just fallen into a glass of Chianti—holds their breath as the bus slows.

It stops in front of the piazza.

"Lorenzo! *I turisti!*" Giuseppina yells, as if he is not standing next to her.

Giuseppina leaps over the bar, barely catching herself on her wedge sandals to sprint out the front door of Bar Celebrità. She runs across the piazza, performing her own stunts by flying over cobblestones, dodging tables and chairs, and then coming to an abrupt halt to wave frantically at the blue bus. The bus lets out a haughty hiss. It shudders. Rattles. Convulsing now, the bus is spluttering out clouds of exhaust, passing the piazza, starting its melt back down the mountainside. Giuseppina yanks down her singlet and bra to flash a busload of wide-eyed tourists, her answer to holding up a *save us* sign from the desolate island of Lazzarini Boscarino. She tosses her head and harrumphs. One might argue that she has given them an alternate vista of the Apennines.

Giuseppina walks quietly back into Bar Celebrità, adjusting her singlet and her brass-blonde bun. Giovanni Scarpazza shakes his head, grimacing at his final poisonous sip of coffee— a feat; very few make it to the bottom of the cup. His dog Aria ducks under the table to avoid the contrails of perfume trailing from Giuseppina. Her very particular perfume reads as an olfactory scream for sex, flowers wilting in her wake.

"We don't need tourists. We have never needed anyone infiltrating our village," says disgraced postman Duccio with a great deal of spite.

"*Silenzio,* Duccio, or I will banish you from Bar Celebrità forever!"

Lorenzo pokes his head out momentarily from the *cucina*. "No, that's not a thing, you can't do that!"

Giuseppina ignores him.

"I think Al Pacino is pregnant again," she announces. Giovanni shakes his head. When is Al Pacino not knocked up? The poor cat had been a peace offering from Giuseppina's husband. Perhaps also a portent of things to come. Her husband had assured Giuseppina the kitten was a pedigreed purebred (though which breed, he never said). He said the cat would grow to be a magnificent tom. Under these false pretenses, cinephile Giuseppina named the kitten Al Pacino. But the odd cluster of fur grew less into a tomcat than a female cat who identified as a dog. Her name stuck despite an evidential number of feline pregnancies. Disburdening a little misplaced maternal instinct, Giuseppina overindulged the cat, who became accustomed to being spoiled and one might say was ultimately spoiled. And who could blame the little cat who had no firm hand to guide her while she held her own among all the village hunting dogs? Who took her guard duties so seriously she developed both stress-induced alopecia and dermatitis. Al Pacino does the best she can under the circumstances, valiantly tackling the terrorism of tourists while generously spreading her spawn over all of Tuscany in an army of cats often mistaken for weasels.

Lorenzo suddenly appears from the *cucina* again, looking haggard. He is a gentleman and a gentle man, Lorenzo, a long-suffering peacekeeper who gets along with everyone. Well, almost everyone. And being the peacekeeper of a town like Lazzarini Boscarino is a little like being a tiny orange water pistol up against all the seagulls of Venice. Duccio and Giuseppina register the fumes of exhaustion lifting from Lorenzo's head. His checkered shirt looks baggy, the skin around his eyes gray.

"Giuseppina, not more little Al Pacinos! Why do you let that cat out, she is undiluted chaos! Keep her inside; she terrifies the tourists."

"Lorenzo, *keep her inside!* What balls! You can't tell her what to do! She needs to be free to be herself, to love, to make her own decisions, to live an authentic life and be celebrated for who she is and the gifts that only she can share with the world!"

"The cat needs that, does she?" Lorenzo heads back into the *cucina*. Giuseppina minces after him. Duccio studies them suspiciously, only his eyes moving like one of Caravaggio's creepier portraits.

Lorenzo trips over the crate of onions aging on the floor. He recovers, snatching up a spoon of the *ragù alla bolognese* sauce, a garlic and meat medley of steam swirling around him. His jaw tingles as his tongue is hit with an herbaceous tang.

"You are stifling me," Giuseppina says with a head toss. "I can't do my job if you are stalking me."

"You can't keep giving away all the chocolate... the drinks!"

"I'm not!"

"Did Leon pay for his grappa?"

"No, I put it on my tab."

"You don't have a tab! And why are you flashing your breasts at our customers?"

"I am very generous."

"And I am missing an enormous amount of chocolate inventory."

"Ridiculous. Your counting must be questioned."

"Giusep—"

"They weren't our customers; they were all in a bus to..." She pauses. She doesn't want to say it, but she cannot lie to Lorenzo. Never Lorenzo. She sniffs. "The festival."

Lorenzo falls silent. Giuseppina sees storm clouds gather behind his eyes. She did not want to mention the autumn music festival of Borghese, the neighboring village. A village with waves of tourists crashing against its shores year-round, a veritable tsunami of them in the summer. A village heralded for its colorful pastel buildings, castles, upscale eateries, and rich history of culture, music, and art. And a music festival that siphons glorious guests from all over the world. Not to mention their professional bartenders who don't give away drinks, eat all the chocolate, and expose themselves to busloads of tourists. But Borghese's Festival Del'Arte and its flagrant success is more of an affront to some. For Lorenzo Micucci, it is personal. Giuseppina hates to see his hopes crushed. He does not need this stress. Lately, he is looking more and more like the last asparagus spear of the season. It matters to Giuseppina. She cares about this man far more than about her husband.

Lorenzo quickly distracts himself by loading dirty dishes into the sink. He lifts a half-drunk glass of Chianti, breathes in its vapors, and gags. He peers at the ruby liquid, perplexed at its pungent scent. He sips and confirms—the wine he doled out last night tastes foul.

"*Che disgustoso!* No wonder no one comes here, I am serving poison!"

What he doesn't know is that mere minutes ago, a fruit fly fell into this wine. If it had been a male fly, the wine would have retained its tart notes of cottony cherry and purple-skinned plums. Alas, it was a female fruit fly, who—as they are wont to do—released a pheromone that has forever tainted and, perhaps more explicitly put, farted in the face of this wine's flavor. Of course, Giovanni's dog Aria would have been able to demystify all of this, if only she spoke Italian. Instead, the utter horror of having served revolting fly-pheromone wine is now lumped onto Lorenzo's growing list of worries.

Watching him pull faces at an abandoned glass of Chianti, Giuseppina becomes concerned about Lorenzo's state of mind. She breathes in through her nose and smiles like a star of the silver screen. "Look, it's all going to be okay, I went to see a psychic at the Versilia seaside."

"Oh no, Giuseppina, not again..."

"I went to ask her about Sofia! Six days no one has seen her, Lorenzo. Leon is going crazy wondering where his wife is. He's barely speaking this morning! Struggling to drink my cappuccino..."

"That is in no way a sign of ill health. It might even indicate the opposite. Don't make drama where there isn't any, okay? Sofia has probably gone to see her family in Florence. Weren't you only recently speculating that she had a lover? She is probably just tired of the goat smell and playing second fiddle to a geriatric donkey. The life of a farmer's wife is not enviable."

"And if your wife went missing?"

Lorenzo rolls his eyes at her. "You are being—"

"If you say dramatic, I will feed you through the pasta roller. Shouldn't be difficult—look how skinny you are!" Lorenzo dodges her pinching fingers and hastily confiscates the pasta roller, remembering the afternoon Giuseppina chased disgraced postman Duccio through the village with a splitting axe. After hiding the pasta roller, Lorenzo heaves rattling crates of Nastro Azzurro and Moretti from the pantry onto a small kitchen island.

"Lorenzo, the psychic was a good one this time! She was very sexy and mystical and had a proper crystal ball and a jingly headscarf and everything."

"And what was she called...Mamma Fortuna?"

Giuseppina gasps. "How did you know?"

Lorenzo stifles a laugh. "What did she say about Sofia?"

Giuseppina draws out the drama of the moment by squinting at the hanging copper cooking pots. "Time will tell."

Lorenzo massages the bags under his eyes. "Giuseppina, to

be clear, you paid a psychic to tell you something nondescript would be happening at some time not disclosed?"

"She told me that the fortunes of our village are about to change."

"For better or worse?"

Giuseppina steps toward the counter. There sits a *mezzaluna* with an enormous smiling blade used to pulverize herbs. Lorenzo swiftly confiscates the *mezzaluna*, handing Giuseppina a wooden spoon to gesticulate with.

"She wasn't tremendously specific." She scoops up the glass of wine Lorenzo pulled faces at. Knocks back the remaining Chianti. "*Puah!* What is wrong with this wine?"

"I don't know, but I suspect it's some sort of celestial conspiracy. It tasted magnificent yesterday. Don't leave me hanging— what did the psychic say?"

"She told me that we have a very special visitor coming to the village. She said that then, there would be a death. And then our village would come into untold riches."

"Riches can mean a lot of things. For example, here in Lazzarini Boscarino we are rich with broke people…"

"She said money, Lorenzo, I'm just telling the story with a bit of flair. She said it is because of the visitor. The money will come because of the visitor. The visitor that is coming to our village…will change everything."

"I wish you wouldn't see psychics—they rile you up, which is dangerous for everyone."

"Lorenzo, relax. The last time I saw a psychic they told me there would be a sudden death of someone in power. And then Mayor Benigno died!"

"Why didn't you say anything then? You might have saved him!"

"Well, at that time, I didn't really believe in psychics!"

Lorenzo eyes the bottle of Chianti next to the olive oil bottles.

The original source of the revolting glass he just sipped from. He takes a sip and then adds a splash to his sauce, finding it to be delicious. *Why did the wine in the glass smell like dead ants?* he wonders. *Mamma mia!* For Lorenzo, this is further confirmation that, cosmically, nothing makes sense anymore. He has been reading about chaos theory and the butterfly effect, and the more he reads, the more it seems feasible to him that every insect of the Amazon rainforest is bending a leg, licking its own eyeballs, or eating its spouse to set off an endless string of catastrophes that, one after another, sabotage his life. The more he reads about the arrow of time (the nonreversible progression of entropy) and its notion that as time flies forward, matter becomes increasingly chaotic and can never revert to its simpler states, the more Lorenzo believes that his arrow of time is nearing a bullseye.

"Mayor Benigno died of natural causes—against all odds," he says.

"And now we have a new mayor, and everything is going to be different."

"Things will only be different if we survive."

Giuseppina grasps her hips. "I have an idea! We can just charge Duccio extra for his espressos. He's a creepy scoundrel and no one likes him..."

"Hey, I can hear you!" hollers the disgraced postman from behind the bar.

"Giuseppina"—Lorenzo lowers his voice to a tense whisper, ushering her over to the pantry and out of eavesdropper range—"I don't want to frighten you, but...We are in a lot of trouble. We have no money, do you understand? Not enough regular patrons, no tourists, and we are heading into winter. If something drastic doesn't happen, I cannot keep us open. And if I can't keep us open, then...I don't know what we'll all do."

A fog of desperation rolls between them. Aria and, indeed, even Al Pacino would tell you about the scent swirling around these two human animals. Desperation has the scent of dying lilies. Dying lilies for a dying village. There is so much that could be said between Lorenzo and Giuseppina, but whether it should be is another thing entirely.

Lorenzo searches the ceiling beams for ways to be tactful, but then chooses to hand Giuseppina the truth even if she has one of her theatrical outbursts. "Babbo's *pasticceria*—gone. Nonna Amara's *ristorante*—gone. Café Volterra—who managed to make coffee that didn't make every patron poop themselves—"

Giuseppina gasps, clutching imaginary pearls. "My coffee is the fuel of this village! The elixir of life! It is why everyone here lives into their late nineties!"

"Yes, it's essentially formaldehyde; you are preserving them all. Taxidermy works in much the same way." Giuseppina lobs the wooden spoon at the hanging pots with considerable force, dislodging several copper saucepans with a clatter. She looks shocked at this turn of events, but Lorenzo—though admittedly no Mamma Fortuna—had seen it coming and is glad he confiscated both the pasta roller and the *mezzaluna*.

"Giuseppina, *per favore*, make the poor priest his coffee; you have left him in purgatory long enough."

"I will tell you something about that 'poor priest'—" she starts but is interrupted.

Strange voices bubble up from the main room of Bar Celebrità. String-plucked notes of a foreign language. Giuseppina and Lorenzo stare at one another, wide-eyed.

Giuseppina grabs Lorenzo's hands and squeezes them. Her face lights up like the Versilia seaside. Lorenzo gives her a tight smile. Between them—a bright citrusy burst of hope.

"Go!" Lorenzo says, and their hands slip apart.

Giuseppina lets loose her bun of blonde. She bursts from the *cucina* with a vociferous "Ciao!" sweeping a hand in the manner of a classically trained *commedia dell'arte* actor. And if the bar patrons squinted their eyes, she thinks they might mistake her for her musical idol Patty Pravo about to slay a love ballad. All she needs is the sultry fog of a smoke machine.

Between the mascara spiders of her lashes, Giuseppina sees a couple. The girl is blonde and tiny. The boy is tall, thin as a lamppost. Pink sweater draped across his shoulders, an Italian phrase book in his hand—be still her beating heart. They have that lovely, mildly grubby youth-hostel aura—might even be on an adventure all over Europe, bless their little baby faces. Skinny, sun-kissed limbs. Travel backpacks the size of cattle. Tiny noses and hairless ears. Oh, the young are so beautiful, all of them. Giuseppina decides on the spot that they are Swedish and that she will adopt them.

"Al Pacino was chasing them around the piazza," says Giovanni. "I distracted her with the end of my *bombolone* and ushered these two in."

"Thank you, Giovanni. Welcome to Bar Celebrità!" Giuseppina says to the Swedes.

The boy—Giuseppina suspects she has yogurt older than this boy—handsome in his teal linen shirt, upturned collar, pink sweater scarf, and a crop of bronze hair, braves some beautifully broken Italian: "These is villages of Borghese...?"

Giuseppina tries not to deflate at realizing that yet another tourist has ended up in the village of Lazzarini Boscarino because they had yet to crest the next hill, as they couldn't see the Lazzarini Boscarino sign because three years ago a tree fell on it and the *comune* didn't have the budget to replace it. And no one could be faulted for being confused after not finding "zar osc no" on a map.

Giuseppina's hands find her hips. Her lips find the monologue she prepared for occasions like these. "No, we are not Borghese, but we are a very beautiful medieval village. Filled with the most passionate and generous people in all of Tuscany, and if you give us a chance, we will lift your spirits and you will leave a piece of your heart here in Lazzarini Boscarino; and even if you leave, we will treasure it always."

The young couple share a glance, deducing that they are in the wrong place. They swap micro nods of guilt.

"You are have coffees?" the golden boy asks with a Scandinavian smile.

"Of course! Very good!" Giuseppina sings. "Two coffees for our beautiful guests!" She resumes abusing the steam wand and throwing coffee-ground confetti in celebration. "Youth! Beautiful youth! This is what this village needs—a little passion, young love! A little life!"

Duccio shouts to the tourists over the milk frothing. "Keep an eye out, she might try to drink your blood."

"Thanks, a thousand thanks," says the tourist, not having understood a word of what was just said.

Giuseppina brings them two hastily made espressos with double the coffee grounds for good measure. She also brings them sandwiches and *cornetti* pastries filled with pistachio cream made to cheer up Leon, but she will just have Lorenzo—bar owner and baker extraordinaire—make him more; never mind.

With a first sip of coffee, the young couple heroically manage to tether themselves to their chairs so as not to leap four feet from the ground while holding in eyeballs that threaten to rocket from their sockets. Giovanni, Leon, and Duccio give them a nod of respect. These kids have developed intestinal fortitude on their travels.

The glowing blonde opens the sandwich, immediately spying the ham. She mimes a sad face, forms an angry cross with her fingers and then pushes her nose into a snout.

"Ah, you are vegetarians!" roars Giuseppina. "How ridiculous!

No wonder you are so skinny. I bet when you have sex, it's like sticks rubbing together—you could catch fire!"

Giovanni erupts into a coughing fit. Aria, smelling the sulfurous spark of shock, buries her head in her paws. Giuseppina roars with laughter as she uses her own fingers to simulate coitus, admittedly a little confusing to the vacationing Swedes without context and over an impromptu breakfast.

It is at precisely this moment, as Giuseppina is enveloping the youngsters in her charm and potent perfume, that there is more commotion on the piazza. A gaggle of local hunters, rifles slung over shoulders, burst through the door of Bar Celebrità. In the lead is Ugo Lombardi, a great gorilla of a man shuffling in with grunts and huffs. All around him are his fellow hunters—Tommaso and three others no one in the bar is bothered about since they are from a neighboring village and are therefore not as important. The hunters stagger into Bar Celebrità lugging a tarp filled with the deceased body of a most enormous wild boar. Tommaso leaves them struggling with the extra weight of the body as he pulls five Bar Celebrità tables together and they slam the boar down next to the young vegetarian tourists. The impact of the boar's mighty body shakes the whole bar, four bottles of Vino Nobile di Montepulciano leaping from a shelf to their deaths. The wild boar's head flops heavily off the edge of a table. Bloody tongue lolling. Formidable tusks still as stone. Glassy, oddly minuscule eyes seem to roll in their sockets, finding the young blonde vegetarian Swede and fixing on her. The Swedes fail to hold back gasps of horror. Duccio yells out an obscenity. Even Aria agrees it is a tad early for the pungent funk of boar spleen.

"You are proper brutes; there are guests in the bar!" shouts Giovanni. Aria barks for emphasis.

"Let the Germans feast their eyes on our kill!" laughs Ugo. "Today, we brought down a monster!"

"They are vegetarian Swedes, you insensitive baboons!" Giovanni hollers.

Lorenzo emerges from the *cucina*, determined to halt the chaos that has manifested in his bar, a chaos that clearly originated with some asshole insect of the Amazon rainforest squatting on a new leaf or laying eighty-six eggs or blinking overzealously. But he stops short at the sight of the great bloody boar.

"*Mamma mia!* Look at the size of it!"

"Right, Lorenzo? Biggest one anyone in the village has snagged!" says Ugo, face beaming red.

"Lorenzo, tell these louts to get out of here—look at that poor girl's face, she's green!" says Giovanni. Aria is now prancing at his feet, riled up by the chili and vinegar fumes of fury steaming from his person. A smell of boar blood pours through the bar, thick as minestrone.

"Of course, of course... guys, this isn't a good time, we have guests, but listen, you'll save some of the meat for me, uh? I'll make *cinghiale al dolceforte*—Nonna Amara's recipe—it will be good for business."

"Of course, Lorenzo! We should have a big party, bring in some tourists!"

"You're not seeing to the guests you have!" snaps Giovanni, chair screeching as he rockets to his feet. He throws his napkin onto the table in an unsatisfying silent gesture of outrage.

Ugo readjusts his rifle. "Keep your panties on, Giovanni! You can't complain about the accomplishments of real hunters. You are an imposter! And a traitor for selling your truffles in Borghese!"

"At least we hunt animals. You are nothing but a hunter of turds!" laughs Tommaso.

"What are you, five years old?" yells Giovanni. "There is no skill in what you do, Ugo. You aim and shoot—where is the nuance?"

"I'm all nuance. I'm a skilled shot, I never miss!" roars Ugo.

"Then why do you carry around so much ammo?"

The boar hunters are forming a pack, getting in Giovanni's face. Aria barks and spins, warning the hunters to give Giovanni space. She does not like their sanguine smell of old pennies, of petrol and the power hungry. Sweat fills the air with a sudden misting of salt.

As the argument escalates in a language he cannot understand, the eyes of a young male Swede home in on particulars. On the hunting rifles swinging on the shoulders of men. On the vengeful pin eyes of the dead boar. On his terrified girlfriend, who is still angry at him for taking a wrong turn and missing the town of San Gimignano, causing them to miss the wine-tasting weekend at a castle that was to kick off their holiday, and who will now probably never sleep with him again.

Giovanni's hands fly as he protests. "Not even the decency to leave your guns outside! This is a bar, you have no respect for Lorenzo, no respect for Giusepp—"

"Hey, hey, hey!" yells Giuseppina, emerging from the *cucina* and yelling in a tone that threatens to resurrect the boar. She holds a platter of tiramisu to fatten up the Swedish youth. "Where are my beautiful guests?"

Giovanni is red in the face, which makes his great white mustache look like a fallen lighthouse. "Gone, Giuseppina! These brutes terrified them!"

"How did they get away without me hearing?"

"They slunk away silently. They were very skinny," he admits.

Giuseppina is devastated.

All she wants is what they have in Borghese—beautiful people from every beautiful place she could only ever dream of, sharing good food, wine, words. She didn't even get to ask them for a few Swedish phrases she could tuck away for a rainy day. And now they are gone. Just like Elisabetta.

Everyone leaves her.

Giuseppina lifts her tray of tiramisu—eight slices since she figured everyone else would want some—and lobs it at the hunters. Ugo, Tommaso, and the other three duck. Tiramisu, plates, and a tray smash against the stone wall, leaving a splattering that brings to mind the kinetic masterpieces of the modern abstract painter Francesco D'Adamo.

"Hey!" protest the hunters, touching their heads and inspecting their fingers for tiramisu.

"Come, Aria, we don't have to put up with this lunacy." Giovanni launches into motion with more oomph than expected, thanks to Giuseppina's espresso. He storms out of Bar Celebrità, wild-eyed and jittery.

Finally, thinks Aria. *Something is out there, waiting for us.*

Giuseppina watches Giovanni stride away, Aria leaping beside him. Her nostrils flare, a warning sign that terrifies the men left in the bar. The skin of her neck flushes a deep pink. "You scared away my beautiful skinny tourists, and you have made sweet Giovanni angry—what's the matter with you brutes? Giovanni is sensitive and struggling with the blues; Ugo, your blood pressure will be boiling by now! You have no business carrying that boar, you're asking for another hernia; and Tommaso, what do you think all this nonsense is doing to the health of your testicles? If they explode again, I am not taking you to the doctor! Padre, you are just an idiot. And poor, dear Lorenzo is clearly having mental problems. You other three don't live in this village, so I don't know your medical histories. But all of you are a bunch of baby boys! Now get out of here. And take your gigantic boar, who has more manners lying dead across my tables than you do."

"I don't have any health problems," brags Duccio.

"You will when I'm done with you," spits Giuseppina.

"Okay, okay, no one wants to celebrate with us, fine," says

Ugo before making an ill-timed comment about Giuseppina's flimsy singlet. Giuseppina snatches up a Nutella and Go! snack, throwing it directly at his head. A perfect hit.

"Say another lecherous word to Giuseppina and you'll meet both my fists!" yells Duccio.

"*Silenzio*, Duccio, or I'll fetch the axe!" quips Giuseppina.

Lorenzo yells from the *cucina*, "Leave the hooves and snout for me too!"

Giuseppina yells at the hunters, "Get out of here, but come back with the hooves and snout for Lorenzo. He is very skinny and delicate!" The hunters nod as they assemble around the boar, dipping into various stretches until they feel limber enough to lift it. "And you better be back here for dinner!"

Giuseppina wipes the sweat from her neck and picks up a pile of euros folded on the table where the Swedes were sat. She counts them. "Ah-ha!" she bellows at Lorenzo. "Twenty euros! See! My coffee is bringing money, tourists, and luck to the village. It is the elixir of life. It is why we will all live forever."

And much like the sneaky ambush of a hot flash, Giuseppina is struck by the words of the psychic she met at the Versilia seaside while vacationing alone to recover from the stupidity of the men she is surrounded by. She lets out a bloodcurdling scream.

"My god, my god, my god." Giuseppina wrings her hands together.

"Please don't use the Lord's name," says Padre, who is now rather weak in the knees from sitting through an entire season of a real-life soap opera without any caffeine. As he signs the cross, he is very close to passing out.

Lorenzo bursts from the kitchen having spilled hot *ragù alla bolognese* sauce all down his front in response to the scream.

"It is happening. It is real." Giuseppina fuses the back of her hand to her forehead.

"What is real?" Lorenzo yells. "Are you hurt?"

"The psychic. We just had a visitor!"

"We just had two visitors. And they weren't here on purpose; they didn't know what 'zar osc no' meant. No one does."

"Lorenzo, listen to me! The psychic said there would be a visitor. And she said that then there would be a death"—Giuseppina gasps, makes a spear of her arm, and aims it at the body of the wild boar.

"What else did she say?" asks the ever-impressionable Padre from the edge of his bar seat, on the verge of losing consciousness.

"She said that riches—and she meant a huge amount of money—would come to our village of Lazzarini Boscarino." Giuseppina holds up the money left by the Swedes.

"Twenty euros?" says Ugo skeptically, wrinkling his nose like a rabbit. There is a lot of confused murmuring between the hunters.

"I mean, that is a lot for Giuseppina's coffee," someone says so softly that only the fruit fly can hear.

"And then," bellows Giuseppina, "the psychic said a final thing. A bad thing…"

"What?" asks Lorenzo, staring at a drop of boar blood, the tableau of tiramisu on his wall, and a massacre of four bottles of Vino Nobile di Montepulciano behind the bar. Giuseppina makes the sign of the cross. Padre follows suit.

"What is it?" asks farmer Leon, who for this brief moment has been roused from fretting over the whereabouts of his wife, Sofia.

"Giuseppina, the drama, you're killing us!"

Giuseppina snatches up a packet of jelly candies laced with CBD and pops several into her mouth.

"Oh, *cavolo*. Lorenzo, I can't remember."

Chapter 2

Having put her heart, soul, and a sizable number of sedatives into her run for election, Delizia was horrified to discover that—when all the votes were counted, then counted thrice more after accusations of both fraud and senility—she had won. And with everything she now knows, the secrets unearthed in a dark room, Delizia finds herself in the worst imbroglio of her life.

Her suspicion is that she will not survive this morning. That even before the dreaded event has begun, they will find her splayed across the floor like one of those bearskin rugs they have next to fireplaces in American mansions. She might have had a chance if she'd slept, but last night she tossed and turned, unable to digest the *pappa al pomodoro* her husband had made to comfort her. The thick soup, with its *costoluto fiorentino* tomatoes, its rustic *pane Toscano*, rich river of olive oil, snarl of garlic, and bright lift of basil sat in her stomach, growling at her with a vengeance. A cup of camomile tea failed her at eleven p.m.

Torturous attempts at meditation left her in the lurch at midnight. At two a.m., some brandy was equally ineffectual. While staring down the end of the witching hour at four a.m., she had considered helping herself to a little horse tranquilizer, but decided she couldn't live with the additional guilt of depriving an enfeebled horse.

And so, eye bags bulging with the weight of unburied secrets, Delizia must now hold her inaugural meeting as the first female mayor of Lazzarini Boscarino in all its history. She scowls at the tables she has pulled together to seat everyone. The embarrassing bounty of pastries. Her husband has outdone himself—*cornetti* with pistachio cream, a *ciambella* honey cake, even *sfogliatella* with delicate leaf layers of crisp pastry. Of course, every last crumb is a blatant bribe to help her win over the affections of the *comune*—the municipality made up of villagers who meet to make governing decisions and bicker over pastries. Delizia shudders at a piece of paper listing the things they must discuss.

1. Sofia
2. Cats
3. Nonna Amara
4. You have to tell them. Do it now.

She stares at nauseating item number four. She is dreading it so much she could not even bear to write it down. Her eyes flick to the seat at the head of the table. Seat of the new mayor. Mayor Delizia.

Time trickles slowly in Tuscan towns, a glowing golden sap. But here in Nonna Amara's *ristorante*, Il Nido, it is as if that sap has solidified. Tables wear dormant white cloth like sundresses made of marble. Above, a steadfast lattice of old oak beams. Lifeless hundred-year-old wood-fired pizza oven, brick blackened by flames that once blistered dough into crisp bubbles. Walnut wood bar with an ancient till where a young Elisabetta used to ring up your bill, Nonna Amara undercharging everyone. Today the *ristorante* lies like a skeleton mourning the loss of its soul. The only flicker of life in the *ristorante* now appears at the base of the door that leads to the *cucina*. Where old sandstone wall meets terra-cotta tile is a tiny hole, no bigger than a dried white bean. Emerging from this secret hole is a small pioneer, black and glossy as an olive. She has been sent out to seek. The ant floats her well-groomed antennae to smell, senses awakening across each fine hair. Nimbly, delicate legs in a twitchy dance, the scout starts her voyage across the vast tile terrain of the *ristorante* in hunt of her treasure.

To the ant, Delizia is the height of a bell tower. The new mayor hiccups. Why in the world did she throw her hat in the ring of three candidates to run the village? A sense of duty, assuredly. Perhaps she felt she could make a difference, a delusion as wild as the constellation of poppies crocheted across the Tuscan countryside. Certainly, it was to make sure that her rival candidate, disgraced postman Duccio, did not rise to power. Adding a little pepper to the predicament, the third electoral candidate wasn't even human. And her husband had encouraged her, had he not? Said it would be good for her to succeed. Maybe what he really meant was that it would be good for her to finally see something through. But she didn't even win by a landslide, barely claiming victory over a donkey of legal drinking age. Whoever nominated him remains a mystery, but Maurizio very nearly became Lazzarini Boscarino's first nonhuman mayor. Winning is really just the beginning, and Delizia already feels as though she has lost.

Worst of all is that she ran for mayor before she discovered what was hidden right under their feet. Something sinister waiting below ground level for some unsuspecting soul to unearth it. And of course, that unsuspecting soul had to be her.

A thought rises like the thin tendrils of steam from the coffeepot set out for members of the *comune*, who will arrive any second now.

What have I done?

It is only temporary, she tells herself. She will stay in the village as mayor until she has found a successor who is neither Duccio nor a donkey, and then she will start again somewhere new. Blend herself into the soup of yet another big city. Start from scratch—it is her specialty. For Delizia might have been born here in the medieval village of Lazzarini Boscarino, but it is not now, nor will it ever be, her home.

She squints at the room through prop glasses she is wearing to appear political. Smells of the old *ristorante* rise up to torture her. Animalic leather of empty seats. Splatters of grease from years of dishes served with love and laughter. Melancholic musk from long-closed curtains. Perhaps even the pungent perfume of dead dreams. And another smell. Her own shame, manifesting as sweat bleeding across her blouse.

She should have taken the horse tranquilizer.

Her first meeting as mayor of Lazzarini Boscarino was supposed to take place in the traditional spot. But since Mayor Benigno's death and the absence of regular meetings, the traditional spot has been overrun. Several generations of *Glis glis*—whose aliases include "European edible dormouse" and the less flattering "European fat dormouse"—are currently exacting their squatter's rights in the town hall. The arboreal rodents, with their bushy tails and eyes like great lakes of outrage, had been affronted by Delizia's invasion. Even more affronted by the broom she waved about to encourage their exit. But there had just not been enough time to clean up the hailstorm of fecal pellets, to patch up holes they had nibbled into the window shutters, or to salvage various nests they made with the shredded remnants of several vital village documents, including the description of ordinances, code of ethics disclosure forms, and, rather poetically, a protest petition for rezoning.

"Fine," Delizia told the *Glis glis* counsel of representatives. "You win."

And so—in an act of irony and heartbreak—Delizia and the *Glis glis comune* at large decided it was best to hold the meeting here in Nonna Amara's shuttered *ristorante*, Il Nido. Delizia, already donning the tie of the slippery politician, chose it partly in strategy. She hoped that holding the meeting here might put her in better standing with the *comune*. Because who in all of Italy could be unhappy in Nonna Amara's *ristorante*? This is where everyone came to celebrate—from the birth of Giuseppina's daughter, Elisabetta, to the golden wedding anniversary of Carlotta and Gabriele. This is where all their babies grew up, finding their first steps on solid ground, staggering around like small sea creatures. First fistfuls of pasta and the gait of geese, waddling toward their first words, and, in the blink of an eye, their weddings. This is where they gathered together to eat manna pulled from the earth—fibrous roots tugged from sweet soil. Nonna Amara's fingers—parsnips in themselves— deftly bringing together ingredients into heirloom recipes made magical by Tuscan terroir. A particular alchemy of sun and soil and the poetry of happy plants. *Bringing together—* Nonna Amara's specialty. Even Delizia, who gave up trying to belong here when it never bore fruit, felt held here. With the shutdown of our *ristorante*, Delizia thinks, we are all uprooted.

Giovanni had helped Delizia remove the nailed boards, unearthing the teal front doors of Il Nido with the stone-arch frame and sun-cracked paint. Sunlight streamed in, the *ristorante* exhaled a stale breath, and memories flooded forth from this place whose old wooden bones creak like a great ship. Out floated a sadness scented like the oils of old paintings. People came from villages far and wide to fill up here at Nonna's *ristorante*. If it couldn't survive, what chance do any of the rest of them have?

Delizia gags—almost throws up on a plate of pastries. She quickly recovers, horrified. The *cornetti* have been saved. But she needs air. And quickly.

Delizia staggers to the window, a playful breeze fluttering her blouse. It bears a clean, calming resin of the cypress trees, and something else out there she is not able to smell quite yet. Something sneaky and sulfureous. A garlic cough, cheese ripe with attitude, a naughty note of fruit. A devilish song for the senses. A secret about to be spilled...

Delizia sighs. The view from *ristorante* Il Nido has not tarnished with time. Colluding clusters of hazelnut and cypress trees. Olive orchards, vineyards, lemon groves. Cascading terraces and the lovely blossoms of pastel pink and yellow houses. This very *ristorante* pops from the hillside with walls as yellow as the yolks Nonna Amara deftly folds into flour. And oh, the *ristorante*'s terrace, beautiful even now in October. Grapevines are sewing their tendrils artfully up the trellises. A bee bumbles along, humming a lovely hymn on its way to gather up gold from the flowers. Flowers that... wait a minute...

Why are there flowers?

The *ristorante* has been boarded up for months. Yet all the potted plants are still here, pruned to perfection. Delizia crouches, squinting quizzically at puddles. The plants have been recently watered. She pictures a paring knife piercing her chest, slipping between her ribs, burrowing out bits of her heart like seeds from a lemon. Darling Nonna Amara has somehow been sneaking in here and tending to the perennial plants in spite of everything. It is too much to bear.

Nausea creeps up Delizia's throat. She whisks off one of her high heels and throws up directly into the insole.

Gasping, Delizia stares down at the street below—empty except for Al Pacino, that sentient scrub brush of a cat, waddling across cobblestone, pregnant and patrolling for tourists.

I could run, Delizia thinks. It is not too late. The meeting has yet to start. Propped against the stone wall below is a bright red bicycle. She can still get out of this. She will steal that bicycle and ride it as if possessed. Down the winding road from the village, cypresses streaming beside her. Toward the fresh-cut-grass fragrance of freedom, into the bucolic fields and the heady smell of hay and manure. Back to doing more palatable things like castrating pigs and artificially inseminating livestock. She and Lorenzo will return to Florence or run away to any big city. A big city allows you to be anonymous, to slink among the streetlights, endlessly reinventing yourself under storefronts and neon signs. But in a tiny tight-knit village—try as you might—you can never hide from who you are.

The truth will always be unearthed.

Voices spar outside the front door of the *ristorante*. Delizia's heart is pounding so hard she sees spots. Her jaw quivers.

They are here.

As the first female mayor, she cannot afford to show weakness. She hurls her soiled shoe out of the window with great fortitude.

Valentina and Rosa appear in the doorway, all crinkly smiles and the spitting image of one another in pink and yellow cardigans, halos of dyed-black curls, and dangly earrings pulling their earlobes to their midcalves. Round and soft and smiling, they are hairdressers as well as twins, proud co-owners of the village's salon, Mozzafiato Hair. Behind the twins, Stefano, once the village driver, who now only drives his wheelchair, flatcap perched on a head smooth and brown as a porcini mushroom. Gentle Benedetto, the grocer, trudges after Stefano, drowning in an oversize tweed suit and looking for all the world like a tortoise Delizia once treated. Neck long and lined, eyes twinkling, Benedetto takes his time placing each loafer, as though conscious that they might crush something with a soul. He approaches Delizia, nodding, and hands her a wet fish. A glance down reveals that she has not been handed a fish, but rather, a clammy hand. She thanks Benedetto. Wipes her palm on her skirt.

Duccio the disgraced postman wafts into the *ristorante* like a sour smell. Following him is Carlotta, a nonagenarian speckled with sunspots. Her hair is a pale mist. Given her church-mouse stature, one might not suspect a lot of spice from this woman, but this would be as much of a mistake as gazing up at the night sky and thinking a star is small. Carlotta has been many things in her nine decades but is most proud of being grandmother to the village policeman.

As the *comune* board members babble excitedly about being inside the *ristorante* while bickering over seating arrangements, Delizia attempts to smile, bright blotches detonating before her eyes. She figures that at least if she dies, she will no longer be burdened by this terrible secret. And she will make it a point to come back and haunt her dear darling husband for being so supportive and encouraging her to run for office.

Valentina approaches Delizia, pinching strands of the thick hair that tumbles past the new mayor's shoulders. "Delizia, your hair...we can cover up these streaks of gray. Come and see us."

"Have you been swimming?" Rosa asks, prodding Delizia's sodden blouse.

"I'm simply a little warm."

Valentina's rouged cheeks lift. "The mayor of Lazzarini Boscarino. Who would have thought, little bare-bottom Delizia. Always running around naked, no one could ever convince you to put on a stitch of clothing. We remember the time you made a *cacca* all over the old café!" Laughter spritzes across the *ristorante* like a good parfum. This does nothing for Delizia's bureaucratic credibility.

"That happened when I was a baby, which was a very long time ago now. Please sit; let's get the meeting started."

"Did your shoe not come with a partner?" asks Valentina.

"Still can't get our Delizia to put on clothes properly!" laughs Rosa.

"Please sit," Delizia says with a gentle insistence.

The twins have an in-depth discussion via mental telepathy before tottering to their seats.

"Where is everyone else?" Delizia asks.

"Ah, they didn't come because Mayor Benigno won't be attending," says Rosa cheerfully.

A tight smile from Delizia. "I see. Well, Mayor Benigno not attending is mostly on account of his death. Let us start with our first order of business—"

"I don't think a woman can be mayor," mutters Duccio.

"—Thank you, those of you who have come, to my first *comune* meeting as mayor." Delizia squeezes her eyes shut to suppress a primal urge to sprint across the *ristorante* and join her shoe in its flight from the window.

Someone coughs.

"Where is Benigno?" bellows Stefano, blinking through his glasses like an unearthed mole. From his wheelchair, tennis ball–yellow trousers are singing about spring. Stefano is known for wearing the brightest and tightest trousers in all of Tuscany. Garments that inspire joy, to Giuseppina especially, who thinks that when strung up along a clothing line, they greatly resemble strands of drying pasta. But gone is Stefano's signature cloud of curls blowing in the breeze, his days of ferrying people up and down the windy village roads in his red Fiat Panda at a ferocious clip. He now lives in the spare bedroom of the good grocer, Benedetto. Stefano's memory comes and goes like May sunshine, but he has never lost his lively spirit and flair for flamboyant slacks. And his is the kind of loyalty that cannot be questioned, evinced by the fact that Stefano cast his electoral vote for the erstwhile mayor, even though Benigno is quite deceased.

Stefano blinks at the *comune* from behind glasses, waiting for an answer about Benigno. And with their silence, the *comune* members gathered in Nonna Amara's *ristorante* decide not to answer so as not to have to deliver the news of a death all over again.

Delizia decides to distract him with a bribe. "Please help yourself to pastries, Stefano. That's a *ciambella* honey cake."

"Where is the..." He spits, a gob of saliva sailing across the table and splattering onto Delizia's blouse. He saws at the air with his wrist since the word he's looking for has fluttered off like a nine-spotted moth.

Delizia holds up a finger to signal she will be right back.

As she is gone, the tiny forager ant, trailing her unparalleled sense of smell, appears at the top of the table, having scaled its leg. Her antennae, mostly the right one as is her preference, has led her here. To where pastries blow a zephyr broadcast of warm egg and sugar. The ant sways her antennae to determine what is before her. Gigantic bread buildings of nutty browned butter, flour, and fruit singing a malty music. Sugary structures towering side by side. A whole city of confections, each edifice the size of a castle. The ant, having found the Lost City of Sweetness, begins her sweeping skitter back to the nest. She is the runner, the scout, and she has hunted down paradise. The queen will be pleased. She will hurry. There is no telling who else might seek such a treasure.

Limping in one high heel to the *cucina*, Delizia ransacks

drawers, muttering to herself. "Knife, I know why I didn't bring a knife. My subconscious was trying to save my life. Who knows who will have stabbed me by the end of this meeting." On the stone lip of the antique sink sits a dusty old bottle of *vin santo*— holy wine. Divine timing if she's ever experienced it. Delizia takes a healthy swig and makes the swift discovery that the bottle no longer harbors holy wine but is a vessel for vintage duck fat. While spitting duck fat into the sink, she makes the political decision—on second thought—not to bring a knife to the table.

Delizia catches her breath and then her reflection in an old copper pasta pot. A wealth of silver threads are woven through her thick hair. The only silver society doesn't deem valuable. Forty-five years of running away from this village, and now she is its mayor. It is a wonder her hair isn't white. She peers in closer, scanning for those pesky little chin hairs. Why are those necessary? Who is she going to look like in ten years— Leonardo da Vinci? She readjusts her dummy glasses. She can do this if she can just tuck her stress under the surface of her skin where no one can see it, she tells herself. If she can just bury it.

"Do not show weakness. First female mayor. Don't drag this out, Delizia, just get to the point. Simply stand before them and tell them the truth."

Delizia removes her lonely shoe and hobbles back to the table barefoot.

1. Sofia

"Cake later. Let us start with the first order of business... Sofia."

"Sofia is missing," interjects Carlotta, whose diminutive size and prominent nose liken her to the Etruscan shrew.

"It's true. She never misses a hair appointment," the twins say in unison. "We must find her."

Delizia draws a breath. Sofia comes to her first in scent: vanilla and the warm smell of a summer storm, when the soil gets its wings. She steals back in time to a memory of Sofia on the piazza outside Bar Celebrità, the evening broken by a great crack in the sky. Rain pelting down in fierce filaments. Everyone on the piazza ducking, scurrying indoors like *Glis glis*. But Sofia stays, laughing—gratuitous howl of the uninhibited—shaking her hands at thunder as if in private communion with the gods. She is twirling clumsily, recklessly really, blunt bob white as the villa across the hill. Dizzy now, she staggers, soaked through, gulping from the wineglass in her hand. Her husband Leon approaches, shelters her with his shadow, urging her to join him inside the bar. Sofia waves him off with veiny wrists. They are the only ones in the rain-soaked piazza. Side by side, a bird and a bear. Leon placing his huge hand on her elbow, bony as a bat wing. Sofia screaming at him, collapsing onto the cobblestones. Her wineglass shattering, and now the storm is in her eyes, in Sofia staring at shards, the wine turning into water. Everyone in Bar Celebrità turning their heads, averting their eyes from the window. It is the polite thing to do.

"Has anyone seen her in the last week?" Delizia asks. When there is no response, she continues. "I spoke to Poliziotto Silvio."

"My grandson!" squeaks Carlotta. "He will find Sofia."

Delizia nods. "...Silvio says that he is looking for Sofia, but that the *carabinieri* don't suspect anything suspicious. Sofia is free to make her own decisions and travel to wherever she chooses. It's not the first time—"

"We think she was murdered!" yells Valentina, her twin throwing arms into the air for pathos. It seems early in a *comune* meeting for a murder accusation, but what would Delizia know? This is only her first.

Duccio, disgraced postman and sharp stone in the shoe of the village, adds, "The *carabinieri* should search Borghese; I bet they'd solve the mystery of where Sofia is then. And by that, I mean that she is drinking and having sex."

The table falls silent as everyone ponders this. Rumors spread like spores across a small village. Whispers about Sofia sneaking around on Leon with someone in the neighboring town of Borghese have long been in the wind. But Delizia will not have her first meeting devolve into gossip. She bristles, envisioning a gaggle of geese honking at one another, necks snaking side to side.

"Other than reaching out to anyone we think might know where Sofia is, I propose that we leave the police to do their jobs and that we take care of poor Leon. How about an *osso bucco* night at Bar Celebrità? It's his favorite. We must make sure he knows that we are here for him during this difficult time."

"Oh! I know!" chant the twins. Valentina takes over: "He is worried about Maurizio's birthday."

"Wonderful, Valentina and Rosa. Then we will make sure to make Maurizio's celebration special. How old will Maurizio be on his birthday?"

"Twenty-two. Is that old for a donkey, Delizia?"

"They can actually live until about forty."

"Maurizio!" cheers Stefano. A moment of silent appreciation for everyone's favorite donkey.

Duccio snorts. "Maybe Leon had enough of Sofia. People can sometimes just snap. Not surprised Sofia cheats on him. Passed over for an old ass. I'd take to the bottle too—"

Delizia snaps. "If you have nothing nice to say, you know where the doors are, you old goose." The room rings in silent surprise. Delizia cannot believe she has just called Duccio a goose. The ageism as well. It does not seem mayoral. A sharp sniff. "Members of the *comune*, I apologize. That was uncalled for and will never happen again. Let the record show."

The *comune* search the room, wondering where and what the record is.

At the other side of the *ristorante*, the scout ant has arrived back at the nest. She has scattered a careful trail of phero-mones, a path of scent crumbs leading from the hidden city of confections to the nest. She arrives, diffusing her signature blend of scents into home base. Ants all around churn and eddy, roused into frenzy by her chemical clues. Through che-mosense, they know she has found the sweetest of treasures. An ant horde rallies and follows the first pheromones of the trail that promises to lead them to utopia.

2. Cats

Delizia moves things along. "The next item on my agenda is to discuss the village cats. There are too many. I would like to implement a spay-and-neuter program—"

"Barbaric!" yells Duccio. "All of them will die little virgins. Why deprive them of the greatest pleasure of life? Even our village cats deserve to make love!" The passion with which he enunciates lovemaking, the forceful, mouth-molding *m*, shoots his upper dentures onto the tabletop. He scoops them up and slips them back against his gums, soft folds of his mouth filling in around their horseshoe shape.

Delizia continues. "It's better for the health of the cats and the village if—"

"You just want to carve them up because that's where you get your jollies."

Carlotta shouts, "Oh, *silenzio*, Duccio, you old goose." She winks at Delizia.

A survival tactic, Delizia's mind unspools into the sky as if snagged by a breeze. It is true she would much rather be making a slow surgical incision, up to her elbow in the birth canal of a cow or blasting bladder stones from the urethra of a miniature poodle. But that is because Delizia is a veterinarian. Or at least, she was, having graduated from veterinary school at the University of Pisa, worked at several veterinary practices across northern Italy over the years, running away before ever laying roots in any one place. Anchoring roots leaves you vulnerable to blight, to pests. Better to pack your bags after being passed over time and time again for promotion to partner by the men running these veterinary practices and the rest of the world. Each time, holding herself together until she got home to Lorenzo and shattered into pieces. She takes a deep breath and thinks of Lorenzo. A wonderful man who unburdens her of old hurts. He diffuses kindness, generous as a great oak tree to those around him. Her husband wants her to take her time here, to heal in the village, but oh, did she protest when he called it her home.

It was a phone call that had brought Delizia back to Lazzarini Boscarino—that most dreaded nighttime mewling, punctuated by the noises of nightfall—soft questions posed by an owl, a song of cicadas. She had answered, still in a thick stew of sleep. A voice like a gravel road rumbled her into consciousness. Ludovica. The wife of Mayor Benigno.

She spoke calmly, spreading out the facts into the darkness and distance between them. A sentence here and there shattered by her smoker's cough. News of the death of Mayor Benigno brought Delizia back to the village where she was born. Where she spent so many summers trying to belong. And now somehow, in a ludicrous turn of events that her husband would surely attribute to some insect farting on the other side of the world, she is its mayor.

Delizia returns to the *ristorante* to find Benedetto eyeing her with suspicion. "What will you do with all these cat balls?"

"We don't keep the testicles as trophies, Benedetto."

Duccio growls. "Cat balls now and then who will be next? Stefano, Benedetto, Lorenzo, Padre Francesco? Castrate all the males of the village, why don't you?"

Valentina leans toward Duccio, earrings like wrecking balls. "At least it would be an easy job in your case, since they are dragging along the ground behind you." This earns her an uncoordinated high five from her twin.

"Like two chestnuts in a wet sock," adds her sister.

With newly heightened civil servant senses, Delizia gauges a need to regain control of the meeting. She claps her hands to silence the *comune*. She does not notice an entire army of ants marching up the leg of her table, questing a tidy trail of pheromones left by the scout ant. A colony of ants so very, very close to nirvana.

3. Nonna Amara

"The third item on the agenda," Delizia says, "is Nonna Amara."

A collective sigh shivers through the *ristorante*. Silence while everyone present thinks of Nonna Amara, her grin with its signature gap. Arms soft as the dough she kneads, bosom large as the bags of flour she bullies around her *cucina*. Nonna Amara shuffles slowly in her slippers, but how fast those thick fingers are. They fly toward a cheek to stroke it, prod a rib in suggestion of a second serving, hold you so hard and so tenderly in a hug that your worries become weightless. The *comune* can all see her sitting outside this very *ristorante* when she has chosen to take a quick rest. "Rest" meaning that she is flagging down as many friends as she can, slicing apart the world's problems with

her positivity. Silver Saint Christopher around her neck winking under the sun. Both legs propped on a crate of aubergines,
varicose veins embroidering her calves like Chantilly lace, like
sentient filaments spidering under dark soil. She is eighty-six,
but it seems she has always been as she is now. Wise. Wonderful.

"Come, come and talk to your *nonna*," says everyone's
nonna, cheeks rosy as autumnal apples. There is nothing she
hasn't heard. No news that can knock her off course. Not the
malmignatte—the Mediterranean black widow spider family
she found hiding in her glove. Not the enraged bull who clat-
tered through a rotting gate, chased across the cobblestones by
a younger Amara wielding a pizza paddle. Not an angry man—a
swarthy Sicilian gangster who came to drum up business in the
village—half her age and twice her size, as she stared him down
and gave him marching orders. And after "rest," back to her
cucina, the language of her love carved into a charcoal-kissed
steak. Flicked with the spears of rosemary grown in her garden.
Smeared without reserve over each crisp disc of crostini.

The *comune* are thinking of what happened to everyone's
nonna three years ago.

The seventh of June.

Nonna Amara had been in her garden when a rumbling
growled up through her feet. She stood, turned from rows of
lettuce toward the mountainside towering behind her house,
trees and rocks looming above. As the growling grew—low
notes of a cello swelling from every crumb of soil—Nonna put-
tered down the stony driveway to inspect her shed. With one
deafening crack, half a mountainside came down beside her.
A river of rock destroyed her terraces, a forty-year-old cherry
tree, and one side of her house. In terrible cosmic mockery,
the landslide took out her *cucina* and her old pizza oven, reduc-
ing her haven to ruins. Forced from the home she grew up
in, she has been staying at Stefano's old house. Next door to

his boarded-up guest room that once housed tourists. Nonna Amara's life shuttering up all around her.

"Give us the good news!" bleat the twins. Gasps. "You will fix the road and the damage to Nonna Amara's house so that she can finally go home!"

Delizia's throat fills with flour. "I'm afraid we don't yet have the funds to help Nonna Amara. But I am the new mayor, and as the new mayor, I plan to prioritize it. I bring it up to assure you all that I will do everything I can."

The twins stand ceremoniously. Their eyes are shining like the backs of beetles. "We have something exciting to share."

"The floor is yours," says Delizia, regretting it more than the time she unwittingly jabbed herself with an animal euthanasia needle.

"We and Carlotta have a surprise," say the twins. "We have pooled together a little…love." Rosa reaches into the front pocket of her cardigan to place a stack of folded notes next to the coffeepot. Delizia holds her breath and counts. Four hundred and sixty-three euros. A lump, hard as a cold chestnut, lodges itself in the esophagus of the new mayor. Four hundred and sixty-three. An amount so small it will do nothing for Nonna Amara's predicament, but it is a large lump sum for the twins. Half the time, they don't charge for their haircutting. And Carlotta hasn't worked since she settled here, which many have speculated was sometime around the Roman invasion. She now survives on what little Gabriele left her. To stop herself from weeping, Delizia forms a small puckered plum stone with her mouth.

She goes to speak. It feels like she is swallowing small bones. "What a lovely gesture for Nonna Amara. I will make sure this money goes toward the fund to fix her house."

Delizia now notices that writhing black tentacles have descended upon her pastries. Ants, female, all of them (for the males are useless), are crawling up the sides of the *ciambella* cake, the *sfogliatelle*. They have conquered the croissants. Ant colonies, Delizia has read, do not value their aged. Whereas in human society, young boys are drafted for battle, in an ant *comune*, old females are banished from the nest and sent to war. Those disabled or long in the antennae are sent away so as not to be a burden to the queen and the younger workers. The more time they accumulate, the more treacherous the tasks placed upon them—from keeper to scout, then patrol force to suicide soldier. Those who die in the nest are eaten. The aged are discarded and disposed of. Delizia stares at a colonization of her croissants. She can no longer feel her toes.

She glances at an agenda beaming at her from bright white paper, but she already knows.

The moment is here.

Her dread has swollen into something warty and burl-like, something monstrous and grotesque. It is time for the last item on the list.

4. You have to tell them. Do it now.

Her voice cracks. "The next item is a little bit delicate. I have been looking over Mayor Benigno's bookkeeping..."

Here is the thing that tortured her all night. And a quiet calamity occurs. A truth pops up in front of her, as if plucked from a patch of soil. She is realizing, standing here in front of matching cardigans and a wheelchair hosting bright-yellow trousers and even Duccio's bitter aperitivo of a scowl, that she is in love with these humans. Twins Valentina and Rosa, who braided her hair and bought her gelato every summer she spent here, a lost little slip of a thing. Stefano, who has traded the wheels of an automobile for those of a chair, who used to ferry her around in his Fiat Panda. Even disgraced Duccio, when he was trusted to be the village postman and he would bring her cherished horse magazines on his postal rounds, going out of his way and adding an extra hour to his route so that she had something to read and a break from pretending Nonna Amara's tree-planting shovel was a stallion. Benedetto, the gentle grocer, a green bean of a man who turned a blind eye to her rebellious phase, teenage fingers foxily plucking contraband from his shelves like fat figs. She thinks of Giuseppina, who brought her tiny floral dresses, danced with her in the piazza on warm summer nights, fireflies strobing across the hillside like fairies. Giuseppina, who channeled the most ferocious of Leon's guard geese when Delizia—younger, wilder—met that oily man at the village. When young Delizia had attempted to inoculate herself with shots of vodka, and that man—a sly-eyed stoat who smelled of cherry tobacco and trout—had tried to take her home, handsy, patting her down as if she were dirt. Giuseppina honked at him, demanded to know what kind of a weasel handles a woman like a side of ham. She peppered him with questions about Delizia, and when he couldn't answer a single one of them—not her last name, her phone number, or what she had had to drink that night—she chased him out of Bar Celebrità, had Stefano drive that stoat out of the village, out of Delizia's life, out of Italy for all she knew. Carlotta, a child during the Battle of Garfagnana, a nun and a nurse in another life, bending to speak to Delizia's imaginary friend with a quiet dignity. She and these wonderful souls all nourished by Nonna Amara. Nourished by the land itself.

She must now tell the humans she loves how dire their predicament is. How their home of Lazzarini Boscarino is about to become an Italian ghost village. Like tiny, tucked-away Lucchio, abandoned because it was only accessible on foot. Like Rocca San Silvestro, a ghost town since the fourteenth century after a curse of wars, economic hardship, and the Black Death. Col di

Favilla, ravished by the Second World War. Buriano, which died twice, first by gradual depopulation, the second demise due to bureaucratic bickering. Tuscan towns and villages scooped out to mere shells. No souls, and therefore, no soul. Delizia stares at these people she loves and staggers as though on sea legs.

Where will they go? No one here is rich in a monetary sense. It's as she's always seen it: the cruelest people have the comfort of money and the good-hearted have none. The raw and rustic truth is that the good folk of Lazzarini Boscarino are not just in debt. They are destitute. This beautiful medieval village will not be taken by Black Death or an act of God. It has been dying a slow death, slipping away a little more every season.

Delizia clears her throat. All eyes upon her. She just has to say it, to tell them. The truth will set you free, they say, but the truth won't set any of these wonderful people free. It will crush them; it will take hostage their hope, and what of their health? Carlotta is in her nineties, for the love of loyalty.

Delizia's heart is a fast-breathing frog. She parts her lips. "The village...is in...it has a little debt. But there is really nothing to worry about. I have a plan."

She has lied.

She has held the truth from the good people who have always belonged in the village where she was born. The feeling of failure falls upon her like a tranquilized horse.

"Look! Ants are all over the pastries...we can't eat these, Delizia," says Rosa.

"What about Nonna Amara's house?" Stefano asks, forgetting they had just touched on item three of the agenda.

The feeling of failure falls more like a herd of tranquilized horses.

To help Nonna Amara, the *comune* must pay for the side of the mountain that looms above her land to be secured, and then the additional funds to fix what the landslide has done to her house. A song to the tune of not four hundred and sixty, but rather two million euros. For the road fixing alone. Delizia wants to find a tiny hole in a stone wall and crawl into it.

The next move must be made. She has already lied to them, so how much worse is offering them a bit of false hope? "I think the best use of our time today is to gather together some ideas on how to bring more people to the village."

"We don't need more people at the village," grumbles Duccio.

"We actually do. All of our children have grown up, some of our children's children have grown up, and they have all done well and taken big jobs in big cities, and who could blame them? This is what we wished for. But with the economy the way it is and our dwindling and, dare I say it, aging population—"

"Speak for yourself!" says Carlotta, shrew pupils pinning.

"We are young of heart and old of face!" laughs Rosa.

"—our numbers are very low, and we need to revitalize our village. We need to find ways to bring an influx of people and money." Delizia pictures Nonna Amara peeling carrots, ruffling the curls of a toddler. A fire is born in her chest, bright as the living hair of every candle at the Luminaria, Lucca's festival of lights. "And why couldn't we? Our village is one of the most beautiful in all of Tuscany. We still have soul in our rural roots. We must become a place that people want to visit. There are villages around us that have built a reputation and, in doing so, bring people from all over the world. We must evolve and be like...Borghese."

Silence swills around the room like good wine in a glass. Borghese is not often mentioned in the village of Lazzarini Boscarino, akin to whispering the name of a fascist dictator or a villainous Venetian ghost who might be summoned by his name. It is especially not expected to be mentioned by Delizia, whose dear husband Lorenzo has a very personal reason to never want the name Borghese to be uttered again. For Lorenzo, the word Borghese means betrayal.

Silence lingers, and Delizia believes she has lost them. "Okay, not Borghese, we will not speak of that place. But what about Bussana Vecchia? It was decimated by an earthquake, thousand-year-old stone towers crumbled to dust. And now? Now it's an artist haven. Artists came and made it whole again." She starts to excite herself. "Civita di Bagnoregio! Also flattened by an earthquake!"

"This is depressing," says Benedetto.

"But people came in and touched things up, and now tourists flock there. What about the town of Riace? They had the same problem we have, a dwindling population. And they opened their hearts and welcomed refugees and immigrants—"

"We're not doing that," snips Duccio.

"—and now they are a vibrant town! And, of course, who could forget the now famous, once doomed town of Calcata? Where, after being lost for fifteen hundred years, the most sought-after and sacred religious relic was found hidden in a grotto. The Santissimo Prepuzio! Jesus Christ's foreskin! The holy foreskin! The only part of himself he left after his divine ascension! And people still flock to a now vibrant Calcata, even though the holy foreskin was lost again."

"No one here has a holy foreskin," says Carlotta matter-of-factly.

"You are missing my point, dear *comune*! We just need to be creative and think about what makes our little medieval village on the hill magical."

A long, sour silence. And then, face furrowed, wise eyes pinning—it is Benedetto who throws out the first suggestion.

"We could have some music nights at Bar Celebrità."

"Good! Yes, if you have an idea, throw it out for all of us to hear and I will write it down." Delizia grabs a pen and starts to scribble over her cursed agenda.

"We could make it illegal to die!" says Rosa.

Benedetto chimes in with, "We could sell some of the empty ramshackle properties around the village to foreigners for one dollar."

"We don't want poor foreigners; we want rich foreigners!" Duccio rolls skeptical eyes.

Conversation cannot always be controlled—much like cats or the rain or old-age pensioners. But it can be lovingly guided, and so Delizia does just this. "Maybe think of what is special about our village that could be attractive to visitors?"

Clouds part in the skies of Stefano's memory. A smile spreads across his face like May sun. "Giuseppina's bosom!" he bellows.

"'Come to our beautiful medieval village and bring home a cat!" adds Rosa.

"No one wants these cats; they are all insane and inbred. It is the mountain air. Makes everyone a little crazy," Duccio grumbles.

"Especially the men," adds Rosa.

Carlotta studies the stone wall as if translating its old contours. "People should want to come and see us. We're a good-looking bunch!"

Delizia feels a warmth watching the villagers brainstorm. Or maybe that is just what it feels like when your heart is breaking, when you feel hopeless. A great crack in your chest, an egg spilling hot yolk over your lungs.

"What if we do a medieval night where we arm everyone with swords?" asks Benedetto.

"Too much," Delizia says gently.

"Knives then; everyone will have a knife and will have to

fight their way to Bar Celebrità for one free Aperol spritz!" Benedetto laughs.

"A naked Vespa convoy!" Stefano throws up his fist in triumph.

"Think more along the lines of wide appeal."

"We can't help it, we are a very passionate people; it might be all the garlic," Benedetto adds.

"Garlic night, a sensual night for the lovers!" Stefano is flushed.

"I've got it! What about Orso?" Benedetto cries, producing a bottle of the grain alcohol he makes, a bear snarling across its label. A liquor so strong it could clean a crime scene.

"What about Mayor Benigno's olive oil?" asks Valentina. "Surely there is lots of it left."

Delizia suddenly cannot breathe.

It is not the talk of his death or the terrible legacy he has left behind that has stolen her breath. It is the mention of olive oil. Grief is a sea. At times placid, still, and gray as glass. And others, squalling and savage. The chaos of a muscular undertow and wicked winds. Delizia finds herself bobbing in a boat on that sea of grief. At the will of the waves. The olive oil, which she can suddenly smell, has caused the ground beneath her to swell, turn into choppy waters. Notes of walnuts, waxy fruit, and a leafy taste on the tongue dragging her back to her first few days back in Lazzarini Boscarino after the midnight phone call.

She had been given a key. An antique of a thing, rusted into something straight from a fairy-tale book. Ludovica had scowled at Delizia as she held out the enormous key in cigarette fingers. She was wearing oversize cat-eye glasses that shielded the fireless coals of her eyes. But Delizia remembered the glare well enough from childhood, from summers when Stefano drove her to the village, back when Ludovica was the village seamstress. Her body still had some of the hard angles Delizia remembered, though she had shrunken, skin leathered by smoke and sun.

"There," said Ludovica. "The key is yours. Whatever you learn in there, it's at your own peril. You'll have to clean up after him. He is dead now, and so I am done doing that for him." She sucked on a cigarette as if to punish it. Then she released a long plume of blue resentment into Delizia's face in what had turned out to be, in their history, a pretty amicable exchange.

Delizia found it shock enough to discover the crypt under the church. Why hadn't she known about the crypt, where two cobweb-covered sarcophagi sit, holding the skeletal remains of some long-dead men of the cloth? A lifetime of knowing this village, but not its dark, underground vault filled with ancient statues of saints and religious relics. Where, in a corner of the crypt, boxes sat like bullies intimidating a rickety table and chair. And—her heart sank as she saw—bottles and bottles of Benigno's beloved olive oil. Hundreds of the dragonfly-green carafes, filled with the sacred ambrosia from his personal groves, each olive tree the true love of his life. Hawking his olive oil was what he always did, and what he was doing instead of making good on mayoral promises. Olive oil as a curative. As an aphrodisiac. A ritual. For a faulty heart. To lube up your limbs or a squeaking door hinge. Each with a handmade label, some of them reserved for villagers. *For Stefano*, in his handwriting, a spiderly tracing. *For Carlotta*. Even one *for Tommaso's testicles*. Here, in a crypt surrounded by mummified bodies and possibly the ghosts of clergy past, is where Mayor Benigno must have read in the light stammering from candles. A forbidden rustic funk all around.

Delizia spent the best part of two dark days down in the crypt, rummaging through the scattered papers and broken bookkeeping of the late Mayor Benigno. Mayor as long as anyone could remember. Why had he hidden himself in a sub-terranean lair to attend to the matters of the village?

Hunched over the deceased man's desk, dizzy from the musk, Delizia traced every inky bit of evidence he left behind. And late one night, in the dark and dank—she found his ledgers. Breathless, she discovered the truth. The sums of money applied for and allocated to the village for the government are missing. Five hundred thousand euros approved of and received, and not a euro accounted for. All the additional personal donations and saving by the villagers, funds for Nonna Amara, the village sign, to fix its road and buildings, any chance at reopening the *ristorante*. All the money to save Lazzarini Boscarino, missing.

What did he do with the money?

Delizia scoured the crypt, his home—Ludovica watching her closely—and found nothing. Ludovica said he left no money. Only his treasured olive oil, the gold from his groves.

And so the medieval village of Lazzarini Boscarino is doomed.

It is dying.

The village ethos is all about the threads that tie its people together. Ties of trust that wind under the soil and around every cobblestone of the village, ringing brightly with the tower bells all the way back through time. Mayor Benigno betrayed the people he had promised to protect. He stole from his own village. He died and he got away with it.

Sickened, Delizia had found his personal journal. Dramatic ramblings about the harvesting of olives and seasons of success for his oil, paranoid scribblings about the reception of various batches, the obsessive chronicles of a blight. A blight, but notably not a word dedicated to his daughter. There were, however, among the entries of fraudulent bookkeeping, several horrifying entries dedicated to his sex life with Ludovica.

Delizia felt her muscles stiffen. It was painful to be in the presence of Ludovica. Delizia was once again a twelve-year-old, staying at Mayor Benigno's house. Slinking down the stairs to spy on him. Overhearing her father consoling Ludovica, vowing that he will always put Ludovica first. That the child means nothing to him. It was Delizia's first failure. That she didn't matter enough.

Delizia stared at the rusty patina on the lonely key. The key to her father. With a yell, she threw it at the stone wall. Lightheaded, she put her head between her knees. Delizia does not know what to do about the missing money. The crypt smells like decay, like a haunting. An oppression of olive oil bottles encircling her. Her father loved the olive oil more than he ever loved her.

The village bells spill their sweeping music across the village, rattling stone and brick and bone. They shatter Delizia's memory and bring her back to the *ristorante*. Valentina and Rosa leap to their feet.

"Lunch!" they chime.

"A good meeting," says Carlotta as she steps tidily toward the teal doors. "And I've been to a few."

Valentina folds Delizia into a hug. Her heartbeat is steady, her hair smells of coconut. Delizia wants to weep.

Gentle Benedetto wheels Stefano—engrossed in following the adventures of a loosened thread from his trousers—toward her. Benedetto squeezes her shoulder, and beams. "Apple doesn't fall far from the tree, eh?"

Delizia hopes the apple does fall far from the tree. She hopes that when the apple had fallen, it careened off a steep slope and down into the village of Borghese to be trampled upon by a visiting procession of world-class violinists. She wants to be nothing like her fraud of a father. Not to have inherited a familial trait of failure.

She swallows her shame like a cold oyster.

Just outside the *ristorante*, she hears a lugubrious tone that is uniquely a disgraced postman's. "I still think the donkey should have won."

The new mayor stands alone in Nonna Amara's *ristorante*, airing out her blouse with quaking fingers. The donkey might well have been the better choice, she thinks. She couldn't even shepherd *Glis glis*, never mind the entire village. How has she just allowed herself to lie, to cover for her estranged father? She should not still be hunting his approval.

She is left alone with the ants. Watching the tiny black coterie wordlessly carting off *sfogliatella* crumbs, sweet trophies ten times their size. She is humbled. Admires their efficiency, their assured action. She wishes they would whisk her away too.

A thought sinks its stinger into her.

We are all on the hunt for something.

Chapter 3

Giovanni jerks the gear stick. His Jeep shudders along a road that winds up and down the countryside. A scowl storms across his face, tidy white broom of a mustache bristling. He is speeding, the Jeep roaring into a higher gear as if an expression of his rage. Giovanni tackles each tight corner as though he is driving a Ferrari.

"*Vai all'inferno!*" Giovanni yells. He has been kidnapped by the past, entangled in memories from a few hours before this present moment.

Aria bumps around in the back of the Jeep on muddy towels. Beside her, young Fagiolo yips with excitement. Born nine months ago, Fagiolo has no inkling of where he is going, though this does not temper his enthusiasm in the least. He has little life experience but enough to know that every moment is his best one yet. He is the same breed as Aria, a Lagotto Romagnolo, though in contrast to Aria's patchwork of brown blotches, all his curls are the color of fresh cream. Giovanni, when first laying

eyes on Fagiolo curled asleep in a whelping box of darker puppies, named him for his resemblance to a tiny white cannellini
bean. Even before his birth there had been so many hopes piled
upon that little bean. The highest of those hopes? That he would
become a skilled hunter of the most desirable Tuscan treasure.

In the back of the Jeep, the dogs pant in breathy rhythm,
woolen curls bouncing. Young Fagiolo darts ochre eyes at the blur
beyond the window, fields ablaze in autumnal colors. His whole
body quivers in anticipation like a wobbly plate of panna cotta.

"Traitor," Giovanni snarls, revving the Jeep around a bend.
He whips past peach villas with green shutters. "I am not the
traitor, Ugo. You are the traitor. *Chiudi il becco! Vai a quel paese!*"

Giovanni is adamant he has done nothing wrong. Anyone would do the same in his position, he tells himself. What
choice does he have? And Lorenzo doesn't think he is a traitor; that is Ugo's assumption alone. Buffoon. Here, Giovanni
forms a perfect picture of Ugo's rifle, its metallic wink, the long
sneer of its shape. He is haunted by a quick breath of boar's
blood. Giovanni feels the old metronome of his heart. Small
fires blaze up the skin of his neck. To distract himself from the
anger burning through his body, he replays the morning and
his preparations for the hunt ahead.

At dawn, he and the dogs had stood on his tiny balcony
admiring shards of thin light striating the cypress trees across
the hills. He fed the dogs breakfast next to his planters filled
with smiling geraniums. Metal bowls piled with spinach, rice,
chicken, carrots, zucchini—sometimes he simmers it all in
soup or broth. The imperative distinction is that the dogs must
be served food Giovanni himself has eaten first. Rarely, he will
force the jaws of an opener along a tin of fresh dog food. Even
then, he might dip a finger in the jellied meat, slip a glob under
his tongue. Giovanni will not allow a morsel that he has not
approved—not an innocent biscuit given by a beloved villager,

not cake crumb or stringy sliver of prosciutto left under a table—near his dogs. Given their gifts, that they are able to seek out gold hidden under the forest floor, his Lagotti are priceless, and Giovanni cannot afford to let them out of his sight. Not since he saw fellow treasure hunter Ilario hunched on a bench outside the chic *ristorante* Novelli in Borghese. Inconsolable, his hands curled into questioning claws as he wailed over the loss of his springer spaniel, Pascal. "Stolen," he sobbed. "Taken from me." Not since another hunter, Augusto, ran through the twilit streets of Borghese, face haunted. His voice fracturing as he screamed. Augusto scared tables abubble with tourists, silencing clinks and bright caws of laughter with his bellowing.

"Murder!" he yelled into the populated piazza, an accusation hurled at bustling patios with umbrellas wearing twinkle lights. Above a group of musicians whose fingers hovered over instruments in horror. Against the pink and yellow walls of glowing store fronts.

"Murder!" And it was true. Someone had slipped poison into meatballs left out for his beloved mutt and star treasure seeker, Pippo.

Giovanni will not allow this to be the fate of Aria and Fagiolo. But there are those who would commit any crime to know where the secrets buried under the soil hide. To find the loot in the loam. To strike gold. This is why Giovanni keeps his hunting grounds concealed. Only he and his dogs know the location of the treasure troves and how to hunt a gaseous ghost.

Stalking. Thievery. Murder.

He shudders. This is what's at stake. Giovanni is so cautious, the last thing he did before loading the dogs this morning was run an inspection mirror under the chassis of his Jeep. A lesson he learned the hard way. Too easy for some scoundrel to attach another tracking device. Too easy to be tailed and have your secrets stolen.

Feeling his blood start to boil again, Giovanni shakes his head. Undoubtedly, his heart is racing because of Giuseppina's coffee and when, after the farcical mess that scared away the young Swedish tourists at Bar Celebrità, Ugo had called him a traitor. How dare he, that oafish lout!

Marooned in his own mind, wallowing in disturbed thoughts, Giovanni wends another tight corner, only this time he does it at the exact same time as a Vespa driver speeding from the other direction. Aria barks. Giovanni wrenches the gear stick, the dogs flopping to one side of the Jeep. The Vespa driver swerves, wheels warping into a sharp zigzag before he salvages control and snakes into the space Giovanni has left him in jerking the Jeep to the right. The Vespa driver shakes his fist, releasing an arpeggio of high-pitched honking. Giovanni, face as red as *pomarola* sauce, roars out colorful descriptions of the Vespa driver's corporeal parts. Fagiolo mistakes this for singing, joining in with a happy little howl of his own.

The Jeep splutters on. From the back window, wise Aria sees the scenery changing. Centuries-old farmhouses and turquoise pools give way to the shadows of branches feathering down onto the Jeep. The road narrows, the Jeep slowing to seesaw over rocks and the unruly tapestry of a forest floor. Aria whines in recognition at thin trunks of poplar, oak, hazelnut, their prodigal spray of gold and green leaves. She barks, a clear, high note of approval. Young Fagiolo follows up with frantic yapping in clueless but genuine jubilation.

The terrain roughens until Giovanni has to throttle the wheel with both hands, the Jeep rasping, wheels spinning over leaf litter and mud. And, when scrubby trees ahead form a palisade and they can drive no farther into the forest, Giovanni stomps the brakes. The Jeep chokes to a stop. Fagiolo howls, a quavering in D minor. Giovanni is still lost in the elsewhere of human happenings. He mutters as he strides to the back of the Jeep, waxen olive-green jacket and Wellingtons squeaking. He opens the back door. Fagiolo springs to his freedom, flying laps around the Jeep, paws barely skimming the leaf litter, the whites of his eyes gleaming.

Wise Aria waits in the trunk. She lifts her nose to Giovanni. Rising from the skin of her person is a volatile scent. The chili-and-vinegar tang of his fury has fermented into a sulfuric miasma. Frustration is as sharp on her nose as the galvanic brew of an incoming storm, the kind of smell that calls on a crack of thunder. She reads the puckered lines above the gentle gray eyes of her owner. A tightness in the brow tells Aria that her person needs calming. She will not give in to the gritty mystery of the dark woods. Not yet. Not until all is right with her person. Sitting patiently, she nudges her head into Giovanni's hands. There is a fellowship between this man and this dog. A bond born of trust and time has blossomed between them. When a dog chooses to love a human, it is a timeless affair of the soul and spirit, a meeting far beyond the mortal body. An eternal entanglement is this mingling of the souls. A loyalty beyond language and all of life's earthly matter. Truth be told, the bond between Giovanni and Aria is the truest treasure either of them has ever found. Aria decided long ago that her own happiness is dependent on Giovanni. To see him chafed and bristling like this is a torment. A torture her earnest brown eyes and sideways smile of a tail are eager to fix. Giovanni strokes his companion until his pulse finally starts to slow. He closes his eyes, fingers threading through many a wiry curl until his frustration dwindles and—Aria reads—smells like the aftermath of a fire.

"Good girl," Giovanni whispers. He opens himself to the tinkling music of small birds. An inhale invites the autumnal grubbiness of the woods, that damp, rich brew. Mineral and microbe spin gold below the soil, where the mortal dance with dead things. These woods smell to him like so many old books, libraries made of leaves. Perhaps what pleases Giovanni most is all the untamed energy rippling around him. A bright, living language, the never-ending painting and poetry of nature. Humility has shrunken him, and better yet, his woes. Woods are wild and chaotic. None of the pruned nip-and-tuck of a well-tended garden. Survival. Fights between the fittest and the fastest. Starvation. Digestion. Skeletons in the soil. How humbling to face a forest as a mere human, a shrunken statue worshipping at the shrine of nature.

The last fumes of frustration burn off with the morning mist.

Giovanni smiles. Grabs his *vanghetto* trowel and his *bastone* stick for warding off vipers. He squints at the woods ahead. A lightness bubbles up from his gut. With a thrilling rush, he is suddenly enlivened. The last few months were unseasonably wet. Marriages might have been made under summer rains. There is never anything promised, no guarantee, of course. And yet, here it is, that interminable bird. Hope. A prickle of exhilaration. What they seek is rare. A ruby among rocks.

It is time to find treasure.

"Andiamo..."

Aria leaps into action, diving to the dirt. Behind her, sounds of squelching boots and the younger dog crashing gaily through the brush fade into a theater of the senses. The curtains rise.

Aria lifts her nose, and the whole world simultaneously expands and distills. A drama unfurls before her. Scents rise and swirl, bullied around by a light breeze. Some hover like small clouds above stones. There are the tentacled and tailed. A few sing. Some are like small poems. Many are ephemeral, quick as a cough. There are those that snarl, some snicker. Animal spoors trail with confidence like the smoke of a cigar.

Some frolic like a dragonfly drizzling itself across a blue summer sky. Others haunt fallen leaves. They are bright and alive, these auras. They speak of sagas. Of sex. Birth. Battles. Death.

The soil itself spells out life in all its fine notes—breath, death, decay, regeneration. A funky subterranean stew of the living and the dead simmering in a crumb kingdom. Where silverfish and centipedes are giants. Alliances form, wars start nearby. Sly fungi barter with the sunken veins of trees, sucking up ambrosia in their straw structures.

Through scent, Aria sees a young fox marking territory the night before, eyes lambent in the moonlight. She sees the deer that left the scat, grazing until something—the body behind a rustle in the night—startles her. A shiver twitches up the delicate tendons of a doe's neck. She bolts, imprinting her signature odor—a cheesy sebum smear from tiny glands between her hooves. A getaway painted in cloven crescents that remind Aria of savory pastries.

Aria lopes across the leaf litter, guided by her nose. She wends around the boles of trees. Tiny trails meander up the side of a beech tree, the scent tale of oily ants. All around float freckles of the last pollen. The grand drama offers a million distractions, but she must home in for the hunt—swiftly tuning out soft-spoken smells—pheromones of flowers, quiet musk of moss, hay-like incense of hazelnuts buried by a forgetful squirrel. She must tune out the sinister. Screams of spilled boar semen and the flesh an owl let fall. Rusted tin roof smell of dried blood. And all around, trees releasing heady waves of resin, each as bright as a burst of laughter.

Among all these stories is the one Aria is after. It starts as a flutter, a mere flirtation. Aria drives her nose just above crisp leaves as the scent gathers strength, daring her. It calls to her in a chemical incantation.

It is close.

A dull sound, deadened by the enthrallment of her nose. Giovanni sees his dog has locked on to a trail and calls out in the pillowy coo of a dove.

"Find it."

Aria's focus is swallowed whole by the hunt ahead. Head hung low, she sweeps her nose across the woodland soil, picking up on the bite and prickle of garlic. Yes. The garlic base notes peal out across the woods like the village bells, savory and strong, and she knows she is nearing her treasure when a whisper of sweet, fermented fruit slips into her. She circles the area—making a wide loop, and then, heart pumping, she tightens her loop. That rich smell is sharper, dense, and delicious.

"Find it."

Aria, heaving with anticipation, finds the spot where the cipher rises from the earth like a Greek siren. Below lies the sentient silk of a fungus. She dips her nose to the dirt, then leaps backward. Lunges forward and dips her nose again to signal to Giovanni that this is *the spot*. Here lies treasure. She rakes at the soil with her front paws, ears jangling. The warm marzipan-and-honey smell of Giovanni's skin lingers near her—a smell that gets fruitier with time, hanging around him like humidity. A sour puff of coffee breath near her as she scrabbles in the soil. Giovanni leaning into Aria, nudging her aside to use his metal *vanghetto* now, deftly parting soil and stones aside, careful, so careful as not to scar the secret under the soil. And then, popping free and rolling out from the hole dog and man have dug . . . *eureka*.

A diamond.

A quiet riot.

A tiny god.

Aria has found a black truffle.

Giovanni turns over the warty gem in his palm. It is the size of a Ping-Pong ball. He smooths a thumb over the knobbled landscape of its surface. Tiny holes tell him that a burrowing mouse has nibbled it here and there, and who could blame it? He lifts the truffle to his nose and sniffs its magic. First, he registers the coat of damp, wormy dirt it wears, but then comes that animalistic horseradish and funk of good grana cheese. Leathery, nutty, yeasty, it has his heart racing, this naughty little oyster of the soil. And because the truffle is at its freshest, plucked right out from beneath the earth, it tells its truth and fills Giovanni's senses with its ephemeral high notes—a quick pineapple kiss of sweetness. Eyes squeezed shut, Giovanni is hypnotized, whorled off his feet with a flood of emotion. Nostalgia wraps him in tepid waves. Fond memories of other truffle hunts. A shared plate of pasta and shaved truffles with Paolo, fingers interlaced under the table. Paolo in the early days, with his summer skin and beautiful black hair. His silly experimental mustache, marbled stomach muscles. The tidy trail of dark hair peeking out from the waistband of his swimming trunks. And further back in Giovanni's memory, a quick haunting. The broad shoulders of his father. Hurricanes in his eyes. Spittle and sharp words launched from blueish lips.

You are a disgrace. A dirty boy.

He remembers the day he was kicked out of his house, out of his family. Giovanni had knocked on the door to Nonna Amara's centuries-old house. She held him as he sobbed. Draping a shawl over his narrow shoulders, she listened to him speak of beautiful Paolo and the hatred his own father had hurled at him. His mother's deafening silence. Nonna Amara picked up the shattered pieces of Giovanni's heart, nourishing him with stories and her handmade pasta. Shavings of truffle nestled between buttery strands of penne. Snowfalls of Parmesan. Nonna Amara raised him as her own, staring down Giovanni's father at the grocer's, telling him to mind his own business in a voice as cool as spring water. Tiny Nonna Amara standing before his broad-shouldered father. But in all these memories, it is thinking of Nonna Amara's house and what she lost in that landslide that brings tears to Giovanni's eyes. The emotion summons a clearer picture of his father raising a belt high above his head, blue lips and face filled with hate. A painter by trade and a bully to his only son for loving boys. Boy. Only darling Paolo. Only ever Paolo for as long as he lived and beyond. Paolo, the beautiful soul he would leave his father for every day of eternity. Giovanni shakes his head.

His father has been dead for many years. No need to resurrect him.

"Good, Aria," the truffle hunter says, pulling a treat from his pocket and slipping it to his companion. Young Fagiolo thunders out from behind a chestnut tree. He slams muddy front paws onto the thighs of his owner. He can smell the tallowy lumps of chicken mingling with crumbles of cheese, and oh, what joy! Treats! *We are having treats in the woods!* He shoves his snout against the jacket pocket filled with chicken and cheese and is pushed away.

"Fagiolo, find it!" calls Giovanni. And Fagiolo has forgotten what it is precisely that he is supposed to find, but no matter, he is racing into the woods again. This moment is the best moment of his life, only to be topped by the next moment and the next. Giovanni is here, Aria is here, and they are in the woods with all these wonderful smells that are so much more than smells—they are emotions, stories, songs, secrets, riddles, thick and rotten gamey smears to roll in. Here is the slime of a carcass to roll in, and how he wriggles until he is wearing the remains of the rabbit, and how glorious this all is. And now he has found a stick he likes. Dropping the stick and with a billowing inward rush of purpose, he remembers that he is supposed to bring Giovanni something, and so he does, racing back up to a pair of olive rubber boots, ready to receive the treats that he can smell sitting in that waxy jacket pocket.

"No, Fagiolo, that is a rock." Giovanni offers Fagiolo a flash of the truffle. Fagiolo tries to eat it. "Don't eat it! Find it, Fagiolo. Find it. Go. Find it."

Fagiolo snorts. He tears off into the woods with a chesty huff of laughter, the rock held by his smiling mouth.

Aria is already on the trail of another truffle. Her nose— reminiscent of a black truffle itself—skims moss, grass, and mud, sifting through the sensory jamboree to answer a call. She darts past plucked dove feathers, this natural to her, in her nature. She glides above the inchoate cabbage coughs of truffles that are not yet ready or ripe. Patient little previews of what is to come. Tiny futures gestating in the woods. Aria traipses over silent seeds and their promise of tomorrow. They sit below a branch once haunted by a hawk. Aria disregards a sensual whiff of mushrooms. An old weasel bone. Ammonia-sharp markings of a badger, billowing out like the sails of a small boat. Cologne of old trees. Acidic activity of insects hiding in the cracks of rocks. Aria sniffs a depression in the leaf litter where something large lay. But the story is long gone, stolen by the wind. Like a lot of good things, scents don't last forever.

Fagiolo is crashing through the woods like an ivory comet. He is so excited, he has forgotten all of his training. His heart sings as he barrels in between chestnut and oak, gummy grin wide, tongue a tiny pink streamer.

"What are you doing, Fagiolo? Come!" yells Giovanni. Showing off now, galloping—at a glance, the spitting image of a fleeing lamb—Fagiolo slips, tumbling into a mud puddle. He rights himself—brown as bark now—and is further delighted at discovering mud puddles! Giovanni laughs, bright barking sounds as his happy mud monster Fagiolo dances across the woodland sludge.

Twenty feet ahead, Aria barks, leaps backward. Dips her nose again. This is the spot. She digs, front paws scrabbling in the soil. Giovanni collars Fagiolo as he bumbles past, bringing him to the site.

"Find it," he says to Fagiolo. Fagiolo, mud soaked, panting, senses that this moment is important. He barks, an ecstatic yap. Giovanni points to the earth. Fagiolo draws a whiff of the loosened crumbs of dirt. There is something below. Something utterly intoxicating. He starts to dig, a frenzied gouging with his paws.

"Good boy, find it! Find the truffle, Fagiolo!"

And Fagiolo can't believe how wonderful this is—the cheesy, aromatic secret hiding here somewhere. Sneaky little something out of sight. Giovanni calling his name—he thinks?—and he is doing a good thing here, scrabbling in the muck. Suddenly, a beige body peeks out from the soil.

"Move aside, move aside, Fagiolo."

The young dog feels Giovanni's hand nudging him from the smelly little lump. Giovanni is now using his *vanghetto* to carefully round the body of the bulb, and with a deft poke, he pops it free. The white truffle rolls down the mudhole toward Fagiolo, and with a swift *sloop*—he swallows it whole.

Fagiolo eats a whole truffle and is inebriated with it.

What a day! What a life!

Giovanni moans, raising his hands in the air. His apprentice truffle-hunting dog has just snorted a good hundred euros' worth of earthen gold.

"Fagiolo!" Giovanni calls after the dog, who is off in a flash, a small, white firework. Giovanni laughs; the puppy can't help himself. There was never any mischief in Aria, even as a piebald pup. But Fagiolo is made of it.

The more seasoned scent reader, Aria finds three more truffles. She enjoys the bright aroma lifting from Giovanni's body.

Her person brushes off a beetle from the largest of the truffles, abuzz with endorphins and relief. Giovanni will be able to sell these. At least one hundred euros for each tiny god. Traitor, that's what Ugo calls him. For selling his truffles to an upscale eatery in the rival town of Borghese. A traitor because he is selling to Chef Umberto Micucci of *ristorante* Novelli instead of Umberto's brother, Lorenzo Micucci, owner of the humble Bar Celebrità in Lazzarini Boscarino. His village. But what choice does he have? Lorenzo cannot afford truffles. *Cavolo*, Giovanni himself cannot afford truffles. The grotesque dirt-covered delicacies in his truffle bag today will fetch at least four hundred euros.

I need this, he wants to scream.

Truffle hunting saved him. In the early days, he would bring the odd truffle home to Nonna Amara and Nonno Vito, back when he had all the truffle hunting skills of Fagiolo, but a willful little dog named Bebe. He watched Bebe munching truffles (at the time, he thought they were potatoes), plucking them up and snarfing them as though she were shopping for bonbons on their morning walks. Bebe and Giovanni taught each other a thing or two about truffles. And truffle hunting saved him when he and Paolo left the village for another, only to be hounded by a neighbor who threatened to set fire to their home while they slept. A man who threw a bottle through their bedroom window one starless night. Nighttime truffle hunts saved Giovanni. When he had somewhere to walk off his horror after talking to the police after his car had been spray-painted with hateful words. All because of loving someone. How could such a personal act merit persecution? Truffle hunting saved him again later, when Paolo spent long hours in Lucca receiving treatment, his thin arms waving off Giovanni. When Paolo weighed nothing, big eyes and bird bones. A beautiful old man he had become, black hair now a flashy silver, an earned wisdom in his eyes, smile lines deep and lovely because he and Giovanni had made them together over all that time.

"Go hunt truffles," Paolo would say, with a blown kiss. "It will give me a much-needed break from your fussing."

Giovanni's last gift from Paolo was Aria, a curly-haired companion for his hunts when Paolo knew he would no longer be able to join Giovanni. Not in this life, anyway. And what a gift she is.

Giovanni walks back from his memories to stare at the scenery around him. The name of these woods, all the secret spots nestled in the Tuscan hills and what they hide will go with him to the grave. Does that make him a traitor? Is he selfish? He has had to protect his heart and his dogs for so long. He'll admit, his life has become small. Smaller still with the shrinking of Lazzarini Boscarino. Retirement, widower. They are just words. He is happy hunting in the woods. He does it in a sustainable way, and selling the truffles to Umberto Micucci only makes sense. He is merely doing what the woods ask of him.

Fagiolo bounds up to him, tail whipping side to side. In his mouth is a porcupine quill. He lifts it to Giovanni for certain approval. Giovanni laughs, gently prying the quill from between the young pup's teeth, each as white as Carrara marble. He may not be showing the same sort of truffling prowess as Aria, but what joy Fagiolo brings. He rampages merrily across the woods, lifting knickknacks from the soil with everyone's spirits in tow.

"Come," Giovanni calls for his family of two dogs. He starts the trek back to the Jeep, truffle bag clutched between his fingers—velvety, soiled, filled with little gods.

Fagiolo bounds after him, a muddy, brown blur. But Aria is stock-still. She raises her nose to the wind, eyes glistening.

"Come, Aria," Giovanni calls again. But his loyal dog does not. Aria is facing farther into the woods. Tail and body frozen but for the butterfly beats of her nostrils. Giovanni turns

to watch. Aria is rarely this absorbed by something after a truffle hunt. Once, when she had insisted on searching on like
this, Aria snuffled after a scent trail and found the enigma
of an abandoned pair of jeans, both pockets stuffed with
euros. Another time, she tracked deep into the woods to an
upside-down Citröen C3 hatchback submerged in a creek, its
passenger door flung wide-open. And the most memorable of
her searches—she found a six-year-old girl who had wandered
away from her family at a picnic and fallen asleep under an oak.
Found her before cold shock coursed through a mother, before
the family ran around yelling a name until their throats hurt,
found her before the wailing of sirens and searchlights and the
terror of a village had been ignited.

Given her history, she has Giovanni's attention.

"What is it, Aria?" Giovanni calls out, goose bumps peb-
bling across his flesh. He squints at the trees, hunting himself
for flashes of neon orange and yellow. For camouflage. For the
bounding chaos. Square-bodied dogs bouldering through the
brush. Barracuda body of a gun. He waits but hears nothing.
Rasping chatter from a magpie tells him there are no boar or
bird hunters nearby.

So what is it that has Aria frozen? The brown-and-white
Lagotto Romagnolo is breathless as she waits for permission to
give chase.

"Find it," says Giovanni gently. Aria darts into the woods.

She is amped, insistent. She is running now. Giovanni lopes
through the woods after her, his eyes out for hunters. Ears
pricked for the chiming collar of a dog. He does not want to
startle men who are armed. Does not want his dogs around
the brutish canines who chase down boars. Behind Giovanni,
young Fagiolo smells the tension in the air and races after
them, close on Giovanni's heels. Aria slows around a copse of
chestnut trees. She zigzags, nose skimming the soil.

"We have enough, Aria, come on home," Giovanni tells her, suspecting she is still truffle hunting. But Aria, always obedient to Giovanni, disobeys him. She hunts on, detective of the dirt, head darting, nose stalking a powerful perfume. She barks. Indicates a spot. Sits up brightly, panting. Young Fagiolo releases a little of the tension building inside him by rolling in a nearby bush. Giovanni approaches as Aria starts to dig. Her whines put him on edge. She has not been this panicked since the missing child. She barks again and backs up, waiting, her whole body aquiver.

Giovanni digs carefully with his *vanghetto* and finds nothing.

"Nothing, Aria; it must have already been dug up or eaten by a boar." Aria barks again, insistent. Giovanni nods at her and continues his excavation. He digs deeper around the roots of the chestnut trees, but at this depth, he is unlikely to find anything unless it was buried here by human or animal. Seeing sparks shuddering through his beloved dog, he obliges her and carries on digging.

"I'm looking girl, I'm looking where you've said."

He digs. He digs. He digs. Until a glimpse of a being reveals itself to him like a pale moon lifting in the night.

"Oh, good girl, Aria; I see it. Very good." He is careful with the *vanghetto* work, gliding it over the uneven terrain of the truffle. Its clusters of beige polyps. And suddenly, every hair of his body is standing on end. Gingerly, oh so gingerly, the truffle is showing itself. Telling the truth. Giovanni has unearthed only part of the top of this truffle—color of a potato, physical semblance to a mummified brain—and it is already five inches in diameter. His breathing quickens. He blows off dust, and works the soil away from the treasure, sweat slipping down onto his forearms. And he gets to six inches. Time evaporates. Adrenaline floods him like a rain-gorged creek. Minutes slip by unnoticed as Giovanni's arms start to ache, and he cannot stop the sweat from spilling into his eyes. Blood beads on his fingers as he uses them to scratch away at the loam; there are spots too delicate to risk using the *vanghetto*. This impossibility is hidden deeper than most, as though a trick, a test. Giovanni performs a surgery under the soil, deftly detaching the truffle from an intricate skein of tree roots and soil as strong as Giuseppina's coffee. The minutes melt into maybe half an hour, but he can't be sure—time plays tricks on those who hunt truffles. The dogs lying nearby. Watchful. Panting.

And with a last satisfying pop, the monstrous treasure is freed from its chest.

Giovanni is speechless. He stands under the sanctuary of trees, filthy as Fagiolo, holding what looks like the fist of a giant. He has never seen, let alone found, a treasure like this. He gags, sickened with the weight of responsibility he holds in dirty fingers.

The clock is ticking. He will now fight a countdown, for a truffle is at its peak ripeness when plucked from its hidden hole. A white truffle is almost impossible to cultivate. It is forged by cryptic collaborations in a cauldron of darkest soil. It has traded with the trees, made discreet dealings with microbes. Fused to the tree roots like a good growth, plum-like, this not-so-tiny god has bulged to hideous perfection, sending out its intoxicating cry to be eaten so that it may spread its spores with the digestive aid of squirrel, rat, pig, dog, human. It does not discriminate. But timing is everything. Every second that truffle is out of the ground is a diminishing. Seconds tick toward the death of this warty diamond. Delicate, demanding; within five days, it will lose its enthralling spell completely.

The very thing that makes this white truffle magical will vanish.

The ruby among rocks will be worthless.

Giovanni, dizzy, leans against an old oak, knotty against his palm. His breaths are hitched, heart hammering as wildly as anything in these woods. Veins running through him like the roots below tighten, a cold sweat lifting from his skin. Lifting his arm—sickle moons of his fingernails black as beetles—he finds his right hand to be shaking violently. His fortunes have, with the keen black nose of his beloved dog, changed shape. His gut gurgles as though a brain, wise and pondering. Giovanni already knows his life will be rewritten with the unearthing of this truffle. His future morphs on the horizon like cloud formations. He is thinking of the shattering of a record. Every white truffle is expensive, a luxury with humble beginnings like the caviar pulled from the slit stomach of a sturgeon. Like a pearl made as the oyster coats an invading grain of sand inside its shell in lustrous layers. Rags to riches. The record paid for the most coveted of them all—the white truffle—was by a Hong Kong businessman who shelled out $330,000 for a beast that tipped the scales at just over three pounds. Pressing his boots into the earth so that he doesn't faint or fall, rooting himself, Giovanni caresses the humungous fungus filling his hands. A fierce living perfume of the largest truffle he has ever seen envelops him.

An earthy aphrodisiac.

Fermented sweat seeped from an earthen grave.

The breath of a gigantic god.

He lifts his hands. This truffle weighs far more than three pounds.

"Oh, Santo cielo!"

Giovanni not only believes he holds a prized truffle. An incomparable lump of gold with no equal. The rarest among rubies. He believes that his clever little companion Aria has just gone and found what is about to be the most coveted truffle on earth.

Chapter 4

The Jeep door claps like a gunshot. Giovanni grimaces. A frantic scan of the lower car park of Lazzarini Boscarino suggests that—*grazie a dio!*—no one is around to have heard it. No one to have seen him careening into an open parking slot like the getaway driver of some heist, stomping the brake pedal so hard he fishtailed. To have witnessed him stumbling from his vehicle—dazed, delirious—cradling gold of his wildest dreams disguised as the grubby knurls of a gargantuan truffle. A truffle so large he has no bag to carry it in, forced to smuggle the pungent secret in an old dog towel.

A look down confirms his hands are trembling. Whether from the weight of unburied treasure or stress, he cannot tell.

He must move like a mountain mist.

No one, not a single soul, can see this truffle.

Since carrying this beautiful monster takes both his hands, Giovanni has had to loop the strings of his truffle bag around his belt and allow the rest of his loot to dangle around his waist

like Christmas baubles. An act that, under any other circumstance, he'd consider sacrilegious.

Aria—sensing a need for stealth—pads silently at Giovanni's
side. She lifts her brown-and-white face up to her person.
Skulking under the stinking brawn of the truffle, his sweat
tells her a story. A salt and tar and smoky poppy seed smell of
adrenaline ribboning from him like steam from scalding hot
tea. Worse—she smells fear. Fear is turpentine and the crushed
bodies of beetles. It menaces him with the shapeless grace of
a gas leak. Aria will stay by his side, keeping watch until the
gray ghost lurking behind Giovanni's eyes dissipates. Until his
jaw unclenches, the rigid stitching of his facial muscles comes
undone. Until the sherry-sweet smell of skin slips into her nostrils and she knows for certain that he is alright.

Giovanni wipes his forehead in the crook of his elbow, blinks
feverishly, and tries to locate his less obedient canine companion. He finds Fagiolo writhing in a pothole filled with rainwater.

"Fagiolo, come here!" comes the truffle hunter's desperate
whisper. "Quickly! We must sneak back home without being
seen. Be subtle, Fagiolo." Fagiolo springs from the pothole, a
curly-coated geyser. He thunders toward his person, who he
thinks has just called his name, but he's never sure because
really he's not much of a listener, but, how lovely, here comes
another moment with his person! Giovanni registers an
inbound canine comet. Ecstatic tongue and boundless glee
barreling toward him.

"No, no, no!" Giovanni has no way to shield the beautiful
burden in his arms. "No, Fagiolo! *No!*"

Giovanni hoists the great toweled truffle above his head
milliseconds before his lively Lagotto makes contact. Front
paws wallop against Giovanni's thighs, Fagiolo embossing his
human with the heart-shaped prints of his paws. Then, a result
of having slept in the car despite a drive that might have broken

records at the Mugello Circuit, Fagiolo rockets off for another lap of the car park.

"*Mannaggia,* Fagiolo!" Giovanni hisses. "Stop clowning around and follow me."

Giovanni gingerly sneaks up the winding cobblestone path that leads from the lower car park into the heart of Lazzarini Boscarino. Sweat stings his eyes. The truffle grows heavier with every step he takes. But, a little luck. Now is when most of the villagers retire indoors to eat a homemade lunch and partake of a *riposa,* a noon nap. So the village sleeps. Autumnal sun streaming in through windows. Bellies warmed by a little wine. The low-pitched prayer murmured by a fan. Still, he cannot be too careful. You never know who might be out for a stroll, and he cannot risk being seen with a secret of this size. Out of the earth, this truffle is a vulgar extravagance. Gratuitous, the most flamboyant of flirts.

A one-of-a-kind treasure too easily coveted.

A diamond of desire.

Giovanni glances up at a blistering blue sky. The bell tower looms above, a majestic vestige of the Middle Ages, when mighty bronze bells were thought to be endowed with supernatural powers. They sit where they have for hundreds of years, poised to peal thunderous chimes in warning of enemies encroaching for battle, of a call to come together in times of crisis, and more recently, of lunch. Superstition slithers up upon Giovanni. He imagines the tower itself is sentient, boring an ancient consciousness into him. Mystically sensing what he has stolen from the soil, what he smuggles in a dirty dog towel, the truffle treasure he has unearthed. He flinches, waiting for the bells to shudder into reverberating chimes, each one loud enough to raise bones back to the surface of the soil.

"Truf-fle! Truf-fle!" the bells will ring out. "A treasure! Giovanni has found a priceless subterranean jewel!"

His heart is a medieval bell. Giovanni can feel the veins of his neck throbbing. His blood pressure medication is at home—he never needs to bring it on a hunt. Ironic thing, really; there aren't any medicines that work for a broken heart. Hunting for truffles is the closest thing to a cure.

But he fears this one is about to kill him.

Fagiolo trundles behind Giovanni, nose gliding over cobblestone. He whiffs corners where Spinone Italiano hunting dogs have spritzed stories about themselves. He smells a bitch in heat. Cats claiming territory. The spot where a mouse was murdered. Hot leather clump of tobacco curled in a cigarette butt like a dead cockroach. He licks the small purple painting left when someone dropped a squashed blackberry. Delicious.

Giovanni winds the first corner of the village's cobblestone labyrinth, peeking his head around a stone wall to spy on the grocer's. Benedetto's scrawled sign adorns the door, the grocer's telltale handwriting reminiscent of an orgy of insects.

Chiuso

"Closed. Good," he mutters. Giovanni pictures Benedetto snoozing on his floral sofa. Stefano dozing in his wheelchair nearby. The small television where nosy priest-turned-detective Don Matteo bleats out pearls of wisdom while solving crimes on his bicycle.

Giovanni turns to make sure that Fagiolo is bringing up the rear. His little white Lagotto is lagging now. Stooping to lick cobblestones.

"Hey!" A vocal ambush from above. "Giovanni!"

Giovanni looks up in horror. It is Giulia. Giulia is here from Florence visiting her brother Padre Francesco, and right now she is hanging out of his emerald-green shutters with a direct bird's-eye-view of the unfathomable fortune in Giovanni's sweat-slicked hands. Giovanni stares up at her, wide-eyed. Draws his lips into a tight line. Nods vigorously.

"Bring your cake to the piazza—Lorenzo has a special treat for us!" she says, donning pearl earrings and a sickle moon smile. "*Ciao*, Aria; *ciao*, Fagiolo!" she adds before being swallowed up in shadow behind the shutters. Giovanni peers at the toweled truffle in his hands. Giulia has confused it for a cake. He blows air out his cheeks. Feels sweat tickling down his temple.

Suddenly aware that his breathing is labored, Giovanni glares at the deep green of her shutters. He inevitably thinks about poison. Shutters are always green because it was a trend and a trick from the eighteenth century, when the colorant of arsenic was used to paint them in an attempt to ward off mosquitoes. Poison in plain sight. Like the poison that was soaked into Pippo's meatballs because a rival truffle hunter was sick of Pippo's success. Tired of his own truffle dog signaling a spot, only to discover that Pippo had found it and taken the grimy diamond first.

Stop it, Giovanni tells himself. His stress is summoning dark thoughts. Paolo would tell him to take a deep breath, to relax. But how can he relax? Pounds of pungent delicacy are bearing down on him.

He shudders to think of what will happen if someone sees the truffle.

Giovanni lowers his head. He slinks on.

Aria in the lead now, Fagiolo just behind. Up ahead is a familiar configuration of patio umbrellas. Voices cricket around the afternoon air. Something unusual is going on at the piazza.

Giovanni freezes.

He must avoid detection or it's all over. He gives a low whistle for the dogs to heel. A hasty plan—he will slip past the piazza, past Bar Celebrità, and up the last little garter snake of a cobblestone street to his house. He will be careful not to stumble over his steep doorstep. Inside, doors locked, he will shut the windows, draw the curtains. He will set out fresh water bowls for the dogs, and then he will sit at his kitchen table, gingerly unwrapping his great golden egg. But from this point, his imaginings shimmer into obscurity. What on this great green earth does he do next? He doesn't know how to share this mucky diamond with another soul. Who to trust? The quiet chaos of it is killing him. The truffle is a terrible liability. A bawdy avatar of banknotes. He just doesn't yet know how many.

What does one do upon finding the world's biggest epicurean diamond?

Giovanni fears what he knows is to come. The truffle will incite hysteria, greed. Worst of all, danger. *Tartufai*—truffle hunters—have committed the most heinous of crimes over *tartufi*. Over forest territory, high-end buyers, the innocent dogs who find them. Where there be treasure, there be pirates. Giovanni suddenly pictures Paolo, the sharpest vision of him since he passed. Paolo is twenty years younger, those Grecian god feet dangling over the sofa while he waxes lyrical about lottery winners.

"A curse," says Paolo with that clarion tone that snitches of a good singing voice. He prods a tabloid emblazoned with the tragedy that befell a winner of the SuperEnalotto. "Terrible things often happen to those who receive a windfall. Sudden wealth can be scary. One can be crushed by their good fortune." Song and superstition flowed through his blood like the Serchio river after a storm.

"It's almost like a certain town that shall not be mentioned," he adds, eyebrows raised. And Paolo doesn't have to mention the town's name because he is forever talking about it without naming it for superstitious reasons. A Southern Italian town labeled "unlucky." A town said to have had an entanglement with witches since the nineteenth century. Where a baby girl was born with two hearts. A town where a lawyer, at the apex of a critical trial in the 1940s, raised a quavering finger and said, "If I am not telling the truth, let this chandelier fall down!" only to have the chandelier plummet and compress him like the provolone of a proper panini. The sort of supernatural nonsense stories that dilated Paolo's pupils and Giovanni proclaimed a lot of old rot.

Mamma mia, what Giovanni wouldn't give to hear about that stupid town again.

Giovanni shakes his head. What made him think of spooky superstitions and a cursed town? He has not thought so much and so clearly about the past, seen Paolo as though he is sitting on the sofa, and especially had thoughts of his father in years. Why now are these memories haunting him? Giovanni, overcome, giddy with the muscular scent of the truffle—his trophy huffing out burly breaths as though it were alive under the towel—steals a glance to his right. The piazza is filled with villagers.

He mouths an obscenity.

"Quick," he whispers to the dogs. He picks up his pace, hobbling to compensate for the gaudy secret between his hands. Aria slinking at his side. As he passes the hubbub, he ducks, using the cover of the low stone wall that encircles the piazza. Knees cracking like stepped-on sticks. He pulls the truffle closer to his chest, dizzy with its intoxicating stench of old eggs, the funk of exotic flowers and faraway fruit. Creeping, inching along, whirling from the stress he has made his life small to avoid. He is almost on the final little stretch of street to his doorstep when the air fills with a cry of "It's Giovanni's puppy, the truffle-hunting apprentice!"

A more irate voice hollers, "Grab him! He stole a whole focaccia!"

Fagiolo emerges from the piazza. Struts up to a crouching

Giovanni to show off his contraband—a whole rosemary focaccia held hostage by moon-white teeth. Hot on Fagiolo's tail is a cat, an apoplectic Al Pacino.

Giovanni stands from his crouch behind the stone wall to avoid having his ankles attacked by a cat who identifies as the local law enforcement.

And as he does, Giovanni's cover is blown.

"Giovanni! You're back. Come and join us!" sings Padre Francesco.

"Fagiolo stole some focaccia, but don't you worry," yells Giuseppina. "Lorenzo made it fresh, and I saw him. Also, I ate a little just now, and look at me—fit as a fiddle!" Giuseppina shimmies her hips as she shoves a sizable piece of focaccia into her mouth as testament. She knows all about the dark truffle underworld and dog poisoning.

"How was your hunt?" yells out Padre Francesco, placing a bowl of grated Parmesan on a long table set up on the piazza.

Giovanni feels his scalp prickle. He clears his throat.

"Come and see, Lorenzo has made a *pranzo di lavoro*. Like we used to have! I brought blackberries for the *zabaglione!*" Padre Francesco spoons a snowing of Parmesan into his palm, then drops it into his mouth with a lift of his biblical brows.

Pranzo di lavoro. Work lunch. An ironic event given that almost everyone is retired, Giovanni thinks. What a thing to have resurrected. Paolo would have loved it.

Lorenzo is dipping in and out of Bar Celebrità, balancing plates of steaming pasta and frilly skirts of salad hosting rounds of mozzarella. Giovanni watches Lorenzo. His stomach hollows out. Good Lorenzo, who is back running Bar Celebrità. Who has supported the love of his life in her mayoral candidacy. Who is bringing back an old tradition that is sure to delight all the villagers with nostalgia most delicious.

Giovanni blinks to clear the sweat from his eyes and sees

Stefano, Carlotta, Benedetto, Duccio, farmer Leon, and the twins have already taken a seat. That at the end of the long table sits Silvio, the village policeman. Legs crossed at the ankle. Sipping a glass of red wine. He listens to hunters Ugo and Tommaso regale him with some tale of tracking, of a chase, a close call, skins, and tusks. Ugo, gruff and leathery, who has branded Giovanni a traitor. Tommaso, who laughed at him and called him a hunter of turds.

Lorenzo looks up while painting aged balsamic over creamy mozzarella. "Giovanni! Come join us. I've reinstated *pranzo di lavoro*. A fixed menu, chef's choice. Today, *parmigiana di melanzana*, and *filetto di maiale con pancetta*. *Insalata caprese*. We are celebrating the first meeting of the new mayor. Come, Delizia will be here any moment."

This is who Ugo says he has betrayed. This good man who has come home, left the glitz and glamour of bigger places to share his gifts with the village. Giovanni feels the truffle in his hands gain an extra pound. He found the truffle. It is rightfully his. But this is more than he knows how to handle.

He holds a king's ransom. And no one can know.

Below the filthy towel and what it hides, Al Pacino has returned to harass him. She flattens her ears and hisses at Giovanni's feet. She swipes at his ankles, lunging at the offensive stench she knows is sneaking out from the towel. Then paws at the ground at Giovanni's feet—best to bury a reek like that. Aria barks; she has never known what to make of Al Pacino. Aria places herself between the cataclysm of a cat and her person, blinking at a firework display of pregnancy pheromones.

Giuseppina hollers from the belly of Bar Celebrità. "Al Pacino, calm down! Giovanni, hurry and join us! Lorenzo has made a *pranzo* that's better than sex!"

Padre blushes and habitually signs the cross.

Giovanni shakes his head, makes a move to leave. Track the

last of the cobblestones that lead to the front steps of his house. He can see the vintage wood of his front door. He is so close to home. All he needs is...

Five thick fingers press against his skin. Padre Francesco has his elbow now and is guiding Giovanni toward the piazza, where wafts of warm basil mingle with notes of toasted pine nuts. The air is buttery and bright. A beautiful autumn day with a light breeze, sun in the sky.

And a bomb ticking under a towel in his hands.

"Giovanni, you can sit here next to Ugo and Silvio," says Giuseppina. Giovanni scowls at Ugo. The man who called him a traitor.

"Oof, Giovanni, I thought I smelled you!" laughs Tommaso. Giovanni can only imagine what the villagers are smelling. He has brought a bull of an aroma into the piazza. Beneath the towel, bellowing fetor and funk in steaming clouds.

Ugo dares to speak to him. "Must have been muddy where you went. Makes me think you were hunting in a certain forest just north of us?" He laughs. "Fagiolo looks like a little brown bear! You, too, look dirtier than normal, Giovanni."

Dirty. Giovanni pictures his father's bluish lips.

You are a disgrace. A dirty boy.

Giovanni feels weak. What has he done? Perhaps his penance for raising it from the soil is that it is resurrecting his past?

"Giovanni, what is the matter?" comes Carlotta's voice.

He can't answer. His chest is wrapped in cellophane. Throat has closed.

Chiuso.

His hearing is muffled. Stress is a snake around his neck.

After Paolo's passing, Giovanni made his life small. A tiny truffle he could keep safe in the palm of his hand. Forty years with Paolo already made him the richest man he knows. He never had aspirations for a castle on the hill or the wild travel fantasies Paolo dreamed of. And suddenly, it's all too much—the responsibility of guarding treasures. Once only his darling Aria, but now also young Fagiolo, who is reminding him of the fun he'd long forgotten, of the risks you take when you love something. Love is a truffle. Delicate. A rarity that takes time to cultivate. A recipe of the right relationships. Sometimes with a too-short shelf life, he thinks. It is an erotic entanglement, an alchemy of chemistry and a seduction of the senses.

This giant truffle is going to blow up his carefully curated life.

He can't do this. It's all too much for him.

Voices volley across the piazza.

"Look how pale he is."

"Giovanni, what is wrong?"

"Sit down, sit down."

"Lorenzo, call Delizia!" yells Tommaso.

"Delizia is a veterinarian; he needs a doctor, not neutering, Tommaso!" shouts Rosa.

"Then call Dr. Vittore!"

"He's only coming to the village next week; he's in Gallicano," yells Duccio.

"Then I will fetch him myself," says Benedetto, donning a flatcap.

"He's fainting; take his shoes off!" bellows Stefano.

"Why his shoes?" asks Rosa, incredulous.

"Here comes Mayor Delizia!" adds Carlotta.

Giovanni is more stable now that he is sitting. Aria fusses around him. The hunters, Ugo and Tommaso, are nearby. The twins. Silvio the policeman.

"Give him space!" someone yells.

"I just need water," Giovanni says, his words frail as wishbones. Padre Francesco hands him a carafe. Giovanni gingerly rests his trophy on his lap to gulp down sparkling water.

He blinks and the new mayor, Delizia, is kneeling in front of him. She has his hand in hers, squeezing gently.

"What is happening, Giovanni? When did you last take your Norvasc?" Delizia studies his eyes.

"That smell!" says Rosa, wafting her hand about.

Valentina adds, "*Caspita!* Smells like my late husband's socks. Giovanni, are you alright?"

"I am. I am alright. I'm going to be alright," he answers. Padre Francesco lets out an exaggerated sigh of relief. Aria has placed her head in between Giovanni's arm and his side, careful to avoid the truffle. This is how Giovanni knows he is not in danger, because she is not barking for help like she has done before.

"Giovanni, don't go scaring us like that," Giuseppina says, wiping her brow with a napkin.

A shadow falls over the distressed truffle hunter.

"What's in the towel, Giovanni?" asks Silvio the policeman. Tall, formidable, wearing his authority as well as his leather boots. Red stripe across his jacket emblazoned with the word *carabinieri*. The boots were his father's. Quite literally; Poliziotto Guido was the village policeman before he died in a tree-trimming accident many years ago. Giovanni marvels that it has somehow been over fifteen years since Silvio donned those boots to follow justice in his father's footsteps.

But Giovanni cannot tell Poliziotto Silvio what is in the towel. He cannot tell any of them what is in the towel. Can he? He hasn't decided what to do or where to go with the treasure. Delizia squeezes his hand again. Giovanni melts under her touch. How much she cares, how much they all do. And looking up at the familiar faces around him, it becomes clear. He cannot do this alone. He's going to need these people to weather what's coming. The madness that will be uncorked when this truffle is held to the light of human consciousness. Just as he needed these people when his person passed. When—drowning under the swell and surge of grief over Paolo—he suffered a stroke. Aria frantically barking on his behalf. These beautiful humans coming to his aid.

It took a village to save him. And save him they did.

As clear as the glass in his hand, he pictures Paolo. Smiling at the supernatural spell the truffle has cast. He remembers Paolo's words. Giovanni didn't want to face the music, even consider what life would be like without his Paolo. But Paolo, thin and pinching a breakfast pastry between his fingers, had cornered him in the kitchen as he tried to enjoy his espresso.

"Giovanni, when I am gone—"

"You are not going anywhere; eat your pastry."

"When I am gone, you must stay social. Lean on all our friends in the village. No moping. You will have to live for the both of us."

"Paolo, don't talk nonsense—"

"Listen to me. You are not alone. You are loved in this village. Don't you go disappearing into the trees like some sad little specter. It's not the way of the woods. In the forest, everything relies on everything else. Or so you tell me. You need to do the same. Besides, you won't be rid of me that easily." Paolo stared dreamily out the window. "I'll be in the breeze. I'll be in the songs of birds and bright shivers through the leaves. I'll be right here..." He prodded Giovanni in the chest.

"Paolo, you don't even like going out into the woods. I have to bribe you."

Paolo waved his pastry in the air. "That's because I have very nice shoes, but when I'm gone, I'll definitely be more outdoorsy."

Giovanni can barely breathe. He hasn't thought of that conversation in so long. And he cannot keep this to himself any longer. For the sake of his heart and his sanity, to be rid of the kind of stress he hasn't felt in a decade, he stands up. Takes excruciating care as he positions the truffle on the long table. And, a little carried away by the moment, all those expectant eyes boring into him, Giovanni whips the towel from the truffle in one dramatic flick.

A collective gasp sucks up the scented air.

"*Madonna!*"

"Giovanni, *Santo cielo*! Is that real?"

"It can't be! You've done a trickery. It's papier-mâché or a puppet," posits Carlotta.

"It's real! Smell it! That is a scream of a scent," says Stefano, his senses awakened. "And look at the thing! It is just like a human brain!"

The villagers stare at the hulking diamond of desire. Its staggering size. Sitting on the table like the unearthed crown of a medieval king. Knobby and tumorous, each gnarled protrusion of it like the burl of a grand old oak. With the whipping off of the towel, they are now all under its scent spell. An aromatic canticle releases tantalizing notes. The scent of a truffle speaks to each soul individually. Plucking at the pain of longing and potential. Some of the villagers smell desire, others dreams, many destiny. Memories and a bit of magic are conjured. The villagers stare, agog, as though it were a lamp. As though they are waiting to meet the djinn trapped inside.

Leon, emerging from the den of his despair, walks slowly toward Giovanni. He lowers his face to the truffle, great white beard hanging like spun sugar.

His voice, the village had almost forgotten it. Resonant as the bells in its tower. "It is a masterpiece. In a class by itself. Out of this world."

"It is a gift from God!" says Padre Francesco, twiddling with his rosary and muttering a prayer soft as a breeze between leaves. Before he can get halfway through it, Giuseppina elbows him out of the way to get a good look at the epicurean emperor.

She inhales, her eyes closing. "Mm. It smells like sex in a very small room. In summer." She sniffs, enraptured. "I love it. It is love."

Giovanni rubs his arms, aching from carrying the truffle. "It is real. I found it this morning. In all my life, I have never seen a truffle like this. And I don't think I ever will again."

A village not known for its silence falls silent. They may not have an exact monetary amount in their minds, but they are aware of the pricey nature of truffles. The villagers picture Giovanni and his truffle talk after the hunting season. At Christmastime, all the villagers tucked inside Bar Celebrità with spiced wine and slices of fruit-jeweled panettone. Snow glittering outside frosty windows. Outside, winter soft and savage. Inside, they are warmed by a crackling fire. Giovanni told them tales about the chain of selling, of how much these dirty little tubers can command. Of the Michelin-star chefs who hand over fistfuls of cash for little devils hiding in the dirt. The villagers listened, rose-cheeked and truffle-eyed.

Giovanni glances at all the faces around him. Everyone but Lorenzo, who is inside Bar Celebrità, preparing his *pranzo*.

It is Rosa who asks the burning question. "Giovanni, what is this truffle worth?"

Giovanni thinks about the potential. The prestige. The glamour. Its rarity. The wealthy hunt for exceptional. Social status is all about exclusivity. Bragging rights. What does the finest caviar fetch? Well, Giovanni knows, because he googled it. White gold caviar, or Almas, is the finest. It comes from the belly of the rare female albino sturgeon, who swims in the unpolluted southern waters of the Caspian Sea and who must be sixty to one hundred years old at the time of harvest. White gold caviar sells for $34,500 per kilogram and comes in a twenty-four-karat gold–plated tin. What about a one-of-a-kind pearl plucked from its oyster? Giovanni googled this too. A Filipino fisherman harvested the salty treasure from the seas around Palawan Island, a gargantuan twenty-six-inch pearl that is now valued at $100 million. Value—the worth we ascribe to things. What would one pay to own the *Mona Lisa?* Or some unearthed masterpiece hidden below soil, in a dark cellar, discovered to be an underground da Vinci? A lost Leonardo. Giovanni rubs his eyes. And he gives the villagers the only answer he can give right now.

"An absolute fortune."

Giuseppina drops a plate of olives. Her scream pierces through even the hardest of hearing among them. "The psychic! It's all coming true! The psychic said there would be a visitor. And she said that then there would be a death. She said that riches would come to our village of Lazzarini Boscarino. The visitor is here! It's the truffle! And the riches…they are coming! Someone is going to die, I am sure of it. Oh. Oh, no. Oh, no, no. I'm getting out the Orso; we all need a shot."

She strides past Lorenzo, who is standing in the doorway of Bar Celebrità holding out a glass of wine for Delizia. The new mayor retrieves it, then leaves Lorenzo standing watch, his mouth tight. She returns to the table. Appeals to Giovanni carefully. "Truffles a fraction of that size have put Italian towns on the map, Giovanni."

To Mayor Delizia, this whole day feels like a strange dream. As if she fell asleep in Nonna's *ristorante* and was carried away to an alternate universe by ants. "This fungal fruit could change everything for Lazzarini Boscarino. But you found it, Giovanni. And so it's your treasure."

The villagers contemplate this while watching Al Pacino drag a large sliver of prosciutto across the piazza.

Nose wrinkled, disgraced postman Duccio has held back his thoughts through this whole charade. He cannot hold them a minute more. "Truffles are a trick of the devil!"

Padre crosses himself and moans.

"This evil fungus is a blight on our village!"

Rosa frowns. "Duccio, what is wrong with—"

"We don't want to be associated with this—look at the thing. Disgusting, rotten tormentor! Revolting smell, hideous thing."

"Duccio—" Delizia tries to calm him.

"Look at that—it looks like an old man's fist! A mutant potato. The knee of a camel! The testicle of a badly preserved mummy! Get rid of it! Burn that tantric tumor. Horrendous witch's wart of the woods! You've lost your minds, all of you. You have let the devil in the door!" Duccio takes two strides, then turns and adds. "It looks like Tommaso's testicles!" He storms off, throwing a platter of pesto pasta into the air before he goes. It crashes down onto the piazza, Fagiolo appearing swiftly for clean-up service.

Everyone is shocked by Duccio's speech. By the massacre of a perfectly beautiful platter of pesto pasta. And perhaps because the village wet-weekend has spoken out against it, the truffle has just become more endearing in everyone's eyes.

"What on earth was that all about?" Benedetto asks. No one seems to know. Except Giovanni. He knows exactly what is happening. The madness has begun. The spell of the truffle has been cast. Here comes hysteria. He has witnessed mania around truffles, even tiny ones. He shudders to think what this one will inspire.

"What are your intentions then, Giovanni?" Mayor Delizia asks.

Giovanni stands with a wobble. Hand on the table to steady himself.

"I believe this truffle is a gift. A gift from the earth, a gift from God, the gift of scientific happenings in the soil. I don't know. But it has grown nearest our village and that is what I intend to tell the buyer. I don't want the responsibility, the ...

chaos of this. This truffle belongs to Lazzarini Boscarino. And it should fetch enough money to make a difference here."

"*Bravo!*" sings Delizia. Giuseppina has returned to dole out shots of Orso.

"It is a miracle!" yells Carlotta. "We have our holy foreskin!"

Those who were not at the *comune* meeting squint in bewilderment.

Giovanni passes on a shot of Orso. "I have to act fast. I have to sell it as soon as possible."

"Who do you trust, Giovanni?" asks Delizia. "Who to take a treasure like this to?"

He nods. "There's a big dealer in Florence, but I don't know him personally. There are high-end chefs in Rome I could approach, but I don't trust anyone I don't know with this, and, to be honest, I don't think I can manage the drive and transporting the truffle. I am the man with my hands in the dirt, not the man in the pockets of the rich and wealthy. There is just too much at stake. It's dangerous."

Delizia stares at gentle Giovanni, light gray eyes shining from his muddy face. The possibilities play out in her head. She is the mayor of Lazzarini Boscarino, and though it will be a personal catastrophe, she has to be the one to say it. No one else will.

She takes a deep breath. "We have to sell it to Umberto."

The piazza falls silent. Unsubtle eyes flick to Lorenzo, who quietly sets down little glasses of *zabaglione*. He does not hide his horror at the mention of his brother. That his wife is the one who brought up his name.

"You cannot trust Umberto with this," he warns.

Delizia feels ill. She does not want to hurt her husband. Her love. Her light. And here she is, calling back the wolf—the brother who betrayed him and broke his heart.

"Lorenzo, what choice do we have?"

"He's greedy, selfish—"

"But look at this truffle. Look at it! Umberto is Giovanni's contact."

"Surely, there is someone else! Anyone else!"

"Lorenzo, *per favore*. We have to act fast. And Umberto is who we have."

"What about Borghese Tartufi?"

Giovanni spits on the ground. "No! Borghese Tartufi are corrupt fiends!"

"Giuseppina!" pleads Lorenzo. "Would you trust your dear husband, Umberto, with this truffle?"

"God no," she says. "Disastrous idea."

"Thank you."

"But…Delizia makes a point. Umberto really does know truffles."

Lorenzo seems to deflate. Lorenzo, kindness incarnate. Every heart sinks at the sight of his despair. Delizia purses her mouth, sighs. She sees her husband holding back all the things he could say—about what was taken from him, about working in bars all over Italy as he supported Delizia in her capricious veterinary career. But he doesn't, this selfless soul.

"Do what you must. But I won't have anything to do with Umberto." Lorenzo widens his eyes, flashes the palms of his hands, and retires in silence to the *cucina* of Bar Celebrità. Before he disappears behind the doorway, he shares an exasperated look with Giuseppina. Giuseppina lifts her hand in a gesture that suggests she has a plan.

"How long do we have before it starts to lose its value, Giovanni?" asks Delizia, setting down an empty glass.

"There's not a minute to lose. It will be utterly worthless in…five days."

They contemplate this to the sound of an amateur truffle-hunting dog munching on spilled olives. "We'd better get to Borghese right away."

The villagers all stand up from the table, thrumming from the excitement of the most eventful afternoon *riposa* anyone can remember. Delizia's heart drops as she realizes that lunch has not even begun. Lorenzo's beautiful *pranzo di lavoro*, in honor of her, will not be touched.

Sabotaged by a secret found in soil.

"Borghese is a danger. We have Borghese Tartufi to watch out for." Everyone has had to listen to Giovanni grouse about the truffle-hunting company in Borghese. A band of swindlers who take tourists out for a truffle hunt, whatever the season. Hunters who are rumored to game the system by stealthily tossing in an older truffle at the last second of a dog's scrabbling. Rolling worthless old truffles in synthetic truffle oil—specifically the devil chemical flavor bis(methylthio)methane. The truffle-hunting company promises to find the tourists their truffles whatever the season. A rigged rip-off to dazzle and rob them blind. "If they get wind of this, and they will—just smell the thing—it all might get dirty." He stares at his soiled hands and lets out a delirious twitter of laughter.

Poliziotto Silvio stands. He pulls off a John Wayne swagger in historied leather boots toward the gigantic truffle. Dons his traditional two-pointed hat.

"Well then, you will need a police escort."

Chapter 5

Tranquil old-world elegance is boasted by a wall of sanded stone. An operatic drama of arched windows. Gold lettering winks from polished glass.

NOVELLI

The building is Tuscan modern. Sexy as a building can be. An olfactory language purrs through cracked windows of this chic *ristorante*. Where the rhyming couplet of coffee and chocolate recite the rich poem of a tiramisu. Where the choicest cuts of meat share sizzling gossip in garlic oil. Crisp consonants of hot salmon skin spat from a hot grill. Nutty drawl of browned butter. And the occasional musk of a grated truffle murmured like an erotic patois.

On the outdoor patio, tourists sip prosecco in glamorous Borghese, because the weather is warm. Before autumn wraps them in the spell of woodsmoke, her golden leaves illuminating their lovely lesson about change.

"Good heavens, what is that?" asks a tourist attempting to pass the three-Michelin-star paradise. He is an Englishman who has recently sautéed his head to the hue of tuna tartare. A smell has caught this tuna in a sensory snare. He is the latest victim of a walk-by sniffing. The *ristorante*'s glass menu display case is populated with nose prints. So many, in fact, they call for a twice daily polishing.

The only thing that ever deters anyone from Novelli is its prices.

You follow the invisible invitation. A vine-wrapped door opens for you as if by magic. Inside, you admire decorative wine barrels. Sommelier-blessed wine bottles backlit with an ambient blue glow (blue being psychologically symbolic of tranquility and self-expression). You are warmly welcomed by someone who is either a maître d' or a runway model.

Waitstaff flitter from table to table as if biddable little Italian bees visiting a thousand flower faces to make *millefiori* honey. Chandeliers shaped like tortellini give every patron a flattering glow.

As you tread deeper into the *ristorante*, the aromatic language intensifies. Because now we are in a cityscape of sharp edges and shining silver.

Novelli's kitchen.

Here is where the owner and renowned chef—certainly the best in Borghese, and one of the most highly regarded in all of Tuscany—is curled over an edible composition. His pewter hair lifting up into pomade curls like frozen seaside froth. A matching beard has been bossed into a tidy triangle. He carries the generous padding a nightly steak propagates, washed down with a midnight Chianti. With steady hands, Chef Umberto Micucci is painting a pastry brush along the borders of a fine china plate.

"And now," he says, lifting the plate, pressing the funky Day-Glo orange frames of his glasses against his face. "Tell me what is missing."

His minions—the picture of youth and cleaver-sharp ambition—hover close, holding their breath. They are the best of the best, these white-wearing chefs, all of them rising stars. A truth, bitter as radicchio, is that this season's culinary inquest has pushed them to their limits. In hierarchical order—his direct report and chef de cuisine, Adroa Mbabazi. Fastest fingers and finest culinary creative Umberto has known. But due to pressures from the competitive hustle of haute cuisine, Chef Adroa is also taking part in a migraine trial and wears a mouth guard to deter him from grinding away his own teeth in the pepper mill of his mouth. Next, Sous Chef Ichika Tanaka. A chef who handles flavors like an intrepid pioneer of the tongue, a wayfarer of the avant-garde and the unexpected. A chef who has also explored the emergency ward three times this year for some equally enterprising accidental self-stabbings and who has taken to wearing her chef hat even outside of the kitchen due to several sizable bald spots. Next is Novelli's pastry chef, Alban Toussaint, a master of sugar work, a chocolatier who once built an eight-foot Eiffel Tower out of cacao, but who is also on medication for "sleep cooking" after having recently set fire to his home kitchenette. And finally, Sauté Chef Farah Ahmad, small and ferocious, the self-proclaimed hurricane in a hijab. Executive Chef Umberto sees the most potential in Chef Farah. She has that drive, the passion it takes to carve out her own spot in the cutthroat culinary world. Or is she a they? Chef Umberto is having a hard time keeping up with all these youthful requisites, like rainbow-colored hair, internet dance trends, and pronouns. And time, doesn't it seem to slip away lately, as silently as the steam from a seafood hot pot? He sometimes remembers the never-ending hours of a single day biking around his home village as a boy. Now, the world is moving faster, and he is moving slower.

When did it all get so complicated?

Chef Umberto stares at his team, who—forgiving the blackened eye bags and a generous peppering of hives—look like auditioning contestants of *Junior MasterChef Italia*. *Che bambini sono!* Relocating to Borghese from all over the globe, they are here because these rising stars of consommé, *culatello*, and chiffonade have a chance, under his tutelage, to become supernovas. To dazzle during *l'ora di pranzo* when Novelli serves a luxury lunch, taxing in itself. But after four p.m., when the evening unfolds her royal navy robes and the Aperols begin to spritz, is when the real adventure begins. Chef Umberto has outdone himself. This year, he has created a world-class nine-course gustatory extravaganza, a culinary celebration of seminal life experiences. *Gastronomica* calls it an "unparalleled epicurean awakening of the soul." Two early patrons have—mid nine-course meal—fainted. Another sobbed so hard she had to be sedated. The chefs have a daunting schedule ahead. Over the next nine weeks, they will introduce multisensory dining experiences.

Week 1: Birth
Week 2: Family
Week 3: Friendship
Week 4: Battles
Week 5: Sex
Week 6: Failure
Week 7: Success
Week 8: Death
Week 9: Reincarnation

Chef Umberto speaks to his hastiness of cooks in a voice rich and robust as ragù. "I want you all to remember that we are sorcerers of taste and scent. Scientifically speaking, smell and the memory are linked by the biological makeup of our brains. Emotion and smells are inextricable because they are stored in our olfactory bulb as one memory. And we must create a visual extravaganza on every plate because we humans smell in color."

Chef Farah Ahmad squints, her pupils hard as the pits of plums. "With all due respect, Chef...what do you mean that we smell in color?"

"What color are you picturing when you first inhale that fresh cut grass? Or when you sniff a rose? What hue do you imagine when you inhale a bundle of lavender?" Each eager chef closes their eyes, transported through sensory experience.

"Do we comprehend?"

"Yes, Chef," they bleat. They even look a little like a flock of sheep, Chef Umberto thinks, in their pristine white uniforms. More like lambs. Feeble lambs with flabbergasted faces, lost in the Apuan Alps.

Of course, he sees that these young chefs are run ragged; he isn't blind. But Chef Umberto knows that to become truly extraordinary, they must be dismantled and rebuilt. Rising stars must sink or swim. And a truth about stars is that the bigger they are, the quicker they burn up their fuel supply. Chef Umberto has to admit, he is exhausted with sustaining the success of Novelli. He is secretly a little bit bored with being the best. And all the little lambs sent his way seem to get younger and younger. Plus, he's having a hell of a time getting their pronouns right, even though he has practiced them within an inch of his life. "*They* is chopping the su vide." "They has severed they's finger while they was manning the mandoline." "*They* is in the process of spilling half a gallon of roux on the floor." Chef Umberto doesn't feel old, but it does feel that everything is changing fast. Does he take issue with these changes? Certainly not. He wants to get it right, to remain relevant; it's just that he can't get his matured mind to retain these shifts in language and sacrilegious online food trends. He still has an insatiable fire inside him, but maybe he is ready for a change of pace. During the few hours he is in bed, he has taken to calling out their names and pronouns in his sleep.

He stares at his sous chef, Ichika Tanaka, and the three separate bandages fused to her fingers. "Remember that each dish is a journey, a nostalgic foray into the past or the possibilities of the future. This is about creating new neurons in the human brain through taste and scent and texture. Through food. Now, what are we going for with this dessert of Week Five?"

"An...intimate affair," braves Chef Farah Ahmad.

"Sex, yes. Very good. So what's missing?" He hears throat clearing. Witnesses lambs blushing. "There is no room for shame in culinary exploration." He points at the enticing dessert, its phallus of a pistachio-dusted plantain, the guava gel–covered cheesecake to represent a pair of testicles. A haphazard slash of passionfruit coulis as an abstract suggestion of the volatile nature of passion. Gold leaf and edible flowers to symbolize fertility. Or is it the Garden of Eden? Or nipples? The young chefs cannot remember.

"I can't hear you, chefs. What is missing from this scene?"

Alban Toussaint, the *bombolone*-eyed pastry chef, makes a suggestion, his voice cracking. "A clitoris?"

Umberto raises his eyebrows and twists his mouth. He nods his head vigorously. "Very good. And what would you suggest we add to the dish to represent it?"

"A pomegranate?" Chef Alban Toussaint asks, thumbing the bottle of Lexapro in his pocket. The other rising stars all pull faces suited to sewage smells. Chef Alban Toussaint had not expected his lack of experience with the female anatomy to hinder the culinary career that is the reason for his lack of experience with the female anatomy.

Chef Umberto shakes his head, ashamed of the young pastry apprentice.

Chef Alban Toussaint tries again, desperate now. "Tempered chocolate...I could mold one."

Chef Umberto squints hard. His orange frames become terrifying portals, threatening to suck young aspiring cooks right through their lenses. "The cacao will overwhelm the dish; it will upstage the subtleties we've spent three days harmonizing." He pinches the bridge of his nose. Scoffs. Shakes his head. "Chocolate clitoris. Tsk."

Chef Alban Toussaint's facial tic returns with a vengeance. His fingers instinctively find the patch of eczema on his elbow and linger on it as though it were a small oasis. Chef Ichika Tanaka is staring at her sous vide–spattered shoes. She is suffering from pronounced PTSD after slipping on a dropped ostrich egg.

"What is your opinion, Chef?" Umberto sets his unflinching focus on Chef de Cuisine Adroa Mbabazi.

Chef Adroa squeezes his eyes shut, wary not to squeeze so hard he summons another migraine. "Lychee?"

The chefs hold their breath, awaiting the verdict of Chef Umberto.

"Hmm. Citrus perfume notes will complement the passionfruit. You're finally thinking, Chef. Now go get some."

Chef Adroa Mbabazi bolts to the walk-in refrigerator as though trying to clock the finish line of the Florence Marathon. In the high-end culinary world, it can be difficult to regulate your stress levels, so the chefs often find themselves racing through relaxing activities—engaging in frenzied knitting, high-speed gardening, and listening to audiobooks at three times the natural pace. In the refrigerator, Chef Adroa

Mbabazi takes advantage of his solitary moment in the subzero environment to squash his face against a wrapped prosciutto leg before his frantic search for a small fleshy fruit.

They are like terrified little *Glis glis*, thinks Chef Umberto, having just watched his chef de cuisine streak across the kitchen as though he were trying to outrun the Frecciarossa high-speed train. It's not his fault if they can't handle a little heat. Yes, Chef Ichika Tanaka may still have the willies from sliding around in an ostrich egg, but Chef Umberto is here to expand the frontiers of food. He is here to push his people and his patrons until either their minds or their pants explode. Like many a live lobster, he often finds himself in hot water. Chef Umberto is infamous for adding unconventional ingredients to his tasting courses. An edible balloon filled with a harmless huff of laughing gas. A lemon with a little dusting of deep-fried Brazilian ants. A squirt of epinephrine injected into foie gras to induce a physical and existential panic attack for the resurrection course. Authenticity is everything. Occasionally, the police come to investigate these dalliances, yes; it's their duty— but after a roasted rack of lamb and three majestic glasses of Brunello, everyone is forgiven. And all of it just brings more publicity, more celebrity, more Michelin stars. In a rather boring way, Chef Umberto finds that he is utterly untouchable.

The striking young woman from the front of house spills into the kitchen like a refracted rainbow. Her tight obsidian dress renders her figure legible. It is a figure that, only last summer, caused a seven-car pileup in Rome, and earlier this spring, caused a tourist to become disoriented and speed his Saab illegally through the Vatican. Chef Umberto finds her youthful beauty arresting but ephemeral. Intense and intoxicating, but without nuance or complexity. A perfume whose top notes are strongest. He enjoys that she is carefree and untethered, light enough to be blown around by a breeze. But she is unworldly.

She wears her inexperience like cheap, ever-present earrings. A million questions tied around her tongue. He finds her exhausting. Exhilarating. A beautiful island surrounded by the gulf of all she has yet to know. She is a blank book waiting to be filled with words.

"Um, excuse me, Chef?" She mouths vowels with her Australian accent as though rolling macarons with her tongue.

"Yes, Marilyn?" Chef Umberto keeps his voice even.

Chef Alban Toussaint eyes a lychee and then Marilyn.

"You are required at the front of house, Chef."

A long, constipated pause. "I will meet them front of house when I am finished here." He looks back down at the plate. Of course, the lychee is making him think of Marilyn, who he was careful not to let his eyes linger on. He hasn't so much as hidden their relationship as obfuscated it, and he doubts anyone even suspects it, given how subtle they have both been.

"It's urgent?" says Marilyn, her voice slightly higher than normal, which, incidentally, is how everyone knows that she and Executive Chef Umberto are sleeping together. Also, the fact that they keep typing on their phones at the same exact time, and the most telltale sign of all—they started actively ignoring one another at work about six months ago, despite their close professional proximity.

Chef Umberto, his tone gentler and lower than normal, adds, "I'm occupied. I will see them when I am finished here."

Marilyn's charming little *struffoli* of a nose wrinkles. "I don't think—"

"*Marilyn,*" he scolds her in a tone used for a child. Chef Umberto forces his eyes to stay locked onto the intimate affair on his plate rather than the intimate affair standing at the swinging doors. Since he is not looking at her, he does not see that she is pouting her naturally pouty lips. "This networking of the creative impulses is an integral process in creating a culinary masterpiece. It cannot, ever, be interrupted. I will be available when we are finished here. Tell the person here to see me that I will be with them when we have given the time this creative exploration asks of us." He lowers his orange frames to the phallus on the plate. He is still very much not looking at her.

Marilyn lets out a mutinous bark of laughter, louder than the yell of her youthful beauty. "Food doesn't ask anything of us."

Chef Tanaka gasps. Chef Toussaint stress-squirts an arc of béchamel sauce into the air.

"*Marilyn*," says Chef Umberto through gritted teeth. In the beginning, their entanglement was an irresistible intoxication. Forbidden fruit. Chef Umberto finds the generation gap is sometimes quite charming, like when over a text he told Marilyn he was listening to the Beatles, and she assumed he had taken up entomological studies. But often it is less charming, like when she misunderstood the identity of his old VCR and forcefully inserted her cheese sandwich into the tape deck. Perhaps he struggles most with the particular horror that, although she is dating a world-class chef, she still insists on eating an inelegant hunk of cheese clapped between sacrilegious slices of white bread.

Marilyn lifts her eyebrows, hands on hips in an act of insurrection. "Anyway, it's not a person here to see you. It's a village."

Umberto has barely had time to digest her words before most of a medieval village storms into his three-Michelin-star kitchen.

His flock of young chefs trots nervously as the intrusion of exhilarated senior citizens bombards their workplace. A migraine blooms in the corner of Chef Mbabazi's mind. Chef Ichika Tanaka slips trembling fingers under her chef's hat, uprooting several strands of hair.

Chef Umberto's eyes glisten with recognition as he spots the twins from the village of his birth. Then Padre Francesco, Carlotta, a haggard-looking farmer Leon, and finally Stefano, wheeled by Benedetto, into his territory. He fails to see Giovanni slinking in last, brow beaded with sweat. A curiosity swaddled in his dirty dog towel. But he clearly spots Poliziotto Silvio striding into the kitchen with an air of authority. Chef Umberto feels his resolve collapsing like an over-baked soufflé. But the *carabinieri* is not what concerns him most in this moment.

"Is *she*...here?" he asks, his flock of chefs hearing fear in the voice they are afraid of for the first time.

"She's not here, but we are!" sings Valentina.

"What about—"

"Your brother is not here either," says Rosa, icily.

His main fears assuaged, Chef Umberto nods at Poliziotto Silvio. The *carabinieri* have been in this kitchen many times before, but always the Borghese precinct. Never the lone *poliziotto* of Lazzarini Boscarino, whose most prolific police work was the apprehension of a pants-pilfering goat when it absconded with a clothesline. And, though he has never spoken of it since, the time Poliziotto Silvio was called into the piazza because a rubbish bin was pulsating with a suspicious object believed to be a bomb but that turned out to be an abandoned vibrator. A cold case that has never been solved. Does it seem likely that Poliziotto Silvio is here to charge him with violating patrons' privacy for the "family week" epicurean experience where Umberto hides a surprise edible portrait of a guest's loved one in a white chocolate-and-cardamom mousse? It does not. But he'd ordered three cases of Brunello, just in case. Nor does it seem likely that the *poliziotto* is here with a health violation charge. Chef Umberto has been very subtle about the thousands of live crickets, mealworms, scorpions, and cicadas he ordered for the week with the theme of "failure." He has demanded complete discretion from his entourage while he navigates his insect experimentation phase.

No, this is something else. He's been at enough award shows to recognize that crackle in the room.

Chef Umberto places his pastry brush on the counter. Frowns. He is a self-made culinary sensation, his sense of dignity built with every brick of his accomplishments. He stands on his Michelin stars. And here, the very village he worked so hard to get away from—in geography and reputation—has just barged into the clandestine kitchen of his glamorous restaurant. It is an outrage. The young chefs and Marilyn idolize him. He cannot have his roots exposed like this. He has done too much to hide his humble beginnings.

"There are too many chefs in my kitchen!" he roars.

Chef Adroa Mbabazi signals for all the chefs to busy themselves at the far end of the *cucina* with prep for the tasting extravaganza that is—a quick glower at the wall clock confirms—just about to start. He and Chef Ichika Tanaka alone will stay by the side of Head Chef Umberto as he handles whatever half the village of Lazzarini Boscarino has in store for them.

"The bravado! What has possessed you to waltz into my private kitchen, just as we are about to start serving a *pièce de résistance* in a replication of the miracles of life?"

Benedetto ruffles his oversize suit. "A real miracle of life."

"I know what this is," says Carlotta. She is bent over Chef Umberto's plate like an antique reading lamp, scrutinizing Chef Umberto's plated delicacy through her Coke-bottle glasses. "It's a dessert holy foreskin!"

Chef Adroa Mbabazi dry-swallows a Xanax.

"Someone needs to tell me right now—" Chef Umberto starts, running a hand through the suspended silver flames of his hair. Flattening signature orange frames against his face. "What is the village of Lazzarini Boscarino doing in my restaurant?"

Valentina opens her mouth to explain.

"Wait…" Umberto's pupils dilate. Saliva pools in his mouth. He feels a small butane torch making a brûlée of his insides. A quick succession of memories slam into him—champagne glasses clinking in his honor at the White Truffle Fair in Alba. His heart filling with foam during a life-changing phone call, as he learned Novelli had been awarded its first Michelin star. Marilyn and the plastic strawberry smell of her, tangled up in his bedsheets as he brings her an Australian breakfast of farm-fresh eggs, bacon, grilled tomato, and mushrooms to stave off her homesickness.

There is only one gourmet comestible that can transfix him this way.

The white truffle.

To Chef Umberto Micucci, success is the smell of a truffle. Woodsy reek. Garlic gas. Sweat on leather. An earthen umami cologne. Naughty sulfuric skunk of the finest marijuana. But what he smells now is knocking his socks off. A bomb has detonated in his *cucina,* diffusing the most intoxicating lust potion. He has never smelled any truffle quite like the little lumps he imagines are waiting for him in that odd bundle Giovanni is cradling. And—what luck. Lately, with all the dry weather and changing climate, truffles have been stunted and strange, most offerings reminiscent of dehydrated *Glis glis* spleens. *Piattelli—little plates*—they call them. The value of truffles has skyrocketed in recent years. The pungent little treasures in Giovanni's bundle might actually be worth their lofty price tag.

"Giovanni, you've brought me truffles." Chef Umberto's nostrils beat like bat wings. He is drugged. Aching with desire. "You've brought me lots and lots of truffles."

A parting of villagers reveals the gentle truffle hunter

cowering at the back of the *cucina*. His scruffy truffle-hunting dog is by his side, a health violation that Chef Umberto is far too intoxicated to address.

Giovanni looks small next to the large mechanical animal of an industrial mixer. His misty gray eyes are bloodshot. Skin cemented with mud. He is cradling a filthy dog towel. The tremors quivering along his arms pique Chef Umberto's interest. As does the shocking amount of grime the gentle hunter is lacquered with. How strange to see Giovanni in the kitchen. Umberto usually greets him at odd hours, under a smattering of stars or during the first stanza of sparrow song. Always in clandestine meetings at the delivery entrance of Novelli. The two of them alone, sifting through a velvet sack of pungent secrets.

Chef Umberto steps closer to the truffle hunter, and the smell slips its shackles around him. A step closer, it swallows him whole. A strong-arm of a smell.

"Show me," he croaks, his eyes watering.

Valentina and Rosa flank Giovanni. Each twin takes a side of towel, and they whisk it aside as though magician's assistants.

Pupils balloon behind orange frames. "Oh, *Santa Maria Maggiore*... that's one truffle. How can it be? I... when... where did it come from?"

Giovanni stays silent. Chef Umberto knows that the answer will go with Giovanni to the grave, but he couldn't help himself.

"A gift," says Padre Francesco, raising a spatula for dramatic emphasis, "from God." Rosa shushes him and confiscates his spatula.

Chef Umberto gestures at the gargantuan truffle. Giovanni nods. The famous chef approaches slowly, deferentially, as one would a monarch or a long-lost relic. His hands are quaking, sweat shimmering across his brow. Behind orange frames, his engorged pupils decipher its shape. A preserved brain.

Peeking through a layer of dirt, a beige color brings to mind ancient bones. A chill whispers across his skin. Chef Umberto is no stranger to the world's most exclusive culinary luxuries—caviar from rare albino beluga fish, scarlet threads of saffron. The umami magic of matsutake mushrooms, rare as a result of deforestation to their pinewoods and a villainous worm called the pinewood nematode. He has cooked with the poisonous fugu pufferfish, nests of swallows stolen from cliffsides, moose cheese made from one of only three lactating domestic moose in the world. He has dabbled with *kopi luwak* java beans, eaten and then excreted by a palm civet, beef from Wagyu bull calves who are massaged and serenaded with classical music, and even the elusive ayam cemani chicken, whose bones and skin and plumage are all black as charcoal.

And truffles?

Chef Umberto Micucci is the King of Truffles in Borghese. He deals directly with the best truffle hunters in the region, often selling the excess up the ladder to further fatten his finances. To truffle dealers all across Italy. A profit is a profit. Business is business. And the sexy little sale of a truffle is Chef Umberto's business.

Chef Umberto lifts a finger in suggestion. When Giovanni nods, Chef Umberto carefully drags the quivering nail of his forefinger along the dirt layer of the truffle. A bawdy stench of success is giving him a searing rush, a wasabi kick up his nose. Volatile organic compounds slip along chosen neural paths in every brain. Summoning specific memories to everyone. A walk in the woods. Raindrops releasing the essence of the earth. First sips of a summer wine, pupils swelling with desire.

The villagers are silent as Chef Umberto, Chef Tanaka, and Chef Mbabazi begin a delicate dance, cleaning the truffle with the softest brushes. Chef Umberto is overcome, steadying himself by holding on to the stainless-steel range. The truffle is not holding much dirt. Merely a dainty layer. Wormless. Not a mouse nibble nor a stone in sight. Which means that this mass is all truffle.

It is solid gold.

Words are eluding him. He bites the insides of his cheeks. Then gestures to his professional digital kitchen scales.

Everyone in the kitchen holds their truffled breath, eye-whites glistening. Giovanni gingerly places the truffle on the scales. It looks obscene sitting on the measuring plate. Grimy and grotesque. Hysterically absurd. An excavated alien with no equal. A lonely subterrestrial.

Breathlessly, everyone watches the digital display.

In the split second he waits for a number, others swim to Chef Umberto.

2007: casino mogul Stanley Ho bids on a 3.3-pound white truffle and wins for the sum of $330,000.

2010: Stanley Ho bids again on two pounds, fourteen ounces' worth of white truffle for $330,000.

2013: Russian billionaire Vladimir Potanin pays $95,000 for a batch of truffles totaling four pounds.

2014: Sotheby's auctions off a 4.16-pound truffle, the largest known to man, and receives multiple offers from Chinese bidders. It sells for $61,250.

2021: at the Alba White Truffle Fair auction, a two-pound truffle sells for $118,000.

Chef Umberto remembers precise figures because he bid on some of these beasts. He has never landed one of the treasured tubers, and here—as if an attracted atom drawn here by his own desire—the most valuable truffle on earth is now rumbling its high vibrational siren song in his kitchen.

The digital number blinks into being. Chef Adroa Mbabazi chokes on air.

Six pounds, fourteen ounces.

Six pounds is the weight of three liters of milk. A drip coffee maker. Two laptops. An adult Yorkshire terrier. A newborn baby.

No one on earth has ever found a truffle this size.

Not one with a fragrance as arresting.

History is leavening like a pale dough, right before their eyes.

Chef Ichika Tanaka yanks out a handful of hair and yelps.

This fungus crown will bring on a price tag all of its own through hysteria. By those who have to have the world's biggest and best truffle. To be the owner of a great white whale.

"How…much?" Chef Umberto says, staring at the filthy truffle hunter he has known his whole life. Umberto pulls on his poker face, heart pounding. He can do nothing to stop the tear of sweat slipping down the side of his face. "What is your price?"

He must not show that he is head over heels, that this truffle is making a junkie of anyone within its sphere of influence. A full moon to make us all a little mad. Because now is when the wheeling and dealing begins over the sale of this treasure, and, as seems befitting of truffles, there is a lot more trickery than in your average negotiation. What Chef Umberto is banking on is that truffle hunters never see the biggest bucks. Chefs buy fresh truffles from hunters directly to use that night, each generous grating of truffle snowing over eggy tagliatelle skyrocketing a patron's bill. If the truffles are pristine, rare, large—they sell to dealers, urban wolves who take them to the highest-end clients and auction houses. That is who makes the real money. The hunters see a fraction of the final amount a gourmet restaurant will pay for their filthy little treasures. Middlemen usually bridge the gap between hunters hobbling around in the dirt and the chefs of three- and four-star restaurants who will pay through the nose to snuffle a truffle. Peddling a product that must be moved faster than cocaine, dealing in anywhere from

$10,000 to $30,000 in truffles per day. But Chef Umberto has known Giovanni since he was a young man, cultivated this relationship like roots and a friendly fungus. Cut out the middleman. Chef Umberto will pay Giovanni handsomely—maybe a few thousand euros—and then he will sneak right past the dealers and take it to an international auction house. And—a good guess—sell it for more than half a million. Business is business. And Chef Umberto is a boar about his business.

Chef Umberto is already famous. He is about to become infamous.

Giovanni has not given his price. Umberto clenches his fists, veins crackling with adrenaline.

"I'll give you twenty-five thousand euros," says the famous chef.

The twins gasp.

Giovanni's pale eyes widen. "I…I need to think…"

Chef Umberto can't have Giovanni thinking; he needs to bargain swiftly. "I'll take the truffle off your hands, Giovanni."

"I know, I just need a moment—"

"Forty thousand euros." He extends a sweaty hand.

Benedetto has to steady himself against the deep-fat fryer.

All the villagers' stares bore into Giovanni. Their mouths are agape in disbelief—*What is he waiting for?*

Umberto is overcome with the moment, with the promise and potent scent waves swimming into his nostrils. Giovanni looks at his shoes. His eyes close. He is calculating the worth of the truffle, *oh, no,* Umberto needs to get ahead of this. Go big or lose the biggest culinary prize of his life.

"One hundred thousand euros, *Signore* Scarpazza."

Cries of shock lance across the *cucina*. Padre Francesco lifts his hands toward the heavens. Stefano, quite overcome with excitement, snatches up a fistful of flour and throws it into the air.

Umberto wipes the sweat from his brow. Pulls together his poker face and fixes it on the truffle hunter.

"One hundred thousand euros. My final offer."

But before Giovanni can agree to the price of the tuber treasure he hunted, the doors to the kitchen of the best restaurant in Borghese wallop open.

The villagers stare wide-eyed at Chef Umberto, waiting for his reaction. The young chefs freeze. They breathe as quietly as possible. There are, after all, small piles of yeast that garner more respect from their head chef. And no one is sure about what will happen next.

Chapter 6

Leave us." Giuseppina's words are fermented in vinegar. She strikes a pose at the doors of the *cucina*. Brassy blonde hair loose, haunting her shoulders. She has changed from a signature singlet into a sequined blue dress. Loud lipstick. A pair of stilettos she hasn't worn since the opening of this restaurant. Her tan howling under the clinical kitchen lights.

Chef Umberto protests. "My chefs can be privy to anything we discuss—"

"Leave us! All of you!"

Chef Umberto widens his eyes at his chef de cuisine, Chef Adroa Mbabazi. They have run through an emergency drill for this very scenario. Chef Adroa does his duty, quickly snatching up as many knives as he can before evacuating the kitchen. Chef Ichika Tanaka follows, scurrying through the swinging doors and into the safe zone and main dining room of Novelli. The other chefs tail them, as light on their feet as prey animals. Half of Lazzarini Boscarino follows, Benedetto giving

Chef Umberto one lingering look as he disappears through the doors. It is the look you might give a live lobster in such a setting. Chef Umberto has half a mind to ask the *poliziotto* to stay, for his own safety. He thinks better of it.

Rosa has the last word before she leaves. "Giuseppina, we will be waiting at the *osteria* next door." A sad truth in the subtext. None of the villagers can afford even an appetizer here at Novelli.

Chef Umberto Micucci now stands alone in a kitchen newly denuded of knives with Giuseppina Micucci and the largest truffle in the world. Not a word has passed between the estranged couple in eight months. Another dilemma for Chef Umberto—the truffle is a ticking clock, a potential for fortunes to seep away every second, and here he finds himself standing alone with the only human on earth he is afraid to hurry.

Sweat burgeons across the chef's lower back. He braves breaking the silence. "Hello, Giuseppi—"

"Don't lecture me!" Giuseppina's eyes are filled with the sort of searing heat that recalls a peperoncino-laden Southern Italian pasta Chef Umberto once served at a chef's table dining event. A dish known as *spaghetti all'assassina*. Giuseppina's scorching glare finds the monstrous truffle sitting on the scales. Then Chef Umberto. "What are you doing?"

"In my kitchen? In *my* restaurant?"

Giuseppina narrows her scowl. "You cannot hide anything from me..."

Chef Umberto lifts his hands defensively. Giuseppina scans the kitchen. Takes in every detail. It has been a long time since she has stepped foot in this restaurant. Today she has broken her own boycott.

"That's new." She gestures at an extravagant range.

"It is. And I replaced the walk-in refrigerator after Chef Toussaint got trapped in the last one."

"Have you seen Sofia?"

"Is that an accusation?"

"Don't be dramatic," Giuseppina chastises. "She still hasn't come home. Leon is losing his mind. We all are."

"That is odd. The last time I saw Sofia, she was at the *osteria* with Nico. And the last time I saw Nico, he was at the *osteria* sitting at the same table, sobbing over missing Sofia."

"Believably?"

"Now that's an accusation. They don't call Nico the Casanova of Borghese for nothing...but he doesn't seem a likely candidate for anything nefarious. Between the bowlegs and advanced rheumatoid arthritis..." Chef Umberto watches his estranged wife strut around his kitchen. Her skin nut brown. Those wild brass-blonde locks. The active volcano that is her spirit. An untamed fire smoldering inside her. She is a most terrifying animal. He smiles at her stilettos, softens. "You've been to the beach..."

"Maybe."

"Alone?"

"None of your business."

"How is my brother?"

She shoots him a look that would extract every layer of an onion. He translates this as "You do not deserve to know." Umberto nods.

Giuseppina's inspection continues as she peers at hanging prosciutto legs and cured pork cheeks. She prods at a sleek fire extinguisher with the toe of her stiletto. Curling over a jar of white powder, she frowns, then yells, "What is this? Cocaine?"

"It's desiccated coconut," comes Chef Umberto's exasperated response.

"*Porca vacca!* Whose testicles are these?"

"No one's. Those are Indonesian fruits called *rambutan*." As Chef Umberto watches Giuseppina snoop around his *cucina*, he rubs the cell phone in his pocket. Once he buys the truffle from Giovanni, he can place the call he needs to in mere minutes. He'll get to savor being the one to break the news of this unprecedented truffle, he just needs to be alone… "What are you looking for, Pina? Are you wearing a wire? Trying to get me arrested?"

"If that were my intention, you'd already be in jail by now, with everything I know!" she foghorns.

"Now who's being dramatic?"

"There are bugs in this kitchen…"

"*Pina.* They are necessary for a culinary transcendence. I stand by my work. I am pushing the boundaries of gastronomical exploration."

"And what have you done to your young chefs? They look like lost lambs!"

"They do, don't they? I was just thinking that…"

"You have browbeaten them into oblivion. Each one has the fortitude of a defrosted scallop. They are only *bambini*, you awful beast."

The tension in the kitchen is thick and ominous. It could be cut with a knife had they not all been confiscated. A thought pops up in Umberto's mind like discharged toast.

"You're not scouring my *cucina* in case I hid Sofia in the chestnut flour bin, are you?"

"Tsk, no. She's just on my mind all the time, and I wondered if you knew anything. I came here to stop you."

"From what?"

"From making a lowball bid for the truffle, you snake."

"You look nice."

"Don't change the subject."

"We haven't landed on one."

Giuseppina tosses her hair. The sequins of her dress wink spasmodically under extravagant kitchen lights. "I have come to the conclusion that your lawyer is blind."

"I'll admit, his driving is a little hair-raising, but legally, he is sighted."

"Well, what's taking so long? What lawyer takes three years to finalize a divorce?"

"Ah, that's why you are performing this interrogation...you want me to sign the papers."

"It's not why I'm here, but yes, I want you to sign them. It's why I filed them and hired Mauro at great expense."

"What is he charging you?"

"I don't know yet; he hasn't sent the bill. He is a delinquent."

"That is an unkind thing to say about your second cousin. When he does charge, let me know. I will cover it. Or I will get you a better lawyer."

"We can't have the same lawyer in our own divorce, Berto." Giuseppina rolls her eyes, pops a whole fig into her mouth. She turns to study Umberto's strong nose, his gravity-defying hair. The crackle of his commanding presence. Eyes underlined in gray from so many late nights. How they blink behind the bright orange glasses she chose for him. "You are seeing someone."

"What? How did you know that?"

"My psychic told me."

"The young psychic from Volterra with the shaved head and the goat tattoo?"

"It is a satyr."

"A what?"

"Her tattoo. It's part goat."

"Exactly, a tattoo of a goat."

"*Porco mondo*, you are as stubborn as a goat. And no, not her; I have a new psychic. Mamma Fortuna. This one can actually predict things. Berto, she saw this truffle coming."

"Ah...now I see. So that's the real reason you're here."

A pregnant silence settles between the two of them. The

silence lingers, carrying on long enough to give birth and raise twins. The *cucina* suddenly seems colder, dropping several degrees. Aromatic gas billowing from the gargantuan truffle dizzies the estranged pair. It has begun a dangerous dance with their hormones.

"Umberto, how much money will you pay for this magnificent truffle?"

"A handsome price."

Giuseppina snatches two saucepans and smacks them together. Ladles fall from the wall. "I knew it! You are going to rip him off and sell it yourself at auction!" she yells. "It's not enough that your ridiculous face is plastered all over the side of olive jars and pints of gelato! Yes, Umberto, this is why I am here. I am here, once again, to save you from yourself!"

She has struck a nerve. Umberto loses grip on his temper, that slippery little thing. "*Pina*, you turn everything into a soap opera! The entire village of Lazzarini Boscarino trespasses into my kitchen begging me to buy this truffle, and here I am obliging! I am willing to take all the heat and the responsibility of this. You think old Giovanni can handle what is about to happen when the world gets wind of this white truffle?"

Giuseppina cackles. "Ha! What a hero you are…playing the role of a truffle broker yourself and taking it to an international auction. Bravo, Umberto, pawning off yet another selfish act as a benevolent cause!"

"It's what any sane human would do in this circumstance!"

"No, any human with half a heart would save his home village! Revive the place he was born, where he met his wife and had his daughter. But not you, you are a monster, Umberto—"

"Why are you calling me *Umberto*?"

"Because it is your name!"

"*Pina*, please—"

"You don't need the money! You are filthy rich!"

"That truffle is going to bring its seller a lot more than money..."

"The truffle money must go to save Lazzarini Boscarino! Every euro! You know how much they need this! This is depraved, even for you. You are about to steal from your own village!"

"Borghese is my village."

"Balls, Borghese is your village! You were born in Lazzarini Boscarino, which is also where you married a goddess named Giuseppina. Why do you have to be such a prejudiced snob about every other village?"

"Ssshhhh, Pina, keep it down, I have a *ristorante* full of patrons—"

"Shushing me? You're shushing me, Micucci? Always with your precious patrons! Always putting them before anyone else in your life! Let us see these precious patrons!"

"Pina, no!" he hisses. "We are treating the *pranzo* patrons to our culinary extravaganza dinner..."

But it is too late.

Giuseppina slaps open the kitchen doors in the ultimate movie-star entrance, sending forth a fresh wave of truffle essence. Patrons lift their eyes from perfect platings to a diva in a dark blue dress. A knife clatters onto a plate. Sharp intakes of breath. Patrons, wearing elegant attire and expressions of surprise sit up straighter. A syrup of dark perfumes, Opium and Poison, perform autoerotic asphyxiation. Slipping rich fingers of scent around every throat.

Giuseppina takes center stage, projecting loud enough to call home any literal lambs lost in the Apuan Alps. "Here it is, your fine dining *ristorante* at capacity, every patron paying what—what are you charging now, what is the going rate of a kidney? And it's not enough for Chef Umberto Micucci! Hear that, precious patrons?" Giuseppina gesticulates wildly, striding around the tables in her stilettos. "Nothing is enough for Umberto Micucci, the chef with an endless appetite. Appetite for food, appetite for sex, appetite for fame—"

"*Pina…*" Umberto attempts to clasp her elbow but is shrugged off. The patrons, in varying stages of their sexual simulation meal, are entranced by this magnetic woman. The smile of her hips, high steps in stilettos. She is a bright blue flame they cannot tear their eyes from. Almost as exciting is the sweaty master chef who appears to be afraid of her.

Attempting to avoid a car crash, Chef Umberto switches gears to speak English. "I hope everyone is enjoying their epicurean odyssey. This feast is about the senses, about passion, about lust and love!"

A woman wearing a cashmere shawl whispers to her husband in an attempt to decipher the relationship between the diva and the famous chef.

Giuseppina appeals. "Berto, listen to me. Do not take the truffle for yourself. I did not marry a monster."

"You married a man with ambition, and you couldn't handle my commitment to my art, so you gave up on me and filed for divorce," he seethes.

"Don't you dare tell me who I married! I fell in love with simple *ribollita* you, not lobster-boiled-in-LSD you, you pompous cretin!"

"Pina, this art is who I am; you know it better than anyone, and when you talk like this, what you are saying is that you don't love who I truly am!"

"This?" She spins on her stilettos, pointing at an edible abstract painting on the nearest plate. "This isn't you"—she snatches up a scorpion impaled upon a stick wearing a fedora made of Manchego cheese and black-truffle mousse—"this is an extension of your ego. This is not who you truly are."

She smirks, and it almost kills him. His heart kicks.

Giuseppina. Pina.

His Pina.

There is no one more alive. She is an astronomical force, all of life helpless to her gravitational pull. A true star. Umberto has cooked for kings and sheiks, presidents and princes, and no one has come close to fascinating him in the way Giuseppina does. She is the rarest of truffles. Changes the air around you. Umberto was doomed to be born in the same village as this treasure. Doomed from the moment he, as a little boy, laid eyes on her. Doomed when, during one of their earliest interactions, she handed him half a *bombolone* and demanded to date him for one whole hour. Doomed because Giuseppina sees right through him; she always has. She holds a mirror up to the man inside, to everything he has spent a lifetime running away from. Umberto reinvented himself by diverting from classic Italian fare, flinging foie gras in the face of his ancestors. Peppering every delicacy with his irreverent personality. Proving with every adventurous plating that he is not provincial. And he has paid the price for it. And so he disappears further and further down the rabbit hole of experimental cuisine. It's what pulled him out of the dirt. Made him money. It's how he runs from his roots. But one smirk from Giuseppina and he is that little boy holding his breath and half a *bombolone*, hopelessly and utterly in love.

The gentleman patron minus one fedora-wearing scorpion stares up at Giuseppina. She smiles down at him, used to adoring stares. But on closer inspection, Giuseppina finds that the eyes of these patrons seem glazed.

"What is wrong with them all, Berto?"

"They are not Italian?"

"Oh, *cavolo*, Umberto, you have drugged them."

"I have not," he hisses, smiling back at the patrons. "I think it's all you. And the fumes from that truffle."

A gentleman at the back of the *ristorante* sniffs the air with his eyes closed. A voice from somewhere near the champagne bar asks, "What is that heavenly scent?"

Giuseppina squints. "They seem…amorous."

"That is the idea," says Chef Umberto, blushing. "It's aphrodisiac cuisine. This is the sexual simulation course. Though I think the giant truffle might be doing the heavy lifting…"

"And what do you call this dish?" She points at a plate.

"Nothing," he says, hurling a nearby menu that clearly labels the dish "Giuseppina."

Another patron moans in delight.

Giuseppina raises her eyebrows and sniffs. "Listen to me. This truffle is a chance to change. The truffle sale money must go to Lazzarini Boscarino. Your sister-in-law is the new mayor!"

"God help her," says Umberto.

"*You* help her. Give her the connection to sell the truffle. Do it for your brother. You owe him after all that you have done."

"No; it's not how this works. I'll pay Giovanni and then it's mine."

"Do it for me." Giuseppina's patience snaps. "For God's sake, Umberto, get your head out of your ass!"

"Why are you still yelling?"

"Because my shoes are too tight!"

In one swift motion, Chef Umberto sweeps Giuseppina into his arms. She shrieks as he carries her back into the *cucina* of his *ristorante*. Several patrons gasp. It is true that the lines of their reality have been blurred due to a microdose of MDMA in the amuse-bouche. But it is the love potion of a giant truffle that is truly evoking their carnal appetites.

In the *cucina*, Umberto places Giuseppina on a cold kitchen counter and gingerly removes each stiletto to massage her feet (another health hazard—but so are all the live scorpions, if he's honest). Umberto caresses her feet, every line of them legible to him. He kisses the swollen soft part of her sole.

"I am not having sex with you over the deep fryer again. That ship has sailed."

He laughs. "Why are you wearing these terrible torture devices?"

"It is an attempt to bribe you through nostalgia. I wore these at Novelli's opening."

"Of course, I remember." He trails a finger around her beautiful ankle. An ankle he would sell his soul to see hanging over the side of their bed once more. It's the simple things you miss.

"How are you managing?" he asks, gently rubbing her toes. He doesn't have to clarify that he is asking how she is coping since their daughter Elisabetta moved. Their miracle among so many miscarriages. Their curly-haired cherub who is somehow now a grown woman with a life all her own. Elisabetta was always the nucleus around which her adoring electron parents orbited. Perhaps, he worries, it was only ever Elisabetta holding them together.

"Withering to dust," Giuseppina tells him. "Lucca was far away enough for all those years. Why did she have to move even farther away from us?"

"Milan!" they chime, wrinkling their faces in disgust.

Umberto lowers his head to Giuseppina. He takes a long inhale, breathing her in. He savors a spice of star anise running through her veins. Some solvent smoldering just beneath her skin. He imagines she smells of a wished-upon star. The heady poison of her perfume, dismantling him slowly—death by hibiscus and honey. She is bread and warm butter. A million memories swim from these scents. They mingle and taunt him, all in cahoots with a tale the truffle tells. Umberto is transfixed. He has, all these many months, been paying his high-powered road hog of a lawyer a fortune to procrastinate with the divorce proceedings. Because he is hanging on to hope. Because Marilyn is a plastic strawberry and Giuseppina is foie gras. She is the finest fiorentina steak. All that they created together— a marriage maturing, gaining complexity and richness with time and Tuscan terroir. But trouble found them. Their fights began to register on the Richter scale. He and Giuseppina are two great acts of God. Two fires that no longer had so much to hold them together, burning each other again and again until it consumed all the good between them. What do you do when you can't live with the love of your life? It is tragedy. Comedy. Shakespearean. Dickensian. Divorce, no matter how amicable, is always hard. Complicated. The splitting of atoms.

One inhale of this woman, one hit of hibiscus and honey, and Umberto feels a longing stretching his soul thin. He is as in love with her as ever. Maybe more.

Umberto smiles. "Elisabetta. My greatest creation."

"Well, it certainly isn't the hat-wearing scorpion."

He laughs. "What if we could turn back time?"

"To when?" she asks.

"To when I walked in the shoes of a younger man."

"Why were you wearing some other man's shoes?"

He laughs again. Squeezes her foot.

"You can't run from your roots, Berto. Make things right. You betrayed your brother; you owe this to him."

"Do you need money?" Umberto asks. "Because you know—"

"I don't want your money. I want you to do the right thing by your own village. I want you to do right by your brother. Lorenzo is about to lose everything."

"You chose my brother over m—"

"If you dare finish that sentence, I will fetch the sausage stuffer and you will suffer the consequences. I sided with Lorenzo because of your insufferable greed. What you did was wrong. He needed help with Bar Celebrità. You ruined him.

You left me with no other option. I will always side with the angels. That's something all my psychics have said about me."

Here she notices that he is paying less attention to her words than to the curve of her thigh.

Giuseppina slaps his side. "Stop picturing me naked."

It is at this highly inopportune moment that the front of house sticks her head into the kitchen and is hit with the warm front of a one-of-a-kind truffle. For Marilyn, the truffle does not elicit some of the deeper emotional responses it has for some souls. To young Marilyn, it smells as if a rugby team from her homeland had spent lockdown in their locker room, kneading aged Roquefort with their feet and then straining it through soiled jockstraps. Gagging, Marilyn manages, "Oh my god! Who farted?"

It is a second later that Marilyn sees Giuseppina, instantly recognizing her from the nude oil painting hanging in a hall-way of Umberto's villa. Marilyn lowers her eyes. She slinks away like a country fox caught in a flashlight.

Giuseppina raises her eyebrows at Umberto. "Nooo..."

Umberto massages his temples. "Pina, please don't..."

"That's her? This is who you are sleeping with? Did you steal her from the prenatal ward?"

"Don't—"

She laughs, a braying that would do odd-toed ungulate and mayoral-candidate Maurizio proud. "How is *la bambina* enjoy-ing your sleep apnea? Or is it that pained groan you make every time you stand up that she finds irresistible? You have become a cliché, a dirty old man, Berto!"

"Pina, don't be cruel..."

"Perhaps it is the allure of your ancient house slippers that gets her going..."

"Pina, it's not serious, I don't want you to think—"

"Or your illegible text messaging—"

"I text fine—"

"Does she even speak Italian?"

He is too embarrassed to answer.

And this is what causes Giuseppina's kettle to boil over. Not that her estranged husband was staring at her thighs as he listened to almost nothing of her pleas, not that the girl sleeping with her estranged husband is barely out of a stroller, but that, sacrilege of all sacrileges, that young vixen has not bothered to learn *la bella lingua*. Stilettoless now, Giuseppina bursts through the doors of the *cucina* and back into the *ristorante*. Marilyn has had the good sense to become invisible. The patrons cheer in delight. Chef Umberto stammers in after the sparkling blonde like a lost Apuan lamb.

"*Porca pupazza!* No, Umberto, it must be your intermittent hemorrhoids that first attracted the young lady. Because everyone is attracted to the delightful bullheadedness of a cantankerous old man! She will soon learn that with the Lamborghini comes middle-of-the-night trombone farts! That poor child!"

"Pina, if you are done making a scene in my *ristorante*, we need to tend to the . . . *situation in the cucina*. Every second counts here, you know this. I need to sell it. You know better than most how this works. It's just business. And this is the Holy Grail."

Giuseppina is as loud as a *carabinieri* siren now. "Every second does count, Umberto. Every second is an opportunity to change your selfish ways and do the right thing by your village. By your brother. *Per favore!*"

The patrons volley their focus between these two. At an undeniable chemistry.

"Do it for me," Giuseppina says.

Umberto stares longingly at his Giuseppina. He remembers the Australian breakfast he fried up for Marilyn and suddenly understands exactly how she must feel living in a foreign land. Umberto feels adrift without Giuseppina. He is homesick for this woman. He marvels at the bullish goodness in her, the spectacular scene she is creating in his *ristorante*. How he loves that she is as bold as a good Brunello. Quick to cry, quicker to laugh. She is the first to dance and the last to leave. He can live neither with her nor without her. These paradoxes twist him into knots. She unravels him.

The Novelli patrons watching are overwhelmed by emotion. By truffled nostalgia wafting in from the *cucina*. The two humans in front of them are a volatile substance. Warring splendidly. They are a chemical reaction, this man and this woman, like the flame of a candle. The patrons don't need to understand one word of Italian to know that they are witnessing a spectacle of the heart. Almost everyone in the room can relate, riding down memory lane on the powerful pheromones of a truffle. Many are quite overcome, tears streaming down upon their scorpions-on-sticks.

Umberto looks at his shoes briefly. He is exhausted. And he knows now that he only wants one thing.

"If I do this..." he says, "will you talk to me again?"

"What are you, five? *Che bambino!*" She laughs. Then she realizes he is serious. She waits for his next words.

These past eight months have tortured Umberto Micucci. And even if he cannot turn back time or get his marriage back, he just wants to see this beautiful face now and then. Be near the spice and drama of a burning star. She is, after all, his muse.

"Alright. I will introduce Delizia to my connections and the truffle will be sold by the village of Lazzarini Boscarino. Where it was born. For you, Pina. For you."

"Brava!" Giuseppina screams and throws her arms around him.

The *ristorante* bursts into applause. Patrons rocket up into a standing ovation. In part because of puckish truffle pheromones and in part because they have confused Giuseppina's magnetic presence as part of a dinner theater performance in their epicurean drama. Giuseppina improvises and takes a bow.

"*Merci, merci*," she says, generously. "*Danke! Arigato!*" She kisses Umberto on the cheek and the patrons roar with delight. The clapping is deafening. Not until after her last curtsy does she say, "My work here is done. I am going to the *osteria* to tell the village, and then I'm going to get Delizia here. It is time for this truffle to take the world stage."

"Can I come and see you?" Umberto asks, worry in every word.

"Fine. I will lift your banishment at Bar Celebrità. You can come, but not too often."

Umberto folds his arms. Throws back his head. Relief.

As she sashays away, all eyes still upon her, Giuseppina turns one last time. "Oh, and let me know when you're coming. I'll set out a high chair for your girlfriend."

She slays him with another smirk. Umberto turns toward the kitchen, his heart radiating. A smile too big to hide with his hand. He tunes out the rabid applause of his patrons. He has made Giuseppina happy.

It is the most sated he has felt in a very long time.

His fingers find his cell phone. Scroll down his VIP contacts. A single press.

And he begins a call that will spread spores of madness across the world.

Chapter 7

Face pinched in frustration, Mayor Delizia glares at the brass lion knockers of an ancient door. Old walnut wood hums under the golden aura of a lantern dangling from a rusted wrought iron chain. Delizia tugs at the hem of her woolen coat and the inappropriate attire underneath. She turns sideways, angling her shoulder at the door. The new mayor squints her eyes. Exhales.

She barrels toward it.

Her shoulder slams the rustic door that has just eaten its own key. She shrieks as the door clatters open to the sound of splintering wood. The impact rips the door from rusty hinges. Delizia bursts across the threshold of the town hall, trips on a broken tile, and splats onto the floor.

For a moment, she lies in the dark cradling her computer. She feels exhaustion burning in her bones and something else. A squishiness through her coat back, as though she is lying on a bed of tiny Taggiasca olives. Alas, they are not olives. They are generous confetti of *Glis glis* pellets. She plucks the thin strand of a silver lining—at least she hasn't landed on her laptop. She reminds herself she is no stranger to animal waste—she was, after all, a veterinarian in a seemingly less stressful life.

Old bones of the building let out an eerie groan. Delizia startles, struggles to her feet. Fishing the flashlight from her coat pocket, she casts a circular beam across the spacious town hall. The rotted door, prone on the floor. A scorpion skittering from her light. Locked shutters. Peeling murals so sun beaten they depict melting ghosts and ghastly deformed figures. In the center of the hall, an enormous medieval table and fourteen chairs, each resembling a throne. Someone has left empty Peroni cans, a knight's helmet, and a longsword on the table. A few Gothic candelabras. In a corner of the hall is an oversize wardrobe that holds costumes and props for a medieval festival that used to take place in this village when there were enough bodies to wear and wield them. Delizia swings the flashlight to illuminate the imposing fireplace.

The beam sends something inside it scrambling.

An icy draft adders across the new mayor's exposed calves.

She sweeps the circle of light along the flayed plaster of the walls and framed pictures, illuminating a yellowed map of the village. Amateur art by homegrown artists in lazily hung paintings. Oil painting of a horse ridden by a baby with the face of an old man and a look of constipation. A Renaissance woman defensively cradling a weasel. A red-nosed clergyman with minuscule hands and one oddly enlarged eyeball. And a woman who appears to be a replica of the *Mona Lisa*, but who greatly resembles a veiled turnip.

She sighs. It is not the Uffizi.

The beam stills on a set of light switches. Delizia treads toward them to the tinkling of broken tiles. With a small prayer, she flicks the switches. The town hall blinks into brightness.

The rickety lights illuminate more town hall horrors. A terrifying papier-mâché of the pope. A decapitated ventriloquist's dummy and a badly taxidermized boar's head protruding from the wall.

"What?" she asks the cross-eyed boar. "It was not my idea to host it here."

Porco mondo, she had urged Umberto to host this critical event in Nonna's *ristorante,* Il Nido, instead, describing the town hall's state of disrepair to him.

"No, Delizia," she mimics Chef Umberto and the brass band inside his voice as she positions her laptop on the long table. "Tradition is tradition; it *has* to be in the town hall. What will the *Americans* think if we deliver the most important culinary news of the century in a smelly old *ristorante?* That your village is provincial? Poor? How do you expect to be taken seriously as mayor?"

Delizia rolls her eyes.

Something is still scrabbling around in the fireplace.

A glance at her wristwatch. 7:52 p.m.

Eight minutes left. She stares at the unhinged door, waiting for movement.

She grimaces at the abominable artwork. If the village had the money, they could restore this space to its former glory. Host destination weddings, worldly brides trailing satin across terra-cotta, savoring rustic romance that stops short of European edible dormouse poo. If only they had the money.

She gasps.

The truffle. She left it outside. Left it in the passenger seat of her Land Rover. Seat-belted and sitting in an airline-compliant carrier for a medium-size dog. In her haste, she had parked at an odd angle outside the steep stairs leading up to the town hall.

A bulb of panic bursts inside her chest. Did she lock the doors?

Delizia rockets to her feet. She runs across the town hall. Back down the stone steps.

She could have been followed. Anyone would question why a mud-colored Land Rover is parked at an odd angle to the stone steps of the old hall at 8:00 p.m. on a Tuesday. She is struck by a quick haunting. Giovanni's voice slips into her ears. Worried whispers, sea fog–gray eyes, the crescents of his soil-darkened nails clawing a glass of red wine at Bar Celebrità. As he leans in, his earthen smell rises, punctuated by wafts of wet dog. With every fretful word, Giovanni unveils the lengths the Borghese truffle hunters will go to. Stories of break-ins and car bombs. How he has been followed and harassed. The fear of what might happen to his darling dogs. Delizia's pupils swell, the scent memory of disinfectant knifing up her nostrils. She has treated truffle dogs in several clinics for ingesting strychnine, antifreeze, rat poison. Stomach pumping. Glassy eyes and lolling tongues. She hears her own voice, frantic and strained as she begs the owners of truffle dogs to keep their dogs indoors with them at night. She ordered muzzles for them, can feel her fingers on the rough leather of two types. One that blocks the dog's mouth from eating food powdered with poison. And the other—a newer model, a Hannibal Lecter–like mask that doesn't allow even a tongue to protrude. This version had to be designed after the truffle-hunting poisoners wised up and started to drop their lethal strychnine directly into forest puddles.

She pictures her Land Rover. The glittering glass of a smashed window. Muddy footprints streaking from the scene. The last notes of truffle breath vanishing into the dark night.

A truffle taken.

Sprinting, her eyes register the Land Rover bouncing closer and closer.

As the passenger door creaks open, she is slapped with a tsunami of scent.

Pinching the skin between her eyes, she groans in relief.

The truffle is still here.

Gingerly unbuckling the seat belt and slipping the carrier from the Land Rover, she staggers back up stone steps to the broken door of the town hall. Halfway up, the toe of her shoe hits a stone step and she stumbles. Delizia drops to one knee, a dull clunk of bone hitting stone. Almost dropping the carrier, she catches herself. She grimaces, fireworks of pain streaking up her kneecap.

A gulping of air is evidence she forgot to breathe.

Six pounds the beast weighs. Six pounds, fourteen ounces, and the backbreaking weight of responsibility.

"Whoever is listening, please let me get the truffle into the town hall without incident, and I shall cut back on cake," comes her breathy prayer.

The sky responds with a belch of thunder.

"Oh, no, no, no, no..."

Clouds open up like a cracked egg. Rain pummels Delizia. She hunches to protect the pungent treasure, hobbling up the last of the stone steps and back into the town hall.

Spluttering rainwater, she places the carrier on the great table as though it were a newborn. Staring at the black mesh and zipper of the carrier, she addresses the subterranean find hidden inside. "You manipulative devil. We are all fawning over your ugly humps. Just as you wish. Everyone that gets a whiff is an utter fool for you."

She peels off her sopping coat. Opens her laptop. Her heart clutches at a totem pole of empty bars.

There is no Wi-Fi in the town hall.

Her watch warns her it is 7:59 p.m. Delizia spits out sentences of stress. Fingers trembling, she connects her laptop to her cell phone.

Eureka. She has internet.

It is 7:59 p.m. *Santo dio*. Chef Umberto Micucci is still not here. Giovanni, who promised to be here as the hunter of this great white whale, is also notably absent.

It is just Mayor Delizia. The world's largest truffle. And a link to a meeting with the American VIPs that starts in twenty seconds.

A burst of black stars detonates across the dilapidated town hall. Delizia blinks. The anticipation is making her faint—she has to move, or she will most certainly pass out.

She leaps up from her chair and crouches next to the laptop, trying to envision what the VIPs will see of the hellish town hall from glamorous New York. What a far cry from the Big Apple, she thinks, as a bulbous-eyed, micro-handed clergyman goggles her from the wall. She flew to New York once for a conference on animal hematology. Fell in love with the fizzing spectacle of it all. Trumpeting traffic, peppy flashes of neon, buildings glittering like tall gods. A million colorful coats striding across streets smoking from their manholes. The bright, living smell of the city—sizzling sausages, sautéed garbage, every perfume prickling the nose. Hope and hot coffee. Urine slicing through it all, screaming "This is mine, this is mine, this is mine." She recalls savoring creamy spoons of cheesecake melting in her mouth, her heart chasing the irrepressible pulse of a city pirouetting around her. What she would have given to have left with the confidence New Yorkers seem to wear so stylishly.

Delizia swivels the laptop to the opposite side of the table. This is to avoid featuring a vandal's enterprising artwork of a graffiti penis wearing a fedora. Spying a broom propped against the wardrobe, she sweeps feverishly at the floor, fashioning hideous little hillocks of *Glis glis* pellets just out of laptop sight.

Delizia smooths her hands over her hair. Her eyes settle on the black carrier that once transported a beagle with a hiatal hernia. She can picture contours of the gargantuan truffle hiding in plain sight as she clicks on the link to the meeting.

"I can do this," she lies to herself.

She is the first to arrive in the virtual room. She stares back at herself from a window on the screen. Eye bags. Wet hair plastered to her head, she is reminded of a guinea pig she once resuscitated after his brief career as an open water swimmer. Sopping summer dress, covered in a vast plumage of thin pink feathers. Highly unsuitable attire for an October night in a dilapidated town hall, but it is all her veterinarian-chic wardrobe had. She wore the dress at her stepmother's sixty-fifth birthday, when Ludovica had eyed her and asked whether she planned to migrate south for the winter.

8:01 p.m. Delizia sits up straighter.

"Hello, hello," she tests, dusting off her English. Clears her throat.

8.02 p.m. Delizia checks her cell phone. A message. It is from a free stress-management app she downloaded. It reads: I am respected and loved by every person in my life.

Her phone clatters to the tabletop. She pinches the skin between her eyes.

Where is Umberto? What happened to Giovanni?

8:03 p.m.

Delizia eyeballs the rain lancing down in silver streaks through the doorless doorway. She shivers.

She texts Umberto. Where are you?????????????????????

Firing off another to Giovanni is an act of frivolity. He only uses his phone as a flashlight while hunting in the forest. Oh, what the hell...

Giovanni Scarpazza, you promised to be here at the meeting to talk about how you found the truffle! YOU ARE THE HUNTER. PLEASE get here.

In her haste, she accidentally ends it with an emoji of an eggplant.

Delizia inhales a brew of mildew, dust, and rodent. And the huffs of truffle squatting in a dog carrier.

A flash of lightning electrifies the hall. Rain is now falling in full sentences.

Something in the ceiling snaps. A torrent of water is unleashed onto the table. Delizia screams. She torpedoes herself across the table's surface, sliding under the freezing waterfall. A passionate shove sends the carrier sliding across the slick table.

"No, no, no—" she yells as the carrier glides to the very edge of the table. Delizia rolls off the table and scrambles to the chair the truffle dangles above. Gingerly, she lifts the carrier and nestles it at the covered end of the medieval table.

She peers into the carrier. The truffle is dry. Hair glued icily to her neck, Delizia blinks away rainwater. She cannot tell whether it is the cold or the adrenaline rattling her teeth.

Failure, that familiar tide, rises sure and fast. It starts to swallow her whole.

Delizia drops down in front of the laptop. Buries her head in her hands. Just as she is expelling a long, primal moan, the screen of her laptop blinks. Muscular voices startle her. Three men in sheeny silk-thread suits loom large on her laptop. Each fills a velvet chair parked around a white Carrara table, marbled like a good mortadella. They grip matching coffee mugs as a roller coaster of rounded vowels soar and dip between them. Delizia is being broadcast from an enormous flat screen in a conference room with a hedge growing from one wall.

Water cascades elegantly down the back wall. Blown-glass pendant lights dangle like octopuses that are either performing aerial art or have hanged themselves. Near the table stands an enormous abstract sculpture that Delizia finds to resemble the lower intestine of a cow.

She can smell the money in that room all the way from Italy.

Her stomach sinks. She can't handle this all alone. These men are here for world-renowned Chef Umberto Micucci. Glamour and iconic orange glasses. The weight of this truffle should not be on her head. She is bitten by doubts. Each is a staple in her skin.

But what can she do? She is the only one here in the town hall, advocating for the whole village. She swallows.

She has to sell the truffle. She has to save Lazzarini Boscarino.

"Good evening, gentlemen. My name is Delizia, and I am the mayor of Lazzarini Boscarino."

The man on the left smiles. His fair skin has the flush of a red mullet fillet. Dirty blond hair so slicked as to appear ceramic. Head hosting ears like large woodland mushrooms.

"Good afternoon. My name is David, I am a private sales specialist here at Sotheby's New York headquarters, and these are my colleagues. Steven, senior director of consignment management. Jeffrey here is our fine wine sales associate and our fine food specialist."

Steven has a pleasing beak of a nose and chestnut hair in a severe side part. He nods, bringing to mind a lackey from a Scorsese movie. Jeffrey, by far the youngest, flicks a hand absently, smiles without involving the eyes fused to his cell phone. His vertical crop of brown hair reminds Delizia of cat grass. She recognizes Jeffrey's steely affect, a silent confidence diffusing from him like the gas given off by expensive cheese. He hasn't even looked at her.

Delizia's ears are set on fire. She swallows down the memory

142142 Kira Jane Buxton

of a million meetings like this, of men flaunting their power at her. Dangling it like a blown-glass octopus.

But this time, instead of her own interests at the cliff edge, it is all the innocent people of the village she ran away from. The village folk who helped raise her. Who love her despite her failures. Acid rises up her esophagus.

She squints at the Carrara table, spots matching car keys. Mercedes? Rolls-Royce? One of her hands flattens the other to squash raucous tremors. She cannot stop inane thoughts like, *I wonder if these men live in those big American mansions with bearskin rugs by the fireplace?*

"Where is Chef Micucci?" asks David. His hair gel winks at her.

The mayor's eyes flick to the hole where there should be a door. "He should be here any second, gentlemen."

"Where are you right now?" Steven asks, squinting as he gargles his *r*s.

"We are in the beautiful village of Lazzarini Boscarino. A village where—"

"No, where are you streaming from? Some kind of haunted house?"

"Oh"—her eyes meet those of the decapitated ventriloquist's dummy head; she feels kinship—"this is our town hall. It has seen better days."

The men in New York share a microsecond look.

A glance at her phone. No message from Umberto.

She has no choice but to start. She prays for a keyhole of confidence to make it through this.

"Okay, gentlemen—"

"You can just call us David, Steven, and Jeffrey," says David.

"Of course. Gentle—uh—David, this is a very exciting time. A truffle hunter from our village, along with his beloved dog, have found what I believe is the world's largest white truffle."

"Your accent is really wonderful, Delilah," David interjects.

"It's Delizia, and thank you. I like your accent too."

"I don't have an accent. Listen, we were happy to hear from Chef Micucci and to schedule a meeting with him, but we only have fifteen minutes here."

Delizia's phone chimes. Her heart kicks. Her eyes lower to a message—

I shine like a diamond.

Delizia clears her throat. Of course, these men only have fifteen minutes. They have Cy Twomblys and Matisses and cases of Château Lafite Rothschild to auction. Millionaires dripping in Gucci and Givenchy to charm. Lives sparkling with champagne and seasoned with caviar.

Fifteen minutes. She fingers her neck. Nods. Glances at her phone.

She has fourteen minutes and forty-five seconds to save her village.

"Umberto and I would like you to hold an auction to sell the truffle."

"Where's the truffle?"

"It is sitting in here."

"Is that a dog carrier?"

"I have one like that for my cockapoo," Steven says wistfully.

Cockapoo. Delizia wonders if he walks it himself. She blushes, ashamed of the thought. Bitterness does not become her. Every drop of it brings her closer to becoming the bottle of grappa that is her stepmother. She pictures her stepmother sitting on a bar top with a cork in her face.

"What is so funny?" asks Steven.

Delizia rubs her eyes. "Nothing, nothing is funny at all, gentle—Steven."

Delizia stands. Her legs are quaking. The thought of lifting the truffle brings on swift terror. That moist, spongy skin. Like

picking up an organ. Handling a human brain. She peers into
the carrier that is entirely filled with the obscene muscles of the
truffle, figuring out how to slip her fingers inside and not accidentally nick off several hundred euros...

A chiming sound. Heels striking tile. Delizia deflates in
relief.

Finally. Umberto.

The Sotheby's men lean in toward the screen, faces brightening at the arrival of the famous chef.

Delizia smiles at David, Steven, and Jeffrey. Footfalls echo.
The expressions of the three men change. Delizia smiles as she
sees their eyes widen. World-renowned Chef Umberto Micucci
often receives a reaction like this. Delizia turns away from the
screen to give the tardy Umberto a furtive look of fury and is
met with an unexpected sight.

Standing in front of the fireplace of the town hall with a skit-
tish stance and an utterly bewildered expression, in full view of
Sotheby's New York headquarters, is a goat. The gate-crashing
goat lets out a small bleat of self-announcement. Each of its
vacant orange eyes face a different direction, like two flung
marbles. He nods his brown-and-white head questioningly, a
dull bell around his neck clanging.

Delizia looks back at the screen with a face like crushed
paper. She looks back at the goat. Then at the truffle. The goat.
The truffle. She must act quickly.

"Get out of here! Go!"

The goat cocks its head, ears jangling like wet socks on a line.

"I'm in a *meeting*," she insists, as though to convince the
ungulate, surely one of farmer Leon's.

"Is that a...goat?" David finally asks, astutely.

"He found his way here by the trail of the truffle..."
Delizia tries to sound mayoral as she shoots up from her chair

and starts waving her arms as though she were guiding an airplane to the gate.

David and Steven are pitched toward the screen, both leaning like the tower of Pisa. Jeffrey finally peels himself from his cellular affairs to squint his eyes, register the wall-eyed goat, then lower them back to his personal screen.

The goat lifts his anvil of a head to sniff at the intoxicating scent that summoned him here. He weighs the risk of nearing a human sitting at the table against the tantalizing contrail of that truffle. A prey animal, he prides himself on his abilities when it comes to risk assessment. He stares at two arms flapping amok in the air. A plumage of pink feathers. This human looks wet and fairly weak to him.

The truffle it is.

Two ungulate eyes swivel. And, with a panoramic sweep across the town hall, they locate it. The goat has followed a funk and found the truffle. It is sitting on a table. It is hidden in that bag. Smelling like it's begging to be eaten.

The goat starts a jaunty march toward his treasure.

"No!" Delizia yells at the goat. But the goat has already decided that the truffle is his—he has leapt over a fence, narrowly missed a speeding Vespa, and trekked across several fields in a storm to be here, after all. It is his to eat.

"No, goat! Back! Get back!" Delizia can hear the panic rising in her voice. Her neck flushes red. She should have cut the video on her stream.

But the goat is undeterred by her admonitions. He strides toward Delizia and the truffle.

Delizia grabs the closest thing on the table, which so happens to be a medieval longsword. She lifts it into the air. The goat halts. He is taken aback. The feathered human is not as wet nor as weak as he'd originally suspected. This looks a lot like the stick his farmer wields, though this one is shinier, unfamiliar, and therefore quite terrifying.

The Sotheby's men stare, faces warped as though by a fish-eye lens as they lean toward their large flat screen.

Delizia shoos the goat with the sword as the ungulate starts a hasty retreat, releasing neither of its eyes from on the truffle. Once he has been exiled from the town hall, the mayor returns. She lowers her sword, sits back down in front of the screen, and rubs her hands together.

The goat releases a questioning "Maa?"

"No!" Delizia yells, before addressing the Sotheby's men. "I apologize; the truffle is attracting all sorts."

The men share a look. Delizia wants to know what, but the screen glitches. David takes a deep breath. He opens his mouth. And is silent. Mouth ajar, he says nothing for several uncomfortable seconds.

Delizia looks at the screen and realizes that she is frozen and pulling a face not unlike the glazed stare of the goat.

"Oh, no, no, no ... Come on, come on, come on ..."

She checks the bar icon—she is still connected. She minimizes the screen. Maximizes it. Still frozen. Still pulling a goat face.

"No, no, come on, they haven't even seen the truffle!"

She hits refresh. She rejoins the meeting, thank god, with full function of her face.

"Oh, there you are, you froze," Steven yells thick and slow, as though Delizia might have forgotten how to speak after virtually freezing.

"Gentlemen, I know time is of the essence. So here." She just does it, just slips her fingers into the carrier, feeling its snakeskin surface, the slight squishiness from the moisture it holds, evaporating by the second. It feels forbidden. A treasure map starting a slow rot right in her hands. She places it on the table.

Its scent billows up from the carrier and hits her hard. For a split second, she pictures her father holding his freshly bottled olive oil. Then—*oh god*—she is flung further back in time; her father is holding her tiny hand at the beach, a waltz of waves against the rocks. A tender moment long lost in her memory. Tears spring to her eyes. The wind is knocked from her.

She sniffs and swallows hard to hold back an ambush of emotion. "Here is the truffle. It is an Alba white truffle—*Tuber magnatum* Pico. It was not found in Alba, but here in our village, and I believe—*we believe*, Chef Micucci, hunter Giovanni, and I—that it is the largest truffle in the world."

There is muttering between the men. Jeffrey looks up from his phone. For the first time, Delizia sees the intimidating voltage crackling from his dark eyes. As he scrutinizes the truffle, they harden into cold shards of coal. The left side of his upper lip curls. Jeffrey lowers his landscaped eyebrows back to his phone.

David assumes his role as spokesman. "Delina, we appreciate you showing us, but your internet connection is pretty weak, and at this resolution, none of us can verify that that truffle is real."

"What do you mean, David? It's right here."

"It might be, but we can't ascertain that given everything... we've seen, and without Chef Micucci here to accredit it."

"I am here to accredit it—"

"Of course, and please understand we don't mean any disrespect at all. We just don't have enough verification. We really thank you for your time today. It's been a treat."

"Please—"

"We here at Sotheby's New York all wish you the best of luck. *Grazie mille.*"

Delizia is dizzy. She feels the color drain from her face. Her throat closes in on itself. She is too tired to hold back her emotion and feels it spooling out from her like dropped yarn. She is about to cry.

The Sotheby's men are standing, stuffing luxury car keys into pockets. Velvet chairs screeching back under a table that is probably worth more than Delizia's house.

Delizia gapes at the truffle. Bulging muscles of a bull. Smell stronger than varnish. It is, at this moment, worth nothing. Its potential is a dandelion wish. The truffle taunts her. False hope shrouded in the scent of heaven. A check that cannot be cashed.

Delizia has, once again, failed.

Shame weighs down her shoes.

And then the clopping is back. Ears pricking at more staccato footfalls. In the screen, a Sotheby's secretary hovers over the End Call button. Delizia turns a beet-red face toward the persistent ungulate.

"Get out, you stubborn goat!"

Chef Umberto Micucci's leather oxfords are like tiny timpani as he marches into the town hall. Through signature orange frames, he appears marginally puzzled to meet the door on the floor.

Here is not the stubborn goat Delizia was expecting.

Out of breath from climbing the stone steps, he shakes his umbrella and sets down a large bag.

"There is a goat waiting outside; I hope that's who you were addressing?"

"You are late!" Delizia hisses at her brother-in-law. Anger arrows through her. This pompous man has crushed her husband's heart, clambered to success on his shoulders, and has possibly just sealed the coffin of his village with it.

"What are you wearing?" Her attire seems to surprise him more than the goat. "You are soaked!" He takes off his coat and drapes it over her trembling shoulders.

Delizia tries to answer but is too angry and will not let him see her cry.

"This place is in shambles," he chides. "Why wouldn't we have hosted the meeting at Nonna Amara's *ristorante*?"

Delizia shoots a bamboozled look to the oil painting of the man-faced baby absconding on a horse.

"*Santo dio*, Delizia—the truffle just sitting on the table like this?" he asks in a searing tone.

"It was in the carrier—"

"It's not a poodle, for the love of the pope!" He pulls an enormous cake stand with a dome from his large bag and settles the truffle inside.

"Chef Umberto!" sing the Sotheby's men in the screen.

Delizia's anger turns to three men in New York. She feeds terse Italian through gritted teeth. "They don't believe it is a truffle."

The chef turns on his world-famous charm, arms outstretched. "David! Steven, Jeffrey. You look well, my friends. You look…rich!"

They all laugh. Blue-white teeth. A shared braying.

Flushed-faced David rubs his hands together. "The internet connection in that hall is lousy, Umberto."

"Ah, the charm of rustic life! This is a village, but it isn't Greenwich Village, my friends." He winks.

They all laugh again. Delizia wants to throw her laptop at the wall.

"So, my friends, you have met The Truffle. And my sister-in-law."

David laughs. "As well as a goat and her swordsmanship! Umberto, listen, we really can't see the thing. And as much as we respect you, it's not the first time we've seen counterfeit truffles. Our legal department works with Interpol and Europol. We've seen every type of food fraud you can imagine—counterfeit champagne, faux caviar, imitation *mozzarella di bufala*. Fake chocolate, tomato sauce, prosciutto di Parma, everything. Where people will pay a premium, there is an underground of crooks and criminals waiting in the wings."

Umberto's words wrap in a wintry frost. "You think we are deceiving you?"

"No, Umberto, we are friends. Never, not at all. I'm just saying the counterfeits are getting clever…it can be very difficult to tell the real thing, even when it is right under your nose."

"Ah. Then you are going to have to put your faith in me, or at least in my brand-new phone." Chef Umberto whips out a sleek cell phone, takes several photos of the truffle and a selfie for good measure. Delizia silently questions her sanity.

"My friends, I am sending you the photos now."

The men check their phones, confer, and for the first time, Delizia sees something move behind their eyes. Pupils pin like night predators. Their posture changes, as though each were a puppet pulled tight by a wire.

"How much does it weigh?" asks Steven. He shifts in his seat. Presses the bridge of his glasses.

"Six pounds, fourteen ounces," chime Delizia and Umberto.

David and Steven turn to face Jeffrey. His pale fingers pinch his phone screen. He is zooming in to the photos Umberto just took. Studying the obscene body of the beast in the town hall.

"Are there blemishes? Worm holes?" he asks.

Chef Umberto shakes his head very slowly.

"It's been cleaned already?"

A smug smile spreads across Umberto's face.

"What does it *smell* like?" Jeffrey asks. Delizia notices a high-pitched hope in his voice. Almost childlike.

Chef Umberto closes his eyes. He removes the infamous orange glasses. It is very dramatic. He lifts the dome of the cake stand, chest rising as he inhales the breaths of the truffle.

Plucking his thoughts from a rain-misted air, he opens his mouth.

"Unforgettable. The spell of first love. Forbidden sex. The winds of good fortune." He takes another rapturous inhale. The men are wide-eyed as they wait. "Like Aphrodite's fig."

David frowns in confusion. Delizia claps her face into her hands.

"Aphrodite's vagina," Umberto says to clarify.

"Wow," utters Steven.

Umberto takes a last hit. "Like the breath of God himself."

David is on his feet. Steven is grinning involuntarily in that wildly creepy way people sometimes do at funerals. Jeffrey drops his cell phone with an unmistakable *dap-clack*.

Jeffrey stares into the screen. He unsuccessfully tries to stifle a smile. "Congratulations, Chef Umberto. You found the world's largest truffle."

The New York businessmen are under a spell that snatches at the bullring of the nose and doesn't let go. A scent that stains the tongue.

The smell of latent success.

Jeffrey is on his feet, gesticulating wildly. "We're going to have to move quickly. We could show it at the Alba White Truffle Fair—they're already midway through it, but the big truffle companies—Sabatino, Urbani Truffles—they are going to want to be involved with its auction." Jeffrey is back on his phone, fingers flying across the screen. "I'm suggesting that instead of the Alba fair, we host a virtual auction. We can get things moving immediately—"

"Of course, I love it," Umberto bellows. "We can hold the auction live from Novelli. I will have my chefs work round the clock to create a truffle-forward menu for the media in attendance. And of course, we would be delighted to host you, my friends."

Steven nods. "I've been meaning to fly out for a meal—"

"Then you must. I'm doing a tasting menu that will blow off your pants!"

"Do you mean our socks?" David laughs.

"Might be both!" Umberto roars.

Delizia feels a heat rising from the top of her head.

"You are a genius, Umberto, there is just no one out there with your commitment—"

With the grating screech of a chair, Delizia is on her feet.

"*Basta!*" she yells. "No!"

Outside the town hall, the exiled goat responds with an emphatic and vibrato "Nooooo."

"No?" asks Jeffrey with a private-boarding-school sneer.

"No." She fires a death glare at Umberto. "The auction will not take place in Novelli or anywhere in Borghese. This truffle is going to be sold where it was born, here in our"—she glances at the slumped papier-mâché of Pope Francis, whose *zucchetto* liturgical hat is actually a glued-on cereal bowl—"our charming artistic and historic village of Lazzarini Boscarino."

"In your haunted town hall? Under siege by rogue goats?" Jeffrey snorts, then holds up his hands to imply he didn't mean any offense. "Your internet isn't reliable enough. I'm afraid that's not going to happen."

Delizia has to think fast. "We will be holding this auction at the castle on the hill."

"A castle?" asks Steven.

"Our castle in our village. If that doesn't suit, there are other auction houses who will certainly be interested in the most magnificent truffle ever unearthed." Delizia feigns gathering her things to leave, reaching for the nearest item— unfortunately, the longsword—as if to take it home.

Umberto squints through orange portals. He is thinking of the castle. "It is a grand place. Magnificent and historic. It has been standing since the eleventh century. Withstood multiple siege efforts and World War II raids. It has a darker history too—it held prisoners for a time and still has instruments of torture—ow!"

He composes himself, rubbing the tender part of his arm that was swatted by Delizia. "I think it would be very captivating to prospective buyers."

"Alright," says Jeffrey. "We have no time to lose then. On our end—"

His words are cut off by an almighty crack of thunder that rattles the town hall. Lightning splits apart the night sky. The boar clatters to the ground, severing a tusk. A gaggle of *Glis glis* burst from the fireplace, escaping through the empty door.

The room falls into darkness.

When Delizia and Umberto find the flashlights of their phones, they discover there has been a murder.

The internet is dead.

"Oh no, Umberto..." Delizia says, fumbling with her phone.

"It's okay, it's okay, I'll finalize the details with them...I'm calling them back on my cell now." He is standing to move, thick fingers stabbing at his cell phone, pressing it to his ear. "Delizia—"

He pauses. Phone flattening his ear. His voice takes on a gravitas Delizia has never heard.

"Find somewhere safe to hide that truffle, start preparing for the auction—it might even happen tomorrow. Make a festival of it, show off the merits of the village. We got Sotheby's excited, which means the entire world—every media outlet on earth—is going to have its eyes on you as the ambassador of Lazzarini Boscarino..."

He strides across the hall. Disappears through the doorless doorway.

Delizia sits in the dark. Stunned.

The goat peers its head into the hall. Bleats pleadingly.

Three sets of eyes stare at her from the fireplace.

She lifts the longsword. The goat ducks out of sight.

The truffle sits in the cake stand. A genie she has wished upon.

Delizia's eyes bore into the dirty crown jewel of reek and imminent rot.

If she can keep it safe until the auction in the castle, this hideous jewel of nature might save her village. As if from some surreal folktale. It is on her head to, in no time at all, put on a festival to show the merits of a place she feels doesn't have any. She must host the entire world at the village she's spent her life running from.

She thinks about where she will hide the monster that might save them all.

The last thing she hears before Umberto vanishes into the night, rising above the wails of a disgruntled goat, is an accent. It is gushing from Umberto's speakerphone as he starts down the stone steps. It's David's voice. Bold apple-pie vowels muscle their way across the town hall.

"No need to apologize, Umberto. Truffles make everyone go a little hysterical."

Chapter 8

The *cucina* of the old house is small and dark. Trinkets of Stefano's past squatting on rickety cabinets. Dusty relics. Cobwebs straddling corners. Candle wax dribbling from wine bottles. And quite hidden, a little being who escapes most eyes. Under the lip of an antique jug, a tiny jumping spider is using her sense of smell to hunt. The little spider picks up contrails of a whining mosquito, plump with the salty-sweet blood of a human animal. Eight glistening eyes inspect their surroundings. Intoxicated by rusted-iron streams of scent, the spider lowers a glassy silken line and spindles hungrily after the mosquito.

The spider huntress is not alone in the cramped *cucina*. Nonna Amara is molding a volcano out of flour, breaking eggs into its crater. Her cooking is a form of worship. Praise folded into an eggy pappardelle. A sermon in every sprinkling of chestnut flour. Time evaporates as she melds Tuscan tradition with the ingredients gifted to her by a garden.

She comes from a long legacy of pastry pinchers, seasoners, and simmerers. Souls who listen to the language of garden growth. Her own Babbo was the proud village baker for all his life. In the *cucina*, Nonna honors her alchemist ancestors, awakening the spirit of their souls with flour fingers and the deepest of roots.

Nonna Amara lifts her head to share the welcoming dawn of her smile. A latticework of lines grace her olive face. Long lobes host sentimental earrings. Saint Christopher winking in silver from her throat.

She pushes a ladle and other weapons of creation aside. Under a light rain of her words, each recipe is woven together—with herbs, meat, starch, or spice—and told in the tradition of a woman born to this village. Each mouthful embodies science and soul and is a bright expression of this woman's heart. Food can be comfort to everyone, so she fills them all up. Creativity digested into contentedness. Recipes traveling down through time and these Tuscan hills to the bowls of her beloveds.

Nonna Amara and the jumping spider enjoying a mosquito meal are not alone. Vittoria—eleven years and eleven months, thank you very much—supervises her grandmother with the unflinching eyes of an owl. Those eyes only avert from Nonna Amara to take notes, tracing each letter with blistering precision. Tongue peeking from her lips, Vittoria gingerly turns back the pages to past recipes she has made with her *nonna*. *Castagnaccio*, a chewy chestnut cake. *Frittata di vitalba*—a springtime omelette made with wild old man's beard they'd picked in the Tuscan woods. *Tordelli Lucchese*—plump ravioli filled with pork, spices, and Swiss chard, pine nuts, raisins, and grated pecorino. *Scarpaccia*—a zucchini-forward flatbread Nonna says was created by retired sailors who likened it to the thin soles of their old shoes. Vittoria has underlined words in her *Cooking with Nonna* book that she thinks might be important. Such as:

Nonna says it is okay if it doesn't taste perfect the first time, practice and patience make for a more delicious dish.

And,

Everything takes the time it takes.

Trust yourself, you can taste what it needs.

Smell everything. Breathe it in deeply and enjoy the story it tells you.

Don't be afraid, every recipe was once someone wandering a trail of curiosity or having a happy accident.

It is okay to make mistakes. In fact, the more you make, the better you will become.

Have fun! It will add to the flavor.

Be kind to yourself, because Vittoria is a wonderful cook and her nonna loves her—Nonna made her write that down and underline it. Vittoria stares at the next underscored sentence and her stomach drops.

There is no need to cry over a cracked egg.

She remembers holding the egg for Nonna, then putting it on the counter where it rolled off the edge. A dull crunch as it hit terra-cotta tile. She howled; Nonna had to rock her back to a place of peace. Vittoria did not have the words to express why the broken egg had broken her until this moment. It was because the egg had been changed irreversibly. There was nothing she could do to return it to its original and perfect state. You cannot put back a shell shattered.

"What are we making, Nonna?" Vittoria asks, spray of tight black curls stirring. She crushes a pen between her fingers.

"Chestnut ravioli with butter and sage." Nonna smirks. "Unless we lose our way, in which case we will rename it *Nonna and Vittoria's Mysterious Blobs in Butter Sauce.*"

Vittoria laughs. "The best blobs in all of Italy!"

"It will be our signature dish." Nonna picks up a fork to whirl the eggs inside a volcano of flour. "We are making it for tomorrow's big truffle auction!"

"Isn't it being catered by Novelli?"

"Visitors deserve a taste of the true Lazzarini Boscarino, don't you think?"

In the company of her grandmother is the only place Vittoria feels safe. Everywhere else—school, home—feels unsteady, as though the soil is sliding beneath her. Cooking with Nonna is when the whirling chaos of being an eleven-year-and-eleven-month-old stills. Warm waves unfurling from the hearth. A sizzling tale spat by pancetta and oil. Her *nonna* seasoning an afternoon. Squeezing love from lemons.

"Have you had any more trouble from that boy at school?" Nonna asks as she teases flour into the eggy lake of the volcano she has made.

"No."

"Well, good. I was about to dust off my broomstick. You see, I parked it over there just in case."

Vittoria looks at a scoliotic broomstick propped against an old cupboard. A smile creeps across her face as she imagines her *nonna* careening across the sky on a broom like La Befana, the winter witch. Nonna is undoubtedly quite magical. She changes the shapes of horrible things. She makes miracles from things she pulls from the dirt. Her laughter turns blood to warm butter.

With a powerful grace, Nonna draws together the eggs and flour until they are a single substance. Then she presses a patient silence into the dough, kneading with her knuckles. Nonna knows when to listen and how to do it with the whole of her heart.

"I like being online more than in school," Vittoria confesses.

Vittoria has taken to hiding in books and the internet. The bullies don't follow her there.

Nonna nods. "Sometimes," she says. "When something is out of the ordinary, people act a little crazy."

"Are you saying that I'm weird, Nonna?"

"I am saying that you are so very special, my sweet one. And if you ever forget it, you come and see me. And I will remind you." Nonna winks.

Guilt sits in Vittoria's throat like a lump of dry dough. Tears well in her eyes. She brushes them away with her sleeve, bending to study a bowl of quince because she cannot bear for Nonna Amara to see what she is hiding. A secret sits inside her like an ugly nugget. She is desperate to no longer carry this burden, to scream it out. But she can't. She cannot tell the only person she trusts.

Because the secret is all about Nonna Amara.

Nonna waves the fork like a tiny silver wand. "And when anything feels too big and out of control, you can always come back to cooking, *Farfallina*. It will ground you, and you will feel the love in every pinch of pecorino." She flicks cheese into the air like fairy dust.

"*Nonna*, you are making a mess!"

Nonna pulls a face, snatches up a fistful of the pecorino, and throws it like confetti. She peals with bright laugher.

"*Nonna*, there's cheese everywhere!" chides Vittoria.

Vittoria tiptoes over to the broom resting against the cupboard. Dangling from the cupboard is a spider. Vittoria peers close. A mosquito dangles from the fangs of the arachnid. She grabs the broom and skitters back to the kitchen counter, skin crawling at the chaos of it. She hates Stefano's house. Rickety furniture and peeling plaster. Rustic fireplace and heaters that groan to life. Dollhouse windows and old oil paintings of fat-bottomed women. Cold stone cellars. Scorpions and spiders.

What Vittoria hates most is that Nonna is living here tem-
porarily. The only possessions of Nonna Amara's are framed
photographs on top of a crowded bookcase. One of Giovanni
and his late partner, Paolo, each with an arm around Nonna.
There are two photographs of Nonna Amara's husband, Vito,
who died before Vittoria was born and is the inspiration for
her name. He has a gentle, grizzly face and looks like Babbo
Natale, Father Christmas. In one photograph, Nonno Vito is
wearing an olive waterproof jacket, boots. Standing in a forest,
he flaunts a palmful of beige pebbles.

"What is Nonno Vito holding in this picture? Stones?"

"Truffles, *Farfallina*. Like the magnificent one that will sell
at our big auction tomorrow evening."

"Oh, like what Giovanni hunts?"

"Yes. Your *nonno* was a seventh-generation truffle hunter,
you know. He knew all the secrets under the soil."

At the word *secret*, Vittoria's cheeks burn. "What really is a
truffle?"

Nonna's hand hovers over Saint Christopher. She stares at
her granddaughter, a slow smile burgeoning across her face.
"Well, it depends on who you ask. There is a whole kingdom
underneath the soil that we cannot see. All manner of fungi
spread tiny threads through the earth—each thinner than spider silk or a single strand of saffron. The fungi are creators and
destroyers of life; there are recyclers and undertakers. Some
are friends and some are enemies in this dark kingdom."

"That sounds terrifying."

"Not at all. Fungi are essential to life. Without fungi, we
would not have wine, beer, cheese, or chocolate! Or coffee!"
Nonna covers her forehead with the back of her hand and pre-
tends to faint.

Vittoria laughs, hands outstretched in mock horror.

Nonna hands Vittoria a bowl of chestnuts to score before

roasting. "Fungi are that important. And they do this work quietly, invisibly. Now, a truffle is the particular fruiting body of a particular fungus. It is the treasure of this kingdom. A subterranean jewel that only grows when there are good relationships underground between certain trees and fungi. Only when the soil is soft and the summer rains are just right. Only when there is a tree that is ready to form a partnership with the fungi and share food."

"This sounds like a folktale, Nonna."

"Yes, but this is all true."

"And Nonno found them in the woods?"

"Truffles are rare, and very hard to find. It is almost impossible for a person to find one alone. They must have a good relationship with a trained dog who has a nose thousands of times more powerful than a human's. Nonno's favorite truffle dog was Briciola. We'll get to see a very special truffle soon enough—the whole village is abuzz over it."

"But the truffles look so ugly. Like potatoes from another planet. Why do people want to dig them up?"

"Ah, that is part of the magic and trickery of truffles, you see. It is true, they aren't much to look at. What they look like—unfortunate little lumps that make a potato look glamorous—and what they represent—wealth, refinement, power—are at odds. People love truffles because of their captivating smell. They are a very, very expensive ingredient."

"Giovanni showed me truffles, but I can't remember what they smell like..." Vittoria stops scoring chestnuts to write "truffle" as a heading. Nonna opens her refrigerator and takes out a plastic container lined with paper towels. She pinches a tiny black truffle, sniffs it, and hands it to Vittoria.

"The black truffle bears a sweet fruit-of-the-forest smell, with a deeper cooked-cabbage undertone."

Vittoria closes her eyes, sniffs. "I like it."

"The white truffle, well. That one is its own entity. It smells . . . powerful."

"Powerful?" Vittoria thinks of strong smells. She revisits being pushed into the corner of the room by her mother's French perfume.

"Very. To me, they smell of garlic and frilly flowers from some exotic place. Many think they smell of stinky socks and underwear!"

"Stinky socks and underwear!"

"And of the very land itself. Of mountains. And skeletons."

"Skeletons?" shrieks her granddaughter.

"Yes. You know, skeletons in the closet. As in *secret affairs*." Nonna is transported to a cold late-November night, under the lonely glow of the moon. She had joined her husband Vito for a truffle hunt with his dog Briciola. After the hunt, they stood next to the BMW of a middleman Vito sold to. The man wore a black trench coat. Nonna hears her gentle husband and the mysterious man haggling over crumbling pieces, invasive bits of stone, the holes made by a worm, shape and size. Briciola panting metronomically in the night. Nonna can almost smell the bossy zephyr of the truffles, moss, and mud, even the metallic wad of cash in the middleman's hand. A flatulent blast of exhaust as he peels off in his BMW. Nonna can feel Vito's hands trembling with thrill, finally understanding the jolt he gets from these clandestine deals. The joy of working with his beloved Briciola to track down treasure in the woods. Quick cash. The secretive sale of a product that must be moved faster than any illicit drug. Nonna catches herself, swimming back from the scent memories. "Truffles are treated as more valuable than gold because they are so rare. And when something is worth a lot of money, it invites greed and corruption. Corruption worse than a worm inching its way through the truffle itself."

"How much money are they worth, Nonna?"

"A *lot*. The rich fly them across the world to shave them across their pasta. You see, the truffle—especially the white truffle—is mysterious. And when something is mysterious, man tries to unlock its secrets for himself. But maybe not everything is a problem to solve or a creature to be cultivated. When we embrace the mysterious, we relinquish our chokehold on control and accept that there is more to life than we can see and know. Isn't that refreshing?"

"I think so..." Vittoria crinkles her face and ponders all this. A shrill scratching as she herds a snowing of Parmesan across the terra-cotta tile with the broom.

"Perhaps it is enough of a gift that we might happen upon a truffle and smell it for a fleeting moment. It is in our nature to seek out awe and magic. To envelop ourselves in wonder. And so much magic lies in the mysterious. Maybe if we don't explain a thing away, it can simply be a miracle."

"*Magic in the mysterious.*" Vittoria presses her pen hard into the paper. "You can grow truffles though?"

"People have figured out how to grow the black truffle— *the precious black*—a bit unreliably. The white truffle is secretive and very tricky to grow. Isn't that beautiful? Nature has all the power. The day they tame the white truffle will be a dark day. The white truffle will become commonplace. And we will once again be suffocating on our self-admiration while we mourn the enchantment of mystery."

"Truffles seem a bit scary to me."

"Some people focus on the dark side of truffles, the competition, jealousy, the thieving, dark deeds. But the truffles themselves don't do this. They are a gift offered to the world with no expectation of reward, only hope. The truffle is the good example with which the fungi show us how to live. Grounded, rooted, they exemplify the power of community and vibrant connection. Truffles are all about trust. Trust that starts at the beginning between fungi and the oak, beechnut, or chestnut tree. Trust between the dog and his human. Trust between a middleman and a hunter over money. Trust all along a complex web of relationships as it journeys from the dirt to a plate. Trust that is popped into the mouth and swallowed. Maybe that is why so many souls go wild for these tubers. Truffles are the taste of trust."

"Maybe," says Vittoria, "they also remind us that what we have been looking for is sometimes right beneath our feet?"

"Brava, *Farfallina*! You are such a bright, clever thing."

Vittoria is enchanted. Her *nonna* is wise. She opens up doors where there were none before. She shares it all—food, love, little morsels of magic. Like when she taught Vittoria to add beet or spinach or saffron or squid ink to pasta, bringing each strand to life in bright color. Or when they made mini panettone jeweled with crystalized fruit and delivered each one to the villagers on Christmas, the snow freckling down around them just like in a fairy tale.

"So Nonno was a hunter of expensive and rare truffles."

"He was. He taught a very troubled young Giovanni to hunt truffles. The thing he loves most. And he loved cats too—just like you."

Even though she's hiding a terrible secret, Vittoria takes a deep breath and fills up with wonder.

Vittoria is not like her mother. Vittoria's mother flits from person to place like a hummingbird moth. She had Vittoria when her other children were long grown. Vittoria knows almost nothing of her father, only that he is from Senegal and that he and her mother never planned to share a life. It is not that she feels unwanted, but rather that she showed up to life too late. But Nonna makes her feel like she belongs. She knows how to untangle Vittoria with a few swift words or a spun forkful of *cacio e pepe*.

Vittoria tries to imagine what the giant truffle smells like.

What trust itself smells like. Her favorite scent is the smell of fresh coffee. Not because she drinks it, but because when she stays with Nonna Amara, she awakens to a bracing perfume of roasted beans, swiftly followed by the heavenly music of her *nonna* humming as she makes her granddaughter breakfast.

"Nonna, how many grams of flour did you use?" Vittoria asks, squinting at her notes.

"About this much." Nonna Amara flaps her arms like an affronted flamingo.

"Nonna," she scolds. "That's silly."

"Sometimes silly is the very ingredient we need!"

"But how will I know how much to put in if I don't write it down?"

"You don't need to worry, *Farfallina*. When you make it alone, it will all come back to you. Trust your wisdom. Write that in your notebook."

Farfallina. Little butterfly. Vittoria prefers it to her given name. She trusts her *nonna*. Tells her everything. Everything up until now.

Vittoria etches a shoal of tidy letters into her notebook. When she looks up, she catches Nonna's smile. Vittoria feels her throat tighten. Words rush out. "I am still looking for the brooch; I think I might have left it in my jacket pocket and I—"

Nonna Amara puts down the dough and swallows the child whole in a hug. To Vittoria, this feels like a warm blanket on a November night. Hot soup for a sore throat. A way for her to feel weightless for a few precious moments. Her *nonna* smells of soap and rosemary. Wood fire smoke that has the good sense to cling to her. She smells soft and safe.

"Never you mind, *Farfallina*. It's just a brooch."

"But you gave it to me, and I loved it, and I never lose things—"

Nonna Amara rocks the child gently, then lifts Vittoria's chin. "The brooch doesn't matter, *Farfallina*. You matter."

And Vittoria feels a rush of energy escaping her. But the secret just under her skin is still there. Sitting. Waiting. Growing.

"We will need more sage," Nonna announces.

"No, we don't."

"What do you mean, *Farfallina*? We only have this, it's not enough…"

"Can we get it from the corner shop, Nonna?"

Nonna Amara blows a raspberry. "Corner shop! Where they wrap it in plastic? I grow fresh sage in my garden. We will walk down there."

Vittoria's throat dries up. "No."

"No?"

"Let's ask Lorenzo for some."

"*Farfallina*, it will only take a moment, as the dough rests and before we make the chestnut filling—"

"I don't want to—" Vittoria's bottom lip is trembling. She sounds childish, and she lowers her head, embarrassed.

Nonna Amara takes her granddaughter's hand in hers, kisses it gently. Reading the light of her young eyes, she adds, "We will go to my garden for sage. And you will see that there is nothing to be afraid of."

"But, Nonna, you're not allowed to be near your house; it's still dangerous."

"You are going to get wrinkles long before your time, *Farfallina*. We will only go to the garden. The mountain has already thrown its tantrum. And there is a nest of *bofonchi*—those giant wasps in the windowsill. I can't go near until Ugo moves them anyway. Tell me the truth. What is going on, *Farfallina*?"

"Nothing."

Nonna looks at Vittoria. "I know you will tell me what is

weighing on you whenever you are ready. But whatever it is, it is going to be okay. Your *nonna* says so."

She opens the drawer of the small cupboard next to the front door. Fumbling, she sifts through pens, loose change, a letter opener.

Vittoria's heart jackhammers against her chest.

She cannot breathe.

Did she put the key back in the right place? If Nonna doesn't find it, she'll know. Vittoria thinks she put it in the cupboard drawer, but maybe she didn't, maybe she forgot to, and Nonna is still fumbling in the drawer and Vittoria is sick to her stomach...

The secret slithers up Vittoria's throat. It squats like an unearthed bulb on her tongue. Quickly, before it transforms itself into words, Vittoria swallows it down again.

Nonna fishes out her house key and Vittoria breathes again.

She fishes out another key that Vittoria hasn't seen before.

Nonna hands Vittoria her coat with the deep pockets. *Deep pockets* can mean that someone has a lot of money. Deep pockets can also be for hiding secrets. For treasures. Hidden things. Small wonders and little miracles. Nonna wraps her head in a scarf, her body in a shawl, and the pair step outside Stefano's door. Leafy autumn air slices across Vittoria's cheeks.

Vittoria feels her *nonna*'s hand, the veins like soft blue snakes. Above, clouds dangle, fat as plums. Nonna lifts her palm to read for rain. Vittoria worries that the woolen shawl is not enough, that Nonna should be wearing another layer to keep her from the cold. They amble, hand in hand, down the cobblestones from Stefano's old house and through the streets of the village. Rolling out from the horizon is a tapestry of olive orchards, vineyards dressed in fiery colors. Houses dotting the forested foothills like scabs. Smoke sneering up from chimneys.

Deep scars of river canyons. A goat sends brassy, long-tailed vowels across the foothills. Rising in the west are the Apuan Alps. In the east, the Apennines, jagged mountains that, in summer, appear postcard perfect. Now, under a brooding sky, they liken giant trolls scowling through masks of mist.

At the edge of the village, they pass Tommaso's house. A hunting dog strains on his leash. Each sharp bark bursts into cold air like an angered ghost. Vittoria shudders. As she passes the wrought iron gate, a sea of black-eyed Susans seem to study her with a hundred botanical eyes.

The old donkey path winds from the village to Nonna Amara's farmhouse, but Nonna veers off the path and toward trees.

"Nonna, no. We must stay on the path."

"*Farfallina,* I like to shortcut with a walk through the woods. The forest is where we go to remember we are part of something bigger than our woes. It will be good for you. You'll see. Come."

Vittoria has read enough folktales to panic over her grandmother walking in the woods.

Dwarfed by trees, Vittoria is engulfed in a deep silence. Despite the cold, sweat beads on her upper lip. She clenches her *nonna*'s hand tighter, concentrating all of her mind on each of Nonna's steps. She studies the woods with wild eyes. She must make sure they are safe. Safe from vipers that may be hiding under a crunch of leaf litter. Safe from spiders who secrete poisons. Maybe even a disgruntled badger or pheasant. And somewhere in these woods lurk the wild boar with tusks like twin daggers. Vittoria's mother once told her that a Borghese hunter died from being gored by a wild boar. She can see him now, lying lifeless on the forest floor, a bloom of deep red blossoming across his chest. But it is not the boar that Vittoria is most worried about. She is most worried about a creature that hunts at twilight in the cold months. One that knows the favor of hunting in harmony and the power of a pack. There are wolves all over the Tuscan mountains. Nonna said she saw one once on her land. Vittoria spins, searching the trees for a great gray form. For the small moons of its eyes, slinking out from the shadows of folklore.

Vittoria starts to stomp her boots down onto the carpet of orange leaves. She splatters mud. She chants incoherently.

"What are you doing?" asks Nonna.

"I'm making my own music!" Vittoria improvises.

Nonna joins in the farcical singing, stomping a couple of times for good measure. Vittoria realizes how ridiculous she looks as she tries to ward off danger and laughs, a balloon burst of a sound. Steam escaping a pressure-relief valve.

Nonna and Vittoria emerge from the deepest part of the woods and trail the donkey path once more. Here, booby-trapped by sharp rocks that Vittoria points at in warning, is the last leg of the path before it forks down into Nonna Amara's driveway.

Vittoria stares up at the mountainside, her eyes wide. All the trees are gone, as though clawed clean off. The landslide has left a mighty gray scar in sheer rock face. A shiver climbs the back of Vittoria's neck. She looks down the grass-and-rock driveway to the terraces, now a terrible entanglement of tall brambles. The thorny war of them blocking out most of Nonna Amara's beautiful view of the forested hills. Right of the farmhouse, there is an unearthly emptiness where the old cherry tree used to stand, polka-dotted with scarlet fruit. Boulders as big as buses hunch on the terraces. Half of Nonna Amara's farmhouse is caved in. Her old *cucina* a tableau of rubble and ruin. The stark shock of such catastrophic damage chills Vittoria's blood. She spies the handle of a copper saucepan sticking out between rubble rocks like a surrender flag. Her breath catches, heart thrashing like a hooked trout.

Nonna Amara had been standing right there. Right in the

devastating path of the landslide, moments before it fell. It had missed her by moments. Vittoria squeezes her eyes shut, shaking her head against an imagining of her *nonna* being swept up by a tonnage of rock. Of all that she loves being buried by an act of nature. She thinks of the jumping spider sucking blood from the limp mosquito.

Nature has all the power. It is what her *nonna* said about the truffles. It is true for the mountains too.

And once more, little Vittoria is overwhelmed by the thought that we live on a fragile blue-and-green marble hurtling through space.

She watches her *nonna* amble back from visiting a persimmon tree, from whispering lovingly to its leaves like an old friend.

"*Farfallina!*" calls Nonna in a fruity voice. "Come see how the apple trees have grown! It's wonderful."

Vittoria crawls through a labyrinth of bramble. She finds Nonna Amara in what used to be a tidy vegetable garden. Summers of aubergine and asparagus. Beetroot, beans, and broccoli. Fruit trees fat with sweet fortune. Flirty green scapes of garlic. Since Nonna's forced evacuation, fangs of bramble have eaten it all.

"Look, apples everywhere. The deer have been at these ones, but we can pick up the last of these over here. What a beautiful blush on this one. I remember planting them. We plant hope in seeds. And we are gifted for our faith with a good garden."

You have not been gifted, Vittoria is too afraid to say, *nature is trying to kill you.* Lip trembling, Vittoria stares down at the dried scat of some creature. The soil is pocked where wild boars have uprooted bulbs. Nonna's pergola has caved in.

"Here, look at how much the sage has taken over here! We are rich with sage! We'll make *salvia fritta.* One day, we should plant another cherry tree."

One day, Vittoria thinks. Planting a tree denotes a faith in the future. The idea makes Vittoria dizzy. Nonna's home has been pummeled and there is not an ounce of self-pity in her voice. Vittoria listens to her *nonna* oohing and aahing over the garden a mountain stole from her and has never loved her more. Vittoria inhales a vegetal waft of soothing sage. She snatches up more sage, rubs its velvet ears in her fingers, and inhales deeply.

Her eyes sweep over the great wound up in the mountainside, trailing down to boulders bigger than buses, a garden choking on weeds. She inhales a longsword of mountain air, and she is quite faint.

"Nonna?" she asks, her voice cracking. "How do we fix what nature has done?"

Nonna's head pops up from the brambles, bright and lovely. Leaves cling to her headscarf. "They need to stabilize the mountainside. What the *comune* say we need, my darling *Farfallina*, is a lot of money."

"So when the giant truffle sells, will it make it so that you can go home?"

"The truffle might make a lot of money, but it will go to other things in the village before repairing my house."

"But why?" Vittoria is shouting. Tears prickle her eyes. "What's the point of it?"

"You're working yourself up, darling. Deep breath. Everything's going to be okay, I promise."

Vittoria nods at her rubber boots. She is an old soul in a junior-size jacket. "Don't be sad, darling. I wanted you to finally see the house for yourself so it doesn't torture you anymore. See, nothing to fear here! Come, I need something from the shed, and then we can get back to cooking. The Best Blobs in Italy don't make themselves!"

Vittoria is suddenly short of breath. The key. The key was for the shed.

Nonna picks up an old oak walking stick peeking out from

rocks that used to be her outdoor pizza oven. She waves it side to side, teasing bramble thorns apart. Emerging from the brush, they stagger to the shed next to where Nonna's old Fiat is parked under an awning.

She winks at Vittoria and opens the shed.

The shed erupts into violent scratching. Vittoria shrieks.

"*Glis glis*," says Nonna at a pair of eyes shining at them from the back of the shed. The shed exhales a breath of musk and neglect. Nonna clicks on a rickety bulb on a wire. The shed glows nicotine yellow. Vittoria sees gasoline cans. Pots of paint. Trowels and shears. Tiny fecal pellets. A rusted wheelbarrow. A Vespa in the colors of the Italian flag. Weedwackers. A large key holder nailed to the wall holds several sets of keys. On the other wall hang several shotguns. Nonna sees Vittoria eyeing them.

"Those are Ugo's guns. I store a lot of other people's stuff in here. Nonna Amara the storage unit." She tsks. "A shed full of sharp things."

Vittoria takes two steps into the shed. Something hanging from the ceiling brushes her face. She screams, stumbles backward. Nonna retraces her granddaughter's steps, reaching onto tiptoes to dislodge the hanging mystery. She holds a length of gauzy mystery to the light and marvels.

"Snake skin," she says. "A big one. Must be living in the shed roof."

Vittoria feels an invisible snake writhe across her skin. She wants to scream. There should not be a snake living in the ceiling of Nonna's shed. A devastating landslide should not have happened. Nonna is the best person that ever lived. How could nature do this to her?

Nonna selects a small woven basket to carry the sage in. She shuts the shed, locks it. Vittoria sees a scurry of movement through the brambles. A *Glis glis* getaway. Nonna takes a few steps from the shed and stares at her house.

Vittoria wonders what she is thinking.

Fistfuls of gathered sage sighing a sweet breath around them, Vittoria and her *nonna* walk back up the driveway and onto the road toward the village. Vittoria had insisted. She was sure there was someone or something watching them in those woods. Lately, it feels that everywhere Vittoria goes, a wolf follows close behind.

They walk up a steep road and find a Madonnella street shrine waiting for them. The Virgin Mary figurine is inside a glass case to protect her from the sun and rain. Her case is painted with golden cherubs, ringed in whimsical fairy lights. Propped up all around the case, wanderers have picked flowers for her, arranging them in Coke bottles and little pots. She is a vestige from the old Roman belief that terrible things happened after dark. When demons crawled up from the depths of the underworld, and frightened Romans placed a deity at every crossroad, lit by the light of an oil lamp. Now, the Madonnelle protect passersby from evil in all its bitter flavors. Nonna places a sprig of sage on top of the case, whispering with eyes closed. A light breeze picks up. Cloaks of crisp leaves flutter around her. Each leaf looks like a little butterfly.

Nonna holds Vittoria's hand, and they walk back to Stefano's house.

Vittoria watches Nonna place the keys back in the cupboard drawer.

She has become terrified of time. She worries about the seasons changing, summer slipping away, trees growing tawny and shivering like bony old men. She has come to detest clocks, which seem like glaring headmasters, stern hands slapping away every second. And thinking about the future makes her tummy turn.

She saw change everywhere as her mother drove her to Nonna Amara's today. In the shed leaves. In so many crumbling churches. And she doesn't want to see change or time passing because it means everything is getting older. Nonna Amara is the only stable presence in her life. Her constant. In the way that eating is a constant and everyone shares the need for nourishment. Time is terrifying because, much like nature, it is a power too great. The minutes with Nonna Amara hold Vittoria together. And though she wishes for an eternity, Nonna is old, and Vittoria doesn't know how many of those minutes she has left.

Two catastrophes have happened that haunt Vittoria terribly. One was when a landslide almost killed Nonna Amara. The other was a fall, Nonna tumbling over a step in the village, scraping the entire length of her shin. A terrifying bruise lingered on her leg for weeks, black and blue as shame. Both catastrophes happened when Nonna Amara was out of Vittoria's sight.

It was not difficult to figure out who was at fault.

Vittoria should have been there. If she had been holding Nonna Amara's hand, it would not have happened.

The solution seems simple. Vittoria must watch over her grandmother in the way she has to avoid certain cracks in the village cobblestones. In the way that every fallen eyelash must be wished upon. In the way that Vittoria must drive the car with her mind from the back seat when her mother is at the wheel. The rules of child logic may not read rationally, but once established, they are ironclad. And perhaps the only force stronger than the logic of a child is the bond between a girl and her *nonna*. Vittoria will be the bravest little butterfly for Nonna Amara, even if it means walking in the woods where there are wolves.

She wasn't watching her *nonna*, and so she fell. She wasn't watching, so Nonna's home was crushed, and she was almost killed.

If her eyes are on Nonna, then nothing bad can happen to her.

Which is why there are tears in her eyes when they get back

to Stefano's, as she says, "Nonna, I'm going into the village, I'll be back soon."

"But what about the Best Blobs in All of Italy for the truffle auction tomorrow!"

"I won't be long, Nonna…"

She steps out the door. Leaving her *nonna* alone is the last thing on earth she wants to do, but she has to.

Moments later, Vittoria—eleven years and eleven months, thank you very much—approaches the Madonnella.

Madonnelle stare into the soul windows of their watchers, reminding them of their civic duties and warning them against committing crimes. Vittoria stares into the patient brown eyes of the Madonnella and prays. For protection for her *nonna*. She smudges away a tear. As Vittoria stares at the Virgin Mary, she is certain she sees those waiting eyes move. She gasps. Wordlessly, young Vittoria asks for forgiveness and confesses to the Madonnella that she has committed a sin. But it is only because she will do anything to keep her *nonna* safe. Vittoria slips her fingers into her jacket pocket and smooths them over her stolen secret—the key to Nonna's shed. The gnarled clot of guilt swells inside her because she is lying to the person she loves the most.

She lets the key drop down to the bottom of her pocket. No one will know. It is well hidden by a handkerchief.

Forgive me, Madonnella, forgive me, she wishes in a whisper. *But I have to do this. I have to.*

Vittoria slinks—eyes searching the woods for wolves—back to Nonna's shed.

Chapter 9

A tiny Italian honeybee lifts above a patchwork quilt of vine-yards and olive groves. She is on a life-or-death mission to find sweet sustenance. She flies fast. A miniature shooting star of yellow and black, bright as the notes of a Vivaldi concerto. Terraces of naked grapevines melt away beneath her, her wings shimmering against air filled with an aura of apple. She must hunt for nectar and bring it home. And she must do it before winter clenches a cold fist.

Her hive depends on her.

High in the sky, two antennae tremble as the lone bee trails a sweet scent. Below her, a rustic farmer's market, where women bundled in shawls sell a harvest just lifted from the land. The bee can smell every great wheel of *parmigiano*, diaphanous pet-als of prosciutto, each warm wave of roasted chestnut. None of these are what the bee is after. She flies on. The stream of sugar intensifies as the bee nears a tall, cold-blooded beast of a building.

She hovers over a medieval castle on a hill.

Below, an old Jeep spasms up a long driveway toward it.

The young bee swoops down toward the castle, history humming across its golden stone. Down into a large cobblestone courtyard, where men and women dressed in white scurry like mice. Some stagger while shouldering enormous floral arrangements.

Medieval castle doors gape open. The bee zips through them into a palatial hall. Her five eyes register a long banquet table decorated with magnum wine bottles. More frantic humans worry around the room, wiping, mopping, pummeling clouds of dust from tapestries, flapping feather dusters at pillows and paintings framed in gold. Some lift chairs to impassioned cries of "No, you idiot! Line them up this way, the whole world will be watching!" and "We don't have a second to lose! It has to be perfect; every inch of the grand hall must be spotless! That's not spotless! What's that? A spot!"

The bee focuses on her sense of scent. The great hall smells of sliced pear and pecorino cheese. And something else.

Something sweet.

Below on the banquet table, the bee spots a steaming pot of farro and bean soup. Red velvet pillow on a pedestal cake stand, quietly waiting to flaunt the world's largest truffle. But it's a platter of *befanini biscotti* that croons to her in a song of sugar, a cookie constellation of sweet dough made to look like the moon and the stars.

Her antennae quiver.

The brave little bee flutters her wings, dipping toward a star-shaped biscotto. In a flash, a humongous hand is hurtling toward her. The bee is in for a head-on collision, human hand trawling the air right in front of her. Insect instincts light up. The bee flips her body in a mid-air turn. The split-second flight maneuver spins her between two fingers as she narrowly misses a swatting by the hand of a pastry chef with a sleeping disorder.

"Chef Umberto, I think we have a bee problem," calls Chef Alban Toussaint with his sallow skin and drooping eyelids.

"What? How many of them?"

"Well, just one…"

"That's not a bee problem, Chef Alban, don't tell me we have a problem when we don't have a problem!" Chef Umberto Micucci turns on his heel to assist Chef Mbabazi with relocating six feet of a sixteenth-century knight's armor suit. As the two men hobble to hold on to cold metal, the knight's hinged visor flaps open. Chef Mbabazi screams. Chef Umberto, startled, loses his grip and the knight loses an arm, metal clattering to terra-cotta tile.

"I'm sorry," Chef Mbabazi says. "I half expected to see a face in there."

"Pull yourselves together, all of you!" Chef Umberto roars, wielding an armor arm. "None of the nonsense ghost tales of this castle are true!"

The little bee lifts toward the flaky frescoes of the ceiling. She lands on a large painting to repose. Hiking over an ornate golden frame, she crawls across the face of a curly-haired count who once inhabited this castle. A recluse who suffered from a psychological condition that caused him to believe he was made of glass, the count walked sideways through the corridors and insisted his servants polish his skin with vinegar daily.

The bee swipes her eyes with her foreleg before crawling to the middle of the mad count's mustache for her rest.

Below the bee, Chef Umberto Micucci conducts the chaos in the great hall, a sheen of sweat glistening across his brow. The pomade taming his iconic vertical waves is leaking down his temples. His eyes ping-pong between the people he has enlisted to prepare the neglected castle for the world stage.

"No, line the chairs up with enough space from the table for the camera crews! The truffle will be sitting here on the banquet table, right in the center. I want every person in this hall and every eye around the world to be able to marvel at it. Chef Farah, take down the last of the wall tapestries and beat the dust from them outside. Chef Alban, you sweep that huge hearth for any more rat bones. The grand hall has to be perfect—do you understand me?"

"Yes, Chef!" bleat most of Novelli's staff.

"You three—clean his antlers!" commands Chef Umberto, pointing to a stuffed stag's head mounted on stone wall. "And comb his fur; it looks greasy."

"Comb his fur, Chef?" asks a young Novelli waiter with nautical tattoos swimming up his arms.

Chef Umberto answers with no answer; he is busy poking several rose bouquets into submission before molesting the tablecloth as if to make croissants out of it.

"Chef, if I may ask…where is the giant truffle?" braves Chef Alban as he wrestles with a towering studio light at one end of the banquet table. Three Novelli waiters pull chairs up underneath the great stag's head and puzzle over how they will lower the mighty stag without impaling themselves.

The famous chef's face stiffens. His nostrils flare. "No one can know where the truffle is right now. It has been hidden away for everyone's safety. You will see the truffle here, tomorrow, as it makes history." He points a trembling finger at the red velvet pillow atop the cake stand. At its snaking trim of golden thread.

His staff are given a moment of peace as Chef Umberto leaves them to buzz around several men he has hired to install Wi-Fi in a medieval castle.

"It has to be fast, you understand? We are broadcasting across the planet!" Orange glasses gleam inches from the eyes of an internet installer. "Oprah will be watching!"

The internet installer feigns fascination with his optical network terminal box to avoid further dealing with an unstable, sweat-shiny chef.

Chef Umberto wipes his brow and smudges his glasses on his designer sweater. He spots Novelli's front of house, Marilyn, cowering under a wrought iron chandelier. She is wearing two coats and his trapper hat with the giant ear flaps. She rubs her fingers together as if to start a fire, exhaling in miniature clouds.

"It is cold as the winter witch's tit in here!" Chef Umberto exclaims. "Chef Ichika, round up some heaters! We'll freeze all the international journalists in this drafty old place."

"No."

"Excuse me?"

"I said no!" yells Chef Tanaka. She whisks off her chef's hat to unveil a head as bald as a plucked quail. "I'm a professional chef, not your cleaning crew. I deserve more respect than you have ever given me. And"—something is swelling inside her, something she has tried to swallow down for so long—"and... and my duck pâté en croûte wasn't dry! It was perfect."

Her lips are quivering. Water wells in each narrowed eye.

Chef Umberto looks around the great hall. All sweeping has stopped. Every eye—including those of faultfinding royals trapped in paintings—is upon him.

"No...you are right, it wasn't dry," concedes Chef Umberto. Everyone in the grand hall pretending not to eavesdrop. Someone clears their throat. The internet installer studies the flat surface of his optical network terminal box at close range. Chef Umberto weighs up his next words. "But the gelée—"

"What about the gelée?"

A sniff. "Did you use white wine?"

"Yes."

He takes a deep breath, stares at the impossible silk of her skin. The luminous beam of her bald head. Such a slip of a thing. But now that she has swept her submissiveness out with the scorpions, here she is, bursting with spice and sriracha. Insouciant eyebrows. A tendon in her neck challenges him to a duel. Ferocity ticking in the black bombs of her eyes. Chef Tanaka truly has the makings of a master chef.

"You should have used prosecco."

The bombs in Chef Tanaka's eyes go off. "I quit." She storms from the castle, trampling the white surrender flag of her chef hat as she goes.

Chef Umberto's eyes widen behind his orange glasses. He takes a deep breath as one of the brightest sunrises on the horizon of haute cuisine bursts from the hall. He slinks after Chef Ichika Tanaka sheepishly.

The little Italian honeybee lifts from the painting and its solvent smell of old oils. She rises above the chaotic hive of humans to flutter down a long hallway. Ancient shields and sconces line the walls streaming beside her. Voices bubble below.

Benedetto in a wintergreen coat steers Stefano's wheelchair down the hallway as Stefano struggles to balance two large oil paintings on his fuchsia trousers.

"I thought we could hang some of my paintings in the castle since we were told the truffle auction is to be televised. I fetched them back from the town hall. You never know who might see them if the whole world is watching, Stefano," Benedetto says in his lovely quavering voice. Stefano lifts one of Benedetto's masterpieces to squint at it. The woman depicted looks familiar, but also reminds him of a root vegetable. He peers down at the second painting lying flat on his lap.

"Is this lady holding a salami?" he asks.

"It is a weasel."

"Hmm." He whirs along the hallway with its smells of cold stone and dust, cut by the chain-link bite of metal from swords suspended on the wall. Stefano is struck by a thought. "Where is the truffle now, Benedetto?"

"Stefano, *che meraviglia*, you've remembered the truffle!"

"Of course I remember it, it looks like my uncle Luigi's feet after he got lost while porcini hunting in the Apennines. But that smell, that is something you can never forget. You know, Benedetto, it brings me back to a night many years ago. The night I lost my virginity here in this very castle."

Benedetto chooses not to press him further. "The truffle might be on display in the grand hall already—let us find out. I don't like wandering through this castle. They say there is a ghost here who is not fond of intruders."

"Bah, ghost…" says Stefano. As he is wheeled down the dark hallway, he catches a glimpse of a hole in the wall perfectly sized for an eye. He pulls his cardigan tight around his shoulders and shivers. "If I were to bury a body, it would be here at this castle."

"Stefano, you should never say things like that," Benedetto chides, and leaves it at that.

The bee flits farther down the winding hallway with extravagant paintings depicting the Battle of San Romano. And a dark depiction of coal-eyed witches and skeletal beasts with the wings of bats torturing men in the spilled oil of night. The bee soars above the robed figure of Padre Francesco, who is wandering the halls alone while flicking holy water at the frescoes. His face contorted in concentration, spitting out bitter pits of Latin into the cold, musty air.

The bee deftly slips into a library ripe with the warm smolder of old books. She alights onto a smooth white marble bust of Fulvia Plautilla, the barely teenage wife of Roman emperor Caracalla, who ordered her murder by his tyrannous command. The bee settles to clean her antennae on a broken bit where Plautilla's nose once was.

Mayor Delizia is holed up in the library. She is hunched over a walnut wood desk that was once covered with maps and the war strategies of an Italian general. Vintage books with gold lettering line the bookshelves behind her.

Delizia swears she can still smell the truffle. A phantom perfume since the priceless truffle is not in this castle library. She has hidden it. And she is the only one who knows where. Did not utter its whereabouts to a soul, not even Umberto. She has not had a chance to tell Lorenzo. The intoxicating fungus is not even in this room and yet she is still crushed by the responsibility of it.

Should she have let it out of her sight? she wonders.

It is as though she had left a baby locked up alone in secret. Even from a distance she is tethered to the thing, the unbearable burden a cold metal around her wrists. Handcuffed to a fortune of fungus.

Delizia is too busy to dwell on it for long. Biting her last nail down to the quick, Delizia stares at her laptop. It has come alive, chiming every few seconds like church bells.

Her phone has also been endowed life, vibrating on the antique desk like something Dr. Frankenstein fiddled with. Last she checked, her voicemail was full.

"Hello, I'd like to speak with Delizia Micucci. I am a journalist with CNN, and I am interested in talking about the giant truffle and the auction in your Tuscan village."

"Good morning, Signora Micucci, I am a journalist with the BBC..."

The New York Times. The Moscow Times. Al Jazeera. *Forbes. Travel & Leisure. South China Morning Post. El País.*

She blinks at emails stacking on top of one another. She has been fielding interview requests all night. The first few came in at three a.m. seeking details about the secret location in the forest.

I am sorry, but our truffle-hunting grounds are top secret. We can only divulge that the truffle was found in our beautiful and historical village of Lazzarini Boscarino.

About the truffle hunter's name and what breed his dog is.

Giovanni Scarpazza. His dog is a Lagotto Romagnolo named Aria. She is a sweet soul and is doted upon in our village.

She wrote to the *New York Post* and *Business Insider* to answer their questions about the castle itself. Who owns it? Currently, no one. In the past, it has slipped through the pale fingers of nobility, marquises, counts and countesses, and wealthy titled families. Unable to sell it, descendants of the Bartolinis, the last family to own it, left it to the village of Lazzarini Boscarino, where not a soul could afford to maintain such an extravagance. As mayor, Delizia's father gave the castle to the government to become part of a program instated by Italy's Minister of Tourism. The minister offered up this historical place, along with 103 other castles, to anyone who wanted them. For free. You, too, can own a free castle, with the caveat that you must restore it to its former glory and with an eye to entice tourists to the area. Dampening its appeal, its wine cellars were once used as torture chambers, and it features its own rather large cemetery. There is also the small matter of its spectral inhabitant. A ghost is said to wander its halls, moaning. It is said that sightings of him are preceded by a woodsy smell. Some say of cedar or rosewood. Or sandalwood, oakmoss, fern, or balsam. Some suspect the ghost was a pirate. Or the illicit lover of a long-dead count. Most suspect he is one of the torture victims who tried to escape the castle prison, making it as far as the wine cellars before he was beheaded. Others suspect this is all utter rubbish.

But so far, there are no takers.

Dear Mayor Micucci, I would like to speak to you regarding a certain ghost said to be haunting the castle hosting your auction tomorrow. I'm reporting for the National Enquirer—

Delizia sat up through all the night reading and responding, cool blue glow of her laptop illuminating her face. A journalist from *Corriere della Sera*, Italy's widest-read newspaper, emailed to ask her about her rare role as a female mayor. How would her father think she is doing?

She fired back, He hasn't chimed in due to being dead.

Send.

It was three a.m.; grace had eluded her.

At four a.m., an internet search revealed that a reporter at *La Nazione* had run a piece that mentioned Duccio's jail time. They did not reveal what Duccio had been arrested for, just that he had served a sentence. Another patch in the quilt of doubt flung over the people of her village. Googling *Lazzarini Boscarino,* she found another fresh piece about Padre Francesco and his alleged excommunication from a church in Rome. And then, the floodgates opened.

Email after email after email. A little medieval village under the gaze of the Appenines, the Apuans, and all the international mass media.

Splashed across newspapers virtual and physical were headlines like WORLD'S MOST VALUABLE TRUFFLE FOUND IN OBSCURE VILLAGE WHERE AGED DONKEY RAN FOR MAYOR AND MISSED BY A MARGIN. The article is complemented with a picture of the flyer for Maurizio's twenty-second birthday party and its rather unflattering close-up of his prominent front teeth. There is no photo of Delizia.

"They are making a mockery of us," she murmurs.

She had wished upon a truffle, had she not? And, like a good genie, the truffle delivered. Here comes the global media, digging up the village dirt.

The embarrassing headlines irked her, but it was the last two voicemails she listened to that sent spiders up her spine.

"Good morning. I am hoping to speak to Signora Micucci,

the mayor of Lazzarini Boscarino. I write for the *Guardian* and am working on a feature about the largest truffle find. I'm currently researching your village and would be so grateful for more information on the disappearance of villager Sofia Rosetti..."

"Mayor Micucci, I am writing about your village for the *Times of India* and would love to talk to you about your late father, and about the missing sixty-eight-year-old woman named Sofia..."

Delizia—eyes twitching, bones burning—is hypnotized by the dancing phone and the sounds of a scandal about to break. Of course, they would find out about Sofia's disappearance. On the one hand, it brings her hope. If Sofia has—and how she hates to add to the rumor mill—run off, there is a chance she will read about herself in the news and come home. At least call poor Leon to put his mind to rest. Getting media attention for a missing-persons case is a blessing, a privilege the truffle's stardom will afford them. But Sofia's disappearance should not cast a shadow over the reputation of Lazzarini Boscarino. Painting it as a place where women go missing. Absolutely not. Delizia must take control of the narrative. She has to figure out how to fan the media flames and also protect the privacy of her people. The allure and glamour of the beastly truffle could change their reputation and put them on the map. It could resuscitate them.

The truffle will sell tomorrow.

Her heart is galloping. Words domino in her mind.

World-class auctioneer. Bidding. Sotheby's. International media. Celebrity attendance. Bid increment. Paddle. Seller's commission.

She pictures superstars dripping in gold, framed by fur coats. Paddles spring up, one after another, faster and faster, as the price of the truffle gets higher and higher. Her heart might burst.

Delizia jumps out of her skin at the knock on the door.

"Come in," she coughs.

She looks at the seventy-four-year-old Italian standing in the doorway. Something about Duccio's face has always reminded her of a candle. Today, an especially melted one. His cardigan is the orange and black of rusted barbed wire. He is years older than the mug shot she had just seen of him online.

"Are you alright, Duccio? You look like you've seen a ghost."

"I thought I did! On my way to see you, I bumped into a robed figure wafting through the halls, but it turned out to be Padre Francesco. He is dousing the place in water. My heart rate hasn't recovered yet."

"Of course he is. Well, I'm glad you're alright. I'm a little busy with putting the auction together for tomorrow though—"

"Delizia, I know that the truffle might sell for a lot of money, but you have to cancel the auction."

Delizia feels a headache blooming at her temples. "Why is that, Duccio?"

"Because...we really just have to."

Delizia wonders if he has seen the article. The careful wording.

Formerly incarcerated. Time served. Undisclosed crime.

She answers him over an endless electronic buzzing.

"Sotheby's are flying in tomorrow morning. Tomorrow afternoon, we will hold an auction here at the castle to celebrate a most miraculous find. It cannot wait. The truffle loses value every second. I am fielding emails from all over the world. Our whole village has come together to help set up for this illustrious event. Everyone is trying to make a little celebratory festival of it. There will be no canceling of the auction, Duccio. We need this."

The candle of Duccio's face melts a little more. "It's just that—this truffle is...it's not who we are. All this pomp and pageantry. This is Borghese stuff. The truffle is a hideous thing, a foul-smelling boil on the buttocks of our village—"

"What a lovely metaphor—"

"I don't think having an international spotlight on our village will be good, Delizia."

A silence menaces the library. Unsaid things crackle between them like static.

"Oh? You don't?"

"The castle is creepy. It's not...us." Duccio frowns at his loafers.

"Is there something more to this you want to share?" Delizia pauses as her chiming devices do not.

Duccio presses his lips together and holds a hand at the back of his neck. Delizia decides not to excavate his past. "This is very good for the village, Duccio. I know you can find it in you to join in and be a good—"

"It is an embarrassment!" He raises his voice. "Have you seen Tommaso?"

"No, what is going on with Tommaso?"

"And Leon has brought a barnyard to the castle!"

"What do you mean Leon has brought a barnyard to the castle?" The mayor is on her feet.

A quick glance at her phone.

You have 46 missed calls.

She closes her gyrating laptop, exhaling to a count of eight. Briskly crossing the library, her jaw a closed clamshell.

The little bee pivots on the marble bust of a murdered Roman bride and finds the sweet sugar stream has gone dead. What she seeks is not in the library, so the bee takes flight once more. She slips through a crack in great oak doors. Down a dramatic spiraling staircase and old portraits of long-dead men. Oil-painted eyes seem to trace her every wing whir. She flies by rooms with four-poster beds. Bathrooms with claw-foot tubs.

The bee shoots into an ancient castle *cucina* with a dumb-waiter. Dead flowers and an old silver pail hang from the ceiling. Old copper plates line the hood of a sooty fireplace, laced in cottony cobwebs. The *cucina* has been used as a storage room, crowded with rusting wine and olive oil bottling equipment.

What she seeks is not in here.

Windows above a large stone sink are open, so the bee slips through into fall-flavored air. A garden opens up in her five eyes. Pots of herbs. Rows of vegetable patches, soggy and browned with the season. Beyond are the vineyards and apple orchards. The garden is riddled with bustling humans.

The bee lowers and lands on the hindquarters of a twenty-one-year-old donkey named Maurizio. She starts a crawl down to his flank. A tail careens toward her, pendulum of a thick tassel swinging straight for her tiny bee body. The bee rockets skyward, donkey tail cleaving the air in her wake.

The bee alights on one trellis that holds the trunk and arms of a grapevine.

Farmer Leon is holding the leashes of two goats. Standing by his side with upright ears and a gentle expression is Maurizio, aged donkey and Delizia's rival mayoral candidate.

Delizia marches up to him.

"Leon, how are you?" Delizia unhinges her jaw to ask him softly, her nose filling with the warming smell of hay and horse dander. The scent ignites an immeasurable yearning in her for long afternoons on bucolic land, tending to farm animals, solving medical mysteries in the clues of symptoms. Leon kisses both her cheeks and Delizia softens under the smell of silage and woodsmoke, fresh-cut grass, and a practical and pleasant sigh of manure.

"I am managing," says Leon.

Delizia looks at the tangle of his great white beard. The hugeness of him. She turns to Maurizio, smoothing a hand along his hindquarters. She steps along the donkey's side, up to his head, running her fingers from his poll—that lovely steady bone between his ears—down to the spiky fur of his forelock. His velvet ears swivel. He blinks soulful brown eyes and presses his head into her chest.

"He looks good," says Delizia, smiling for the first time today.

"I don't know what I'd do without him," says Leon. Maurizio, the village donkey. All but its mascot. "Are you coming to his birthday party?"

"I wouldn't miss it for the world."

"Lorenzo is cooking up a feast for it, *primi, secondi, contorni,* everything."

Delizia floats in Maurizio's calm glow. She cups his velveteen muzzle with her hand, enjoying the prickle of his whiskers.

"Still nothing from Sofia," Leon says in a voice that makes her think of a great ship, creaking under the weight of its own wood. A ship lost at sea. "The Borghese *carabinieri* keep questioning me. And I tell them the same thing every time. She never came home that Friday night. Her keys, purse, gone with her."

Delizia leans her face against Maurizio's. "What about her family in Venice? Have they heard anything from her yet?"

"Last people she would go to. She was estranged from her family."

Delizia's mind flickers back to a conversation she had with Sofia at Bar Celebrità. It was warm out since they were on the piazza, and late enough that Lorenzo was clearing the last glasses from tables. Slender Sofia waved her glass of fizzy wine, exposing the thin blue veins of her wrists. "My sister and I share everything. Clothes. Food. Secrets. Men." She lets loose a high-pitched laughter without warmth.

Is that what Sofia had said? Who to trust?

"She has a sister, doesn't she? What about her?" asks Delizia.

Leon shakes his head very slowly. He is not making eye contact with Delizia. His eyes are on Maurizio, ruddy hands clasping the goat ropes so tight Delizia sees them whitening around the knuckles.

"They keep me going, you know. Especially Maurizio; he is a sensitive soul. Gentle and good. I brought them to be part of the truffle auction and festival. To show them to the world. If a truffle can be admired, think of how impressed they will be with my animals." He steps closer to Maurizio's face, dwarfing Delizia. "You know, sometimes I think Maurizio is the only one who truly believes I had nothing to do with Sofia's disappearance."

Maurizio swishes his tail.

Delizia says nothing. She is faced with the dilemma of not wanting her village to be ridiculed on the world stage. She must tell Leon to take the animals home so that the village doesn't look like they are reenacting the world's most pitiful nativity scene. But peering at the old farmer's bloodshot eyes, she knows she cannot. The media are on a hunt, sniffing out tantalizing tidbits as though they were truffles. Everyone an internet detective. Everyone snuffling for clues about the disappearance of Sofia. A scarf of suspicion twirls around his neck. Tightening with time. This man she has known her whole life. A man who is good to his animals. A man who had called her one recent night to help with the birthing of a breech calf, the two of them fighting in a stable under the stars, slick with blood and mucus. And after, sipping brandy on a stack of hay, bone tired, silently celebrating a beautiful newborn calf. She stares at the huge animalness of Leon and finds herself thinking about Sofia's slender neck. The white bob. The wildness in her. She embarrassed him often, openly berating him, wine on her breath.

Could it all have just become too much?

She shakes her head. She is exhausted. These thoughts mean nothing. And so, in addition to every top-tier journalist in the world attending the auction, there will also be a donkey and at least two goats. Delizia despairs as she looks down at the smaller ungulates. A familiar brown-and-white goat studies Delizia suspiciously from behind Leon's legs. They both know he is searching for where she is hiding her longsword.

A conspicuous rustling announces the arrival of hunter Tommaso.

Maurizio, a donkey famous for his even temper and tolerance, takes great offense at Tommaso's attire. He brays, stamping his feet. Leon leads the old donkey and his goats away from the torment of Tommaso and along a path into the apple orchard.

"I told you, Delizia, Tommaso has lost his mind," growls Duccio.

Delizia wants to ask Tommaso what on earth he is wearing, but the words won't escape her clenched jaw. She stares at Tommaso in his homemade head-to-toe suit, lumpy and bulbous.

"I spent all night making it, in my medium of choice—papier-mâché." His voice is muffled because his head is mostly obscured by a beige lump of dried newspaper and glue.

"He has come dressed as a testicle!" complains Duccio.

Twins Valentina and Rosa arrive, their arms full of an old doll collection. "Are you supposed to be a testicle?" they chant.

The small amount of Tommaso's exposed face burns bright red at the medically insensitive accusation. "I'm obviously a truffle!"

"You are obviously an imbecile!" shouts Duccio.

"Enough," says Delizia. "Cut it out."

"They should throw you back in jail, you old goat!" Tommaso the Truffle jeers.

Duccio grabs a burly nub protruding from Tommaso's

truffle costume and yanks hard. Tommaso teeters, somehow stabilizing for a second before he falls to the dirt. He throws his weight at Duccio and topples him to the ground. The two men roll and yell, flailing their arms to the dull crunching of fist meeting papier-mâché.

Valentina and Rosa land on the same idea at the same time, snatching up fallen apples and hurling them at the tussling men.

"Spray them with water!" yells Rosa, realizing the apple throwing is fruitless.

Duccio manages to wriggle on top of Tommaso and starts slapping at his face.

"Enough, both of you!" roars Delizia. She grabs the back of Duccio's orange-and-black sweater and pulls him off Truffle Tommaso. Tommaso splutters and moans, rocking up onto his knees with the effort of an upturned tortoise. Delizia stomps a foot. "Everyone needs to pull themselves together! What do you think the media will make of this? That we are a village of buffoons! I won't stand for it. Act your age, and for god's sake, dress"—she looks at Tommaso—"normally! Be good to one another. There are already reporters arriving at the castle; some are scouting the village as we speak. Now. I have a million emails to answer. Where is Umberto? I need to bend his ear..."

As if on cue, Umberto emerges from the castle with an enormous oil painting of Jesus. Padre scuttles behind him protesting his savior's eviction from the castle. Carlotta shuffles after them, seemingly amused by the argument.

"Umberto, he must stay on the wall! The world will think we are heathens!"

"Best to be honest," says Carlotta.

The bee has had quite enough of the hullabaloo near her grapevine trellis and lifts toward a tree deeper in the ancient orchard. She lands on an apple, skittling across its glossy skin. Searching for a way into the sweet flesh.

Ludovica, wife of the late mayor, trudges through the orchard just below where the bee traverses an apple. She is dragging a cart filled with bottles while sucking a cigarette.

"How much do you think the thing will sell for?" Ludovica lowers her voice to a whisper in case there are spies in among the apple trees. "Umberto told me it could be more than a million euros."

Giuseppina prances next to her. "A million euros! And the whole world will love our beautiful village. We will host them all after at Bar Celebrità! What's all this you're carting? Wine?"

Ludovica blinks. Sniffs. "It's Benigno's olive oil."

Giuseppina glances at the bottled passion of Ludovica's late husband. A finite thing. She is handing over the last of his love. Giuseppina stares at Ludovica's sharp cheekbones. How her houndstooth coat hangs from her. "Oh, Ludovica. How are you doing?"

"I'm okay." A long draw on the cigarette.

Giuseppina dares to ask. "Did you ask Delizia if she'd want some of it?"

Ludovica exhales a smoke stream of unspoken things. She looks around the garden—the herb patch, fallen leaves, wheelbarrows. Three waiters using shoe brushes to groom an enormous stag head. The melancholy and mud of a garden out of season. "You know. I don't think she'd care to have any reminder of her father. And she certainly doesn't want to spend a minute talking to me."

She winks at Giuseppina and yanks the cart toward the castle.

As Giuseppina watches, Giovanni appears in the garden

wearing a flatcap. Aria bounces by his side. Giuseppina kisses his cheeks.

"Giovanni! Delizia is looking for you, my darling." Giuseppina bends down to scratch Aria's head curls. "I think you are in trouble. She says you didn't show at the meeting with Sotheby's. What naughty little things were you up to? Tell your Pina everything."

"I couldn't do it. I just…I don't like the attention. On me. On the village."

"But you are here now."

"Against my better judgment," says Giovanni, gentle gray eyes watery. "I don't think anyone understands how dangerous this truffle is, Pina. As word gets out about its worth and where it is…I just, I worry. I've seen things. Terrible things. The truffle world can be treacherous."

"Darling Giovanni. Have faith. Where is my baby, Fagiolo?"

"In the Jeep." He gestures to the driveway. "Too much temptation for him. He really has a thing about goats."

"Where is the truffle now?"

Giovanni puts his hand on Aria's head. "Delizia has hidden it. Hasn't told anyone where."

"How exciting! Hidden treasure, right here in our village."

A ruckus snatches their attention. Tires fighting gravel.

"Who is that, driving like a speed demon?" Giuseppina stares at an unfamiliar Fiat Panda, hands on hips.

The car screeches to a halt in the castle's circular driveway. A green driver's-side door slams shut, spitting out a man in a blue vest and shiny black shoes. He has fair hair, a raining of freckles, and the look of a man who has waged battle at a board meeting or two.

"Oh no. Quick!" whispers Giuseppina. "To the orchard!" She takes the lead in an escape from the freckled man.

"I see you running!" the man in the blue vest calls after them. "Giuseppina! Giovanni!"

"Don't make eye contact!" hisses Giuseppina, grabbing Giovanni's hand as she lunges toward the orchard.

"Giovanni Scarpazza, I insist on speaking with you!"

"No thank you!" Giovanni calls back, squelching through a patch of long-withered sunflower stems. But Rico Valentino is here on a mission of passion that propels him. He catches up with the pair easily, ending their getaway in an instant. They are trapped, standing in what was a bed of strawberries in summer. Behind them, another shriek arcs out from the great hall.

"There is no need to be immature," huffs the freckled man. "We need to talk about the truffle, Giovanni."

"It has nothing to do with you, Rico."

"It has everything to do with me! Why on earth didn't you come to me first?" His eyes are pale and fierce.

"Because, as I said, it has nothing to do with you."

"Where is it?"

"That's none of your business."

"Of course it's my business! I am the president of the Borghese truffle hunters! The truffle was found on Borghese Tartufi hunting grounds—"

"*Your* hunting grounds?"

"How do you even know where it was found, Rico? Get ahold of yourself," says Giuseppina, her posture straightening. Two enormous paw prints on either breast thrust forward like official badges.

Rico frowns at the paw prints and continues. "I have every right to know where it is. And to see it myself! This organization is the backbone of Tuscan truffle hunting—"

"Get out of Giovanni's face, Rico," warns Giuseppina.

Aria lowers her head and barks at the president of Borghese

Tartufi. His energy is humming, as constant as a car engine. She doesn't like the effect it's having on her human.

"Where is it, Giovanni?" Rico insists, wiping mud from his shoe.

"He just told you it is not your business, Rico," says Giuseppina over Aria's barks. "And you are distressing Aria."

"I am not part of your organization, and I have no interest in talking to you, Rico. Please leave me alone."

Rico steps closer to Giovanni, a forefinger aimed at his face. "There is already an international auction being set up and Borghese Tartufi has not even been consulted. This is not how it is traditionally done. You need our verification, our connections! If there even is such a truffle. If it's even real!"

Giuseppina's eyes narrow. "Rico, I've asked you to back off. Now I am asking you to leave us alone, you mosquito of a man…"

"Why didn't you come to me with the truffle, Giovanni? I have to hear about it in the news? Not even a phone call? What size is it? Tell me. There are all sorts of absurd rumors swirling around, and if I can just see it, I can verify—"

Giuseppina loses it. She pushes Rico's bony chest. "Enough. He asked you to leave nicely and now you are being a bully, so I'm going to bully you and see how you like it." She slaps at his chest and arms. He tries to block her, but Giuseppina is bigger than he is and gets a great many swats in. Aria puts her body in front of Giovanni to protect him.

Carlotta and her grandson, Poliziotto Silvio, appear from the garden patio, as well as several well-dressed foreigners. Reporters. No one, not even the bee, can see that now up in the grand library windows of the castle stands Mayor Delizia. Not a soul sees her waving her arms frantically and performing the charade of dragging her finger across her throat.

But the argument is abruptly stopped. Not by Poliziotto Silvio or the mayor's furious gesturing behind glass. As a small crowd gathers around a charismatic bartender slapping the president of Borghese Tartufi, an old engine roars to life. Giovanni startles, spinning toward the circular driveway. Toward a familiar growl. Ahead, reflected in the truffle hunter's eyes, is his trusted old Jeep.

Giovanni sees his brake lights burning red.

His mind struggles to catch up to what is happening.

Cold fingers of terror slip around his throat as he remembers.

He left his keys in the ignition.

Giovanni looks around at the castle, at Giuseppina, tries to find sense in the sky. And then it hits him.

"Someone is stealing my Jeep!" yells Giovanni. He scoops up Aria, places her into Giuseppina's arms.

Giovanni is running.

"Fagiolo!" he hears himself scream, syllables jostled by pounding footfalls. "Fagiolo is in the Jeep!" Fear sends shocks up the back of his neck. Boots slipping on crunching gravel. His breath ragged.

Noses for news, a media crew leap into action, reporter shouting instructions. Another trains his camera on the stolen Jeep as it speeds away from the castle.

"Someone stop the Jeep! Giovanni's puppy is in there; they're taking the puppy!" screams Carlotta, her voice tight with terror.

Poliziotto Silvio is running right behind Giovanni. He overtakes the truffle hunter, bolting toward his *carabinieri* car. Fumbling with his phone, he connects with the Borghese police department.

"At the castle...theft...Giovanni Scarpazza's Jeep...his truffle dog is inside..."

A drone lifts, whirring above the fray—a cold, mechanical insect here to document disaster.

Giovanni scans the circular castle driveway in desperation.

"A car, I need a car…" he is muttering, eyes fighting to focus.

Leon appears from the side of the castle like an old god of the sea. "Here, go quickly." He tosses a pair of keys at Giovanni and points to his vehicle.

The tiny light-blue Piaggio Ape sits silently on three wheels. Somewhere in between a Vespa and a car, as petite as the Italian bees it is named after. Giovanni squeezes into the Ape, onto its seat upholstered with a pair of old jeans. A clap beside him. Giuseppina has squashed herself in next to him. She is cradling Aria—panting, shivering—in her lap.

"Seat belt," Giuseppina says to silence Giovanni's pending protests. And then she says a small prayer to the Spirit of Safe Driving. There is not time for anything else. Giovanni turns the key in the ignition and, lifting the skinny silver excuse for a clutch, he jerks the little blue Ape into motion.

Giovanni, Giuseppina, and Aria test the upper speed of an Ape as they fly across the driveway, away from the castle. The skinny road leading from the castle snakes down among trees and rocky mountainside. Giovanni can see—*yes, I see you*—on a turn up ahead, the red lights of his Jeep—*if you touch a curl on Fagiolo, I will*—and Giovanni forces the Vespa-vehicle into fourth gear despite its insectile screams. If the Jeep gets away, he will never find Fagiolo. His little Lagotto will become part of a devastating statistic of stolen truffle dogs. Giovanni blinks away tears. Slams his foot onto the gas pedal.

They round a bend at top speed and come front-wheel-to-front-wheel with a Vespa in the colors of the Italian flag. Losing control, the Vespa driver zigzags violently, snaking to the right side of the road, narrowly missing the Ape.

"You again, *bastardo*!" Giovanni shakes his fist, Giuseppina and the Ape engine screaming. "That hideous Vespa is out to kill me!"

A snake of serious cyclists flash middle fingers as they are almost run off the road by a speeding Ape. Giuseppina almost passes out as Giovanni overtakes a Toyota Yaris, veering into the left lane as an oncoming Ford Fiesta blasts its horn at them. Giovanni jerks the three-wheeled Ape back into the right lane just in time.

"*Porca miseriaaaaaa!*" yells Giuseppina, head smacking against the side of the Ape with every tight turn as she cradles Aria.

An assault of honks startles them. Giovanni squints into the rearview mirror. Poliziotto Silvio is on their tail, waving at him violently. Giovanni jerks the Ape tight to the right of the road, skimming the thin metal railing that is all that stands between them and a forty-foot drop. Giuseppina lets out a long sky-high note made vibrato by the jostling, as though she is practicing for the lead role in a Puccini opera.

Silvio salutes them as he overtakes the Ape, turning on his *carabinieri* siren and its piercing two-tone inflection. The Ape zigzags as Giovanni struggles to keep control at top speed.

The *carabinieri* car roars ahead of them.

The road narrows further. Trees and grass on one side. A fatal drop on the other. There is no room for overtaking, and this becomes a problem as a large delivery van barrels toward the tiny Ape. One of the vehicles must slow down and pull over to allow the other to overtake, but the van driver is late for a delivery, his job on the line. And Giovanni is myopic in his hunt for the Jeep; he will not slow down. He will not let the thief take his Fagiolo.

"Giovanni, pull over! Pull over!" screams Giuseppina. The hair-raising game of chicken comes to a swift end as the driver of the van swerves right, vanishing into the open gates of a villa.

Two more switchback bends and the Ape enters a small town at the base of the hill. Where the main street hosts a café,

a pharmacy, and a *tabaccheria*. Where bottles of wine sit on barrels outside of an *enoteca*. Where a stolen Jeep has shot down the
narrow main street, swerved to miss a pedestrian, and narrowly
missed rows of wine bottles stacked on barrels only to smash
into a short stone wall running the length of the street.

"*No, no, no, no, per favore, no*," cries Giovanni.

Through the tiny Ape windshield they see Poliziotto Silvio's car screeching to a halt behind the accident. Silvio leaping
from his car and running to the Jeep door.

Giovanni no longer hears Giuseppina's wailing. Later, he
won't even remember stopping the Ape in the middle of the
street or leaping from its driver's-side door. He won't remember
running, the sound of his huffing, his footfalls on the street,
Aria panting beside him. But he will always and forever remember one vivid image—Poliziotto Silvio emerging from the back
of the Jeep cradling a clump of curls named Fagiolo.

"He's here, he's alright!" yells the *poliziotto*. "The thief ran
away on foot."

Giovanni feels something rupture in his throat. He runs
to Fagiolo, Aria fused to his side. Aria is afraid of the crashed
Jeep. Afraid of the sinister storm of panic clouding the air,
thunderous drumming of pulses, Fagiolo's legible terror. But
most of all, she is concerned about the quickening of the blood
around her human's heart.

Poliziotto Silvio pulls out his Beretta, leaping over the short
wall to track the thief.

Giovanni's teeth are clattering. He runs his hand all over
Fagiolo, who melts with relief under the touch of his person. A
miracle—the little white Lagotto is not hurt. Giovanni whips
a leash from his pocket. He can barely slip it over Fagiolo's
head because his hands are quaking so violently. Fagiolo stares
at him. Tail between his legs. Licking his lips. Face ablaze,
Giovanni hates himself for helping with this farce of a festival.

For going against every instinct to stay away. He knew better than to become entangled in the trouble of the giant truffle. And he swears this right here and now—the bridge of his trust toward humanity is broken. Permanently collapsed.

Nothing but rack and ruin.

Giovanni Scarpazza has just become an island.

Shopkeepers and pharmacists and pedestrians stand in the street, some snapping pictures. Poliziotto Silvio is pacing, yelling into his phone. Which means the thief got away.

Giovanni strides away from his wrecked Jeep and from people. It is decided—he is turning his back on the villagers of Lazzarini Boscarino. From the people of Borghese who came to help with the festival. Reporters and drones and deception.

"Giovanni!" Poliziotto Silvio calls.

"Leave me alone," the truffle hunter yells back.

The stunned crowd watches the back of his olive jacket, flashes of his muddy boot soles. The last of his family slinking by his side on four legs, their noses burning with the smell of his devastation.

"Giovanni, come back, please!" Giuseppina yells, tears filling her eyes. "Please, Giovanni, don't leave. Don't leave." Her hands find her cheeks, voice thinning into a whisper. "Don't leave me."

As a truffle hunter who has lost hope in humanity starts a long, lonely walk home, panic and preparations carry on at the medieval castle on a hill. The little bee, unable to penetrate the skins of shriveled apples, flies over the huddle of distressed humans. Away from terrible tendrils of stress writhing into the sky. The bee flies back into the grand hall. There, she homes in on the sweetest potpourri. The great hall smells as though it has snowed sugar in here. Dropping down in flight, five eyes read the shapes of chairs, studio lights, knight's armor. Popcorn and pheromone fumes of the pregnant cat that very recently strutted around this hall, knocking objects off the banquet table. An overturned pot of farro and bean soup, merging with a pond of cold black coffee.

And near that pond is a tipped sugar pot.

Sweet grains spilled in a small mound.

The bee lands. There is mercy in this mess. She will carry a few sweet crystals home for her hive. Sustenance for workers, drones, and their queen, every beloved bee. The Italian honeybee flies home. She follows the sweet smell of belonging, a thing to warm the hive on the most brittle and starless nights. The wind stirs her wings, and all around, life hums vibrantly under a Tuscan sky.

Chapter 10

The village is dressed in night. Stink bugs plink against old lamps spilling honeyed light onto dark corners and cobblestone. Across the valley, somewhere on a hilltop sequined with lights, a dog is barking at his own echo.

Giovanni skulks through the silent streets of his village, a broken heart moving through the night. Shadows shroud the stone walls, each like a fat black leech. Giovanni keeps his eyes on cobblestone and the dull rubber of his truffle-hunting boots. He is counting on this darkness. That every other villager is under the spell of a television show, sipping a *digestivo* by a crackling fire or, better yet, tucked tightly in their beds.

That no one will see what he is about to do.

Aria pads on his right, Fagiolo leashed on his left. The long walk back from the town where the chase ended has tired his young dog, and after today's cataclysm, Giovanni will not let Fagiolo out of his sight.

Giovanni passes Lorenzo and Delizia's split-level house. In

a second-floor window, haloed in light, he sees Delizia pacing. She is animated, one arm conducting an opera. The other pressing a cell phone to her ear.

Giovanni tiptoes past her house, then picks up speed once he is sure he wasn't seen. The horror of the day unspools in his mind. He might never have seen his Fagiolo again. How could he have let this happen? He knew the hysteria the truffle would conjure, that the whole village would be seduced by its dazzling promise. And it has only just begun to incite madness and mayhem. No. The sands of his complicity have run out. And there is only one thing left to be done.

In the here and now, dog nails tick against cold stone. It is otherwise silent enough to hear snails painting in silver.

Giovanni and his dogs pass a red bicycle propped against a wall. Potted plants, charmless and colorless in the night. Strange and unnerving shapes made by the shadows of Stefano's trousers strung up on a clothing line. Giovanni and his dogs approach the stone fountain in the village center, where water gushes from the pouting marble face of a man. In the dark, he looks like a goblin.

Giovanni is about to break a promise, but he no longer cares. He is numb. Besides, secrets slip in a village. Secrets like past prison sentences and extramarital affairs. Secrets like where a key is hidden.

Giovanni remembers it well. The memory swims to him easily—an afternoon on the piazza outside Bar Celebrità. He is sitting at a table with Mayor Benigno. Summer sun sparkling in their drinks. Mayor Benigno clasps a large *porchetta* sandwich, wafts of perfectly roasted pork causing the curly-haired dog at Giovanni's feet to salivate. Frustration molds the old mayor's face into a frown, his white hair gleaming in the afternoon light. Collar of his checkered shirt peeking out from under his bright blue sweater. A stain sits on his right sleeve—olive oil, *porchetta,* who knows? One leg crossed over the other, his shiny leather shoe bounces in agitation. He is sleepless over anticipating yet another unseasonably hot summer and what it will do to his beloved olive trees. They are everything, his olive trees. His passion, his pride. Silvery spray of their leaves, lovely arthritic trunks. A sea of green harvest netting below them to catch thousands of the pleasing green and purple gems. Plastic crates, his lucky work gloves, telescopic wand. These days, he uses an electric tree shaker to free the tiny fruits, but as a young man, he proudly scuttled up a rusty old ladder, wielding his trusty rake. The skin along Mayor Benigno's forearms pebbles into bumps as he thinks about quickly—it must be done quickly—rushing crate loads of those beautiful little fruits to his *frantaio,* the enormous olive press with its imposing great stone wheel. Pressing oil is life's greatest pleasure, he thinks, Campari sparkling in his stomach. He is smiling as he pictures the silky fruit juice—green as antifreeze—anointing a stainless-steel drum. The air blossoming with its bright peppery smell.

But the scorching summers are changing the nature of his oil, and it threatens to drive the mayor to madness. Worry gnaws at him from the inside out. The heat is causing some of his fruit to fall prematurely from the trees. His has always been superior, a nectar of the gods, the greatest olive oil in all of Tuscany. Could last year's batch have succumbed to heat? Or is he imagining a greasier mouthfeel? A little less fruit and a little more fustiness? He will need an impartial person to test last year's nectar; he has no choice. He has to be sure it is not just his own paranoia poisoning his palate.

Mayor Benigno puts down the *porchetta* sandwich to bury his face in his hands, envisioning the upcoming autumnal harvest. Could he bring Giovanni to the bottles for a tasting? He hesitates. He keeps his treasured olive oil hidden. In mildewy darkness. Can he trust the truffle hunter with his lair?

The secret spot where he hides all the delicate matters of his mayoral duties? He hasn't even told his wife Ludovica about where he hides out for such long hours. Mayor Benigno studies Giovanni's eyes—gray as mountain mist—kind, sun-kissed face, tidy white mustache, coppola hat. A man who has spent so much time in a forest, he seems a shadow of his former self. As though he is being slowly swallowed by the understory. And, once again, Mayor Benigno chooses his olive oil over everything else.

"Come, taste my olive oil and tell me, Giovanni." He takes a stress-sip of his Negroni. "But I will need you to swear to tell me the truth. Whether the quality is changed by the heat. And"—he leans in; Giovanni cannot escape the sweet-sour breath fumes snaking into his nostrils—"I will need your promise. You must never tell a soul about where I keep my oil. And once I show you, you must never come back to it. Where I hide my legacy must always remain secret."

In the here and now, shrouded in shadow, Giovanni stands at the bronze-studded doors of the village church. Above, in a small alcove of the great stone edifice, a marble Roman soldier sneers at him with one fist raised.

He thinks about turning back. It's not too late to change his course.

No. This is all his fault, and he has to fix it.

He replays the moment Delizia arrived at Novelli to pick up the truffle and take it to the town hall for her meeting with Sotheby's. Her cell phone ringing. Delizia fishing around for the phone. And an old skeleton key poking out of the purse. A key he'd been shown once before.

Giovanni exhales. Pushes open the church doors.

At this moment, a short walk away from the church, Delizia finishes a phone call with David from Sotheby's, who is thirty-five thousand feet in the air, on his way to Italy. Her mind is whirling with details and to-dos for tomorrow's historic auction, but her stomach is sinking. She has hidden the truffle well, she knows it. Still, she should just go and breathe it in for a moment. One moment with the truffle before everything changes.

"Lorenzo," she calls, "I'll be right back…"

In the church, Giovanni is baptized by a holy perfume. Beeswax of altar candles. Dust and decay. Wood polish on pews. A cloying cough of incense. The smell of sanctity. And another powerful scent.

The giant truffle.

The first flicker of guilt he feels in his heart chambers.

Each step squeaks on marble. He lightens them.

Giovanni and the dogs pad silently past the pews. Saints spy on them from paintings and stained-glass windows. An apostle made of marble, entombed in alabaster robes, stares at Giovanni with a pleading expression. He holds something in his hands under those stone robes.

Secrets abound.

Giovanni suddenly feels quite sick. His heart beats like the wings of a wood pigeon.

Aria whines.

He shushes her with a look.

They are just statues, he tells himself. Paolo would tell him there are spirits watching him, that what he is about to do will cost him his soul.

Well, Paolo isn't here to stop me.

Beautiful Paolo, who believed in a spirit world and some shadow realm Giovanni tried to talk him out of. Wonderful, perfect Paolo, who doesn't get to be here in this moment that he had seemingly spent his every sparkling moment on earth preparing for. Paolo would be warning him, telling Giovanni to stop while he still can, using his astrological inkling and spiritual sensibilities. It doesn't matter that Giovanni never believed in any of it. Because Paolo believed in it. And he believed in Paolo.

The last time his shoes touched the tile of this church was at Paolo's service.

Anger awakes inside Giovanni, rising up onto fiery feet. Aria lifts her black truffle of a nose. Stress is making grasshopper shapes that leap from the truffle hunter's skin. An aggressive perfume, inescapable as a mouthful of moths.

They pass the pews and stand in front of the altar. Electronic candles flickering for eternity. A jeweled chalice. Sacred oils in golden pots. Bottles of wine and holy water. Pacifical and processional crosses. Communion platter. Brass bells.

And above, at the back of the church, Jesus dangles—helplessly, horrifically—from a great cross.

Giovanni swears he hears a whisper. He spins. Fagiolo pivots, licking his lips. Giovanni places a hand on his head to reassure him, then moves his dogs like water toward the back right of the church. Where velvet purple curtains he'd spent a lifetime believing were merely decorative hide a door.

On the floor, a few feet from the base of the curtains, the alms box sits, a big black treasure chest of a thing. Collecting cobwebs in its wait to swallow up donations. It is chained to the wall. But on one side, undetectable to an eye, is a panel. A panel Mayor Benigno showed Giovanni one summer afternoon. A secret unfurling before him like a flower. Tiny springs sit in a push-to-open mechanism. When pushed, the panel pops open into a tray.

Giovanni extends a dirt-mired finger to push.

In that tray lives a skeleton key.

Giovanni genuflects next to the alms box, knees creaking their complaints.

His lips part. Gray eyes widen.

The key is gone.

Does Delizia still have it? Giovanni feels his jaw tighten. Despite a brittle church draft, sweat slips down his brow. Using the box to hoist himself to his feet, he pulls back the velvet curtains. The metal door is open.

He looks back through the empty church. Jesus nailed to the cross. Cold, eternal eyes of the apostles. Judgment in the stares of saints. Angelic bodies of the dogs at his side, he slips into the secret door.

Delizia strides across cobblestone lit by moonlight. The feeling of uneasiness has grown, and she is anxious to be soothed by the truffle's funky pheromones. Ahead, a shadow sits in the middle of the path. As she nears, she makes out the black-and-white body of Al Pacino, pregnant belly splayed on stone as she recovers from a night hunt. Delizia stops to pet her. Al Pacino is patient with a couple of head pets, then starts to swat at her wearily.

Pools of light bleeding across the concrete stairs down into the crypt tell Giovanni that someone has left the light on. Or someone down there has turned the light on. But he already knows his hunch was right. The truffle is calling out to him in thick, gamey gusts. He breathes in the power of it, feels instantly intoxicated. The crypt *is* where Delizia hid the giant truffle. But Delizia isn't down there now because he just saw her in her upstairs window.

So who is it?

Giovanni pads down the first of the steep concrete steps down to the crypt. Bawdy puffs of cheese and semen and socks and wet grass and garlic and musk and madness and despair and dreams hit his nostrils.

Find it. Find the truffle.

Aria lifts to her hind legs. She paws at Giovanni's leg, hard enough to scratch the skin beneath his rainproof trousers. He bends to look into his partner's eyes and sees they are filled with wild delirium. Worry lifting from her every wiry curl prompts him to place a hand to his heart. It is bludgeoning his rib cage.

His heart pills.

He forgot to take them in all the pandemonium of the day.

Staring into Aria's eyes, he can hear the broken washing machine of his old ticker. Pulsing his vision. Aria paws at him.

She pleads.

And then, from down in the crypt, a series of sounds. The chimes of high heels striking concrete. The sounds of a stride across cement.

Someone is down there.

Someone else knows about the key.

Someone else has come for the truffle.

Giovanni looks one last time at the loving desperation pouring from his dog. Catching whoever is down there in the middle of their midnight truffle theft could be dangerous. He nods. Obliging Aria, he gingerly slinks back up the stairs. Back through velvet curtains. Slipping silently through the medieval church and into a night air that slices at the lungs.

It is not long before he realizes he has been followed. It is his anger, still wrapped around his throat. Being back in the church after so many years—those sanctimonious smells, a robe of guilt wrapped around him as a young boy—has brought back feelings of inadequacy. Belittlement by his father. Abandonment by his mother. Shame for being born to love the best person he ever met.

He touches a quivering finger to his chest. Go home. He should, to take his pills. But he doesn't want to go home where there is a vast, Paolo-shaped void. Grief waiting for him at the dining table with pockets full of sorrow and all the time in the world. Giovanni does not want to be at home alone with the crowded cityscape of his own mind.

Fagiolo and Aria are salivating for their beds, but he just can't do it. He turns the dogs away from the steep little street that leads to their front door.

And he heads for the nearest woods.

Delizia shivers as she strides through the dark church. She approaches the alms box. Finds her father's key is missing. She hurries down the stone steps to the crypt.

The truffle is gone.

She can smell it, but it is not behind her father's olive oil bottles where she hid it. Delizia can't get enough air. She sits on the stone floor riding out the panic attack that sinks its fangs into her.

Someone took the truffle. What do I do? What am I going to do?

Giovanni and the dogs move through the cold, mossy air, following an arc of light from his headlamp and his cell phone. In the distance, in all that dark, a deer barks. Giovanni keeps an ear out for rustling. An eye out for the slender bodies of snakes.

He keeps Fagiolo, fatigued into obedience, leashed. The words he frees are for Aria.

"Find it."

Aria does not move from his side. Her back end lowers to the leaf litter in an act of civil disobedience. Giovanni lowers to her, lets her run her damp nose across his chest. She sniffs his face, wet truffle of her nose grazing his cheek. He cups her ears gently.

"I'm alright."

Her sniffing continues, intensifying as she inspects his ears.

"Find it," he insists. He sees she is not satisfied that he is safe, her hazel eyes two copper coins in the light. But he needs this. Hunting truffles will heal him. He gestures to indicate that the request is not up for discussion. Aria reluctantly leaves his side. Her snout snuffles at twigs and needles.

He strides through the forest on a hunt for a fungus. Lungs filling with the crisp, cold air, suspicion sharpens his thoughts. *Who was in the crypt?* Not Delizia, who hid the truffle in there; he saw her through her window. Who else knows about the secret spot? About the skeleton key? High heels striding across cement with confidence—that's the only clue he's got. Ludovica? Did the mayor's wife know? What will they do with the truffle? The monstrous truffle that he had planned to steal back. To put an end to all the madness before it devastates his quiet little village. Giovanni was going to leave it in the forest, an offering. An atonement. A chance for the fungi to forage new relationships in the soil and redeem itself. Thoughts of the media burrowing their noses into private village matters and the farce of tomorrow's festival swarm him like gnats, kicking up his heart rate. The tightness in his arms is bothering him, so he takes off his jacket.

Up ahead, Aria stills. Giovanni angles his headlamp at her.

Aria's body is rigid.

"Find it," he insists.

Aria does not move. His beloved truffle dog is staring out into the vast black mystery of a forest at night. She is somewhere in between standing and a sit, head tilted. One paw is raised. Giovanni feels a chill purr across his skin. He lifts his cell phone and its orb of blue light. Squinting, he can only make out a mass of branches that look like veins. Each branch horrid and desperate, like the twisted fingers of a drowning man. The light of his cell phone lands on Aria. Every brown and white curl of her is motionless. Eyes fused to a mystery Giovanni cannot see in the dark. She has found something. Giovanni feels his calf muscles cramping. His veins hum with adrenaline.

"Aria. Find it."

Aria is off like a shot. Giovanni and Fagiolo follow, using their dome of headlamp light to slip between trees. Branches scratch at Giovanni's arms. Truffle-hunter boots stomp on stones and shrubs.

They catch up with Aria.

She is still. Sitting. Staring into the night as though at a ghost. Giovanni sifts his fingers through the soil around her, panting himself now. His headlamp slips, slick from the sweat of his forehead. Between his thumb and forefinger, he pinches a snail shell. Flinches at the slice of a sharp stone. Paws at a wet mulch of leaf litter.

"Where, Aria? Where is it?"

She does not indicate. Her hazel eyes stare straight ahead. Trained at the darkness. Fagiolo whines, a thin, desperate sound. Giovanni is instantly flooded with regret. Something is out here. Something is wrong. The forest dampness seeps in through his sleeves and settles into his bones.

If there were a boar ahead, Aria would have barked to tell him. A badger. A stag. A wolf. He has trained her to alert him to these animals. But she has dragged him here, and he cannot fathom why.

"Stay," he says; his voice sounds too high, tremulous. Giovanni drops Fagiolo's leash. As he holds the image of his frozen dog in the light of his headlamp, Giovanni trudges over stick and stone, moss and mud. He squints into the blackness ahead, searching for eyes shining back at him. For what has set his dogs on edge. What Aria has found. He runs his cell phone light up several tree trunks. He sweeps the phone from left to right at arm's length. The light illuminates what might be beech, oak, poplar, and all the blackness between them. Illuminates his beautiful, fixated Aria. Brightens over a mass on the forest floor. Giovanni's breath hitches. He trains the light on the mass. His eyes read the pile into legible shapes. Morphing a bundle into pieces he can recognize. Limbs. A leg. Giovanni sweeps his eyes down the pale calf where the foot is held by a red shoe. A women's shoe. Shiny. Blotched with dirt. His eyes backtrack up the calf to a floral material. Thin, summery dress, out of season. A small leather purse lies nearby, pebbled with beads of moisture.

Giovanni cries out. He lunges toward the body on the forest floor.

He drops down beside the woman. Touches his finger against her neck—cold and stiff. Her face is pressed down into the mulch. A fallen leaf is caught in the back of her trademark white bob.

Giovanni's breath spells out one word in a cold cloud.

"Sofia."

Chapter 11

Delizia is crumpled on an ancient crypt floor. A torture—the vanished truffle has left pungent phantoms lingering in the air, invisible as feelings and just as powerful. An alchemy of folksy funk mingling with church smells—myrrh and the mothball smell of a grandmother's fur-filled closet. As Delizia breathes them in, the stolen truffle takes her back in time...

"Delizia, do not panic."

These words instantly spark panic. Words said over twenty years ago by a younger Stefano from the driver's seat. His mane of endangered curls are swiveled around to face Delizia in the back of the car.

"Take a deep breath. Yes, you are late to your own wedding. But I'm here, and I can drive very, very fast. You're going to need to hold on tight."

Stefano is in his wedding-guest attire—leopard-print shirt, medallion, zebra-striped trousers. The limousine driver Delizia hired to chauffeur her to the church has not shown up. So the best driver of Lazzarini Boscarino has.

Stefano Perlini feels born for this moment.

Between a surprise heat wave, the missing limousine driver, and her boa constrictor of a bodice, Delizia can barely breathe. She looks down at meringue waves of a wedding gown cascading all around her and is struck by an epiphany—surely the closest sartorial relative to the wedding dress is the straitjacket.

"Are you ready?" asks Stefano. Their eyes meet in the rearview mirror. His—the eyes of a determined wolf. Hers—the eyes of a cornered *Glis glis*.

His question, it turns out, is rhetorical.

Stefano slams a crocodile-leather loafer onto the gas pedal, an attack worthy of the ferocious reptile each shoe once was. A red Fiat Panda tears across the Italian countryside as if driven by a deranged lunatic. Windows down. Vasco Rossi growling from the radio. A chaos of curls fluttering in the wind. Delizia rolling around the back of her chariot, white-knuckling a grab handle.

A fuzzy golden-green sea of sunflowers and poppies whips by the windows. Blurred blobs are citrus trees. Villas. Glistening pools. For several infuriating minutes, they are held up by a *comune* meeting of sheep in the middle of the road. Sheep and an irate shepherd, who seem undeterred by the adenoidal honking made by a Fiat Panda and a man dressed for camouflage in the Serengeti.

Once the road is clear of ungulates, they race on. Stefano achieves a full channeling of Enzo Ferrari as he screeches to a halt where two large tour buses emblazoned with WALKING TOURS OF TUSCANY are blocking the main entrance to the village of Lazzarini Boscarino. Stefano shakes the purse shape he has made with his fingers and screams at a tour guide handing out bottles of Pellegrino to tourists whose smiles are hidden under sun hats. The tour guide yells back at Stefano, making violent propeller blades out of his arms for emphasis. Stefano gives up and tears up a cobblestone side street as Delizia rolls from one side of the Fiat to the other like a large taffeta tumbleweed.

Moments later, the red Panda is forced to stop for waiters carrying platters of food like ants in formation. Invisible ribbons of Parmesan and *scorzone* summer truffle dance in the air. Young folk have flocked from abroad for the chance to gain work experience in Tuscany, lucky to learn the secrets of life and how to put love on a plate from Nonna Amara and her elderly father Babbo themselves.

Stefano honks at them. "Get out of the way!"

A young waiter screams back, "You get out of the way! We're catering the wedding of the mayor's daughter!"

"*Sei un cretino!* I've got the mayor's daughter *in here*! *Move!*"

The waiters flatten themselves against enchanting age-worn doors.

Stefano mutters, "*Mi hai rotto i coglioni!*"

With an insectile whine, the red Panda races up along a last winding street and jerks to a stop. Zebra-striped legs spring from the Panda to open the door for the bride. Delizia gathers up armfuls of taffeta and tulle, waddling out from the Fiat. She eyes the short walk up a steep cobblestone hill to the church.

And then she hears the thin whistle of a football careening past her head.

"Hey, hey, hey! She needs her head, she's about to brave marriage! Get out of here!" yells Stefano, briefly chasing after a gaggle of laughing schoolboys.

Delizia looks up. She sees ribbons around the church doors in "tied knots." She sees a boisterous crowd of summer tourists spilling out of Bar Celebrità, there to watch the football match. Several pull out digital cameras to capture the young

Italian bride. And then she sees nothing—Stefano has thrown a blanket over her head. Blind, breathless, she is marched up the hill by a man in skinny safari trousers. Delizia teeters in ivory shoes she felt matrimonially obligated to buy. And they have almost reached the church when an age-old battle ensues. In the time-hallowed war between high heel and cobblestone, the cobblestones almost always win.

Delizia yelps. A dull crack. Her ankle rolls to an unnatural angle.

"*Oddio.* Can you make it up the hill?" Stefano removes her head blanket.

She nods and the odd pair hobble-hop the rest of the way up the hill.

Outside, the church has been decorated like something out of a fairy tale. Banquet tables wearing white cloth. A pergola with dogs and cats hand carved into wood has been whittled just for her. Fairy lights and flowers. Delizia tears up at either the loveliness of it all or the terrible throbbing from her ankle. She smiles at silver platters waiting to be anointed with antipasti from Nonna's *ristorante*, closed today to cater her wedding.

Laying four eyes upon Delizia, twins Valentina and Rosa throw their hands in the air in delight. They have been pacing outside the church for twenty-five minutes in matching pink hats.

"Darling, you are so beautiful and so late!" they chime. "Everyone is in the church waiting, sweating like fat fruits in a *limonaia*!"

"Do not panic, darling," says Rosa. "But something has happened to the cake."

The twins are quick to assess what the heat has done to Delizia's hair.

"It has fallen like the Roman Empire!" wails Valentina in a muffled tone, bobby pins pinched between her teeth. Rosa attacks Delizia's hair with a teasing comb. Rosa ambushes her with an aerosol can and a never-ending stream of hair spray.

The twins and Stefano help Delizia to the doors of the church. She searches. Her heart sinks. But it had already known, hadn't it?

"Where is he?" asks Delizia on her wedding day, moments before she walks the aisle. "Where *is* he?"

Valentina and Rosa shake their heads. Stefano holds up a finger and then slips into the church. He returns with Ludovica in a long black dress she made. She has trouble making eye contact with the bride.

"Where is he, Ludovica?"

The bent wires of Ludovica's fingers are quivering, but her words are confident, almost cruel. "Your father thought it would be better if he didn't walk you down the aisle. He says he is fine sitting with me in the church and he would prefer not to sit next to your mother."

Delizia bites her inner cheek. She will not let her lower lip tremble. "Maybe you could share him today?"

Ludovica blows a stream of imaginary smoke. "It's not my choice. He won't listen. I don't control what he does or who he loves any more than I control who you love."

Delizia hobbles away from the church doors. The twins and Stefano try to follow her. She assures them she just needs a moment. Visitors from Stefano's guesthouse wave at the beautiful bride as they walk by, fingers filled with pastries from Babbo's bustling Pasticceria and Café Felice. Self-pitying tourists stave off disappointment with an afternoon *passeggiata*, having discovered that Nonna's *ristorante*, Il Nido, is closed for the day. A line of German hikers descends the distant hills like a colorful caterpillar.

Under the shade of a hand-carved pergola, Delizia wipes away a tear while staring at the Apennines. She cannot wait to get away from this village, her father's village. She cannot wait to start her new life and a veterinary career in Pisa, a place where no one knows her. Where she can prove herself away from the pain of the past.

Warm fingers gently pinch her elbow. "*Bellissima* Delizia. What's wrong?"

Sofia. Whitening bob bright in the sun. A floral dress. Delizia tries to respond, but if she does, she will cry off the makeup her mother spent all morning on. She wants to say that everything is going wrong. Her father. Her ankle. Something about the cake. This village rejects her, bruises her heart again and again. It has never let her belong.

Delizia manages, "I wish the wedding were somewhere else."

Sofia hands her a tissue. The farmer's wife looks out at stone farmhouses stitched into a green quilt of hills. "Mayor Benigno does not deserve such a lovely daughter. You must put him out of your mind. Everyone in Lazzarini Boscarino loves you. We are proud of our Delizia, who is about to marry the most wonderful man."

Delizia smiles at the thought of Lorenzo. Love foams through her, lemon bright.

Sofia hands her another tissue. "I know you want to run away from this village, and you will. Your life is just starting. Everything ahead of you. The whole world just waiting." Sofia loses herself in the middle distance. Suppressed dreams dance behind her eyes. "But today, be here in your village. Enjoy the moments. Take in how much everyone loves you, because the moments fly fast and will be gone before you know it. Now, what do you think? Shall we get you to Lorenzo?"

Sofia gives Delizia a fierce hug, arms slim and soft as the necks of swans.

"*Andiamo.* Deep breath. Remember—moments. I even brought a little surprise for the celebrations. You'll see."

"Thank you. But I have another problem."

"What is it, darling?"

"I have no one to walk me down the aisle. And I don't think I can walk."

Delizia tugs at the white waterfall of her dress to reveal an ankle purpling and swollen as a turnip. Sofia holds up a finger and sprints to the church.

Moments later, Delizia is propped up at the back of the church. Delizia smiles at Giovanni on her left, scrubbed of the woods and in a smart charcoal lounge jacket.

"I saw the pergola you made me," Delizia tells the village builder and impassioned truffle hunter. "I love it."

Giovanni smiles. "I'm so glad. Cats and dogs carved for our future vet."

Paolo, on her right and resplendent in a plum suit, leans in. "He's been working on it for months. Smells permanently like a pile of wood. I'll be glad to have him back!"

"Ssssssshhhhh!" hisses elderly Padre Salvestro from the other end of the church.

"Sssssshhh yourself, Padre!" comes the voice of a very pregnant and overheated Giuseppina from the pews.

Ecclesiastical silence settles again.

"You shaved your mustache!" Delizia whispers to Paolo.

"Giovanni made me. And I didn't want to upstage the bride."

They laugh, which elicits a frown from the perennially frowny Padre Salvestro at the end of the aisle.

"Oh, Padre Salvestro is going to hate this," whispers Delizia.

"*It's not traditional!*" Paolo perfectly mimics the old priest's sanctimonious tone. Paolo's dark eyes are sparkling, his beautiful black curls combed, winking under the church lights. He squeezes Delizia's hand and somehow dissolves her despair. "You say when you are ready, *bella.*"

Delizia braves a look at the pews. They are packed. All the villagers have shown up for her. Babies bouncing on hips. Children squiggling and squawking. Giuseppina blows her a kiss. Duccio manages a half smile. Benedetto and his wife, Bianca, beaming. Carlotta and Gabriele. Her father-in-law, Niccolo Micucci. And somewhere near...

No. She will not look at her father. She is exhausted with the hunt for a key to unlock him. She will focus forward, to the end of the aisle. Brother and best man, Umberto, is ruffling the groom's hair. Squeezing his shoulders. And there is Lorenzo, dashing in his dark blue suit. He is the home she thought she'd never have. One look at those smiling eyes and she feels the delicious swell of her heart. Her future lies before her, an illegible forest. But she found gold in this village. She and Lorenzo will build a beautiful life away from here, and one day, she will come back and show them that she is a success.

Delizia squeezes Paolo's hand and nods. Paolo, known in these parts as "*maestro*," lifts a hand to his musicians waiting breathlessly to begin.

The sweltering silence is broken by the Lazzarini Boscarino Quartet as they honor Pachelbel in silken notes, the horsehair of their bows soothing violin strings. With pride and devotion, Giovanni and Paolo carry Delizia down the aisle. Warm waves of aftershave as they kiss her cheeks. Paolo smiling at stuffy old Padre Salvestro. And with the priest's wooden words and a spearmint kiss, Delizia becomes a Micucci.

Moments from after the ceremony come back to Delizia like swifts arrowing across a summer sky. Rice raining down over them as Lorenzo carries her (and her turnip of an ankle) through the church doors to a cheering crowd.

"*Viva gli sposi!*" "*Per cent'anni!*"

Leon and Sofia standing next to the surprise they brought—a baby donkey. Delizia watched him being born, her earliest foaling experience. A quilt over baby Maurizio's back, stitched by Sofia over many months with the words *"Auguri, Delizia e Lorenzo!"* Giuseppina dancing with a ring of children. Umberto fussing lovingly over the bump that will become Elisabetta, urging Giuseppina to sit down and—*porco mondo!*—drink some water. Bringing her three slices of cake and then interrogating her about bizarre ingredients and the dreams he has for an upscale *ristorante*. Howling laughter. Sofia strangling the neck of a bottle of prosecco, clambering onto tabletops to dance regardless of her distinct lack of underwear—a shock that nearly ends Padre Salvestro. The masterpiece *millefoglie* cake made by Nonna Amara. Gasps at a cat-shaped dent in the cake, a trail of icing paw prints further evidence of the crime. Paolo slow dancing with Nonna Amara, a thing as sweet as the sugared-almond *bomboniere* wedding favors. Everyone dancing the tarantella—named for its lively steps that mimic a man being bitten by a poisonous spider—in honor of the Southern Italian relatives present. Stefano and Benedetto instigating a comical kicking competition, thin legs jutting out like chorus girls. A wedding night filled with music and laughter under whispers of bat wings and a spectacle of stars.

Delizia takes a break from limp-dancing and sits under her pergola. She commits moments to her mind in a memory palace, diaphanous as sea-foam and smoke. They will be called back at times in her life by scent—a whiff of spearmint, freshly carved wood, the skunk of a summer truffle. Sofia was right. Moments fly fast, gone before you know it. Moments that gather more meaning with reflection and time. One day, buildings and time-old traditions and loved ones will be gone. But moments tucked into a mind and held by the heart live on in a human.

Tiny tucked-away treasures.

Soon, the wonderful wedding will be over. Delizia will leave

Lazzarini Boscarino for a fresh city and start. Winds of change will carve the fate of the little village.

Time will pass.

Time as ephemeral as a truffle.

Delizia comes back to the cold crypt floor.

Someone took the key, Delizia remembers, paralyzed with despair.

The truffle is gone.

She staggers up the stone steps of the crypt. Through the church. Mayor Delizia stands under a velvet sky in the village of her birth feeling alone and utterly lost.

Her eyes are drawn to strobing red and blue lights blinking up the road to the village. *Carabinieri* cars streaming like sharks in shadow.

Delizia hurries to her car, wondering if the *carabinieri* found the truffle thief. Wondering how they already knew it was missing. She winds down the road leading to Lazzarini Boscarino— the road she and Stefano once raced along on her wedding day, a road she could drive with her eyes closed. Trees at the edge of the woods are haunted by red and blue, red and blue. She pulls over behind three *carabinieri* cars.

Delizia steps toward Giovanni, her chest a clenched fist.

The truffle hunter's sorrowful face fills her with deep dread.

Giovanni envelops her in a hug, smelling of freshly dug soil.

Chapter 12

Leon's farm sits in the Tuscan hills just outside the village of Lazzarini Boscarino, a tawny tapestry of wheat fields rolling from the horizon. The foothills have settled into the quiet sepia colors of an old photograph. Chestnuts, mushrooms, and grapes ripen wordlessly all around. Birdsong visible in the air. The old farmer drags rough fingers down the length of his great white beard. He speaks the language of this land. Morning mist lifting from the backs of his horses is subtle poetry. Cypress trees flank his house, propped-up quills awaiting an artist. Chickens confetti the garden, while three Jack Russell terriers digest breakfast on the paved courtyard. All is quiet save the gentle grunting of pigs in their pen, the clanging of goat bells, and the song a creek sings, mountain spring water purring over stone. Leon casts his eyes to Luna, his great white Maremma sheepdog, lying by the fence. She is guardian of his sheep, born to keep vigilant watch for wolves.

We all have our place on this farm, he thinks.

Just not Sofia.

The thought is a knife stuck into the meat of his heart.

Leon sits on the old stone water trough watching his almost-twenty-two-year-old donkey, Maurizio, disappearing beads of morning dew and blades of grass behind velvet lips. A cup of espresso dwarfed by Leon's calloused hands, clinging to the ritual of his coffee and this peace, the last before it all starts. His last few moments of morning freedom. The medicine of the mountain air. All around him, Tuscan hills pose with heartbreakingly beautiful indifference. The folly of man does not concern them. They have all the time in the world.

Leon does not.

The terriers break into barking. Shaggy Luna is on all four paws, staring out beyond the fence. Her ears pricked. Voices lunge up the driveway at them. And a car is approaching.

And so it begins. Leon takes a deep breath. Places his espresso cup on the lip of the water trough. He walks to Maurizio. The donkey lifts his head and presses it to his human's chest in greeting. Leon breathes in the salve of his sawdust smell.

A *carabinieri* car, in its telltale raucous blue, seesaws up the rough driveway. A slam of the driver door. A solemn-faced Poliziotto Silvio steps out, looks over at Leon, and raises one hand in greeting.

Farmer Leon nods.

He booms out a command to silence his terriers. Calls out to Luna to stand down.

Poliziotto Silvio opens the trunk of his blue *carabinieri* car. He pulls out a large piece of equipment. It takes some wrestling to wrangle the wheelchair into a functional shape. Benedetto emerges from the back seat of the car to help the policeman settle Stefano into his wheelchair. Stefano looks up at the farm and its bucolic fields without recognition. He is sporting an exciting pair of mustard-yellow trousers and a plaid coppola hat. Chickens scatter at the sight of Poliziotto Silvio wheeling Stefano over the uneven terrain, or perhaps because of the mustard trousers. Benedetto follows the wheelchair carrying flowers and a large casserole.

Leon waves them into the farmhouse.

He sighs, boots tracking mud into his *cucina*. Only *his* now. Huge hands trembling, he attempts to disappear into making a pot of coffee. Nonna Amara has insisted that all the villagers descend upon Leon at his farmhouse. A gathering of support before he sorts out the details of her funeral. But he is a man built for pulling a plow with a tractor, for pushing large-boned livestock and hauling grain bins. He is not equipped to wade through the waters of grief. To herd human emotion.

Valentina and Rosa burst through the front door with baskets of fruit, flowers, and wine.

"Leon"—the twins cling to him, dwarfed like dolls—"we are here for you, anything you need."

Leon nods. The twins share a look. He seems like himself, good old bear-big Leon. Stoic as the old stone of his farmhouse. But they both spy the red map of blood vessels in each eye. The tremor rattling his hands.

Carlotta enters the farmhouse with a tray of olives, meats, and artichokes. Carlotta kisses her grandson Silvio on each cheek, then stands near the old stone sink holding Leon's hands in her own, staring into his eyes. She says nothing. Leon, a man who cannot stomach attention, starts to sweat. Over the warm caramel wafts of brewing coffee, he smells his own body odor mingling with a loud smell of lilies. He can barely breathe over all the things that aren't being said.

Everyone is in his house, slipping on the sadness. Awkwardness saddled to their backs.

What to say in the face of a tragedy? Tongues are tied, everyone tiptoeing on eggshells.

Sofia. They are silent about the cause of her death, judgment simmering under the surface of every skin. Some even feel complicit. No one can help catching glimpses of where Sofia lingers in the farmhouse—in the felt hand-stitched hearts that hang on every doorknob, made with her fingers when they were steady. Bright pops of color in her oil paintings of sunflowers and the Cinque Terre, fashion magazines—*Grazia, Vogue Italia, IO Donna.* And there is something else swimming under the grief and shock and the guilt of every villager who thought that either foul play or Leon was involved. An insatiable ache. A tortuous white-hot burning desperation to talk about what else happened last night.

About what happened to the truffle.

But this is not the time nor the place. It would seem that something has managed to overshadow the largest truffle in the world.

Tragedy.

"We'll pour the coffee," chime the twins to shatter the silence. They gesture to the kitchen table with its mountains of lilies and chrysanthemums, each bouquet made of even numbers in the mourning tradition. "You sit."

"I can't," says Leon, opening up his fridge to slot the casserole in among farm-fresh eggs.

Nonna Amara arrives soon after with her granddaughter Vittoria, and everyone stands. She hands off fresh focaccia, and then Nonna makes the rounds in a sequined black cardigan and skirt, kissing cheeks, embracing her beloveds. She is holding the village together with her heart, loving everyone out loud. Vittoria, wearing a jacket and a pout, slinks out of the kitchen and down the hallway. Head hung low, she disappears into shadow.

Giovanni and his Lagotti are next to bluster through the front door. He nods excessively at Leon for lack of knowing what to do. The truffle hunter spends several minutes prodding the hazelnut chocolates and cheese platter he carried here among a field of flowers on the kitchen table, all while thwarting Fagiolo's multiple attempts at grand theft pecorino.

To Giovanni, the *cucina* seems muggy, clogged with a thick and unbearable sadness. Too many bodies and not enough words. He looks up to find a twin on either side of him. Valentina bends to a cheese plate and whispers, "Giovanni, you found her. Are you alright?"

He nods. He is ambushed by an image of Sofia's red shoe, a moonlit sweep of calf. The single leaf in her white hair.

Rosa continues, "I don't know how Leon is staying so strong. She was sick of being a farmer's wife, cheating on him with a man from Borghese, and then she disappears and all the suspicion falls on Leon. It's enough to drive a man mad."

"Sshhh, keep your voice down, and don't drag that up now, Rosa," says Valentina. "*Of the dead, speak well.*"

"I'm just telling the truth—someone has to speak it! Someone has to say *something*!"

On Giovanni's right, Rosa lifts a bottle of Chianti to examine it—a ruse. "Something else happened last night, Giovanni."

The twins lean in, each close to one of his ears. They whisper in unison.

"The giant truffle was stolen."

Giovanni feigns horror. It was an outcome he suspected, having been down in the crypt at the same time as the mystery thief. Every hair on his arms lifts.

Giovanni waits for Nonna to reach up and squeeze his shoulder then shuffle past to ask, "Do you have any idea who took it? Or why?"

The twins shake their heads.

"Everyone is a suspect in my book," says Rosa, fluffing chrysanthemums.

"Rosa, don't be paranoid. We all know it was Duccio."

They fall silent as Leon places another pot of coffee on the crowded kitchen table. He lowers his gaze to avoid eye contact with his crush of visitors. As he lumbers back to the *cucina* sink, Benedetto appears at Giovanni's side, bending to pet Fagiolo and whisper in Giovanni's ear.

"It's all over, Giovanni. The auction is off—someone took the truffle last night. Stole it from its secret hiding place. Lorenzo called me early this morning to ask if I had any idea who might have taken it. Can you believe it?"

"I—"

"Such a terrible shame for us—my grandson told me that peculiar things can sell for a mint at auction. John Lennon's molar, Churchill's dentures, Elvis's hair, Queen Victoria's underwear all sold for spectacular sums, he tells me. Someone bid $1,209 on a potato chip shaped like the pope's hat!"

Carlotta pops up from behind Giovanni and adds her voice to the whispering. "This is not the time to be talking about the truffle. We must respect our dearly departed Sofia." She pauses to close her eyes and exhale. "But did I hear you say the auction is canceled? Giovanni, what will happen? Borghese is teeming with reporters who flew in from all over the world last night; every Borghese hotel is fully booked. They are all heading to the village for the auction this afternoon!"

Before Giovanni has a chance to answer, the front farm-house door whacks open to reveal a voluptuous woman dressed all in black.

"Leon!" is all she manages to blurt out before dissolving into tears.

"Pina, dear, Pina." Nonna embraces the blonde bartender. Benedetto pours her an espresso with a shaky hand.

The arrival of Ugo and Tommaso is announced by the stomping of boots. Both men are decked in camouflage and are immediately embarrassed by the flagrant display of emotion as well as their last-minute choice of salami and *biroldo* blood sausage as a bereavement gift.

Poliziotto Silvio drains his espresso cup, looks around the *cucina*. "Where is Padre Francesco?"

"Told me he couldn't make it this morning," answers Carlotta. "Says he had a baptism to perform."

"A *baptism*?" Poliziotto Silvio frowns. "For what baby?"

Duccio is next to walk into the *cucina*, wearing a long woolen coat and a suspicious scowl. He awkwardly approaches Leon, who is still holding a rather hysterical Giuseppina, wailing unintelligible words. Duccio holds up a plaster figurine of a donkey. "Once Sofia said she liked this figurine, so I thought she could have it. You know, when they do the funeral, it could go with her. In her coffin or maybe, maybe not, you know, it could go outside on the grave." He blushes.

Leon nods and gestures to the bounty on the table. Duccio places the plaster donkey among a mountain of lilies.

Giovanni slinks to a corner of the *cucina*, creating the greatest distance he can between himself and hunters Ugo and Tommaso. Nonna Amara appears at his elbow, leaning into his side. Giovanni braces himself to be whispered at once more.

"Giovanni," Nonna says in her scolding voice. "You are glowering at Ugo. Knock it off."

"What if it was Ugo who tried to steal Fagiolo?"

"Giovanni Scarpazza, don't be absurd."

"He wasn't at the castle yesterday, and he's a jealous buffoon—"

"Keep your voice down. This morning is about Sofia. And all of us being here for Leon."

They both look over at the big, bearded farmer, who has

opened a cupboard beneath the sink. He drops coffee grounds in a small trash can labeled *organico*. He pauses. Then he reaches a burly arm behind the trash and starts pulling out mostly empty booze bottles from their various hiding places.

Nonna watches Leon pouring out the remaining drops from hidden bottles of alcohol into the stone sink. Her eyes shimmer with tears. "We knew and we didn't know. And we love her no less." She sniffs. "We let her slip away from us, Giovanni."

"Oh, Nonna, we did try to help her; she no longer wanted to be around us. We feel it could have been different if we'd just been there, and I was—I was so close, Nonna, but this was building for many years—"

"We let her slip away from the village. If we had held on to her tighter, she wouldn't have died alone. In our village, we take care of one another, and that is how we survive. With love."

"Even if she'd been here in the village, we could not have saved her."

"But we could have held her hand. We should have walked her through the woods."

Giovanni puts his hand on Nonna's arm. "Sofia was very jaundiced when I found her. Silvio seems to be quite sure that her liver gave out, but we will get the whole story soon enough. Poor Leon. He has been losing her for a long time."

Nonna hijacks the train of conversation and changes its route deftly. "I want you to talk to *Farfallina*. She has a secret that she's hiding from me. And she needs someone to talk to if she doesn't want it to be her *nonna*. I'm not letting another of my beloveds slip away from me. And stop fixating on Ugo. Today is not the day." Nonna squeezes her eyes shut in a long, hard blink.

"Nonna, you're tired..." says Giovanni.

"I'm fine, don't you fuss. Ugo woke me up in the middle of the night with his Vespa."

"Ugo has a Vespa?"

"Rides the thing somewhere most nights."

"It's not painted in the colors of the Italian flag..."

"*Sì*, gaudy-looking thing."

Giovanni wrinkles his nose in disgust. Each of his ears seems to set on fire. It was *Ugo* who nearly drove him off the road just before he found the giant truffle in the woods.

Nonna raises her eyebrows in warning. "Leave Ugo alone. I wasn't sleeping anyway. Too much excitement in our little village. Now, have something to eat and go talk some sense into our *Farfallina*." She pats his arm gently.

Nonna wanders off to chase grief away from the *cucina* table.

Giovanni snorts, his fury at Ugo coursing through him. He storms out a back door of the *cucina*, ushering his dogs outside to relieve themselves.

He accuses me of being a traitor to the village. Almost kills me by running me off the road. Maybe Ugo stole my Jeep?

Of course, Ugo stole the truffle. He doesn't want his village to become famous for a truffle found in an act he doesn't deem worthy of the title "hunting."

He is so infuriated that an old Italian insult he hadn't heard uttered in an age flies from his mouth.

"Fuck your dead relatives and your grandfather's, and your mother's, and those of three-quarters of your apartment block!"

"Charming!" Carlotta pokes her head out the back door. "Come back to the *cucina*, Lorenzo has brought pastries and Delizia is here!"

She lowers her voice to, Giovanni notes, yet another dreaded whisper. "Giovanni, you have to ask her about what's going to happen. Obviously, she's canceled the auction...but we haven't heard anything official! Everyone stayed up so late setting up the castle—Delizia must be going insane!"

"*I* have to ask her?" asks Giovanni.

"We've all been whispering in the *cucina* and have secretly elected you!"

Giovanni rolls his eyes as they make their way back to the *cucina*.

Giuseppina is slumped at the *cucina* table, nursing an espresso. Delizia and Nonna are huddled together, voices low. A surprisingly large coffee stain festoons the sweater the mayor was wearing yesterday, and there is toilet paper stuck to her shoe, but no one dares mention it. Her husband, Lorenzo, is plating a mountain of pastries when he is startled by a donkey at the kitchen window. Leon, face brightening, opens the top of the stable door that leads out to the pergola where his grapes grow, allowing Maurizio to hang his head in the *cucina*. The donkey receives a hero's welcome.

"Maurizio!" chime the villagers.

Delizia approaches the old ungulate, feeding him an apple from the table.

"He never forgets a friend," says Leon. The sentiment sets Giuseppina off, causing her to wail again. Lorenzo ushers Giuseppina to the bathroom.

"Everyone leaves me, Lorenzo," Giuseppina cries.

"Sofia didn't leave you, Pina. This is not your fault," Lorenzo assures her while shooting a sad glance back at Nonna Amara.

Giuseppina is halfway down the hallway when she yells back, "Everyone leaves me. There is a curse on our village!"

"Pina, there is no such thing as a curse," Lorenzo pleads.

"If any of you are in trouble, any kind of peril, you come and see me, okay? You are all forbidden to die, do you hear me? Delizia, make it a law!" is all Giuseppina manages to convey before the bathroom door cuts her off.

Delizia smooths her hand down Maurizio's forehead and turns her attention to Leon. They both look haggard. The new mayor feels her stomach drop with guilt. She let suspicion in over Sofia's disappearance, even though she knows Leon is a good soul. How easy to get swept away with suspicion. To allow hysteria to deafen one's instincts.

Giuseppina returns from the bathroom with a toilet roll and raccoon eyes.

It is at this moment, in the *cucina* of the old farmhouse on the hill just outside of Lazzarini Boscarino, while the villagers gather to bolster Leon after his wife was found dead in the woods, that Stefano—his thoughts wispy and frayed as the mist around a mountain—speaks up from his wheelchair.

"Leon?" he asks. "Where is Sofia?"

A collective gasp. The *cucina* tightens.

All eyes on Leon.

Leon exhales. As he does, some hybrid of a guffaw and a hiccup escapes him. *Finally*, he thinks. Normalcy. Life, messy and ungainly and real as the dirt, grit, and guts of a farm. He can breathe the air of his close *cucina* again. Everyone in the room has been so afraid to say the wrong thing, they've said nothing at all. The silence was suffocating him. Leon doesn't want to be treated like an ornament. He wants the mess and mud of everyday life. With grief there are no perfect words waiting to be plucked from the sky, just a sea of sad feelings, everyone bobbing in the same boat.

Leon puts a hand on Stefano's shoulder. "She died, Stefano. She went into the woods, and she didn't come back. Giovanni and Aria found her, and I am grateful."

Stefano, free from any social filter, asks, "Was she drinking?"

The villagers are breathless. Carlotta tries to silence Stefano with a charade of threatening gestures. Stefano is oblivious. At times, his forgetfulness causes him to conjure creative fabrications and fictions. But sometimes, he simply releases a river of truth.

"Yes," answers Leon. "She was. I didn't know how to stop her."

Stefano nods. "She always did drink too much. But we loved her."

Leon grunts. Nods.

"I think we should have a gathering for her."

"That's what this is, Stefano," says Nonna gently.

"Well, then," he says. "Let's toast to Sofia. Our friend who lost her way. And to all of us and our beautiful village. May we eat well. Drink well. And enjoy every minute of life. It is, after all, the Italian way." Stefano's face contorts with confusion as he finds his hand to be without a cup he is quite sure was just there. Benedetto hands him a cup of coffee to toast with.

Tears tumble down Leon's cheek. Truth is a bird set free. He can finally start to grieve. Giuseppina wails like an ambulance hurtling through the historic center of Rome.

Leon's fellow villagers close in on him. Hands and heartbeats all around.

Stefano casts a dubious glance at the villagers clinging to the old farmer before adding, "Now. When are we going to talk about what happened to the truffle?"

Carlotta chides him. "Stefano, now is not the—"

Leon's deep baritone interjects. "I would very much like to talk about the truffle. Delizia, what is happening?"

Delizia seems to suddenly age a hundred years. She glances down and notices the long ribbon of toilet paper on her shoe. It does not factor high enough on her worry list to deal with and, with the way things have been going, seems to be one of few things that make sense. "Last night, someone stole the truffle from its hiding place near the church."

Giovanni finds it interesting that she doesn't specify that it was hidden in the crypt.

"No!" yells Giuseppina, having not heard the news.

"We all put so much effort into the festival!" shouts Tommaso, reliving a long night of glue and brown paint and papier-mâché.

"I helped Borghese waiters clean a stag head mount with cotton swabs!" bemoans Benedetto. "And we put all our hopes into the auction!"

Delizia steals the espresso from Stefano's hand and downs it. "We are still going to hold the auction."

A shocked silence.

"How can we hold an auction if there is no truffle?" asks Valentina.

Duccio lets out a cruel cackle. "Are you going to try and pawn off Tommaso as the real thing?"

Tommaso lobs a Nutella *bombolone* at Duccio and hits him squarely in the head.

Delizia does not have the energy to deal with them. "I've spent all night trying to figure out what to do next, and who might have done something so devastating to us—to every one of us who calls this village home. Borghese *carabinieri* are busy searching for the truffle thief. They may find the culprit in time for the auction, but if not, I have decided on an alternative answer." A sniff. "We will sell it as an NFT."

Pairs of eyes pinball around the room. Searching for a clue of any kind.

"A what?" asks Rosa.

"What did she say?" Nonna Amara asks.

"Speak up!" Carlotta yells.

"Delizia has lost her marbles," says Stefano unironically.

Delizia digs her fingernails into her palms. "An NFT. A non-fungible token."

"Is that another type of fungus?" asks Benedetto.

Lorenzo laughs.

Delizia fries him with a glare. "An NFT is an asset that has been tokenized by a blockchain."

The villagers stare at Delizia and now indeed wonder if she has lost her marbles. She is not even speaking Italian anymore.

The mayor continues, "The real truffle is gone, but I took many professional photographs of it, which means it can still be sold as a digital piece of art and a collectible. I don't expect you to understand fully, but just to trust that this means we are going to hold the auction as we intended."

"What?" screams Ugo. "Ludicrous!"

"*Va bene!*" yells Tommaso, triumphant that his truffle costume will have its day.

"And in the meantime, I've called Borghese Tartufi, who will bring some real truffles to sell," says Delizia.

"No! Delizia, they are monsters!" Giovanni's face reddens.

"They have what we need, and they're excited to be part of the auction, which is more than can be said for you. Now, I need your help, Giovanni. You and Aria will help me track down the missing truffle."

"No, Delizia, she's trained to find a truffle in the ground; the stolen truffle could be anywhere—"

"Then find me another enormous truffle!"

"How! There is no other truffle on earth like that one!"

Everyone falls into quiet contemplation. Delizia takes advantage of their stunned silence. She puts down the contraband coffee cup and picks up her purse. "I have to leave—Leon, I am so sorry—but I wanted to let everyone know the auction will proceed. I am meeting with Sotheby's; they've landed and are on their way—"

"Do they know there is no truffle?" asks Lorenzo, who appears as stunned as everyone else.

Delizia's face darkens. A vein dances some sort of excitable jig across her temple. Her left eyelid quivers.

No one dares utter a word. Delizia moves toward the door.

"Wait! What about all the articles about us?" Duccio lunges across the *cucina* and flaps a newspaper at her. "Look at this, in a national newspaper no less!" He throws down a Tuscan newspaper that has featured an article about "the colorful characters of Lazzarini Boscarino, a village of old-age truffle snufflers." "It mines our lives for sensation! For entertainment! I am mentioned, Padre's excommunication from the church in Rome has come up again, and it even says that Carlotta was a nun and a prostitute!"

All eyes on Carlotta, blinking slowly as she takes a bite of *bombolone*.

"You were a nun?" Benedetto asks Carlotta, incredulous.

"It's an abomination! This is private information!" roars Duccio. "How are they even digging up this dirt?"

"A reporter asked me," says Carlotta, twirling the pearls around her throat. "And I told him the truth. You should try it for once in your life."

"Just admit it, Duccio, you stole the truffle!" Giuseppina yells. "You hate truffles! Now, where is it!"

"The truffle isn't even here and it's still making everyone hysterical!"

"Do not use that word around me ever again," warns Mayor Delizia.

"What did you do with it, Duccio?" yells Giuseppina, now on her feet.

"Don't yell at me!"

"Come clean and tell us what you did with it!"

Duccio grunts in frustration and storms out the stable door toward the pergola and a hunt for peace. A sharp slice of cold air replaces him in the *cucina*.

"Just wait until the Sotheby's snobs find they've flown all this way for a photograph!" laughs Ugo.

Something inside Delizia—perhaps the last threadbare twig of her resolve—snaps. "*Basta!* I am sick to death of your incessant bickering!"

Ugo's tone is baiting. "Maybe if you'd have hidden it better—"

"You know what I don't need? Another moron of a man calling me a failure!" The silence after Delizia's yell rings in ears. "All of you, pull yourselves together. There is still time to apprehend the truffle thief. We have"—she wrenches her cell phone from her purse—"five hours. And if it was any one of you that stole the giant truffle, so help me God, you're going to want to make this right."

Tommaso stealthily adds a splash of sambuca to his cup. He waits until Delizia is almost at the front door and out of earshot. "It's a good job Padre Francesco isn't around to hear her taking the Lord's name like that."

"He really hates that," Ugo laughs and does an impression of Padre Francesco crossing himself. "It's quiet without him clacking around the place. *Clack. Clack. Clack.*"

Goose bumps pebble across Giovanni's arms.

"What did you say?" he asks Ugo.

"Just saying that I'm enjoying how quiet it is without Padre's shoes around. *Clack. Clack. Clack.* Louder than Giuseppina's stilettos."

Clack-clack. Clack-clack. Giovanni's skin tingles. The sound grabs him by the shoulders. It swings him back to last night.

Night pouring over the village like cold coffee.

An unmistakable chime of heels striking the stone floor of the crypt.

He had thought they were the high heels of a woman when he had slunk back through the church, abandoning his plan to steal back the truffle.

Giovanni knows it as well as he knows his own dogs—the owner of those shoes is the truffle thief.

"Delizia!" bellows Giovanni.

"*Mamma mia*, what next?" Benedetto wipes his face with the paper towel he had just used to enjoy a *bombolone*, rouging his cheeks with hazelnut spread.

Giovanni raises his hands. "I know who took the truffle!"

Gasps. Maurizio lets out a well-timed bray.

Delizia turns from the door to face the truffle hunter. Her eyes burning with intensity. "Who, Giovanni?"

"It was Padre Francesco. I heard his shoes down in the crypt last night."

"You were in the crypt last night? Why?"

Giovanni lets out a long exhale. "I was going to take that truffle back to the woods. Because I was afraid of what would happen if the world saw it. Especially what would happen to our village. Like, for example, someone attempting to steal my dog."

Cries of "Giovanni," "How could you?" and "Pass the sambuca" arc around the room.

"I'm sorry, I thought I was doing the right thing. But someone was already in the crypt, and I heard the *clack clack* of their shoes, and that's who must have taken the truffle."

"Where is he now?" Delizia's tone is taut, a wire about to snap.

"He told me he had to perform a baptism," says Carlotta.

"On whose baby?" asks Giuseppina.

"All our babies are grown up," adds Stefano.

"*Oddio*," says Delizia. "It couldn't be . . . Giovanni, what happens to a truffle if it gets . . . baptized?"

Giovanni's face turns as white as his mustache. "The truffle cannot get wet. Any water—holy or otherwise—will destroy it."

Maurizio lets out a disapproving snort.

"To the church!" Delizia pivots toward the farmhouse door.

Everyone is on their feet, except for, of course, Stefano, and Benedetto, who has to sit down due to a bout of vertigo.

Nonna Amara's voice cuts through the excitable murmuring. "Wait a minute! Wait! This is a gathering for Sofia." One hand is clutching the Saint Christopher around her neck, the other, her heart. "We are not leaving Leon in his time of need."

All eyes on farmer Leon. He is hastily donning his jacket and boots.

"Oh, er, thank you, everyone for honoring Sofia. But right now...I...it's...we have to save that truffle." Leon cannot wait to bolt out the door.

Delizia allows a moment to pass. Then says, "To the church! Save the truffle!"

Pattering feet signify a mass exodus of feverish villagers from the farmer's house.

Chapter 13

The villagers and the truffle dogs pile into Delizia's Land
Rover, Poliziotto Silvio's *carabinieri* car, and Giuseppina's
Cinquecento. They tear down Leon's driveway back toward the
village. Vehicles jerk to a halt outside the church. Car doors
clapping. Breathy panting from the dogs. The Lazzarini Boscarino villagers race into the old church.

"Look! There!" yells Lorenzo.

Padre Francesco is standing at the altar. He is wearing his
white-and-gold vestments. A surplice of liturgical lace. Flames
flicker atop golden candlesticks. In his hands, like an ancient
globe, is the great white truffle.

The rest of the villagers pour into the church—even Duccio, who had been sulking on the piazza and heard the village
cars screeching to a stop. They all take in the scene at the altar.

"*Cavolo*, Padre!" yells Delizia. "*You* stole the truffle from the
crypt under the church!"

Padre Francesco's eyes are round as communion plates.

At this moment, Giovanni sees the deep golden bowl of holy water the truffle is hovering over. "Padre—don't get a drop of that water on the truffle, for the love of God!"

Padre's face drains of color.

"You will destroy it!"

Padre Francesco stares at the truffle in his hands.

"Put it down, Padre! The moisture, it will make it rot. *Please.*"

Padre Francesco's hands start to shake. He gingerly places the truffle onto the altar.

"How did you know I took it?" Padre looks bewildered.

"Your shoes, Padre. I heard your shoes down in the crypt," says Giovanni.

Cogs inside the clergyman's mind spin and whir. "So you were there too! What were you doing in the crypt?"

"Don't deflect, Padre! You were the one about to drown it in holy water!"

"My intentions were pure, I promise!"

Delizia is marching past the pews toward the altar. "I'd better not find a patch of damp on it, so help me, Padre. Baptizing a truffle... *sei pazzo!*"

"It's not a baptism!" says Giuseppina, arms folded. "Tell them what it is, Padre."

Padre's eyes roll as though he is very much considering lying.

Giuseppina jabs her finger toward a cross nailed to the wall.

"I..." Padre Francesco looks at his traitorous shoes with their well-made leather soles and hard heels, then at the cross on the wall. "I was performing an exorcism on it."

"An exorcism!" shrieks Giuseppina. "Another one!"

"What do you mean 'another one'?" asks Giovanni.

"Tell them, Padre," spits Giuseppina, folding her arms.

A pause. "I performed an exorcism on Giuseppina after church one Sunday."

"With her permission, I hope?" asks Lorenzo, his voice climbing higher.

"Well, I—" Padre looks up at the cross as if for a way around telling the truth.

"No," says Giuseppina, hands on hips. "He told me we were going to further discuss the sermon, and then he chased me with a cross and sprayed me with holy water."

"Padre!" If Lorenzo's voice were an airplane, it would have just reached cruising altitude.

Giovanni grabs a handful of Aria's curls for comfort. "Why would you do such a thing?"

Padre Francesco lowers his face. "Because I found her to be so bewitching. I became confused and I assumed she was possessed by a dark spirit."

"Ha! A sexorcism!" laughs Duccio.

"Shut up, Duccio!" everyone chimes.

"Well, none of this would be surprising to you if you illiterates read all the merciless newspaper articles about us. Here," says Duccio, fishing out one of several crumpled newspaper clippings from a hidden jacket pocket.

He hovers an article in the air. POPULAR ROMAN PRIEST WHO PERFORMED OVER ONE THOUSAND EXORCISMS VANISHES. Below, a photograph of Padre Francesco (his eyebrows are unmistakable). He holds a cross above a woman who appears to be vomiting feathers and flower petals.

"Rome! You told us you came from a church in Venice!" Carlotta protests.

"I think the exorcism part is what we should focus on," says Giovanni.

"I became the go-to priest for exorcisms. And it was taxing and became a sort of circus. I agreed to the filming of one exorcism, which went viral on social media. I ended up with a huge fanatical following that did not fit my calling. So I left because I wanted a simpler life and to serve God somewhere beautiful."

"But why did the truffle need an exorcism?" asks Giuseppina.

Padre confesses. "The truffle is a gift from God. But I saw darkness around it. A force of evil galvanizing, and I would not see it possess the good earnest people of this village—"

"Arguably, it already has," Lorenzo quips.

"—I took matters into my own hands. This is my gift. And I used it to protect our gift from God."

"*Mamma mia.* Everyone in this village has lost their mind," mutters Delizia as she inspects the giant truffle up close. Giovanni is at her side, scrutinizing the surface of their dirt diamond. Satisfied it is not damaged, he gives the mayor a nod. Delizia is hit with an almighty rush—the greatest relief of her life.

"I am sorry," says Padre, his magnificent eyebrows furrowed. "I was going to leave it at the church for you to find after I'd finished—a little miracle. I honestly didn't know the holy water would destroy it. I haven't doused it yet, but it has been blessed. And I do believe the dark spirits are gone."

"Not from Duccio. He could use a quick spritz." Giuseppina points at the baptismal bowl.

Duccio glares at her.

Delizia hoists the truffle up for the villagers to behold. "*Signore e signori,* let us ready ourselves for a most magnificent auction. We have our truffle back!"

The villagers clap and cheer. All but young Vittoria, who yells out at Padre Francesco from the pews, her voice tight from holding back tears. "Shame on you, Padre. The truffle's going to help my *nonna!* You almost ruined everything!"

Padre's thick, biblical eyebrows knit together. "I'm sorry, Vittoria. But how was I supposed to know holy water would harm it? I don't have a crystal ball!"

A scream rips apart the peace. A clatter as Stefano drops the chalice he was inspecting. Fagiolo barks.

Everyone's eyes on the source of the scream.

Everyone's nerves frayed like a cat-scratched carpet.

Giuseppina. Black mascara lines down her face bring to mind a badger. Her hair wild, her expression one of acute, sudden shock.

"*Mamma mia*," she yells, fanning herself with a funeral service pamphlet she had plucked from Leon's *cucina* counter.

"What is it, Pina?" chime Rosa and Valentina.

Giuseppina raises the pamphlet for dramatic emphasis. "The psychic!"

Benedetto nervously crams a peppermint into his mouth.

Lorenzo massages his temples and pops a painkiller for his lockjaw. He pleads, "Oh, no, not this again, please Pina—"

"Listen to me, all of you. I went to see a psychic at the Versilia seaside. Mamma Fortuna. The real deal. Even has a photograph of her with the goddess Raffaella Carrà, in case you had any doubts of her validity."

"Oh, wow!" says Rosa, convinced.

"We talked and she told me about our village...she knew its future, our fortunes..." Giuseppina holds the room captive with her charisma and a glossy eight-and-a-half-by-eleven trifold brochure touting a comprehensive list of funeral services. She waves it like a wand. "The psychic told me that we would have a very special visitor coming to the village. That this visitor will change everything. She said that then, there would be a death. And that after the death, our village would come into untold riches. The money will come because of the visitor. The visitor that is coming to our village...will change everything."

"My cousin Agnesia is coming to visit from Florence... could the visitor be cousin Agnesia?" ponders Benedetto. He is thoroughly ignored.

Giuseppina continues, "Almost everything she told me has come to pass. A special visitor will change everything. That visitor is the giant truffle—"

"Oh, for goodness' sake—" moans Lorenzo.

"Lorenzo Micucci, shut your beak and let me finish. You see, there was one last thing she said would happen, and I can't remember what it was, but it's so important. I just have to know. If we know what happens, we might have a chance to change the outcome."

"Was it an unfavorable outcome?" asks Rosa.

"Something dangerous?" asks Valentina.

"It was bad, I remember that. I'd had a wonderful *cacciucco* at a seaside restaurant for lunch right before I saw her and washed it down with a couple of Chiantis..."

"This explains a lot," says Lorenzo.

Giuseppina throws the funereal pamphlet at him. "How long do we have until the auction?"

Leon looks at his watch. "Five hours..."

"It's too far to Mamma Fortuna's," says Carlotta. "Call her."

"She doesn't have a phone; she says that radio waves interfere in her communion with the dead."

"Their being dead might also interfere in her communion with the dead," quips Lorenzo.

"I wouldn't be quick to judge a psychic, Lorenzo," says Padre. "I can tell you that I've seen some very dark and disturbing things in my time, none of which can be explained scientifically. I think Giuseppina is right to return to the psychic."

"I want to know what the psychic said last! What's going to happen to us?" says Tommaso.

Giuseppina marches toward the front door. She gives Leon a kiss on each cheek and salutes her fellow villagers.

Lorenzo appeals to her. "Giuseppina, no, no, no! This is nonsense, it is a waste of time and your money. Mamma

Fortuna is taking advantage of you—that's what they do, these swindlers. And you won't make it to Versilia and back in your Fiat Cinquecento on time. You'll miss the whole auction. We need you here."

"Think of all the magic you must miss because you've got your head up your skinny scientific bottom!" cries Giuseppina. "Have faith, because I have a plan!"

———

The villagers gather outside the church. An ethereal fog burns off the hills on the horizon in every shade of red and yellow. They watch breathlessly as Giuseppina squeezes herself into the driver's seat of her tiny teal Cinquecento. She wrestles the window crank handle, peeling off with a screech. Cats scatter. Giuseppina tosses her hair and punches an old cassette—sun withered and dented from overuse—into the tape deck. Raffaella Carrà croons from the cassette, coming to life in song, shimmying her hips in a silver catsuit.

"Aaah, aaah, aaah, aaah, a far l'amore comincia tu..."

Giuseppina sings along with her idol, louder, *con passione*. They drive fast, she and Raffaella Carrà, much too fast for these winding Tuscan country roads. The little teal Cinquecento chugs, its faulty speedometer needle swinging wildly, steering wheel shuddering, and because the heating is on, it struggles up every hill, roaring with the effort of ascent.

Bucolic smells of cattle and chestnut and mushroom give way to the sophisticated smells of Borghese—garlic from fine *ristoranti* and, perhaps Giuseppina imagines it, clean mountain air mingling with the metallic scent of money. The Cinquecento beetles through lush greenery lining the streets of Borghese until Giuseppina follows a winding private driveway that leads up to the grand wrought iron gates of a magnificent villa.

The gates are open.

Giuseppina revs the engine and screeches to a stop in front of the beautiful sunflower-yellow villa guarded by cypress trees. She marches past the covered pool, its outdoor bar and exquisite patio with potted plants and topiaries and umbrellas. Either side of her, manicured lawns and terraces sleep in their off season.

As she ascends the slope of stone steps to the imposing arched double doors of the beautiful edifice, she passes an elegant sign hanging off a stand that proudly reads MICUCCI. She pauses briefly, then gives it a herculean kick and sends the sign flying.

Her finger stabs at the doorbell. Then stabs at it six more times for good measure. And because she's in a hurry, she also pounds her fists against the expensive wood of the front doors.

The villa's arched doors open. A woman in front of Giuseppina is wearing a bikini despite the season. A towel is piled high on her head. Perhaps most surprisingly, her face is bright blue. Her eyes grow wide. In one hand she is squashing the two cucumber rounds she just peeled from them. The rest of her face is covered in the blue clay of a face mask. She is young, attractive, and Australian.

"Good tomato," she stutters. Her Italian is very poor. "I've just been on the phone with my genitals."

A pause. "Do you mean your parents?"

"Yes."

"I speak English, so let's stick to it, shall we? And good tomato to you too, Marilyn."

Marilyn swallows, an audible gulp.

"What is that smell?" Giuseppina wrinkles her nose.

The young woman who is sleeping with Giuseppina's husband flares her nostrils, mouth puckering as she contemplates. "Oh! That's beer. It's on my head."

"Hmm."

"I'm getting ready for the auction. Lager makes the hair shiny. The smell might also be yogurt; I mixed some of that in too because it's moisturizing."

There is a long, torturous pause.

"Umberto isn't here," says Marilyn, blue face mask cracking.

"Thank goodness for that," Giuseppina responds, toying with the slim-limbed Australian like a field mouse.

Marilyn's long-lashed brown eyes track to the left repeatedly, looking for either an escape or something to defend herself with. "Are you here for his wardrobe again?"

Giuseppina smiles. She'd almost forgotten that the last time she was here at the villa—her ex-villa—she'd stormed up the grand staircase to Umberto's walk-in closet. Then, armed with a pair of gardening shears, she'd cut one sleeve off every shirt he owned. *Un bel ricordo.*

Giuseppina smiles, then lets her face stiffen into seriousness. "Car keys. Now."

Marilyn nods. "Jeep?"

Giuseppina shakes her head.

"The Ford?"

Giuseppina pinches her eyes into a Clint Eastwood scowl.

"The classic one? The uh...Lancia Lambda?"

Giuseppina raises her eyebrows, a power move.

Marilyn's voice hitches. "Of course."

Marilyn scurries back across the entryway of the villa toward a decorative crystal bowl sitting on a nineteenth-century table. The bowl sits next to two ornate candle holders. Near a vintage velvet armchair with golden legs. There is a pop of cheer from that perfect bright blue vase. Rustic but elegant, the entryway asks you to come inside and enjoy classic sunbaked Tuscan elegance in its iron accents, terra-cotta tiles, and artful trompe l'oeil touches. Watching the terrified foreigner rummaging inside the decorative bowl, Giuseppina admires how beautifully decorated it all is. How expertly balanced. After all, she did it all herself.

The young foreigner finally fishes out a set of keys. She hands them to Giuseppina, thin fingers trembling and clammy. Giuseppina nods and thanks her. She wafts away from the spacious villa. Struck by a thought, she turns back to the terrified Australian cowering under an enormous doorframe. Marilyn winces.

Giuseppina calls out to her. "You are a very beautiful young woman. You don't need to do all that crap to yourself. I hope at least you are doing it for you, and not for him."

Marilyn's loneliness is wound around her folded arms. She blinks back tears. "He's going to break up with me, I feel it. Reckon I'll be heading home soon."

Giuseppina pauses. "You are so young to give yourself to someone. Let Italy hold your heart for a while. First you will fall in love with life, and in time, with yourself. Live your life for you first."

With that, Giuseppina Micucci turns, whips on a pair of cat-eye sunglasses and a silk headscarf from her pocket. One sharp flick of her head like a dressage horse, and she climbs into her estranged husband's favorite car.

His Lamborghini.

"*Ciao*, my old friend," she says to a charging bull emblem, smoothing her fingers across the steering wheel. She breathes in the lovely cologne of leather and lubricating oils. She opens the console to find it stuffed full of euros.

The Lamborghini Aventador growls—a panther—as Giuseppina starts its V12 mid-rear engine. With a roar, Giuseppina peels out from the driveway, a streak of glistening gold rims. Its body in Lamborghini's signature matte black—*nero nemesis*—sends a shock of adrenaline through the veins of anyone who sees it. And gives it its nickname, the Dark Knight.

Giuseppina races the Dark Knight around hairpin turns at high speed, growling from gear to gear. Her movie-star scarf flutters flag-like behind her.

"I'm on my way, Mamma Fortuna!" she bellows into the wind. "But you probably already know that!"

Chapter 14

A Lamborghini lock chirps like a Eurasian blackcap bird. Giuseppina runs from the exotic car, across the spacious piazza of the Versilian town of Pietrasanta. The coastal town, gentrified into a mecca of modern art, bounces up and down in Giuseppina's vision. Gulping, she inhales the ocean, mere miles away. The piazza is populated with modern art sculptures. She sprints by bicycles propped against peach, pink, and pappardelle-yellow buildings. Shoes slapping against cobblestone, Giuseppina salutes the great fourteenth-century Duomo di San Martino's alabaster face, its one rose-shaped window like an omnipotent eye made from Carrara marble mined in the snowcapped Apuan Alps. At its side, a sixteenth-century *campanile* bell tower rises to clouds silver as fish, soft as prayer.

The sprinting bombshell in a black sequined dress captures the attention of those on tourist time. Eyes lift from designer dresses in storefronts.

Giuseppina blows them a kiss, ever the entertainer.

Pumping her arms, she passes them. Still, their aromatics ambush her, a thing never consensual. Citrus lotion. Cigar smoke. A cloud of Acqua di Parma. Invisible emanations mingle with lunch preparations across the grand piazza, warming morning air with the basil, garlic bullying olive oil, pizza ovens blistering disc-shaped bodies of dough.

Giuseppina does not have time to savor fine scents and shopping. She is a woman on a mission. An ecstasy of urgency purrs inside her like the engine of the Lamborghini she sped here in.

Slipping from the piazza and down a quaint side street, she scuttles under an art installation of umbrellas strung between coral and apricot buildings in the alleyway. Tourists goggle up, wrapped in the wonder of it all.

They are very much in Giuseppina Micucci's way.

"*Scusate! Per favore,* this is an emergency! Coming through!" Giuseppina growls. She is jabbed in the boob by a selfie stick and leaps just in time to avoid stepping on a small judgmental dog wearing a plaid sweater and matching leash.

Not the Pietrasanta of my youth, she thinks, this touristic success story. A village risen from the ashes, evolving to appeal to modern times. The offseason tourists are obstructing her path, but they do give her a quick hit of hope.

Giuseppina's run ends in front of an unmarked door.

She is finally here.

With an ethereal jingling of strung bells, she opens the door and slips inside. Tendrils of incense rise to greet her. The waiting room is decorated in neutral tones, a gentle precursor to prepare you to walk through the door at the back. The door to the psychic's space. A lone skull sits on a stack of old books in evidence of the occult. A reek of dying flowers Giuseppina locates in an old bouquet, necks drooping. The door to the psychic's space is shut.

A solitary figure sits at a large desk.

Quite unexpectedly, Giuseppina finds the figure to be that of a young boy. He sports enormous old-soul eyes. Just above them, severe eyebrows that convey perpetual disappointment. His mop of unruly brown hair has multiple parts, bringing to mind the disheveled style of the Peruvian guinea pig. He wears a buttoned white shirt and an austere expression beyond his years. Rather like a pocket-size politician or a scientist that has been discredited by everyone in every facet of his life.

"Good morning. Where is Mamma Fortuna?" Giuseppina pants.

The boy—no more than thirteen and small for his age at that—studies the glittering sequins of her black dress with an expression that lands somewhere between the vast plains of confusion and revulsion.

"What is your name?" the young man asks her.

Giuseppina's eyebrows lift at his authoritative tone. "My name is Giuseppina Micucci, and I am here to see Mamma Fortuna. It is extremely urgent."

"Mic-ucci," he spits plosive consonants out like the seeds of a *melone*. "Micucci, like the famous chef?"

"It is spelled the same way, *sì*." Giuseppina sniffs. "I don't have an appointment."

"That is obvious, given that Mamma Fortuna doesn't take appointments." The boy eyes her suspiciously before performing a well-rehearsed script. "Mamma Fortuna is very busy helping many souls. You are welcome to wait here. I must inform you that you might be waiting awhile."

"I don't have a while."

"That is not my problem."

"And who are *you*?" asks Giuseppina, taken aback by his aristocratic arrogance. She prides herself on being adored by children and vows to crack this little nut with her charm.

The boy does not answer, lowering his eyes. The only sound is a pencil rasping its way across paper. Giuseppina would ordinarily take the time to enjoy the scenario, but time is the very thing she doesn't have. Frustration stitches itself silently across her brow. The mysterious boy lifts his enormous dark eyes to her and points at two chairs next to the front door.

Giuseppina emits a *hmm*. She sits.

Smoothing one hand over the other, she spies on the waiting room. Candle flames flicker like serpent tongues. She stares longingly at the framed photograph of Mamma Fortuna and her idol, the late Raffaella Carrà. Beautiful Raffaella Carrà, with her iconic blonde bob and her effervescent soul. Another beloved Giuseppina believes left her.

A wall clock mocks her with a great flat face, tattooed in the phases of the moon. Its hands callously slap away seconds. Every second is more moisture wicked away from a giant truffle. Every second is a second closer to the auction that will save her village and the people she loves. A second closer to a thing happening, a thing she cannot foresee but feels twisting up her insides, a terrible thing she must circumvent in any way she possibly can, even if it means stealing her estranged husband's Lamborghini and speeding to a psychic for the slightest clue.

She glares at the young boy, concentration cemented across his face.

"Is Mamma Fortuna in her room, or is she out right now?"

"You will just have to wait for her quietly."

The cheek of this boy! Giuseppina glares at three pencils peering out from his breast pocket. What is it that he's doing that is so utterly absorbing? Curiosity arches its back and claws at her until she gives in.

"What business are you attending to over there?" Giuseppina asks, gesturing to his papers.

"If you must know, I am drawing a recreation of the *Vitruvian Man*."

Giuseppina's lips part. Nothing comes out.

"It is a famous drawing by Leonardo da Vinci," he clarifies.

"I know what the *Vitruvian Man* is."

He squints at her skeptically. Draws a breath. And he begins. "It was drawn in 1490 by Leonardo da Vinci, my favorite of the old masters. Da Vinci's intention with the *Vitruvian Man* was to use geometry to depict man's connection to nature. Man fits inside a circle, which is the divine symbol, and he also fits inside a square—that one is the earthly symbol. It is about man's connection to the earth and divine connection to the universe. Da Vinci used geometry to show man as a 'microcosm' and the universe as a 'macrocosm.' Do you know what that means? It means that man is the universe in miniature. Would you like me to read you what da Vinci himself said in his notebook?"

"I am guessing you are going to whether I—"

"Da Vinci said, 'By the ancients man has been called the world in miniature; and certainly this name is well bestowed, because, inasmuch as man is composed of earth, water, air, and fire, his body resembles that of the earth.'"

Giuseppina tries to stuff down her surprise. "I suppose the question is, why would one try to recreate one of the greatest masterpieces of all time?"

"I am studying its principles."

"How old are you?"

"How old are *you*?"

"It's impolite to ask."

"I agree."

Giuseppina snorts, *con passione.* The small philosopher is swallowed back up by the demands of his intricate drawing. Giuseppina counts to five slowly so she doesn't scream.

A stealthy sniff under her arm brings the musk of her stress sweat. Her mind replays the chase after Giovanni's stolen Jeep. The last tattered moth of her patience flutters away.

"Young man, I understand that Mamma Fortuna is very busy, but *you* must understand that I won't be here very long. My village—"

The serious boy points at his pencil, then lowers his face to mirror the Vitruvian man's scowl.

Giuseppina stares at the door to the room where Mamma Fortuna reads her fortunes, willing it to open.

"I can appreciate you exploring the scientific and the spiritual, however, this is an urgent—"

The young man presses his finger to his lips. "Please be patient and quiet. You are interrupting my concentration and stifling my creativity."

Giuseppina is on her feet. She will not be patronized by a tiny despot with the hair of a springer spaniel.

As if divined, the door to the psychic's room bursts open. Out flies a woman with wildfire in her eyes. She lunges forth, swatting violently at the air. The woman is in battle, wielding a Dyson cordless vacuum as a weapon.

"Out!" she yells. "Out!" Mamma Fortuna brandishes the high-end vacuum as though it were a machete and the waiting room were choked by Amazonian foliage. She drops the Dyson to waft air and an invisible intruder out of the front door of the studio. Mamma Fortuna slams the front door of her psychic studio shut to a frenzy of bell chimes. She delves into the pockets of her palazzo pants, yanks out a bundle of sage to light with the flame of the nearest candle as if it were a grenade. Tendrils of sage smoke curl into the air from the lit bundle in her bright red talons. She waves her wrists, calming, earthen breaths of herb clearing the room.

Giuseppina is speechless—a thing quite rare.

The room falls silent except for persistent scratching indicative of a young man assiduously tracing the genitalia at the epicenter of his magnum opus.

Not entirely sure of what to ask, Giuseppina waits for an explanation.

The boy does not look up. "A bad spirit has trespassed. It happens."

"If you give them an inch..." Mamma Fortuna does an impressive pantomime of being trampled upon. "Come into my room, it's safe now."

Giuseppina steps into the psychic's space. There is no one else in this space, but somehow, it feels crowded. Powerful aromas of sage, lavender, oregano, tallow, and musk bicker with one another. Neon signs glow across the walls, pillows with symbols of snakes and an incalculable number of hands with eyes in them. Dream catchers dangle from the ceiling like cobwebs over crystals and genie lamps and charts of the zodiac signs. Giuseppina finds herself hypnotized by a vintage Victorian chaise lounge flush against one wall. Peacock blue, dulled with age. Lumps of its insides—downy wisps of stuffing—lie all around it. The chaise looks to have been slashed a great many times. Most alarmingly, there is a large knife sticking out of its tufted fabric.

"Don't be alarmed," says Mamma Fortuna, popping a mint in her mouth. "The ordeal is over. Found that at a flea market, got it for a steal. I probably should have been suspicious, but it had such character. The chaise was really speaking to me. And then I realized it was actually speaking to me, and so I had to free the spirit stuck inside it. It's fine now; it was all an amicable affair, but of course I'm out one chaise lounge. It's always the valuable things they attach to. Never get stuck in any IKEA stuff."

Now that she is no longer obscured by a battle blur of

cordless vacuum and bad spirit, Giuseppina can see that
Mamma Fortuna is dressed differently than the first time she
came to this studio. Last time she had sat in this room and had
the fortune of her village voiced, Mamma Fortuna's hair was
tucked into a headscarf covered in jaguars. Now, it is free, flar-
ing out to her shoulders. The color is an arresting blue-black,
surely born in a box. Her nose and chin are prominent, her
eyes wise, dark, deeply hooded. The psychic exudes an intoxicating power, glowing splendidly as a desert flower that blooms
one night a year. She has ditched her bohemian robes for a
Chanel suit. Her makeup is valorous, Cupid's bow lips painted
the kind of raucous red reserved for Ferraris and the bottoms
of amorous baboons.

She closes her eyes and exhales. "I'm sorry for your loss."

Giuseppina gasps. "Sofia! You psychically sensed that she
passed!"

"No, darling. You are wearing funereal black."

Giuseppina nods. "I don't have a lot of time, but I must
know: Who is the juvenile fascist in your waiting room?"

"Ah, that diminutive dictator is my grandson, Giorgio."

Giuseppina sits on a purple velvet chair but springs up
again, having also sat upon a small chakra-healing Tibetan
singing bowl. She places the bowl and her purse on Mamma
Fortuna's desk. "Aren't you worried about him being near bad
spirits?"

Mamma Fortuna pulls a compact mirror from a desk drawer
and applies another layer of lipstick in nature's warning color.
"Worried? Even the scariest of spirits won't go near him. You've
met him!" She lowers her voice. "I pay him a fortune to sit at the
front desk for me, and he blackmails extra euros out of me or
else he will tell his father what he sees happening in here. Half
our family are agnostics, and the other half are gifted spiritual
communicators. Giorgio is busy capitalizing on the rift." She

stares into the mirror. Smacks her lips together. "He tells me he is saving up to visit the Galleria dell'Accademia in Venice to see one of Leonardo da Vinci's fragile drawings during one of the short stints they risk its delicate paper to be in the presence of the public. Spends all his time talking about moving to Venice or Rome, embarrassed by being a boy from Pietrasanta. Can you imagine? Between you and me, that boy has lived many lives, and he is terrifying in all of them." She puts away the mirror. "Now, to what do I owe the pleasure?"

Giuseppina glances at an enormous framed print of Caravaggio's *The Fortune Teller* behind Mamma Fortuna and reminds her of the last time she was here.

"Mamma Fortuna. You told me there would be a special visitor to our village. That they would change everything. The visitor came. You then said there would be a death, and there was. Our friend Sofia died alone in the woods. You said that after the death, our village would come into untold riches because of the visitor. And this is about to happen. *Today.* And you said one more thing...and I cannot remember what it is. But I believe something is about to happen. I am no fortune teller, but I can truly feel it, and—I am terrified that it is something awful. I'm just here to be reminded of what you said. And to do whatever I can to save my village. You must tell me."

Mamma Fortuna snorts. "Darling, you cannot expect me to remember a reading I gave sometime over the summer. I am in communion with the living and the dead all day long. I am a human, not a hard drive. And a postmenopausal one at that."

Giuseppina gives her an empathetic eye roll.

"We will have to do another reading."

"Something bad is going to happen, Mamma Fortuna. There is a lot of energy stirring in the village right now. You were right about the visitor, who it turns out is a giant—"

Mamma Fortuna cuts her off. "Ah, ah, ah, ah! No details.

Keep it vague; I don't want details. My reading is clearer without them."

"You read the future in my tea leaves last time, and the tarot cards. Everything you said would happen did. I must protect the people I love. The more I know and can stop any...bad things, the better. My beautiful village is dying, and I can't bear it. I am desperate. I want to know the truth."

Mamma Fortuna laughs, a cackle that hearkens from some long-gone time and place. Giuseppina pictures a roaring bonfire, embers sparking into the sky, wrists bound to great wooden stakes, a phantom smell of burning flesh.

Mamma Fortuna's jaw clenches. "People never come to a psychic for the truth. If only you knew all the things I am unable to say. It is my gift and my burden to be judicious in what I share. I try to only tell the truth that is beneficial." She pauses. "Sssssssshhhhh!"

Giuseppina is about to protest that she hasn't made a sound before realizing that Mamma Fortuna is shushing another invisible presence. "You will wait your turn, like everybody else!" she yells, standing to forcefully waft air out into the waiting room. Then slams the door. After pulling down the hem of her Chanel blazer, she flicks her dark hair and sits once more. "They think that because they've passed, they deserve special treatment."

"You have been busy."

"Since the pandemic," says Mamma Fortuna. "Everyone needs a psychic, and all the channels are a constant torrent of communication—every hour of every day. I mean, what am I, Netflix? I tell you, the veil between the worlds of the living and the dead is as thin as a G-string. Here..."

She reaches under her desk, then places a mysterious object swaddled in thick velvet cloth onto the desk. Whipping off the violet cloth with a flourish, she unveils a crystal ball.

Giuseppina is mesmerized. "The velvet cloth—to shroud its powers?"

"No"—Mamma Fortuna points to the light streaming in through her windows—"the ball keeps setting fire to my curtains." Giuseppina notes that the curtains are indeed singed to half their length, black at their bases.

Mamma Fortuna closes her eyes and glides her long scarlet nails above the crystal sphere.

"I see the color blue. You have left a life of luxury for a life of authenticity. A loneliness lives in you. You believe those you love always leave you. But we must be careful of the stories we tell ourselves and sort fiction from fact. You are a spiritual star, a great attractor with loved ones and in life. Open your eyes to it. Do you know who you remind me of?"

"Who?"

"Raffaella Carrà."

Giuseppina's heart lifts to the ceiling, light as a bubble. "No!"

"*Sì*. I met her. She had a big heart and a goodness she was very generous with. Still is."

Giuseppina's smile stretches so wide her cheeks spasm. Mamma Fortuna once more lowers her dark eyes to the crystal. A smile blooms across rich, red lips.

"I see that there are elemental forces at play in your village. Powerful. The most powerful of all forces. An unseen intelligence. Mother Nature has bestowed a gift upon your village, an offering—"

"The great white truffle!"

"Sssshhh...don't give me details, it interferes with what comes through." She frowns, then closes her eyes again. Her pale fingers tremble and twitch, as if reading the terrain of a tiny planet. "This natural force will bring great success to your village. That is its intention. Its playful purpose."

Giuseppina swears she can suddenly smell leaf mold and

humus. Worms and dirt. And a breath of earthen gas and a hint of sweet rot.

The taunt of a truffle.

She opens her mouth to say that it has already begun, but Mamma Fortuna opens one eye to squint her into silence. She continues. "I see that there are other forces at play in and around your village. An awakening of greed. Birds of prey have begun to circle. There is danger."

"I knew it!" Giuseppina whispers, perched on the edge of her seat.

"There will be a battle with a ghost."

"A battle with a ghost! *Cavolo!*"

"But there's something else, something bigger..."

"What is it?"

"Someone will seek vengeance."

"Who? On whom?"

"Ssssshhh. Someone will seek vengeance. You are the only one who has a chance to change the outcome. If you do not stop them, there will be another death."

"What must I do, Mamma Fortuna?"

"You must try to stop them, as I just said."

"But how? How will I know who it is? I mean, obviously, it's Duccio, but to be certain?"

"They will soon make themselves known. They have been lurking in darkness. And very soon their intentions will be brought to the light. You don't have long."

"But...what does the crystal ball say the outcome is? Do I get back home in time and manage to prevent the death or don't I?"

"Oh, no, darling. The future is not fixed. It flutters and shivers and morphs with your every thought and action, dancing ahead of you like a hologram. The insight I share is to empower you and summon your success. The power to evolve and sculpt your future all lies within you."

"Well, how long do I have? I have to drive all the way back!"

"Time is an illusion and a construct, but even so, you must hurry."

A resonant knocking sounds out. Mamma Fortuna stares through the door to the waiting room. Her eyes become glassy. She doesn't move.

The knocking intensifies.

"Are you going to answer?" Giuseppina's eyes are wide. Her jaw tight.

"Oh, I wasn't sure the knocking was from this realm," the psychic replies absently. "Come in!"

The lordly countenance of grandson Giorgio pokes into the room. "The *carabinieri* are here. Again."

Mamma Fortuna nods. "They come to see Mamma with their missing-persons cases. You must go fast, Giuseppina. Get back to the village. Be prepared for the battle with the ghost. Stop the one who will seek vengeance. Drive that Lamborghini like a stallion with an unbroken spirit."

"How did you...?"

She points to the car keys Giuseppina placed on the desk in front of her. "The raging bull emblem is very iconic."

Giuseppina kisses the psychic's rouged cheeks, inhaling an hors d'oeuvre of patchouli oil. She leaves Mamma Fortuna covering her crystal ball to prevent it from committing arson again. Two *carabinieri* sit in the waiting room, stylish in blue uniforms designed by Armani in the 1980s. Spines broomstick straight, the bearded men share sheepish glances as though embarrassed to have resorted to the paranormal for a lead. But they too are losing time. One of them holds a flyer and a mystery of a girl inexplicably gone. And when it comes to a person who has vanished—stolen from their life and loved ones, when the dogs lose the ephemeral story of a scent—these men shelve their pride and personal reasoning. No stone left unturned.

Giuseppina nods at the *carabinieri*. She wrestles a wad of cash from her purse, placing the requisite forty-five euros on the desk near young Giorgio's drawing. She counts out an additional hundred euros she took from the console of the Dark Knight. Hands it directly to the young Renaissance man.

"For your trip to the Galleria dell'Accademia."

Giorgio's face lights up like a Christmas tree. He counts the euros in disbelief. Giuseppina slips her silk scarf over her blonde bun, glides on movie-star glasses. "Of course, go to Venice and the Galleria and all the beautiful big cities, Giorgio. But you must also make a plan to visit the little village of Anchiano. That is where Leonardo da Vinci was born. He is from Tuscany, born only thirty minutes from my beautiful village. They even have a hologram of him there at his childhood home. When you get to the beautiful stone home hugged by ivy, ask for Gianluca. Tell him Giuseppina Micucci sent you. And remember this, Giorgio—magnificent beings are sometimes born of humble beginnings."

Giorgio's eyes sparkle with awe. He is spellbound. As Giuseppina struts toward the door under the admiring gaze of two *carabinieri*, Giorgio springs from his seat. Giuseppina clasps a hand around the door handle and finds the Renaissance boy at her side.

"Signora Micucci, I want you to have this."

He hands her his masterpiece and homage to the *Vitruvian Man*. She smiles. He has even etched da Vinci's own four-hundred-year-old words under the naked man. His tidy lettering resembles a city skyline.

Learn how to see. Realize that everything connects to everything else.

Giuseppina brushes her hand against Giorgio's cheek. "I will display it in my village bar for everyone to see. *Grazie e ciao*, Little da Vinci."

Giuseppina Micucci races against time toward a borrowed Lamborghini on a mission to save her village from vengeance. Mysteries swirl like spores inside her mind. Warring ghosts. Who seeks vengeance. Who might die. Whether they are outsiders or among her beloved villagers. She pops a contraband CBD candy and picks up the pace.

Through a window in the waiting room, young Giorgio watches Giuseppina running in the alleyway under multicolored umbrellas. The starry-eyed boy is pinching his hundred euros so hard his fingers turn white, thinking of what she has just gifted him, this woman with a little magic of her own.

A woman who can change the future.

Chapter 15

Camouflaged in an olive-green jacket and boots, a hunter slinks between the twisted limbs of olive trees. He has slipped past detection. Not a soul knows where he is. Under the cover of shadow, he is a spy. His eyes land on several glossy vehicles. Alfa Romeo. Mercedes....no, a Maserati. Rolls-Royce. Each glides up the long driveway toward the medieval castle on the hill. The truffle hunter skulks closer to the medieval castle through the belly of the olive grove. Away from the exposed driveway and the path of watchful eyes.

Giovanni Scarpazza does not want to be seen.

Boom.

Giovanni searches the sky for a storm. But the clouds have burned off, and there is nothing but dazzling blue.

Boom. Boom. Boom. Da-boom.

Drums. A beat throbbing in his bones.

Giovanni follows the percussion, pulling the leash in his left hand taut as they reach the front row of the olive grove. Fagiolo stills, squinting at sunshine. Aria leans against Giovanni's side, lifting her head to study him with every sense she has.

The truffle hunter yanks out a pair of binoculars and spies on the front of the castle from a safe distance. Curiosity is killing him.

Magnified lenses zoom him in to eleventh-century castle turrets stabbing at a boasting blue sky. He lowers the lenses to luxury cars revolving around the fountain of the circular driveway. Black limousine doors yawn open. Out spill glittering gowns. Thousand-euro suits. Silk dresses with the back slashed off. And the jewelry—he has never seen such enormous jewelry. Diamonds like dove eggs. Great gold bracelets shackling wrists. Gentlemen in chauffeur hats and dove-white gloves extend a hand to their passengers. Not a single guest seems to be able to exit a vehicle without assistance, regardless of their age or blatant glow of good health.

Who are these people?

A silver-haired man wears a willowy young woman on his arm, just above his Rolex. *No dirt here,* Giovanni thinks, picturing the black smiles of his own fingernails, *everything designer.* The labels are a language Giovanni doesn't speak, but he can spot the graceful polish of high-quality leather, the tidy tailoring of an extravagant suit. He spies one of *ristorante* Novelli's catering vans parked near a topiary tree. Private security guards are positioned around the edifice like gargoyles.

Where are the other Boscarini?

A shrill whirring fills his ears. Lifting the lenses, he finds the source—four drones appear, watching all the glitz and glamour like big black birds of prey. Moving the binoculars again, Giovanni captures the source of the drumming. *Sbandieratori,* a troupe of Tuscan flag throwers, are performing on the castle lawns. The performers dazzle in chain mail and brightly colored medieval costumes, tossing flags expertly to the blare of trumpets. And that gorilla of a drum, every beat pounding against ancient castle stone, conquering these Tuscan hills.

"*Ma che diavolo!*" Giovanni hisses. These are the Borghese flag throwers! Borghese is once again stealing wind from the sails of Lazzarini Boscarino. True, the only surviving members of the Lazzarini Boscarino *sbandieratori* are Benedetto and Stefano, who are due for a knee replacement and have forgotten what flag throwing actually is, respectively, but it's the principle of the matter, isn't it?

The binoculars now bring Giovanni close to bodies of the beautiful and the rich posing against a media wall, camera flashes illuminating designer handbags and teeth white as polished bidets.

All of this for a pungent lump of fungus.

What is happening inside the castle? Giovanni wonders.

He squints into the binoculars, blinking away his own eyelashes, to spot a freestanding sign that reads SOTHEBY'S IS PROUD TO PRESENT THE WORLD'S LARGEST TRUFFLE. Below gold lettering is a graphic of a man and his curly-coated dog truffle hunting in the forest. Giovanni realizes that this is a representation of him and takes great offense that the man is clearly geriatric, bald as a bunion, and sporting a nose that would scandalize Pinocchio.

But Giovanni also feels a stab of guilt. He is supposed to be right there, mingling with the elite in this castle. After all, he is the man of the hour. The finder but not the keeper of a most magnificent tuber. He is the official living proof and the provenance of the largest truffle ever found. Millionaire guests and the global media want a slice of him because he is a key ingredient in the rustic romance of the truffle. Truffle hunter Giovanni Scarpazza, the rags origins of the riches success story. Foodies and famous folk are going to raise their paddles, and his presence could raise the tantalizing final price of the

truffle. Enchant the bidders who have a right to selfies with the
lonely old goat who tromps around in the mud with his dogs.

Pressure against Giovanni's leg summons him back through
the binocular lenses and to his place under the olive tree. He
finds Aria is on her hind legs, paws pressed to his knee. She
has picked up on how flustered he is before he has—Giovanni
finds he'd been scowling into the binoculars hard enough that
his eyebrows hurt.

"I'm alright, Aria. But we want no part of this circus."

It pains him, but what happens to the giant truffle is no
longer his business. And yet. An inescapable sadness stirs in his
belly. Paolo pops back into his head. Shiny suit, sips of prosecco,
his curls glistening with pomade. Uninvited, a waft of Paolo's
favorite cologne visits—grassy vetiver warmed by oakmoss and
a fleeting cackle of citrus. Oh, Paolo would have loved an event
like this.

Curiosity paws at Giovanni once more.

Where will his magnificent truffle end up? A millionaire's
mouth? What country will it be flown to when it has made its
mark on this castle?

What will it do to the people walking into that castle with its
violent perfume, all those bewitching pheromones?

What legacy will the truffle leave for his village?

Giovanni snorts, startling the dogs.

He thought he was immune to the tantra of *Tuber magnatum*
Pico. But he carries a secret—he is inextricably tied to this truffle. It grabbed him by the nostrils and never let go. He can't stop
smelling it at an impossible distance, worrying about where in
that castle it sits right now. Pulling that monstrous white whale
from the soil resuscitated him like some holistic miracle drug.
An oasis in a sea of sadness. Its powerful pheromones awoke
something in him. It has brought him back his Paolo with a
clarity he'd lost to the numbing agent of grief. Because of that

truffle, he has begun to feel again. And so Giovanni can't help but be consumed by wondering who will win the truffle. He feels burdened by responsibility. After all, he is the one who coaxed that gigantic truffle from its secret spot and brought this madness upon his sleepy little village.

No. Enough. Giovanni Scarpazza will walk away.

He will return to his roots.

He will truffle hunt.

Giovanni Scarpazza belongs to the dirt, not a castle.

He leads the dogs away from the hysteria of humanness. They slink back through the olive grove. Away from a castle and the momentous auction that will decide the fate of his home. Rustic olive trees give way to a realm of hornbeam and alder. Towering oaks on fire with fall colors. Rain boots trudging across a lake of scarlet leaves. The forest is uncivilized, sharp on his senses. Its wildness swallows him whole. Forest fragrances start to untangle the truffle hunter.

He hears songbirds chirp of his presence. The whispered language of leaves.

Deep in the womb of the woods, it is Fagiolo who first picks up on a scent. Nose low, gangly gait. He snorts into the leaf litter. Pivots on all paws sharply.

A current rushes up through Giovanni's chest. A sylvan thrill.

"Find it."

Fagiolo races off in between tree trunks and Giovanni feels his heart tighten. He whistles. The little white dog comes bounding back and Giovanni can breathe again. Fagiolo has returned, certain that he has found treasure. He is beaming, barely able to keep the large piece of wood between his smiling teeth as he shows it off to Giovanni.

"No, Fagiolo, that is a branch."

It is dawning on Giovanni that he only has one truffle-hunting dog. A disappointment, but he loves his cream-colored pup no less. One truffle hound and one happiness hunter. A kind of balance, he supposes.

Fagiolo races off to find the next treasure. Giovanni bends to part the leaf litter. A warm mushroom breath rises to greet him. He has found a cluster of porcinis squatting like cherubs in cloche hats. Plucking one, he holds it to his nose and inhales its beautiful aroma, warm as baked bread, billowing earthiness of freshly dug potatoes and old books.

Fagiolo crashes across the brush to lick the entire length of his human's face. Giovanni holds up the impressive porcini.

"Look at this, Fagiolo. *Che meraviglia.*"

Fagiolo lunges. Giovanni barely sweeps the mushroom away from the bright white canine and his bright white canines. Having delighted in the joy he saw in his human while sniffing the porcini mushroom, Fagiolo has a new mission. He bounds around the base of trees, returning to Giovanni to bring him every single porcini mushroom he can snuffle out. Entangled in small and wondrous woodland moments and far too busy receiving Fagiolo's porcinis, Giovanni doesn't realize that they have not reached the dark heart of the forest. He looks up. Fagiolo has led them to Nonna Amara's land.

He hasn't been here in a long time. He and the dogs follow the walking path to Nonna's house, finding most of the terraces smothered by brambles. Giovanni stares up at the naked face of the mountain. Giant rocks left over from a landslide. He breathes in clean mountain air and savors the stillness. He grew up here. Nonna Amara—soft slippers and ferocious love—made sure that he had a home here and in the hearts of all the villagers. That the bigotry and intolerances of men like Giovanni's father and old Padre Salvestro were not tolerated.

"Fagiolo! Come here!"

Little Fagiolo is bounding around the property. Giovanni

calls for him again, feeling his heart tighten as Fagiolo slinks in between brambles and out of sight. Giovanni picks up his pace. He dips under a depression in the brambles, wades through a sea of sage and Nonna's persevering vegetable garden.

Fagiolo is suddenly a statue. Every muscle of his body is tense.

He looks back at Giovanni. His pupils have shrunken to pinpricks.

A shudder runs across Giovanni's skin. Every hair on the back of his neck rises.

"Find it."

Fagiolo bolts. A blur of white arrowing across the ground.

Aria watches the young pup. She sniffs the air. Captivated by the invisible. Giovanni holds his breath. An elixir of excitement and deep dread emulsifies inside him.

Previous finds rise up to haunt him. Little girl lost in the woods. Jeans stuffed with cash. The largest truffle on earth. Sofia's pale, lifeless body.

Giovanni considers calling off the hunt. Heading home. It would be better for his heart.

But the skin across his arms has hardened into pebbles. His breath has quickened. He is fizzing with excitement. It is too late. He is already high.

"Find it, Fagiolo."

Fagiolo treks ahead, slower now, caution in his gait. Giovanni loses sight of him behind a mass of brambles. He finds a path around them.

Fagiolo is ambling up a clearing in the terraces.

Giovanni watches the little white Lagotto park himself under a tree. He sniffs at the air, placing his head on his paws. Giovanni frowns. Even with the overgrowth, he recognizes every inch of this land. But not this tree. He is enraptured by its beauty. Branches reaching for the clouds like a candelabra.

The lively flames of its leaves. Its soul-stirring hues of scarlet and tangerine against a bright blue sky. The tree stands alone on the terrace, a gentle giant. A survivor.

And it dawns on Giovanni.

He does know this tree.

This is Paolo's persimmon tree.

Giovanni laughs. A sound so alien it startles the dogs.

He approaches the tree. It is covered in sunset-colored leaves now, but soon it will bear plump fruit—*cachi*—each like a swollen sun. He cannot believe the tree is here. Paolo, they used to joke, was allergic to the outdoors. He preferred parties and the opera, Puccini and Prada. Just his luck to fall in love with a truffle hunter who also happened to be the village builder. Giovanni teased Paolo mercilessly about his lack of a green thumb, so Paolo came up with a scheme to prove Giovanni wrong. He would grow his favorite winter fruit. Planting a persimmon tree became his project. Every evening, he would saunter off onto Nonna's land, designer shoes trudging across the dirt. But the persimmon tree never seemed to grow, no matter how much he watered or sang to it. Giovanni had laughed at the thought of Paolo standing on the terrace, singing to a little tree stump. Giovanni offered to intervene, but Paolo refused and eventually gave up on Project Persimmon, conceding that he was more suited to haute couture than horticulture.

Giovanni approaches the tree like a newfound family member. Paolo's words swim back to him. *Besides, you won't be rid of me that easily. I'll be in the breeze. I'll be in the songs of birds and bright shivers through the leaves. I'll be right here...*

"Hi, Paolo." Giovanni feels silly talking to a tree, but his heartbeat is slowing and syrupy. He feels peace with his hand pressed against its trunk, rooted. "I miss you every second of every day."

A breeze picks up, rustling the leaves of the persimmon tree that glitter like the scales of a great red dragon. Paolo was here. His beautiful hands in this dirt. Sharing the song inside him with a little sapling.

The truffle hunter sits under the umbrella of Paolo's persimmon tree. Sits with his dogs, letting the land hold him. For the first time in an age, he is not drowning in his grief. Perhaps it is the purifying mountain air. Perhaps it is the extraordinary patience of the persimmon tree. That his sadness is allowed to breathe here, to be free, like the little songbirds who bounce along its branches, pecking at early persimmons. Perhaps it is because he truly feels as though he is somehow in the presence of Paolo.

Giovanni's heart swells thinking of the designer shoes and the ridiculous hats Paolo would wear to water the tree. It is easy to make martyrs from memories. But Paolo was perfect as he was. A loud chewer, afraid of all bugs, and a terrifying driver. So gloriously, messily, gorgeously human.

Giovanni laughs again. A great release. Fagiolo bounds over to Giovanni and licks his face.

"I'm okay, Fagiolo. You found a real treasure today, didn't you? Perhaps you're not the best truffle dog, but you are a little soul savior."

Giovanni thinks about all the threads of life weaving together in the woods. About science and spirit, nature and nurture. About his giant truffle. The hardest part of all of this is that Paolo hasn't been here to see it. The madness. The mayhem. And so he tells Paolo's persimmon tree all about finding the white truffle. Once his tale has been told, he stares up at a great spray of flame-red leaves. If Paolo were alive, they would be at the castle. No one would be more excited about the auction. No one would be more devastated over Sofia's death. No one would be more proud of Giovanni.

Fagiolo stands. Barks. *It is time to go!*

Giovanni stands, slips extra treats into the slimy mouths of his dogs, crouches to tousle their head curls. A sharp whistle. Giovanni is striding away from Paolo's persimmon tree, his dogs trotting tight by his heels.

Once again, Giovanni can see his future shifting on the horizon. He will not become embittered. He will see through the fate of the giant truffle and do what he can for his village of Lazzarini Boscarino.

"You will have to live for the both of us," Paolo once said.

And so Giovanni is heading to the medieval castle after all.

He leashes Fagiolo and guides the dogs back through the woods, his own heartbeat clattering in his ears. Giovanni can no longer hear the birdsong or the liquid rustle of a creek. His mind is abuzz with human happenings. With excitement.

He leaves the forest and follows the road up to the castle, where there are fewer sticks and porcini mushrooms for Fagiolo to obsess over. The dogs prick their ears up at an obnoxious clamor far behind them. At a sound like an enormous swarm of angry insects. A panther-black Lamborghini streaks into view as it growls up and down the Tuscan hills at a terrifying clip, undoubtedly heading for the castle. Clearly some rich asshole ready to make a name for themselves by buying the biggest truffle on earth.

"Ricco idiota."

Giovanni Scarpazza strides on, staring at his boots. Footprints stamping over invisible forces below. Roused from the anesthesia of grief, he is impassioned. Alive. Making his mark on the earth.

Ominous drumbeats shatter a great weight of silence.

And, with one pat of the persimmon leaf in his pocket, a truffle hunter strides toward a castle.

Chapter 16

Delizia steals one moment. One breath. One break between back-to-back interviews. One instant to still herself. The castle crackles with anticipation. Black-tie and blowouts. Lipstick and lace. A grand hall humming with excitable chatter. Tinkle of champagne flutes. Laughter lifting to the ceiling like prosecco bubbles. Vivaldi skipping out from hidden speakers.

And waiting in the wings—history, about to be made.

The mayor is running on adrenaline. Her bladder is as swollen as a medieval water flask, but she doesn't have time for relief. Smells sneak up on her as silver platters pass. Umberto and the Novelli team have outdone themselves. Tiny pots of truffle custard with crab and caviar. Prosciutto rolls with black-truffle burrata. Truffled foie gras bites wrapped in gold leaf wink at her. Antipasti made with fresh shavings of truffle that have journeyed from the dirt to the dining hall. Delizia smells perfume pulsing, boneless, across the great hall. Sour surges of body odor bleeding through a suit. But prevailing above the swarm of invisible aromas in a medieval castle on a hill is an unstoppable aphrodisiac.

Effortlessly overpowering all.

A hulking great Goliath of a stench.

The not-so-tiny god.

Delizia is giddy. The truffle's breath is more powerful than it has ever been. As if it knows this is the moment. The critical time to show off and save her village. Delizia closes her eyes and whispers a prayer to the truffle, to help her succeed—*madonna mia*—at something for once. To compensate for the unforgivable theft and betrayal by her father, the late Mayor Benigno.

She and the villagers just have to keep it together for the next few minutes.

Twelve minutes and eight seconds, to be precise.

Sell the truffle. Save the village.

So close to victory she can smell it.

Delizia Micucci has never wanted anything so much in her entire life.

The auction must go perfectly. Everything must go perfectly.

A multicamera global live stream is poised to begin. Imposing flat screens cling to stone castle walls that have stood watch since the eleventh century. Each colossal screen is a window to another world.

Hong Kong. Dubai. Seoul. New York.

Crisp white cotton dishdashas. Glinting cuff links. Razor-sharp blazers. Photographers checking camera settings. Agents ready to receive calls from buyers whose identities remain a mystery. Bidders in different time zones with Bluetooth apparatuses affixed to their ears. Fingers fly across cell phones as international truffle enthusiasts prepare to flex their funds and fight for the largest specimen the world has ever seen.

Delizia's heart stutters with the savage ache of longing.

And here—in the great hall of a medieval castle in Lazza-rini Boscarino, all around Delizia—Sotheby's specialists, deal-ers representing buyers. Media. Celebrities. Actor Riccardo Scamarcio agrees to a selfie with Gucci-clad fans. Chiara Fer-ragni in a plunging V-neck minidress, rapper Fedez in a slick suit, tattoos peeking out from his collar. Young models glowing in medieval attire the colors of an Italian summer.

And every soul in the grand hall under the sensuous spell of the truffle. Vibrating with the tantalizing mystery of what fortune it will command and the identity of its final possessor.

Chairs are lined perfectly. Everything ready, everyone wait-ing for the auction to begin. Delizia's eyes lift to the dramatic countdown timer Sotheby's erected in between the interna-tional flat screens.

Eleven minutes, twenty-eight seconds...

Center of the great hall. The banquet table. Everyone after a sniff and a selfie with the giant truffle. A truffle that Deli-zia has covered up for dramatic effect. Everyone aroused by its smell but yet to lay their eyes on the great white diamond that came from the dirt.

Delizia searches a sea of people for Giovanni.

Mingling bodies. Bright white smiles. Diamonds lanc-ing light across the room. *Allora*, there is Chef Umberto—silver hair, orange frames, black eye bags—huddled with fel-low superstar chefs, Carlo Cracco and a bespectacled Massimo Bottura. With them, blonde comedy actress Luciana Littizzetto pulls a face and cracks a joke. The famous chefs crumple into belly laughter.

But dazzled as Delizia is, she is haunted by uneasiness. Burning sensation in her throat. Twitching fingers.

Instinct.

Protective instinct for her people. She will not see them

exploited. Seen as some sort of elderly entertainers for a colosseum of the elite.

Where in the hell are her villagers?

Delizia's eyes find Benedetto, Stefano beside him in his wheelchair.

Oh, no. They have cornered a Korean reporter, who is staring at Benedetto's paintings with the bewildered look of a goat staring down a longsword. The reporter—bless her—nods thoughtfully at the painting of a clergyman with one bulging eye and a potato for a head. Her poker face has a harder time with the smirking parsnip that is supposed to be the *Mona Lisa.* Stefano, resplendent in a pair of shimmering leopard-print trousers, is flirting wildly with the camerawoman.

Oddio, what part of Delizia's impassioned speech to the village about "not making a spectacle" wasn't clear to them?

Delizia tries to flag their attention, stop these unsanctioned shenanigans, but her efforts are thwarted both by their commitment to flaunting their respective talents and age-related macular degeneration.

Delizia's eyes skim over magnificent floral displays. The knight's armor, polished like a Hollywood prop. Duccio in the midst of a heated on-camera tirade to some TV reporter.

Imbecille!

Delizia has to stop him. She dances her way in between mingling bodies, smiling at guests to hide her horror.

But it is Tommaso who snags her attention. He is difficult to miss. A line of wealthy guests are waiting to take a selfie with the man cosplaying as either a truffle or a testicle, depending on your interpretation. Digital camera clicks sound out amidst muffled protestations of "I am a truffle!" Tommaso shuffles awkwardly to pose near bouquets of flowers for maximum social media aesthetic. A woman in a satin dress implores him for a selfie with the banquet table in the background. Tommaso obliges, waddling his bulky papier-mâché body toward the table. He is almost to the table when—top-heavy—he trips. Onlookers shriek. Missing the edge of the banquet table by inches, he falls directly onto—or rather, into—an antique Savonarola *x*-shaped folding chair and gets stuck in its diminutive medieval measurements. Delizia silently fumes as she races to his side and, with the help of several guests, attempts to extract Tommaso.

"What are you doing?" she hisses into his eye-hole area.

A barely audible "I am the truffle mascot. They are loving it!"

"Where is Giovanni?"

A muffled "I haven't seen him. I can't see much of anything, honestly."

A small cheer from the guests as Truffle Tommaso is freed. Delizia spots Ugo farther down the banquet table. Looming perilously close to a champagne tower, he is impersonating a charging boar in front of three beautiful women. His arms flail recklessly close to the pyramid of perfectly stacked crystal glasses. The idiot is wearing his camouflage and has brought both a rifle and a dead duck with him, each sitting near the base of the stacked champagne glasses. The dead duck elicits a pang of jealousy in Delizia, with its limp body and commitment to unconsciousness. There he rests, unburdened by the weight of responsibility, no flock of other ducks relying on him to save them from duck destitution. Her jealousy is swiftly elbowed out by anger. She moves to confiscate the rifle—*che idiota, che grullo!*—she was very clear about lying low and letting the truffle speak for itself—but she is stopped by a reporter who snatches her hand and gives it what is commonly known in the dog world as a kill shake.

"*Sì, grazie.* We are, of course, delighted to be hosting the auction and the most prestigious guests here in our beautiful village of Lazzarini Boscarino. I am indeed proud to be mayor, and no, I no longer practice veterinary medicine, though it will come in handy should anyone need neutering!"

A pause for translation. Laughter.

"It is true, but we are privately grieving our friend Sofia Rosetti and ask for your discretion at this time."

"Ah, I thought you'd ask about that...well, if the ghost is here in the castle, keep your eyes open! He might not like sharing his space!"

"Ah, *sì, ovviamente*, the truffle hunter will be here any minute, you won't be disappointed!"

Delizia politely escapes the reporter and breaks out into a cold sweat. Where is Giovanni? Her eyes find Carlotta in a purple skirt suit. She is tiny under a spectacular ice sculpture of a Lagotto Romagnolo and appears to be in deep and utterly oblivious conversation with Donatella Versace. Delizia flinches. Sweat pearling across her upper lip tells her she is already too late. Still, she must try. She waltzes her way in between heiresses and tycoons to stop Carlotta waxing lyrical to the high queen of fashion about Lazzarini Boscarino's holy foreskin. Delizia reaches the pair in the middle of Carlotta's sentence.

"—that's when our local *poliziotto*, Silvio, evacuates us all— every villager—from the piazza and bravely sidles up to the bomb in the rubbish bin, only to discover that the whirring inside isn't actually a bomb—it's a discarded vibrator!"

"But whose?" Queen of the Versace empire asks.

"Mine, of course!" Carlotta peals with laughter. And a cold case is finally solved.

Delizia concedes defeat. She scans for the next fire to put out.

Another squint and scan for Giovanni. Instead, she spots Lorenzo next to camera equipment of imposing size. He is whispering something to her stepmother, Ludovica. An unlit cigarette between her nicotine fingers brings on acidic memories and a hot poker of anger. Delizia quickly averts her eyes and tries to blot out thoughts of Ludovica. She cannot go there. In this moment, criticism will kill her.

"Have you eaten anything yet, darling?" Nonna Amara is gazing up at her lovingly. Delizia's eyes sting, a truffle of a lump in her throat. "You certainly have pulled together a miracle." Delizia's pulse evens at the sound of Nonna Amara's voice.

"I will eat and sleep and resume a normal breathing pattern as soon as the truffle is sold, Nonna."

She kisses Nonna's soft cheeks. Breathes in her sweet smell of *brigidini* waffle cookies and good sense.

"Tell me, have you seen Giuseppina yet?" asks Nonna.

Delizia stabs her own palms with her nails. "What is going on with our village? This auction is all for them! Giovanni, star of the show, is missing. And now Giuseppina!"

"And Leon," adds Nonna. "I haven't seen him since this morning."

Nonna registers the redness flowering across Delizia's face. She gently squeezes her hands. "Go and enjoy the auction you have made happen for us. We are all so proud of you. The others will come. And if not, they will have Nonna to deal with."

Delizia looks into Nonna's blueing eyes. This is who the truffle will save. Absurd that an edible spore might be able to give her back her home, a thing that no one human has been able to do. Nonna gives the mayor's arms a gentle squeeze and shuffles away to look for Leon in the crowd. Delizia's eyes fill with tears of terrible yearning, of fatigue, or perhaps of a truffle's exhalations toying with her.

Swarms of people are now milling around the banquet table. Borghese Tartufi, the truffle hunters of her nemesis village, are in fine form. President of Borghese Tartufi, Rico Valentino, is holding court. Sweaty and smug, he is showing the foods of the gods they have brought to auction. Big, beautiful truffles too. *Tuber melanosporum*—the *nero pregiato* or precious black. *Tuber magnatum* Pico, the white or Alba truffle. Oils and salts of *Tuber borchii*—the *bianchetto* truffle, a gorgeous, garlicky, rust-colored truffle not in season until February. But Delizia smiles. There is only one truffle that is the reason they are all here, and it was not found in Borghese.

The not-so-tiny god sits on a velvet pillow under the giant bell of a cloche draped in dark cloth. Every eye in the castle awaiting its reveal.

Delizia's eye starts to twitch.

She spots another reporter all but running from Duccio.

Delizia blinks twenty times. Her eyes refuse to believe what is happening. She starts toward the idiot postman when Chef Umberto Micucci is suddenly at her side.

"Delizia, may I introduce Stanley Tucci?"

The American actor extends a hand and a "*piacere.*" Delizia registers kind eyes, signature smile, an endangered old-world charm. The pleasing chestnut of his head. But Delizia has a fire to put out. Mumbling an apology, she is abandoning Stanley Tucci, jostling her way through the great hall.

She hunts down the disgraced postman, snatching his bony elbow. "What did you tell that reporter?"

"The truth!"

"Duccio, I asked for one thing." She pinches the fingers of her left hand together, shakes them at him. "I need everyone to keep their shit together so that this auction goes off without incident, and I don't see how you—"

A camera flash. Delizia and Duccio instinctively smile, then resume scowling at one another.

"I told them our village is making a Faustian contract by selling the truffle."

She slaps her forehead. "Do you know how many reporters

have asked me personally about you? About your time in prison? I told them all it wasn't my business. Because you asked me, and I honored that. And I asked you not to accost the reporters with your conspiracy theories, didn't I?"

"You did, yes. I suppose I should keep it to myself," he grumbles.

"Stop. Talking. To. Reporters. To anyone. Silence your mouth by stuffing it with foie gras, knock back some prosecco, and just let the truffle do its magic. For us."

"Fine, but—"

"I don't have time for buts, the auction starts in…*porco mondo*…six minutes…where is Giovanni?"

A jolt of fear. He promised he wouldn't stand her up again after the virtual Sotheby's meeting. He wouldn't do this to her again. Would he? Guests have traveled from afar to meet the man who found the world's largest truffle. The truffle hunter who will provide its provenance. Everyone wants to hear the success story born in soil. A story that could make the truffle price soar.

Duccio squints at the hobnobbing crowd. "It would appear Giovanni had the good sense to stay the hell away from this farce."

Delizia gives him a look that would split a pork chop. She fumbles in her purse for her cell phone.

Her fingers find a napkin. Lorenzo's handwriting like a drunken army of ants staggering across the thin Bar Celebrità tissue.

We are all so proud of you. Ti amo.

Her finger scrolls down a million message alerts. Nothing from Giovanni.

But one quote from her mantra app: My sense of humor makes the world a better place.

She stuffs the phone, the note, and all the emotions it threatens to release back into the black hole of her purse.

Camera flashes. Bursts of laughter blossom up from somewhere nearby.

A hand clasps her elbow.

"Ciao, Mayor Micucci! Congratulations!"

The three Sotheby's men.

David. Steven. Jeffrey.

They all appear shorter in person. She air-kisses each near
the cheek. They smell respectively of shaving cream, cherry
vape, and tennis balls.

"Gentlemen, *buona sera*, welcome to Lazzarini Boscarino."

"We haven't seen much of it; we're staying at a nice hotel in
Borghese," says Steven.

"Of course you are." A diplomatic smile.

The three men smirk at one another conspiratorially. David
says, "*Grazie, signora.* I have been working on *mio Italiano*."

"How wonderful," says Delizia dryly. "We are minutes out,
how is it all looking?"

"Look around you! Do you feel it? There is an air of an
Agatha Christie novel...but instead of figuring out whodunit,
we are all trying to figure out whowilldoit." David smiles,
blinding everyone with slightly oversize teeth. "Who will be
the proud owner of the most magnificent Alba white truffle on
earth? This is an incredibly exciting moment, Delizia. For Sotheby's, for you. We have some of the most influential buyers from
all over the globe represented here. Bidders representing the
royal family of Qatar. Chefs from the most prestigious restaurants in the world—Chef Humm from Eleven Madison Park,
Chef Thomas Keller of the French Laundry, Chef Umberto
Bombana of Otto e Mezzo in Hong Kong. Not to name-drop.
Many wish to remain anonymous. But I can tell you that some
Hollywood royalty are bidding. Also"—he winks—"Jay-Z."

"Beyoncé's husband?" asks Delizia.

"Yeah, he's super into truffles."

He points to a screen where several Japanese bidders confer excitedly.

"And valuation is unprecedented. Current market price for *Tuber magnatum* Pico is $299.99 per ounce, $3,889.99 for a pound. But everyone on earth wants claim to *your* truffle. To own the Picasso of luxury foods. We know the potential buyers and the level of excitement over this one-of-a-kind find. I'm very proud to share that we project this Alba white will sell for over 500,000 euros. Our official projection is 550,000."

Delizia's mouth runs dry. Doubts flit around her mind like great black bats. She is so afraid to believe this wild fairy tale happening in her village. To believe in a forest-found miracle. "You've done an incredible job rousing international interest on such short notice, gentlemen."

"It was relatively easy. Everyone wants a chance at the extraordinary. An original. It helps to have a sob story, pull at hearts," says David.

"So true, everyone is charmed by the saga of the dead village and the resurrecting magic of a one-of-a-kind truffle," adds Steven.

"My village is not dead."

"Needs resuscitating though," Jeffrey adds to the conversation. He plucks a porcini bruschetta with truffled triple-cream brie from a waiter traveling at high speed, pops it into his mouth, and rolls his eyes in ecstasy.

A tray of champagne glides into grabbing distance. Delizia's arm strikes like a viper, snatching and downing the glass in one.

"We do have one major issue, Delizia—where is the truffle hunter? Influential people are lined up to talk to him. They want to know about the truffle's provenance." David leans close to Delizia's ear, engulfing her in the nutty exhaust of a peanut butter protein bar. "That truffle hunter is the key to the truffle's desirability. If he's here—the price of the truffle could skyrocket. Our guests are eating up the romantic story of the down-on-his-luck, desperate guy who strikes gold."

"He is not down on his luck or desperate. His name is Giovanni Scarpazza, and he lost his partner. Truffle hunting is what saves him from his sadness."

Steven snaps his fingers. A blunt-bobbed assistant appears, her fingers flying across her cell phone screen as she nods. "Why didn't we know this before? This is good, so good—Kelly, are you getting this? 'Truffle saves him from sadness'?"

Kelly nods. She looks up sheepishly. Delizia and Kelly share a millisecond look. A secret look that has been shared between women for millennia.

David starts up again. "You look so worried, Delizia, please don't. All the hard work has been done. Now, we sit back and enjoy the spectacle. I don't know about you, but I'm a good Christian." He steadies himself and unleashes his tirelessly rehearsed Italian sentence, "*Quando scorregiarci, possiamo pregare.*"

His New York colleagues are dazzled by David's commitment to learning *la bella lingua*. Delizia stares at him. She believes he meant to say, "When we are discouraged, we can pray." Only he has not used *scoraggiati*, the word for discouraged, and has instead boldly proclaimed, "When we *fart*, we can pray."

David sighs, bored with waiting for a compliment. "We will talk after history is made. See you on the other side. *Buona fortuna.*"

"You too, David." As Delizia turns to leave them, she adds, "Gentlemen, start your farts."

The Sotheby's men look bewildered but chalk it up to a language barrier.

A sudden change in the room. Staccato shrieks. Bodies in motion. Delizia startles, turns to see what the commotion is about. Standing at the entrance of the great hall is a man wearing a weatherproof jacket and a flatcap. Dirt-freckled rain boots. At his side, brown-and-white Lagotto Romagnolo, Aria. Lagotto Fagiolo leashed on his left like a little white lamb. All eyes on the enchanting creatures of the woods. They have brought a balm of the forest with them. Softwood and tree stumps. Wet dog. Damp moss and a marzipan note of wild mushrooms. The truffle hunter squints at an assault of camera flashes. A roar of jostling voices as the world media descends upon a man who just wants to disappear. He slips off his flatcap and nods, gentle gray eyes locking with lens after lens. The truffle hunter who started it all. Man of the hour with mud across his forehead.

Giovanni Scarpazza has shown up for the people of his village. Delizia is bowled over with love for the man.

A velvet voice pours from the speakers. "*Signore e signori,* please take your seats. The time has come. The auction is about to begin."

In each wall-mounted screen, seats start to fill. Across the world, bidders drain espressos, flap papers, fuss with their ties, psych themselves up for the great game.

Delizia sees Giovanni answering questions to a rapt audience. Elegantly dressed people take selfies with the Lagotti, who are all happy tails and tongues.

She exhales. It is perfect.

Delizia watches women turned into birds of paradise by wizards Valentino, Oscar de la Renta, Roberto Cavalli—melting into lined chairs in anticipation of the auction. She eyes the banquet table. Champagne tower. Beautiful bundles of truffles, elegantly labeled. Bottles of Barolo fit for giants. Benedetto has snuck his two paintings at the end of the table with a napkin labeling them in quavering scrawl, *Padre Francesco* and *Woman with Her Weasel by Local Lazzarini Boscarino Maestro, Benedetto Pucci.* Delizia feels a swell of love for him too.

And just as Pavarotti is belting out the final notes of "O Sole Mio," a panther-black Lamborghini screeches to a halt in front of the castle.

Giuseppina strides into the grand hall.

"*Diavolo!*" she screams.

Every eye turns from the truffle hunter to the captivating woman in the black sequined dress. Silk headscarf in peacock colors. Cat-eye glasses. Every eye following her accusatory finger. All eyes now on Duccio, the disgraced postman and recipient of her wrath.

"You seek vengeance!" she roars.

"Seek what?" he bleats, voice lost in the crowd.

"Vengeance, you old goat! *Figura di merda!* You have been lurking in the shadows and now that it is time to sell the truffle, this is your moment. There will be another death if I don't stop you."

Murmuring rumbles the great hall. The tongues of translators performing linguistic gymnastics. Delizia is frozen with horror, mouth agape, antipasto pinched between her fingers.

Duccio turns to a sea of wide eyes. Cameras train on him. Stanley Tucci is filming him for his Instagram Live.

"What are you talking about?" hisses the disgraced postman.

"Silence, you perpetual sad sack! I went to see a psychic, and I know what you're up to. And I won't stand for it. I am here, heart and soul, to stop you."

"I'm here, aren't I? Here supporting this embarrassing farce, even though I'd rather be—"

"You are here to sabotage the auction!"

Gasps from the Italians in the crowd. Pauses for translations and then more gasps. Nervous laughter. Another sound, possibly a fart.

Delizia running across the hall, abandoning her napkin,

a blob of truffled brie sailing through the air as she violently waves her arms to stop two of the people she is trying to keep from sabotaging her auction.

"Mamma Fortuna said there will be a battle with a ghost—" Giuseppina growls.

Duccio's face clouds over. "Calm down, Giuseppina. Your outbursts are insufferable; no wonder Elisabetta left!"

The slap echoes across the grand hall and is heard on four different continents. A slap so hard, Duccio's ponytail falls off. Giuseppina stares in surprise at the stick-on ponytail on the floor. A pause. And then applause patters across the grand hall like rain on a tin roof. Once again, Giuseppina has been mistaken for a performer.

The confrontation is interrupted. Music swells. Movie-trailer music that sounds suspiciously like the theme song from *Pirates of the Caribbean.*

"*Signore e signori,* welcome to the Sotheby's auction for the largest truffle in the world. And now, please welcome your auctioneer, Giacomo Volterra!"

Auctioneer Giacomo Volterra strides to the podium with a miraculous head of dark hair and cinema-star good looks. Little gold gavel in his hand. He pauses to pick up a platter of sizable black truffles, pretending to eat them. Laughter from everyone but Borghese Tartufi president Rico Valentino, who rises humorlessly, only sitting down again once the platter has been placed back on the table.

Delizia is stopped to pose for a photograph before she can get to Duccio and Giuseppina. It is her husband Lorenzo who dives in between the diva and the disgraced postman.

"If you're going to argue, for god's sake, do it privately," hisses Lorenzo.

Giacomo Volterra charms the international crowd from the podium with clever quips.

And then it is time.

"*Signore e signori*, it is my pleasure to introduce—the world's largest truffle."

An angelic woman dressed in a red-and-yellow medieval *gamurra* gown steps forward. Dons white gloves. She stoops, her cleavage plunging like the gorges of Garfagnana.

She lifts the cloth.

A shriek.

Camera clicks. Flashes of light.

The truffle posturing like biceps behind glass. The angelic woman clasps its glass handle and lifts, freeing the truffle from the bell jar.

A yell. "Bravo!"

Excitable cries.

Six pounds, fourteen ounces of hulking beige matter. An unearthed treasure. A colossal secret freed from the soil. Looking for all the world like a mummified organ. It dwarfs the apples around it, there to show its size. Hideous in juxtaposition with all the beauty glorifying the castle but holding every ounce of power.

A grotesque wart to be worshipped.

Deafening applause. The global media are on their feet. Even those in the screens standing.

The smell of the god hits hard. Waves of pheromones dilate every pupil in the great hall. Gamey, damp forest funk. A musk that summons saliva to pool in mouths.

Everyone thirsty for its erotic exclusivity. The hall tight with unspeakable longing. Hearts thumping. Parting of lips. Nipples stabbing through silk. Penises stiffening against Armani trousers.

Once a humble bulb buried under humus, the truffle has charmed its way up the human societal ladder to become an avatar of desire.

It is at this moment that—having snuck past security—a pregnant black-and-white cat leaps up onto the banquet table. Al Pacino starts an arrogant waddle toward the exposed truffle.

Gasps of shock and delight. Nervous laughter. Cell phone camera clicks.

"Al Pacino!" Giuseppina screams.

Camera flashes illuminate the cantankerous feline as she nears the truffle. The cat opens her mouth and grimaces so that the smell-taste Jacobson's organ on the roof of her mouth can take in the truffle's pheromones. Al Pacino then darts over to a smaller bowl of Borghese Tartufi truffles and tries to bury them with her paws. Laughter from the crowd.

"Quality control cat!" someone yells.

Rico Valentino of Borghese Tartufi stumbles up from his seat to the table, face on fire. He scoops up a swiping Al Pacino and rushes her to the front castle entrance. Shoos her down the steps.

"Get out of here, filthy cat! No!"

Al Pacino hisses. She aims a green-eyed death glare at the human. Outrage! Insubordination! *No?* Who dares tell a cat *no*! She has never once been denied in such a way. It is an affront to her feline pride. She glares at the man who threw her out, a man who smells like desperation and the little turds in the bowl she tried to bury. Enraged, she turns her backside toward Rico Valentino and waddles away, contrails of contempt lifting from her tail. A feline scorned.

"Don't touch my cat, you slimy weasel!" Giuseppina yells at Rico Valentino. Lorenzo is suddenly at her side, addressing both her and Duccio. Everyone else staring at the banquet table in a truffle trance.

"Come with me, *now*," says Lorenzo. As the world is infected by the spell of its fungal superstar, Lorenzo ushers Giuseppina and Duccio out of the great hall. Down a corridor that yawns open into ancient bedchambers. Dusty tapestries clinging to stone walls. Bed and furniture shrouded in protective covers.

And a healthy representation of the global media.

"*Scusate*," says Lorenzo and ushers his villagers back down the hallway along several winding corridors as long-dead aristocrats sneer at them from stone walls. They shuffle down stone steps. The temperature plummets. Giuseppina squints into a darkened lair.

Her eyes fill with fear. "No, no, no, *grazie*, I'm leaving. There is a ghost down here who apparently is ready for battle." She makes to leave.

"Giuseppina, there is no ghost. Only old resentments that we are going to put to rest once and for all, right here—and yes, here, because at least there are no reporters," says Lorenzo. And because she cannot bear to disappoint Lorenzo, she stays.

The castle's torture chambers are cold enough to crystalize bones. Which seems apt. A metallic smell rises from crumbling stone. In one corner looms an upright sarcophagus with a swinging door.

Duccio peels back the door. The sarcophagus is filled with spikes.

"Is that a...?"

"An iron maiden," whispers Giuseppina, recoiling.

Lorenzo swipes a finger across the iron maiden's dusty surface. "The Bartolini family had planned to turn it into a torture museum before they abandoned the castle, I think."

Giuseppina hugs herself. "Why are we in the torture chambers? We will miss the auction!"

"The auction is going to start with the Borghese Tartufi truffles and the wine. Our truffle will be the last to sell, so we have a moment to sort this out. What has gotten into you two? Delizia has put her heart and soul into the most magnificent event ever held in our village—"

"I don't know, our fig festival is a delight—" mumbles Giuseppina.

"We are going to sort this out once and for all because you are bickering like *bambini*! Making a scene in front of the whole world!" No one has heard Lorenzo this frustrated.

"Lorenzo, Mamma Fortuna said—"

"Giuseppina, not the psychic stuff again, please. Leave out the spiritual, stick to facts. Say your piece. Then Duccio, you will say your piece, and then, *basta*."

Giuseppina lifts her head with the pride of a warhorse. "Admit it, Duccio, you are trying to sabotage the auction!"

"I've been honest all along about not wanting the auction to happen! But all I've done is speak sense to a reporter or two. I'm not out for murder, *ma dai*! I hate this parade, this superficial delusion of what our village is, of what Italy is! A fever dream of Armani, Ferrari, and Aperol, when, in reality, none of us can afford those things. We struggle and suffocate under a corrupt parliament and politics, sky-high taxation, population implosion, unemployment and poverty, and I'm tired of the poetic lie that we are solely a land of art and cuisine and culture. We are more complex than a villa-with-a-view-and-a-pool holiday! The truffle is who we are—not sitting on a velvet pillow in a castle, but a force of nature finding its way out of the dirt."

A moment of silence as they contemplate this.

He continues, "The world should know the truth about us, not some false fairy tale. This auction is an aberration; you have to trust me."

"How can any of us trust you after what you did!"

"It was a long time ago, Giuseppina! And I paid for what I did with a year of jail time as well as you chasing me around the village with a splitting axe."

"You were lucky I was in heels."

"They hardly slow you down."

"You're lucky you survived, you idiot! If I had caught you, I would have made you into meatballs. All those letters from loved ones, all that important mail—mail from my darling Elisabetta—all because you are a miserable malcontent."

"I hid the mail because..."

Silence falls across the torture chamber like first snow.

Duccio the disgraced postman has never spoken about his motive for hoarding three years of mail. Towering piles of mostly unopened letters he selected and stuffed into his shed. Their discovery that led to his arrest.

"You kept the mail because you are a miserable human who can't stand to see anyone else happy."

"You should be grateful! It was making you all miserable. Every bill that Carlotta couldn't pay. Every letter of rejection from the government denying aid for Nonna Amara's house and to stabilize the mountainside. Every letter from Elisabetta in Milan that made you cry for two days because you miss her so much."

"Ugh," moans Giuseppina, "Milan." She spits on the floor. "Don't try to play the martyr, you have never cared about anyone but yourself."

"Fine. The real reason I hid the mail is because I wasn't getting paid enough. Stupid, *certo*. But it was invigorating to make the reckless choices of a younger man. Hiding it became a habit. You know why I hate that truffle? Because I worked hard for a lifetime and made peanuts. And here comes this hideous stumbled-upon tumor that will fetch a fortune. How is it fair?" A sigh. "But...what I did was wrong, and I know I've never apologized, and...I'm sorry for keeping your mail from you. It was wrong."

Lorenzo moves to sit and ponder, realizing at the last moment that he is about to impale his buttocks on a spiked inquisitorial chair. Instead, he perches on a small stool next to the torture rack. As the three villagers sit in shock and contemplation, the silhouette of a man and two dogs materializes in the arched entrance. Giovanni and the Lagotti step into view. All three wear a wild-eyed look as though they have escaped a pack of predators.

Giovanni is out of breath. "I've escaped the media because they are covering the bidding on Barolo upstairs. What did I miss?"

"We've just discovered down here that, despite years of evidence to the contrary, Duccio has a heart. We found it here in the torture chambers," says Giuseppina. "He just *apologized*."

Duccio rolls his eyes and grumbles.

A glance at his watch and Lorenzo is on his feet. "Okay, now that we've discovered that Duccio has a conscience and you two are no longer at each other's throats, can we please put this behind us, support Mayor Delizia in any and every way she needs, and get upstairs now? Our truffle is going to be auctioned any minute. We can't have anything upstage the sale of that truffle."

Four villagers nod in agreement.

And at this very moment, four villagers and two dogs feel a change in the air. The torture chamber suddenly ices over. Everyone feels a ghostly presence.

A dark silhouette looms at the arched entrance. The figure has the drawn spirit of one who has suffered.

Giuseppina claps her hands to her mouth.

The ghost of the prisoner. Tortured in these chambers. Mamma Fortuna said there would be a ghost. A ghost. A battle.

Fagiolo whines.

"The auction is starting," says the apparition, voice a rustle of dead leaves.

Lorenzo, a man of science, squints at the tortured presence and engages with it. "Delizia?"

She does not answer.

"We're coming up right now, darling," he says, frantically ushering the villagers toward the arched entrance. Voice lowering, he adds, "Hurry, look at the state of her!" The villagers shuffle along, anxious to distance themselves from an iron maiden.

And the strained figure in the torture chamber entrance wafts back up the corridor. Toward the electricity of the great hall.

And the final fate of the world's biggest truffle.

Chapter 17

The giant clock reads 6:00 p.m.

Stress saws at Mayor Delizia's bones. Nervous excitement is steaming up the great hall.

Auctioneer Giacomo Volterra electrifies at the podium behind the banquet table. A conductor, ready to start the symphony. He lifts a white-gloved hand. One small smile. And he blows the lid off the bidding.

"The largest truffle in the world, found here in Lazzarini Boscarino, Tuscany, at 50,000 euros."

Words from around the world arrow through headsets.

Bidders hoist paddles.

"Fifty-one thousand euros, do I have—thank you—" Giacomo points at a paddle lifted by the sleeve of a three-piece suit. "Fifty-two thousand euros, do I have 52,000—yes, thank you, 52,000, 53,000—yes, I have 53,000 euros for the giant truffle, do I have 54,000?"

Numbered paddles pop up like carnival-game targets. Delizia, breath hitching, searches the seated crowd. Security guards have left their stations, mesmerized by the bidding. Nonna Amara and Vittoria are sitting close to the banquet table. Surrounded by hedge fund types. Enraptured. Near her sits Ugo. Did he lock up his escape-artist hunting dog, Spinone Italiano Bruno, tonight? She hopes. She prays.

"Do I have 56,000 euros, thank you, madam—57,000—" Giacomo's voice runs as smooth as the Serchio river. He is a master of invisible money, deftly driving the bids to a crescendo swell. His eyes flick to a flat screen. *"Signore e signori,* a new bid has come in at Sothebys.com, I have 62,000 euros, do I have 63,000?"

Delizia clutches at her blouse, skin on fire. Little stars speck at the sides of her vision. Her neck and face burst into flames.

She is under attack.

Hot flashes are notorious for this.

She lowers her head into her hands. Another sensation. A hand on hers. She looks up to her seatmate, a woman with ice-blonde hair in an updo. Ruby earrings the net worth of a small European country. The lady hands Delizia her paddle and gestures that she use it to fan herself. Delizia nods and does, the first few waves of cool air whispering across her scorching skin.

She spots Giuseppina, Giovanni, Duccio, and Lorenzo sitting together, right next to the Borghese Tartufi team and its president Rico Valentino. Odd. Giovanni detests the Borghese truffle hunters. All around them, paddles trading off like the sun and moon on time-lapse. International offers flood in as bidders raise their hands through flat screens from different time zones.

Delizia thinks about the 550,000-euro estimate. She flaps

the paddle in her hand furiously to cool herself. The thought strikes her—if the bids slow, she can raise this paddle. *No, she mustn't.* It is paddle number 72. It belongs to the blonde beside her. Still, if it's just to drive up the price a little bit...

"There is a new bidder at Sotheby's.com, I have 75,000 euros, do I have 76,000 euros, thank you, Henry." Giacomo nods to a bald man in the middle of the seated crowd. Giacomo opens his mouth to drive the bid higher than 75,000 euros, and just as he does, he is silenced.

A shout detonates across the great hall. "One million euros!"

The great hall gasps.

A joke, surely, hiking the bid sky-high.

Heads turn to find the bellower.

Dark glasses. Shaved head, stubble, and a scowl. Green cotton blazer, sculpted stomach unhindered by a shirt. Slouching in his chair is Sabatino Accardi, the infamous heir to a confectionary company. The Italians know him as Rino Ricco because the press can't get enough of his lavish lifestyle and capricious, daredevil antics—from highest-stakes poker playing to the parties thrown for controversial world leaders, even wingsuit adventures where he throws himself off various cliffs like a flying squirrel.

Giacomo gestures a white-gloved finger toward the heir. "It appears we have a jump bid. One million euros, thank you, Signore Accardi—do we have 1.1 million euros? One point one million euros for the largest white truffle on earth, do we—"

Midsentence stream, Giocomo Volterra is cut off again. Another voice rises over the auctioneer's.

"One point four million euros."

All heads turn to a woman in a striking suit the color of poppies or freshly drawn blood. Black hair falls to her shoulders, straight as silk. She wears her late twenties like a crown. Her poise and power as conspicuous as her beauty.

Elyse Zhang. One of the most sought-after bidding agents on earth. A treasure hunter who lives out of a Louis Vuitton suitcase as she travels the globe in the name of the most discerning of collectors.

Delizia cannot breathe. She is suffocating in the afterburn of a hot flash. Blown over by scents of success. The blonde's Bulgari perfume. And the truffle.

Garlic. Honey. Earth.

Nausea rises like the bidding. Delizia throttles the paddle. Fans herself harder.

Giacomo Volterra calls out, "We have 1.4 million euros, do we have—"

"One point five!" yells Rino Ricco.

Paddles in the great hall and on each flat screen—Dubai, New York, Seoul, Singapore—have stilled. Everyone is pitched forward. All ears.

"We have 1.5 million euros, do we have—"

"One point six." Elyse eyes the enormous truffle.

"One point seven," yells Rino Ricco. He stands, thrusts his chin at Elyse Zhang. "I'm not going to back down. Give your buyer my best."

An excited shriek from the crowd.

Elyse Zhang does not respond. Her eyes give nothing but a glint to torment him. A slim hand over her mouth. She whispers something to the real bidder. An anonymous entity at the other end of the phone, somewhere in the world. A penthouse suite. Mega yacht. Mountain chalet. Private island. Some mysterious paradise.

Rino Ricco is not a man who is used to being challenged. "Who am I bidding against? Tell them to man up and show themselves!"

A toothless smile is all he gets. Elyse Zhang holds the secrets, and it is torturing him. The cat-eye eyeliner. Freezing him with those unforgiving eyes. That pigeon's blood–red suit. Cartier panther ring and its emerald eyes. Elsa Peretti snake necklace clasped around the pale cream of her throat. Elyse Zhang came here to annihilate.

Elyse Zhang pauses to listen to the cryptic human in her ear. She is still as the *Madonnina* statue as she responds with a dulcet "One point eight."

Rino Ricco whips off his pitch-black glasses. Olive skin reddening. This is his favorite kind of game. "One point nine."

Someone in the crowd chokes on absolutely nothing.

Rino Ricco's unbuttoned green blazer parts, his bare chest glistening. "Tell the ghost on the line I won't back down."

Everyone startles at a scream so loud it echoes across the hall. Giuseppina is on her feet. "The ghost!" she yells. "The ghost is battling!"

Uncomfortable laughter.

And then silence. Even the *Glis glis* in other castle rooms have ceased scrabbling. Stomachs in knots. White-knuckling of paddles. Everyone waiting to see what Elyse Zhang will do in the face of a threat. For what the ghost on the line will do next.

The tidy smile of the world's best bidding agent melts away. She shoots Rino Ricco a look. Eyes narrowed in on their target. She is *Vogue*. She is a beautiful villain. She is untouchable elegance itself. And she is not going to take any of his rogue-cowboy shit.

Her eyes—god, those ice-storm eyes—return to Giacomo Volterra. Her expression softens. Elyse Zhang gives the most minute of nods. And then an answer.

"Two million euros."

Applause erupts across the hall. Giacomo Volterra raises his hand to calm the crowd.

"*Signore e signori*, we have a bid of two million euros for the truffle. Do we have 2.1 million euros, 2.1—"

Rino Ricco's bared chest rising and falling. Addicted to adrenaline, he's a fire chaser, he'd admit it. And right now, he is alight with the diesel of desire. It is the heat in the room, his hot head. It is her with her class. The moons of her eyes. It's the pheromone perfume. It's that fucking truffle.

"Two point four million euros."

Before the auctioneer has a chance to acknowledge the bid—a crisp comeback from Elyse Zhang. "Two point six million euros."

The great hall falls so silent a distant cow's moo sneaks in through the door. In the castle *cucina*, a *Glis glis* falls off the fireplace ledge and onto a tray of Novelli antipasti.

"I have 2.6—I repeat—2.6 million euros…" Giacomo pauses, giving the confectionary company heir a moment. A fighting chance.

Rino Ricco is staring at Elyse Zhang as though there is no one else in the castle. No magnates, no world media, celebrities, or world-class chefs. He tears his eyes from her to take in the truffle one last time. The fungal crown jewel puppeteering some of the most powerful humans on earth. He smiles at Elyse Zhang—a white flag of a smile. Later, there will be op-eds, articles, poems, and memes—oh so many memes—made of the way he looks at her. He sees a paralyzing force of nature. Her magnetism strong enough to collapse a star. The moons of her eyes commanding the tides and tethering him to earth.

Rino Ricco bows his head to Elyse Zhang. Looks up again with a rapscallion curl of his lip.

He says, "Three million euros."

Screams. Eruptions of pent-up nerves in outcries and laughs. A man on his way to the restroom faints.

Giacomo almost stutters, "Well, we, I have three million euros, do we have 3.1?"

All eyes on Elyse Zhang. She is listening. Phone pressed to the seashell of her ear. A minuscule nod of acknowledgement to her invisible bidder. Eyes up at Giacomo.

She shakes her head.

"Sold!" bellows Giacomo Volterra, "For three million euros—a world record for the largest white truffle ever found."

The applause is riotous.

Delizia stands. She is swarmed by media. She fans herself with the paddle. Her head is filled with numbers. Paddle number 72, Sotheby's 10 percent gavel commission, two million euros needed to secure the mountainside above Nonna Amara's house. Three million euros. The castle walls are closing in. She needs space. There isn't enough room to breathe. A stampede of smells. Aging truffle. Cologne. Hot plastic of lights and camera equipment.

In her delirium, the pandemonium around her thickens into viscous slow motion. She sees—like a sluggish squeeze of honey—the crowd descending upon Rino Ricco as he flexes for the cameras. He has made history. Just another game.

But something catches the edges of Delizia's attention. Distant buzzing, like an oncoming insect. She stares at mostly empty chairs. A few people taking photos of the truffle and bottles of Barolo. The buzzing is getting louder. Delizia tunes out a bombardment of questions. Instinct—her eyes set on the entrance to the great hall. And what happens next happens faster than she can react to. The buzzing intensifies. At the castle entrance, a vehicle. It revs into the great hall. Vespa. Painted in the colors of the Italian flag. The Vespa zigzags into the hall, skidding on polished marble floor. Screaming. Guests running to other rooms of the castle. Most media running too. Some training their cameras on the rampaging Vespa. On the mystery driver causing hysteria. Their identity hidden by black leather, gloves, helmet.

Not far from Delizia, Giovanni Scarpazza holds back Fagiolo, straining and barking on his leash. The truffle hunter watches the Vespa run riot, horrified. Those colors. Italian flag. Thoughts click together like jigsaw pieces. It's the Vespa that nearly ran him off the road the day he found the giant truffle. The same Vespa that nearly drove into him as he chased after the dog thief.

Ugo's Vespa.

The Vespa chokes to a halt, driver struggling to control it. The driver is wrestling the throttle with a gloved hand. Giovanni's eyes flick to the rows of chairs. Everyone has run from the seats, now empty.

Almost everyone.

Nonna Amara is trying to make her way through the chairs. Shuffling in her sensible shoes. Vittoria helping her. The Vespa revs again. Giovanni wraps Fagiolo's leash around the base of an antique throne chair. He runs to Nonna and Vittoria, ushers them to the side of the great hall.

"Go to one of the rooms," Giovanni tells Nonna and Vittoria.

"What is happening, Giovanni?" Nonna's voice is small and scared, and it knifes his heart. Vittoria's face is frozen in terror.

Giovanni looks at the Vespa. At the far end of the banquet table. At media filming the intrusion. Tommaso, still in costume, is attempting to flee with the other guests.

Everything is happening so fast. Nonna recognizes the Vespa from her shed. "That's Ugo's Vespa," she says.

Giovanni looks over at the banquet table. He sees Ugo. Not on his Vespa but near the banquet table where the giant truffle sits. He has grabbed the rifle he hid under the table during the truffle auction.

Oh, no.

Ugo's face deep red from drink. He yells, spittle flying. "Hey! That's my Vespa!"

Giovanni is running. Nonna calling after him. The Vespa is in motion again, roaring forth, skidding across the slick marble toward the banquet table. Ugo has his rifle raised. He screams in warning. Taking the safety off the rifle. Lining up the black helmet in his sights. Giovanni trips as he reaches Ugo. Catches himself. He smacks the body of the rifle upward. The gun goes off with a deafening blast. Screams. A stampede. Everyone running from the great hall. Ugo stumbles backward, bellowing obscenities at him.

Giovanni screaming at the hunter. "For God's sake, put the gun down." Ugo's arm slackening, his eyes as large as serving platters. Rifle hanging at his side. A Vespa careening into the chairs, bullying its own path toward the table. Toward them. Giovanni grabbing Ugo by his camouflage shirt, pushing him away from the table. Both fall to the ground. Screams and camera flashes. The Vespa driver screeching to a halt before it hits the table. The driver snatches up the giant truffle. Tucking it under one arm.

Shimmering leopard print catches Giovanni's eye. Stefano's trousers. Stefano has wheeled right back into the middle of the hall again, weaving through the fallen chairs.

"What are you doing?" Stefano calls out to the Vespa driver. "Put the truffle back!"

He has placed his body and his wheelchair in the Vespa's only getaway path.

"Stefano, get back!" yells Giovanni, but he is on the ground, too far away.

The Vespa lurches away from the table, smashing aside more chairs. The driver is fleeing with the truffle, back toward the castle entrance. Stefano stretches out his arms to stop the thief. More screaming. Vespa front wheel skidding from side to side. The driver doesn't have control.

"Stefano!" bellows Benedetto.

As the Vespa speeds toward Stefano, a figure sprints out from the side of the hall. Giuseppina screams as she yanks the wheelchair backwards. Stefano feels wind on his face as the Vespa roars past, right in front of him. Another lurch and a blur of green, white, red is streaking back out of the castle entrance. Media chasing the Vespa. Giovanni picks himself up and sprints, faster than he has in years. The driver's helmet bobbing down the steps as they escape the castle. Vespa tackling the gravel. Freedom of the open road not far now. But out of nowhere, a black-and-white cat leaps in front of the Vespa. The driver yells out. Driving straight toward the cat. This cat has gumption, this cat has a grudge, hissing and holding its ground. A Vespa's high-pitched whine as it roars down the driveway, veering a sharp left to avoid the pregnant cat. A scream as the Vespa spills, throwing the driver. Black leather and helmet, body of the driver rolling into a series of fast tumbles across the gravel. A dull smash. Vespa on its side. Wheels spinning. Vespa driver face down. Unmoving.

And a once-giant truffle shattered into pieces all across the ground.

Giuseppina saw it all from the castle doors. She claps her hands to her cheeks. "*Cat* vengeance." She slumps onto a step, dizzy.

Giovanni is running down the steps.

Suited security guards are bolting toward the downed driver.

They reach the driver first. Vespa whining nearby. Someone cuts its engine. A security guard pulls off the driver's helmet. Everyone gasping in surprise to see Rico Valentino, president of prestigious Borghese Tartufi, writhing on the ground. Security guards swarming him. Cell phones pressed to ears, calls to medics and police. Camera flashes.

And rising above the chaos, the crying of a young girl.

Giovanni goes to her, cradles little Vittoria.

She heaves out words between sobs. "It's my fault—I wanted money—to help Nonna—I wanted it for my *nonna*—to have—her—house back—Sofia died, and everything is changing and—and I don't want to lose my *nonna*—"

"This isn't your fault, darling."

Giuseppina flies down the steps of the castle. She hears the sirens screaming toward the castle. "Rico Valentino, I will make meatballs of you."

She sees Vittoria in Giovanni's arms.

"Vittoria, you are alright, you are alright."

Vittoria looks up at her with red eyes. "It's all my fault the truffle is ruined—I—stole Ugo's Vespa from Nonna's shed, I was driving it when I shouldn't have been—I was selling things to make money for Nonna's house—and yesterday I parked the Vespa in Borghese and someone stole it—"

Truths plume into the air like the essence of a truffle.

Giovanni rocks Vittoria. "Never mind all that. We're all safe, and that's what matters."

The crowd has gathered. Photographers snapping pictures of the man who stole and demolished a three-million-euro truffle. Close-ups of crumbled lumps of truffle, as glamorous as the driveway gravel. Cries of excitement. And then, filmed for all the world to see, guests in thousand-euro shoes descend upon the driveway. Squatting and snuffling on all fours, noses lowered to the dirt, grabbing chunks of the once-giant fungus like the truest of truffle pigs.

Benedetto helps Nonna Amara down the stairs. Vittoria is slipped into her *nonna's* arms.

"It's okay, *Farfallina*, I am here. Your *nonna* is here."

Vittoria lifts her head from Nonna's cardigan to mewl, "I sold the brooch you gave me, Nonna, I didn't lose it, I've been selling things at the Borghese music festival to get money for your house—yesterday, I rode Ugo's Vespa into Borghese again—I parked it, and someone stole it—"

"It's okay, *Farfallina*, it's okay," Nonna says gently.

"—I don't want to lose you, Nonna, I don't want any change, I don't want anything to change—"

"Sssssh, ssssssh." Her *nonna* has tuned out the castle, the crowd, the whole world as she speaks to her granddaughter. "My darling, *Farfallina*. You must not worry about that. Fears don't prevent death, they prevent life. My love for you is so strong that I will always be with you. And that's a thing that will never, ever change." She gives her granddaughter's hand a delicate kiss. "Here, so you never forget." Nonna Amara removes her silver Saint Christopher necklace, clasping it around Vittoria's slim neck.

Delizia, her body and mind numb, pushes aside cameras and reporters. She crouches to check on Giuseppina. Her purse slips off her shoulder, falls to the ground where so many truffle pieces lie. Dazed, delirious, she picks up her cell phone. It blinks at her. Another message among millions on the screen. But a name stands out. She reads the texts.

"Oddio."

Sotheby's men flapping around her. Reporters. Cameras. Drones whirring above. Questions about the broken truffle. About Rico Valentino. About three million euros. From the corner of her eye, she catches Rino Ricco in an argument with a Sotheby's specialist. A trace of red—Elyse Zhang melting into a limousine. Guests are leaving. Sotheby's David, his woodland-mushroom ears scarlet, is in her face.

She tunes him out.

"Out of my way, please. Giovanni!" Delizia calls out. "I have to go. Leon is in trouble."

Her focus is singular. Nothing else on earth matters.

Delizia is running toward her Land Rover. Guests groveling on the ground. Reporters buzzing like a kicked hive.

And just a few yards from it all, a pregnant black-and-white cat watches. She feels better about the disrespectful banishment from the castle she suffered when all she'd wanted was a little lick of the truffle.

Get out of here, filthy cat! Puah.

Vengeance is delicious. It's cream and catnip and a warm sunspot.

She slowly saunters away.

For there is other mayhem to make.

Chapter 18

Leon is not answering. The lights are on. Delizia rams her fist against the front door one more time. Nothing. The dogs—even Luna the Maremma sheepdog—are barking. They are in the house. Odd. She howls Leon's name into the night. A tawny owl responds from the treetops with a high-pitched "Who?" And then Delizia is running away from the farmhouse. Her head is filled with snakes, heels sinking into the damp grass. Ahead, in the darkness—Leon's stable. It is aglow. She picks up the pace, rolls her ankle. Swears. Kicks off her heels to hobble the last of the distance to the stable door.

A shove and the rickety stable door shudders open. Delizia bursts in. Smells greet her first.

Hay. Manure. Silage. Timeworn wood.

A naked bulb dangles from the shed ceiling. It casts a yellow orb of light on a scene. Leon is lying on a mound of hay. He is in a navy blue suit. Suspenders winking in silver. Next to him lies the prostrate body of a donkey.

Delizia is fighting off her jacket. She is still wearing her auction dress underneath.

She drops her medical bag. Sinks to her knees.

Leon's voice is hoarse. "Did you bring the antivenin?"

Delizia scans Maurizio's body for bite marks. She focuses on his nose and legs, the most common places for a snake to strike.

"What makes you think it was a viper?"

"I've seen them around here. Big ones. Put the dogs in the house so they didn't get bitten."

"Tell me what happened."

"I was getting ready to come to the auction and I…I can't explain it, I just had this feeling in my gut, so I came out to the stable and found Maurizio."

Delizia runs her hand over the donkey's firm cheek. A sweet waft of hay brings on olfactory hallucinations. Memories come at her like scattered bats. Maurizio giving the laughing children of the village rides. Maurizio and Sofia at the fig festival. Sofia kissing Maurizio's velvet nose, walking him across the piazza on a hot summer's day. Maurizio, the star of every Christmas play, Leon dressed as Moses. Her father in a red suit and big white beard—he is Babbo Natale with a big bag of presents for the *bambini*. Almost twenty-two years of their beloved Maurizio, a donkey that stole the heart of every human he has ever met.

Leon's deep voice is tremulous. "When I couldn't get you, I tried calling the vets in Borghese, but they are on vacation in Greece. For a while he would struggle to his hooves, then circle for a few minutes, bite at his flank, and then he would lie down again. He just kept doing that over and over. He seems too exhausted now."

Delizia sees that Maurizio is curling his lip. She runs her hand over his neck. Damp with sweat. She pulls back his lip and touches his teeth. A clue. His gums. Tacky. Brick red in color. She must check his vitals. She wrestles a stethoscope from her

bag. Listens to the *whomp whomp* of his pulse. Counts his respi-
ration rate. Holds his tail out of the way to take his temperature
with a rectal thermometer. Another clue. His belly. Distended
as a drum. Delizia puts her ear to his taut stomach and listens
to the gargling of his gut—a sound like the river after a rain-
storm. Pinching the fur of his neck into a tent, she eyes the skin
for elasticity.

Leon is squatting now, pitched forward. His eyes bloodshot.
"What is it?"

Delizia's eyes shudder from fatigue. She blinks hard. She
must play the part of a detective. Study symptoms. Analyze evidence. Piece together the mystery so she can administer the
right medicine. And fast. She looks around the stable.

"Has he had a vaccination recently?"

"No."

"Is he on medications?"

"No."

"Have you floated his teeth recently?"

Leon takes a moment to remember when he last filed down
the sharp edges of Maurizio's teeth. "No, I—not recently."

"Has anything—and I need you to really think about this,
Leon—has anything changed about his diet?"

"No." Guilt and grief twist his face. "I just don't understand."

Maurizio is nodding his head. His ears droop like days-old
lilies. Nostrils flare. He groans.

The top half of the stable door creaks open. It's Lorenzo.
Benedetto. Giuseppina. Giovanni. Even Ludovica.

"What can we do to help, Delizia?"

"Bring me some towels and a pail of fresh water."

"Delizia, could it be because he misses Sofia so much?"
Leon is mumbling now. "Maurizio was her favorite...maybe
the only reason she didn't leave me. And he loved her." Delizia
lifts her eyes from her patient long enough to observe Leon.

A great bear of a man, and all she can see in him now is a lost little boy. Drowning in a sea of sadness. "Delizia, is he dying?"

She does not answer. She must focus. She can't think about what it will do to Leon to lose Maurizio. What it will do to the villagers to lose their beloved Maurizio after the tragic fate of the truffle. So much loss. She has to focus.

Delizia is on her feet, gingerly stepping over Maurizio's head. She looks at his water trough. Clear, clean water. She sifts through hay, sniffing it. His bed is a large mound of wood shavings. She sifts wood chips with her fingers, feels the bite of a splinter. Its warm aroma summons sawdust memories of hamsters and pet mice. Her fingers find another texture. Smooth; a little sticky. She lifts up a long sliver of plastic.

"*Oddio*," Leon whispers.

"He's eaten the plastic bag his bedding came in," says Delizia. She is grappling for her medicine bag. "He has impaction colic. Lorenzo, get my mobile IV kit and a bag of fluids from my car." She pulls a nasogastric tube from her medical bag. "And I'm going to need some help restraining Maurizio."

The villagers shuffle into the stable, hay rustling under their shoes. *Dalle stelle alle stalle.* From the stars to a stable in a day. Soft hands press Maurizio's head and neck to hold him down. Maurizio's eyes—spidered with red—searching, desperate. Delizia intubates him with a nasogastric tube. Sends mineral oil and magnesium sulfate into his stomach to help him pass the plastic. She administers dioctyl sodium sulfosuccinate to soften his stool after calculating the dosage and then recalculating it another four times. A miscalculation could be fatal. Next is an antispasmodic and anticholinergic for his intestinal spasms and to help sedate him. Maurizio's breath is the ocean at high tide.

"And now?" croaks Leon.

"And now we wait. I think there's a good chance he will pass it, but only time will tell. I want him on psyllium and alpha agonists for pain management over the next few days."

Leon nods. A tear paints his cheek silver.

Lorenzo leaves Maurizio's side to embrace Leon. Giuseppina, Benedetto, Giovanni, and Ludovica hover over Maurizio, willing him to heal. Whispering words he can't understand, but he can feel.

Delizia excuses herself. She needs air. The night air is so fresh it is mint on her lungs. The tawny owl calls another tremolo hoot. Delizia shivers in the wide expanse of the field before her. No longer trying to hold every thread of fate, the last stitches of her resolve unravel. She pictures pieces of truffle scattered on the ground and bursts into tears. Heaving with silent sobs. Failure has found her again.

A presence by her side. Coiling cigarette smoke.

"What do you need?" Ludovica's voice is an ashtray.

"A time machine. A lot of money."

"I don't have either of those."

Delizia laughs at her stepmother's literal thinking and lack of humor. She pictures a desert. Sand for miles. She sniffs. Ludovica hands her a tissue.

"Is this my stepmother come to tell me I'm a failure?"

"A failure? You've only just got the job and you've already given the village so much. Your father would be very proud. And it might not mean anything to you, but I am very proud. I've known you most of your life, and you have never, ever been a failure."

Delizia dabs at her eyes with the tissue, makes a Rorschach with mascara.

Ludovica squints into the night to avoid eye contact with her stepdaughter. "This village meant the world to your father, even if he wasn't very good at being its mayor. I found out what he did with the money."

"What?"

"Bad investments, some gambling. Tried to double it and lost it all. He was reckless. And a fool." A drag on the cigarette. "I miss him."

"Are you alright?"

"I am." Her cigarette light flares like a devil of a firefly. "Grief is a tax. One you pay if you were lucky enough to love." She stares at her shoes. And she digs deep. "I thought... I have been meaning to ask. Maybe we could have a coffee together some time?"

There it is, after all these years. The tiniest thread—hypha thin—reaching forth, struggling through the soil in search of connection. Delizia sees her stepmother's hands shaking. She looks away. Marvels at the black silhouettes of the Tuscan hills. With so much loss, what is left but forgiveness and new beginnings? She pictures an olive branch. "Okay."

"Good then." Ludovica starts to walk away. Time has softened her, taught her what matters.

Delizia suddenly remembers seeing Lorenzo whispering with Ludovica at the auction. "Did Lorenzo put you up to this?"

"No. But I told him I was unhappy. And he encouraged me to be brave and tell you how I really feel. All these years I've let my own pride get in the way. I wanted us to be friends, but your father made that complicated. I should have said something sooner, but you were in Pisa, and...well, it's all just time and excuses." She crushes the cigarette under her foot. "You've got a good man, Delizia. He loves you, and you deserve that love."

"I can always count on him. No matter how wild the winds get."

"He has a way of grounding everyone, doesn't he?"

Delizia nods. She watches her stepmother shuffle back toward Leon's house. In her blindness, a myopic hunt for her father's affection, she didn't see that she'd had it from her stepmother. Spiny Ludovica. Prickly, in pain. Treading in a sea of self-preservation. Afraid of failure. Delizia sighs. Family has always felt like a forced entanglement. Her stepmother became a stranger to her. So easy to sever the thin threads connecting them. But they still have time to reach out to each other. Commit to the tiny act of drinking one coffee together. The beginnings of a mutual relationship.

At four a.m., the villagers are in need of rest. Lorenzo holds his arm out for his wife to hold.

"I'll stay," she says. Lorenzo kisses her on the forehead, tells her he will pick her up when she is ready to come home.

Mayor Delizia and farmer Leon. Sitting in the open stable doorway, side by side, watching the glinting sequins of the stars. They cradle mugs of Vecchia Romagna, the brandy golden and glowing in their chests. They are too tired for talk. Maurizio's chest rising up and down as he rests.

A stir of movement in the darkened field ahead catches their eyes.

Delizia frowns. A dark shape is slinking toward them. A bleeding black shadow.

Leon's hand on her arm to keep her still. Silent.

Thirty feet ahead, a wolf steps into moonlight. Drawn onto the farmland by the distress of a donkey.

Light pours down on the wolf like thin milk. Its fur is an autumnal forest. Reds of a rusted old lock. Browns of chestnut shells and olive groves beaten by the sun. Wheat fields of cream. Delizia holds her breath. Loses herself in the bright coins of a predator's eyes. The wolf's primal presence is an ancient thing. It spills a great lake between them. It makes a home on her skin.

Her mind is quiet. It is the soul's time to speak.

Delizia feels a cage door open inside her. Her heart is shucked like shellfish, a feeling of belonging rolling out to the horizon like a well-fed river.

She is a part of this.

Forests of oak and beech and chestnut. Alpine splendor. Secret kingdoms of flora and fungi. The living sentences of rich, invisible stories that run deep underground and soar up into the stratosphere. The undulating velvet of these hills where the wolves thrive. Where a man can grow olives and a good life. The sun sweetening the skin of a tomato. Where a magnificent truffle can be born. Delizia has never been less afraid. She is a small animal in awe of the miracle of life. Embedded in a glorious network since birth, she has always been enough. An unbreakable sense of belonging rooting her in place.

Hope wraps its tentacles around her and lifts her to the stars.

Leon makes a gentle grunt to let the wolf know that humans are here. The wolf bolts, cantering back toward the mountains. One last look with quicksilver eyes. And the wolf is swallowed up by the trees.

"I have never seen anything so beautiful," Delizia manages to whisper.

Leon nods. "We almost lost them. They've made a comeback." He sips his Vecchia Romagna. "Loss brings everything into focus, doesn't it? The fragile beauty of life. A desire to live fiercely. It sweeps away the dirt of anything unimportant, exposes the truth. The wolves know how to live in harmony with the land that nurtures them. They are thriving."

Delizia nods.

She has never felt more at home.

Chapter 19

Bar Celebrità is abuzz. Warm lighting and wine bottles. Prosecco pops. Bright waves of laughter. Cozy old Bar Celebrità. F. Paradise Mambo's perky "Buona Sera Signorina" in the airwaves. A scent beating its broad wings, starting a slow flight across the bar. Truffles sit in bowls on tabletops. Homemade birthday banners are tacked onto the walls. Nonna Amara has made a *castagnaccio* chestnut cake. It is, after all, a party to celebrate Maurizio's twenty-second birthday.

Maurizio, donkey and celebrated mayoral candidate, stands at the entrance of Bar Celebrità wearing a dashing plaid blanket and a glow of good health. Leon strokes his nose, feeding him carrots and crumbles of fresh truffle. Giovanni pats the donkey's flank as he passes around antipasti made by Lorenzo, each recipe incorporating the little witchy warts he and his dogs found in the forest.

Vittoria is squatting on the ground, scratching the bright white belly of Fagiolo, who rolls and squirms with delight.

Around her neck, a silver Saint Christopher glints, his staff raised to provide protection. And another silver saint necklace gifted to her by Giovanni. Sant'Antonio, the patron saint of truffles. She is learning to let go of fear and savor the scent of each moment. Aria is at Vittoria's side. She does not need to guard Giovanni, for the sinister scents of fear, anger, and loneliness are gone. He is healing, she senses, finding a new trail to happiness. She can relax her watch. But she will read the rhythms of his heart for the rest of her long life.

Aria is rolling around Giorgio, the grandson of a psychic in Pietrasanta. Vittoria and Giorgio only recently met but became fast friends, bonding over animals and art and having a *nonna* who is made of magic. Just two old souls remembering how to be young again.

Spirited shouts and hoots spark up from the table where twins Rosa and Valentina, Padre Francesco, and the formerly disgraced postman Duccio are playing a card game of *briscola*. Padre has just been accused of cheating.

Lorenzo emerges from behind the bar. He picks up a beautiful white truffle—the size of a Ping-Pong ball—and hands it to Stefano, who sniffs, allowing the tuber to awaken long-buried memories. Lorenzo pats Benedetto on the shoulder and steps over to Giuseppina, who is staring at the picture of Raffaella Carrà.

"Should I be worried about how quiet you are tonight?" Lorenzo asks his sister-in-law.

Giuseppina sighs. "I know you don't approve, but I just wanted to believe that all of what Mamma Fortuna said would come true. She said the truffle would bring our village great success. And it hasn't."

"You don't need my approval. And she got a few things right, didn't she? Battle with a ghost—the mystery billionaire bidder."

"And the vengeance! Al Pacino sought vengeance on Rico

Valentino for throwing her out of the castle. Jumped right in front of his Vespa and caused him to crash!"

"If you say so. I suppose there was a death, wasn't there? The truffle." He smiles. "I regret being hard on you about the psychic. There can be space for both the scientific and the spiritual. Maybe I should open up my mind to the mystical like you do. How sad if I were to miss a bit of magic in my pragmatic life. My favorite work of art depicts both, you know. It is an artistic and mathematical representation of man's connection to nature and man's connection to the universe, which I think can be interpreted as the scientific and the spiritual. What, why are you looking at me like that?"

He stops speaking because Giuseppina's eyes are the size of satellites. Her mouth is agape. Speechless, she pulls the drawing young Giorgio did of the *Vitruvian Man* from her purse.

Lorenzo studies it. "Ha! What a coincidence. Who did this? It's very good."

Giuseppina, a smug glow warming her cheeks, points at young Giorgio. "The grandson of the psychic."

Giuseppina flicks her blonde hair, pinning the drawing to the wall with a flourish. She raises her eyebrows at Lorenzo and saunters away from him saucily, turning once to hit him with an "I told you so" look.

Chef Umberto Micucci is hunched at a table. He is silent and pensive, traits he is unaccustomed to. He is pretending to check his phone while pretending not to sweat. Nearby, his ex-girlfriend Marilyn is laughing and chatting with Carlotta. They are speaking in Italian, Marilyn having recently committed to learning *la bella lingua* and embracing everything Tuscany has to offer. She is letting Italy hold her healing heart, falling more in love with life each sunrise. Carlotta has just taught her the words for "hiking" as well as "holy foreskin." Carlotta is beaming with pride over her grandson, Poliziotto Silvio, who is being celebrated by all the *carabinieri* of the neighboring villages for his excellent police work that led to the arrest of the president of Borghese Tartufi, Rico Valentino. Not just for the brazen theft of the truffle. Or the stolen getaway Vespa. Silvio was sure there was more, but there was no evidence to tie Rico to the theft of Fagiolo. Until Poliziotto Silvio contacted the visiting foreign reporters and acquired drone footage of a Borghese Tartufi member stealing Giovanni's Jeep, who was quick to implicate their president, Rico.

Giuseppina slaps Umberto on his shoulder. She pokes two fingers toward her eyes and then toward his brother Lorenzo, who is now pouring drinks at his bar. Umberto nods, gestures that he doesn't want to be rushed. These things are delicate. He has to pick the right moment to have a heart-to-heart with his brother. To apologize for using money that was meant for both of them to build an empire. For stealing recipes from Lorenzo and Nonna Amara, running off to culinary school, and leaving his brother to pick up the pieces. Apologies are difficult for Umberto Micucci. They smell pickled and briny, that sometimes sewage stink of the sea. But he will do it. He can do it. Apologize first and then make the first steps to rekindling their relationship. Later, he will be so bold as to offer some expansion advice and discuss investing opportunities for the future of Bar Celebrità. And his big proposal—to ask Lorenzo if he is interested in joining creative forces for the future of Novelli. It always should have been a family affair. But for now, a sip of the best Negroni he has ever had and an imminent apology.

Lorenzo is now dancing in and out of his *cucina*, topping up prosecco glasses and preparing to serve his wild boar ragù (Ugo's boar) with pappardelle pasta (Nonna's pasta). He stirs his *spaghetti all'ubriaco*, the "drunk" spaghetti he has cooked in wine until it turns a deep purple, then checks on Delizia, who is perched at the bar. She had been staring up at the bar's new TV. At a news report of a missing Pietrasanta girl who has just been found thanks to the help of a local psychic.

"You doing alright? Your brother is staring at you," says Delizia.

"I noticed. He looks sheepish, haven't seen that in an age."

"Will you forgive him?"

"I think it's time we talked. We're both getting a bit old for grudges. You were right about bringing the truffle to him. I'm happy to see he still has a heart."

Delizia smiles. How is it possible to love Lorenzo more than the day she was carried down the aisle to him?

"Thank you for believing in me."

"I always have. I always will. You can do anything you put your mind to, Mayor Micucci. We are all so lucky to have you." There he goes, shining his light for her across every stormy sea and darkened sky. Calling her home.

Delizia kisses her husband. Cradles his cheek and then watches him shimmy over to Benedetto and Stefano with a bottle. Benedetto is flush with pride, having sold his paintings *Padre Francesco* and *Woman with Her Weasel* for twenty-six thousand euros at the truffle auction. Stefano gives him a look of adulation. He is resplendent in brand-new fuchsia trousers that were bought with a little of the sale money.

Delizia sips her prosecco. She picks up one of Giovanni's truffles sitting in a bowl on a table. Admires the precious organic structure. A taupe jewel made by a brilliant conflation of connections. The very symbol of synergy. Each of these truffles is a treasure that would not exist without a coming together of forces. It is a reward for unity. She looks at the people of her village. Laughing. Celebrating. Food bringing everyone together. In harmony with each other and the land that nourishes them.

Delizia has a secret. She has not yet told anyone. She's kept it in her pocket all day. She just got word that the nomination file she submitted to the World Heritage Committee has been accepted. She will now wait for three advisory bodies mandated by the World Heritage Convention, including the International Council on Monuments and Sites and the International Union for Conservation of Nature, to evaluate Lazzarini Boscarino. But it is well on its way to becoming a UNESCO World Heritage Site. Which is when her village will be eligible to receive funds for its protection and conservation. This place where the people are as magical as the ant and the swallow and the wolf. A place filled with hidden treasures. Delizia has also put out feelers and made her first connections with the Italian Ministry of Agriculture, Food Sovereignty and Forests and the Ministry of the Environment, to protect the forests surrounding Lazzarini Boscarino. The truffle-hunting grounds. She enjoys a novel feeling—warm waves of success. She is just beginning to scratch the surface of what she can do for her village.

She thinks of their giant truffle. The loss of a three-million-euro fortune—Rino Ricco wasn't going to cough up for crumbs. Donations were made to Lazzarini Boscarino, but the media made a laughingstock of them. And then, a little tendril of kindness coiling through the darkness—someone set up a GoFundMe page for Nonna Amara. To reciprocate, Vittoria started filming their time together in the *cucina* and sharing recipes online. *Breaking Eggs with Nonna Amara e Vittoria.* Money from subscribers and sponsorships is flooding in to fund the repairs for Nonna's house. Vittoria says it will bring tourism too, that it is the future. Nonna says Vittoria is the future.

Delizia believes the truffle did not die in vain. Its end as humble as its beginning, it still managed to beautifully manipulate humans into protecting the land of its birth. Taught the village to embrace its nature. That is its legacy. It has indeed,

Delizia thinks, saved the village. The truffle has the last laugh. Chuckle. Breath.

Delizia watches Ugo and Tommaso both attempting to calm Ugo's Spinone Italiano, Bruno, without much success. Bruno vaults onto a tabletop and snarfs down a bowl of pasta. She laughs. She'll tell them all her secret. Maybe after the cake and a toast to Maurizio on his birthday.

Birthday donkey Maurizio is still blocking the entrance to Bar Celebrità. So almost no one notices when the top of a head peaks up above Maurizio's buttocks. Leon, hearing pleas to enter, moves the donkey a few steps farther into Bar Celebrità to let the stranger in. A young man. Maybe thirty-five. Dark skin and a disarming smile. Dressed for a dinner party.

"Good evening. I am looking for Mayor Delizia?" His Italian is good for a foreigner.

The villagers fall silent. They already know he's a reporter. In the days following the auction, reporters circled the village like vultures. The villagers declined interviews. Shooed away any birds of prey.

Giuseppina strides up to the young man. One hand on her hip, the other on her favorite donkey standing in her beloved Bar Celebrità. "You're here to snuffle out the story of a laughingstock village. To photograph its clowns."

"I understand why you'd think that, but I'm not. I'm a writer and a filmmaker. I read about the truffle and Lazzarini Boscarino. It brought back memories of a trip with my father to Tuscany, right before he passed. We visited small villages, and it was life-changing for me. I think—a long time ago—we came here. We were driven around by a man with wild curly hair and bright yellow trousers."

Stefano smiles. He remembers.

"And I remember eating the most wonderful pastry of my life, baked by an old man everyone called Babbo."

Nonna Amara shivers in delight at the mention of her father.

"I'm here because I think the most fascinating thing about this village is the village itself, the relationships that make it rich. I'd like, with your permission, to write about it. I think... and apologies if I sound glib... that your village might be the true truffle."

Giuseppina looks him up and down. Her eyes linger on the laptop tucked under his arm. She squints at his tie suspiciously. "Good. But you have to drink to celebrate Maurizio on his birthday. He was almost mayor, you know."

The young man is dragged off by his sleeve. Introduced to Mayor Delizia. Nonna Amara insisting he eat a plate of antipasto she has just piled together. Giuseppina handing him a glass of vin santo wine with a crisp *biscotto* to dip in it.

"Here," she says. "You look too thin. We don't want Padre Francesco to do an exorcism on you."

In a bar nestled on top of a Tuscan hill, friends celebrate the passage of time. They are surrounded by the stone of old walls made rich and rustic over many seasons. By other charming little towns and villages, tucked away like truffles. Beyond the labyrinths of steep, cobbled paths and centuries-old houses, wheat fields rustle with maddening mountain air. Wheat waited upon—fed, fertilized, watered, and weeded—by the doting hands of farmers. Wheat fields give way to groves of olives. Where poor-postured trees are pruned, watered, and worshipped by humans. Neighboring the olive groves are bewildering beautiful vineyards. Vines planted in tiny lines like library books. Each a pulpit for a person to kneel before. Farther out still are the forests. As archetypal and mysterious as an ancestor.

Beech. Oak. Fir. Chestnut.

Chestnuts are swelling to peak sweetness. Ripening, dropping, humans on their hands and knees to gather these little

gemstones of Christmas culture. And everywhere, the shiny
skulls of mushrooms erupting from the earth. Each is a masterpiece. Porcinis with their bread bun hats. Frilly yellow petticoats
of chanterelles. Tiny trumpets of oyster mushrooms. Slimy little sirens who quicken the hearts of *fungiatt*—the mushroom
hunters.

The forest performs an irresistible earthen symphony.
Humans have always done the bidding of biota.

As above, so below. A sink into the soil. The rum-dark rhizo-
sphere is breathless and bursting with activity. Hidden sagas of
creation and destruction. Sugar-pink earthworms. A starburst
of springtails. Giant bus body of an ant. Fungal fingers—thin
and strange—spidering through the dark. Hunting.

Fungi are the forgotten alchemists. They are king and scav-
enger in the vast kingdom that humbles a human eye.

Here is the base of an ancient oak. This oak has watched
little boys become blue-eyed *nonnos*. A fungus found this oak.
Fungus and a tree forming an alliance. In secret, they swap
sugar and water. These clandestine dealings have borne fruit.
A truffle has swollen to a never-before-seen-size. Muscular and
monstrously overgrown. Deep below the footfalls of fallow deer
and porcupine and wolf, it has ripened in the dark. Thickened
and thriving in the land of love and lemons.

It is time.

The truffle recites a sonnet made of scent.

A call for an animal to come and find it.

An olfactory dare.

It waits.

It waits.

Cast of Characters
Il Cast dei Personaggi

Delizia Micucci: Former veterinarian and now the first female mayor of the village, though she would rather be trimming the toenails of an aggrieved bull. Married to Lorenzo.

Giuseppina Micucci: Spiritual thunderstorm and bartender at Bar Celebrità. If New Year's Eve were a person, it would be Giuseppina. Estranged wife to Umberto.

Giovanni Scarpazza: Gentle village truffle hunter who is grieving his late partner, Paolo. Truffle hunting with his faithful dogs, Aria and Fagiolo, is his passion.

Lorenzo Micucci: Long-suffering owner of Bar Celebrità. Sensitive and scientific, he is husband to Delizia and reluctant brother to Umberto.

Nonna Amara: Soul and sunshine of the village. Sensational cook and owner of long-shuttered *ristorante* Il Nido. Eighty-six years young, she is here to hold a hand and mend a heart.

Vittoria: Eleven-year-old aspiring cook. Nonna Amara's beloved granddaughter. She is a worrywart who adores her *nonna* more than anything.

Umberto Micucci: Famous chef of Michelin-star *ristorante* Novelli, whose ego is larger than the Apennine mountain range that runs the length of Italy. Estranged husband to Giuseppina.

Duccio Berardinelli: Disgraced village postman. Identifiable by his silver ponytail and perennial scowl.

Carlotta DeLuca: Village nonagenarian with a spicy history and love for a good caper. She is most proud of being the village policeman's grandmother.

Poliziotto Silvio: Carlotta's grandson and the village policeman in a village with no crime.

Benedetto Pucci: Good-natured village grocer who is mild of manners and slow of step. Unintentionally abstract painter.

Stefano Perlini: Retired village driver and wheelchair user who is famous for wearing flashy trousers that can be seen from outer space. He lives with his friend Benedetto the grocer.

Rosa Bandini: Twin to Valentina; prides herself on being born twenty minutes earlier. Hairdresser and co-owner of Mozzafiato Hair.

Valentina Bandini: Twin to Rosa; prides herself on being born twenty minutes later. Hairdresser and co-owner of Mozzafiato Hair.

Ugo Lombardi: Larger-than-life village hunter who's full of braggadocio and boar-hunting stories, rifle always at the ready.

Tommaso Pellegrini: Village hunter who has a milder temperament than Ugo, though is secretly a better shot and has, less secretly, a crafting passion for papier-mâché.

Padre Francesco: The village priest is a peculiar man with majestic eyebrows you could swaddle dormice in.

Leon Rosetti: Farmer and a great bearded bear of a man. Leon is dedicated to the land and his animals. Married to Sofia.

Sofia Rosetti: Social butterfly who loves a glass of wine and a bit of whimsy. Married to farmer Leon.

Mayor Benigno: The late village mayor whose passion for making olive oil rivaled the greatest of Tuscan romances.

Ludovica: Stylish retired seamstress. Wife of the late Mayor Benigno and has a strained relationship with her stepdaughter, Delizia.

Mamma Fortuna: A fortune teller from Pietrasanta who puts the Chanel in psychic channeling.

Al Pacino: Female cat who suffers no fools, patrolling the streets for scoundrels and salumi.

Aria: Lagotto Romagnolo and seasoned truffle-hunting dog. Dedicates herself to hunting for truffles and her owner Giovanni's happiness.

Fagiolo: Giovanni's Lagotto Romagnolo puppy and truffle-hunting apprentice.

Maurizio: With his soulful and soothing presence, Maurizio is everyone's favorite donkey.

Acknowledgments

Tartufo is a novel about good relationships. I am so lucky to have many good relationships and to be gloriously entangled with the most wonderful humans.

To Bill Clegg, thank you. You never fail to astound me with your literary brilliance, the care you take with every read, as well as your impeccable advice and encouragement.

My endless gratitude to all the geniuses at the Clegg Agency—Simon Toop, Marion Duvert, MC Connors, Rebecca Pittel, and Julia Harrison—who make magic of messy drafts and made it possible for this book to find its way in the world.

My deepest thanks to Kassie Evashevski, you are an incomparable champion of writers and their words.

To my incredible editor, Karen Kosztolnyik—I love working with you. Thank you for understanding this novel right to its very roots and for elevating it with such meticulous and wonderful edits.

Anjuli and Alayna Johnson—you two are the very best in the business of books, and also the loveliest humans.

My gratitude to Theresa DeLucci. And to the peerless Andy Dodds for being the best publicist a writer could wish to work with.

I am grateful to the spectacular *comune* at Grand Central Publishing and Hachette—Ben Sevier, Danielle Thomas, Andrew Duncan, Joseph Benincase, Matthew Ballast, Beth deGuzman, and Alexis Gilbert.

Thank you to Jarrod Taylor for a book cover so beautiful I fear it will cause someone to fall off their bicycle.

My thanks to Alana McGee at the Truffle Dog Company. And especially to James Nowak and his Lagotto Romagnolo, Dino, for my first truffle hunt, which was every bit as magical as I had imagined and an experience that I will never forget.

I am grateful to Dr. Charles Lefevre, the very lovely Leslie Scott, and everyone involved with the Oregon Truffle Festival, where I learned how to truffle farm, toured truffières, and solidified my identity as a true truffle pig.

An enormous thank-you to Mike Davis at Seattle Truffle Company for his generosity, spectacular stories, and the truffle hunting at his truffière with Aldo the Lagotto Romagnolo. Mike, you put the fun in fungi.

Thank you to Connie Green, the head huntress of Wine Forest Wild Foods, for all the truffle talk and expertise. I am grateful to you for sharing your wisdom with me.

I am so thankful to my fellow scribes and friends. A very special thank-you to my wildly talented friends Janet Yoder, Billie Condon, and Corry Venema-Weiss. A deeply heartfelt thank-you to Stacy Lawson, who is a champion of literature, of people, and of naughty golden retrievers. Stacy, I am in awe at the community you have built and how you bring people together. Warmth from that generosity ripples through this book.

I am forever grateful to Susan Urban—thank you for the care you took reading an early draft, for your wise literary instincts and encouragement. And for taking care of my pampered pooches so I could go on an adventure to learn about truffles.

For fierce friendship, I would like to thank John and Wendy Whitcomb, Vicki Olafson and Mark Michaels, Bergen Buck and Morgan Barton. *Gli amici sono la famiglia che scegliamo noi stessi.*

My boundless gratitude to Nora Tonarelli. Thank you for taking the utmost care with your read through, for superb suggestions, and for making this a better book. Thank you for being such a wonderful friend to our family for all these years.

To all the friends and family we have made in Tuscany over the now many years. I am grateful for the times we have shared stories over an Aperol spritz or a pizza, for the particular Tuscan magic and memories. Here's to making more!

In loving memory of my own *nonna*—Nana—who inspired Nonna Amara with her irrepressible love and the way she brought everyone together.

To Robin Quick, my best friend, who took me to a book launch many years ago and said, "One day, this will be you." I thank my lucky stars for our friendship.

To Rinny, Simon, Nathan, and Liam, with my love and my never-ending thanks for the inestimable support and encouragement as I was writing this book (and every other).

Em and Pops—*come ringrazio i miei genitori?* You follow bold dreams and tell better stories than I will ever write. Thank you for showing me what it means to be a kind person, to make good connections, and to live *la dolce vita.*

And to Jpeg, my true treasure. *Grazie per tutto. Ti amerò per sempre.*

About the Author

Kira Jane Buxton's debut novel, *Hollow Kingdom,* was a finalist for the Thurber Prize for American Humor, the Audie Awards, and the Washington State Book Awards, and was named a best book of 2019 by NPR, *Book Riot,* and *Good Housekeeping.*